200% UN. _ _ _ _ _ _
NIGHTMARE FUEL

TOM RUSSELL

VELOX BOOKS
Published by arrangement with the author.

200% Unfiltered Nightmare Fuel copyright © 2023
by Tom Russell.

All Rights Reserved.

This book is a work of fiction. People, places, events, and situations are the product of the author's imagination. Any resemblance to actual persons, living or dead, or historical events, is purely coincidental.

No part of this book may be reproduced, stored in a retrieval system, or transmitted by any means without the written permission of the author and publisher.

CONTENTS

As Is Correct	1
Burn After Meeting	6
Edgar Hogarth	23
Dorothyrescue.mov	38
A Conversation With Zee	51
Misfortune Cookies	57
What I Found In Father's Box	74
Great Aunt Hortensia	88
Subject: WTF	103
The Zit	107
Fatberg	114
R-Squad	142
Normal People Need Not Apply	152
Distemporal Assets	169
The Evidence	182
Don't Laugh	198
Spontaneous Human Malnutrition	205
RE: Your Resignation	219
What To Tell 'Em When They Ask	226
Lord Orwell Harkenwild)	243
he Last Mrs. Danforth	282
What Awaits	298

AS IS CORRECT

My Dad is a chair. To be specific, he's a fully upholstered bright orange angel accent living room chair. The kind with wooden legs you'd find in any 3-piece suit from the '70s. He's pretty comfortable, truth be told. A little lumpy in places, but his padding is soft. Warm too. He's *always* warm. There's also the telltale *ba-thump ba-thump ba-thump* coming from his back cushion. A steady rhythm at my lumbar to remind me I'm sitting in no ordinary chair.

He wasn't always a chair. Until last year, he was Kevin, the accountant. He was 51, slightly overweight, and generally seemed to enjoy life as a human. He was married to Mom. He still is but, well, as you can imagine it's a little complicated now.

It was funny at first. He came home from work one day and just sat in a corner of the living room.

When we'd ask him why he was sitting on the floor and not the $4000 cream leather couch, he'd just smile and say "It feels right here". It stopped being funny the morning he didn't go to work. Turns out he hadn't slept the night before. He'd been watching a movie with Mom but hadn't gone with her to bed. She left him sitting in his spot, unsuspicious of the "I'm not tired, I'll be up a little later" lie. She and I both begged him to get up, but he refused to move. Phoned in sick at work, the whole deal. Just spent the day sitting on the floor in his corner. We kept asking him what was wrong, why he wouldn't get up except to use the bathroom, and he just kept saying "No… no this feels right".

Mom phoned the doctor around the third day of this. He'd stopped eating or drinking, you see. Stopped getting up to use the bathroom too. Surprisingly though there weren't as many…

umm... accidents, as you'd think. Once he'd allowed the last of the food and drink to leave him it seemed to stop coming. We also didn't hear his belly growl despite going a day and a half without food. The doctor couldn't make sense of it. Their first guess was that it was psychosomatic, but that wouldn't explain the absence of digestive activity exposed by the stethoscope. They said they'd be back to take some blood samples in a few days after they liaised with some colleagues. Unfortunately, as I said, this was last year. 2020. We never heard back from the doctor thanks to the virus-that-shall-not-be-named. I guess "guy with gut troubles who refuses to move" is low on the priorities list during a global pandemic.

Somehow Mom managed to wrangle long-term sick leave with Dad's company. Decades of loyal employee-ism combined with Mom's attendance of every company BBQ and softball game helped Mr. Bannerfrag buy the "unexplained stomach concern requiring hospitalization" excuse. I'll never forget that phone call. At the time, Dad losing his job was the worst-case scenario for both of us. He'd always been the breadwinner. Neither of us could support ourselves without him, we'd lose the house in under a year. Dad didn't seem too perturbed by Mom's frantic pacing, or the lies she wormed through the phone to Mr. Bannerfrag. He just stared at the wall serenely, hovering his butt half a foot from the carpet, balancing with his legs bent and his hands flat on the ground behind him.

That night I fell asleep listening to Mom yelling at Dad. He never yelled back.

We started noticing the physical changes a few days later. That's when we realized this *wasn't* psychosomatic. Unfortunately, our shitty "best insurance deal on the market" doctor wasn't picking up the phone. We'd get passive-aggressive emails informing us they were "waiting to hear back from colleagues", but that was it. This was not good. Especially not when the joints in Dad's arms and legs had fused. The not-goodness of the Doctor's silence increased a thousandfold when we sent photos of Dad's hands and feet flaking off like discarded spider husks the following week. Did the response change? No. We got a *very* snippy email about shortages on ICU wards and the "critical international situation". Mom's shouting match with the Chief of Medicine, the one she demanded her way up the phone chain to speak to, didn't change things. We were on our own.

Mom spent all her time in the living room with Dad. I'd help her wash him, try and make him eat, talk to him when she'd tire out and fall asleep on the rug. Every day of this routine brought with it new changes in Dad's body. It started with his limbs, as you can probably guess. When his hands and feet fell off, there was no blood. They flaked apart, crusty, dry and brittle throughout. Even the bones of his toes and fingers had the density and consistency of dead skin. The wrists and ankles they left behind were smooth and hard. It was difficult to tell whether we were looking at flesh or exposed bone. The dark shining surface seemed to blend into his normal arm at the base of the stumps. This discoloration would rise further up his limbs daily, and before long I awoke to see Dad's head and torso fused to the wooden chair legs supporting my weight while I write this.

Well, I use the term "Dad's head and torso" in the loosest possible sense. By the time his limbs were completely replaced, the rest of him had undergone a slow, harrowing transformation of its own.

His shoulders, and the arms attached to them, descended lower and lower. They found their final resting place at Dad's pelvis, sat squarely behind his rigid legs. The chest area they'd left behind had its own problems. Day by day Dad's neck retracted further inwards. It didn't stop when his jaw met collarbone, either. It pulled Dad's head deep into his ribcage. His face flattened as the skull supporting it sank, forcing his eyes to point in opposite directions. Eventually, they slid down to where his nipples once lay, resting glassy and vacant on his pecks. The change wasn't quick enough to break his jaw though. Instead, it bent outward, its hinges spreading wide across Dad's broad chest. Each morning I'd find Mom sobbing over a fresh unnecessary piece of himself he'd discarded. Hair, ears, nose, his... umm... his *thingy*... all of them flaked off and crumbled to dust in her hands.

He lost the ability to speak as his head withdrew. Unsurprising though, right? He made his intentions clear before he went. The last words he ever said to me.

"Don't cry... I am chair... always was chair... *happy* as chair..."

That was the worst part, I think. Knowing that, whatever the fuck was happening to Dad, he wasn't resisting it. That when he'd got that initial urge to sit in the corner and not get up, he didn't fight it. That he was *happy* this way. The implication being that when he was human, when he was a father and husband and accountant, he wasn't.

Sadly, I still don't know why or how Dad became a chair. I didn't post any photos, you see. Mom wouldn't let me, didn't want the embarrassment. Wanted to keep Dad's dignity intact. Thing is, I agreed with her and kind of still do. I'm *glad* I didn't go to the socials with pics of Dad at various stages of his journey. The temptation was there to see if anyone could help. Nobody could have though, could they? Dad would have become just another internet circus freak. I've done enough research and digging over the months to know that whatever happened to Dad, he's the only one.

Well, almost only.

Mom's own changes started around the time Dad's skin was rethreading into orange fabric and his eyes had hardened into plastic buttons. Her change was a little different. It started in her torso, stretching her day by day while she remained in crab-pose. I must say, she makes a *great* couch. Her transformation may have been a little more distressing, but the end result is better. (Sorry, Dad, it is what it is). I think the worst part with Mom was the despondency. Dad was so serene as he changed. Mom though? Mom wouldn't stop weeping. Quiet sobs, tears that fell for a few days even after her own eyes had become flat plastic. She wasn't crying because of the change, I think. I think it was because she wouldn't get to see how beautiful I'll look when I go through my own metamorphosis.

Thing is, I get it now. Dad was right. He *was* chair. Mum *was* couch. I *am* coffee table. I always was. I was scared at first when I realized. The truth hit me like a piano dropped from the Empire State Building. I was scrubbing the last of Mom's remaining human skin when it struck through every bone in my wrong body, just as it must have done both Dad and Mom.

I spent that whole night sitting on Dad, tears falling down my cheeks, staring at my spot. I didn't want it to be true. I screamed for it not to be, more than once. I couldn't deny the facts I knew deep down to my bones, though. That spot, the space on the rug in front of chair Dad and couch Mom, is for me. It's mine. Where I belong.

Unlike blissfully accepting Dad and weeping resigning Mom, I fought it for a few days. I'm not like them; I'm only 17. I have… had… dreams, ambitions, goals. I wanted to go to college, settle down, marry some lucky guy, be a mom. I wasn't ready to give up my human form. I spent my nights begging for more time. Nothing answered. The urges didn't abate. My awareness of reality now that the illusions had been swept away was too great. When I have slept this last week or so, my dreams have always been the same. I dreamt of *true* reality, of how I now know things should be. I dream of me in my place, my body elongated and wooden and flat as is right, as is correct, as is natural. I have long, blissful slumbers filled with the feeling of hot ceramic mugs on my tabletop and thick carpet beneath my four legs.

I can't fight it anymore. I'm posting this here but also printing it out to leave as a note for the removal guys. I want them to be careful with us when the bank repossesses the house and we end up in storage. Please keep us together, if you can. We're a set. Dad's sick leave ended months ago. As you can imagine, the foreclosure notices have been piling up. I stopped caring about the pile of mail under the door around the time that Mom's ribcage split and flattened into her wide, pinstripe-velvet upholstered back. I haven't been hungry in days, or thirsty. I'm not even sure if I'm breathing now that I think about it. I'm still scared, but I've come to accept that this is the way things have to be. I don't know why, they just do. Maybe it's a curse, maybe this house is buried on some ancient ritual site, maybe it's just some freak anomaly of physics. Who knows? Whatever the reason, I have to suck it up and accept the way things are. This body, this walking wobbling mass of skin and bone and jibbly bits that I love so much, isn't right. It isn't mine. I'm not meant for it anymore. Once I post this and print the copy for the removal guys, I'm going to get in my spot. Then it's just a case of closing my eyes and waiting. I can already feel my limbs pulling inward, my thighs and upper arms sliding to where they'll meet at my navel in a few days. There's a tugging on the back of my knees where they'll bend in on themselves, and all twenty of my fingers and toes grow number with each hour that passes.

Do I have any regrets? Thousands. There's so much I'll never get to do, to see, to go, to be. I can't hide from the truth, though. Not anymore.

I am coffee table.

BURN AFTER MEETING

I'm pretty sure I lived with a literary genius. A once-in-a-generation mind akin to Dickens or Shakespeare, with contents as dangerous as Robert Oppenheimer's or Salman Rushdie's. Whereas Dickens and Shakespeare helped shape the world though, Roy Bardiquet would have no doubt ended it.

Roy's stories and poems had readers laughing, crying, enraged, even sleeping at his whim. To this day I can't explain exactly how he'd do it. He'd set out his goal, then create a string of vowels and syllables with which he played his readers' hearts like musical instruments. His romance poetry had the most reserved of folk spontaneously professing undying love to bemused soon-to-be sweethearts. His tales of nation-forging heroism on the battlefield inspired more than one lad to drop out of university and enlist. His dramas thematically exploring death and loss left none who poured through them with dry eyes. Those times weren't what made me burn down our student accommodation while he was still inside. No. It was the stories he wrote after deciding he wanted to make people scream which did that.

I've been in prison for a few years now. Arson and murder, in case you were wondering. This is it for me. It's worth it though. I may be legally guilty, but my soul carries the weight of zero regrets. Sure, you could agree with the shrink and call me a walking delusional martyr complex. I don't care. I know my life behind bars is a sacrifice I've made for the good of humanity. Fuck knows what would have happened if those stories were ever published.

Suffice to say, Roy had a way with words. I met him in the first year, his room being next to mine in our flat. By the second, he and I were moving into a shared house with two others—Lisa and Ted. And, coincidentally, the latter's testimony to my outstanding character managed to knock all of two years from my sentence.

Throughout our friendship, I could tell that Roy was... different? No, not different. Different is the wrong word. Gifted. Yeah, let's go with that. He was gifted in a way that few have the privilege of encountering.

At first, I felt lucky to know him. Word about the tall guy in the duffle coat who made the famous guest lecturer break down into floods of tears got around quickly. I don't want to reveal her name, because I don't want any media hassle caused by a show-trial when they sue for defamation (the public hate me too much for it not to be used to add another decade to my stretch). If the words *"vampire baseball"* mean anything to you, you'll be familiar with her work. Roy broke her after accusing her of being, in his words, *"a peddler of emotionally empty pigswill that's an insult to the trees which died for the paper it's printed on."* When she'd challenged him to do better, he pulled out a napkin. He wrote a haiku. I never read it, but I saw the video of the famous guest lecturer reading it once, twice, and then throwing herself on the floor in hysterics. I laughed with Roy as she ran out of the room in the clip, wailing *"it's too beautiful, it's too beautiful"* over and over again while the lecture hall howled and cackled along with us. And so it continued for the first six months or so. Roy would have drama and English Lit girls falling all over him. I'd be there with the closest available bed to his asexual brand of impenetrable genius.

That all changed after the incident.

It shocked the whole campus. About six or seven lads, one of them an underage visitor only down for the weekend, died at an after-party. Not died in a quiet-yet-tragic way, either. They died in the kind of way that meant journalists swarmed around our campus for a solid two months. The kind of way that caused over three dozen students to drop out the next day. One lad killed two of the others, one jumped out a window, and there were rumours that the two survivors were so traumatized they mutilated themselves.

Nobody knows what exactly happened, but the university staff couldn't stop the photographs of the bloodshed and carnage left behind being circulated around various WhatsApp and Facebook groups. I never saw the pictures myself; the sight of my future housemate Ted looking at his phone and instantly projectile vomiting across the room was enough for me to know my relatively squeamish stomach couldn't take it. I wish Roy had shown the same restraint.

"Probably a bad batch of acid or something," Ted had said, while Roy gazed at the phone in his hands. "Either that or the others snapped when they saw what Luke did. I heard he cut their…"

"Could you send me these?" Ted was as surprised by Roy's sudden interruption as I was.

"Umm yeah… sure." He'd replied, shooting me a sidelong glance as he took the phone back from Roy. "What do you want them for though, buddy?"

"Research," Roy muttered, already heading to his room.

He had that face on, the face he always wore the night before handing in an assignment that summoned gaggles of fawning female admirers to our flat. I should have twigged then that no good could come from *that* face mixing with *those* photos. I was too stoned at the time, though, and too content to get back to my Tekken match with Ted to worry about the activities of our pet genius.

I didn't know it then, but that night was the start of the nine-month countdown which would end with Roy dead, our flat burned to the ground, and me the monster-of-the-week in the papers.

The first three months were pretty unremarkable, if I'm honest. The first changes were in the fawning groupies Roy would attract to our living room. Guys started to appear alongside them, for one thing. Not that I had an issue with that, but it was a noticeable change. The overall vibe of his acolytes morphed, too. Whereas before he'd lured bouncy art chicks, the tone of his ensemble realigned until I was trying to see Tekken over the shoulders of goth-girls and sunken-eyed wannabe H.P Lovecraft types. However, after the first month or two, this new crowd also started shrinking. The dwindling numbers of curvy goths and disheveled imitators wore increasingly harrowed, worried looks on their faces. Like the darkness they'd come for was far brighter than the kind Roy delivered. A rabbit in the headlights look, the look of the *in too deep*. It was the same mix of expressions the drama and literature girls I used to wake up with wore when Roy's new artistic direction drove them away.

I found out why at the end of the third month. Roy was once more locked in his room, halfway through a days-long writing session.

"What's going on with him?" I asked Ted, jerking a thumb over my shoulder in the direction of Roy's room. "I know he was always a shut-in, but I've not seen him since Thursday. He's stopped bringing girls over, too."

"Yes, because THAT'S what we should be concerned about." Lisa butted in before Ted could reply, rolling her eyes. "God forbid Rick the engineering student doesn't get laid."

"*Ha-ha.*" I let out a wry laugh. "Yes Lisa, very good, you got me… you figured out it was I that hid the body in the floorboards!" We all laughed at the in-joke for a few moments, then Ted finally answered my question.

"Dunno, Rick, mate, in all honesty. He's been off since… well, since those photos from that night in G-Block. The one with Luke McCallis—"

"I know the one you mean, dumbass. That hit everyone though. You can't tell me all my—I mean all his… umm… friends I guess, from his classes dropped out?"

Lisa shook her head. "No, they're still there. Us Journos have a shared lecture with the Creative Writing guys. Travel writing. Roy's stuff lately… Ted, Rick, I think something is actually wrong with him…"

Lisa was leaning forward in the beaten-up living room chair, pleased she finally had an attentive audience for her concerns. The conversation lasted long into the night. It ended about 2 AM, with the three of us stood outside Roy's bedroom.

"Roy?" I hazarded, knocking softly on the door. "Roy? It's Rick. Ted and Lisa are with me… Lisa was saying-*OW!*" Lisa jabbed me on the arm. She was shaking her head, eyes wide and afraid, crossing her open palms in the air to tell me to schtum. "I mean… you remember Rachael? That girl from your course I got on with?"

"That narrows it down…" Ted chuckled quietly, prompting Lisa to deliver another shut up arm jab. I rolled my eyes at Ted and kept speaking to Roy through the door.

"Well buddy, I tried to catch up with her and invite her over, but she says she's… concerned? Worried? Scared?" Lisa nodded at me when I said the last one. "Yeah, she's scared, Roy. She said the stuff you've been reading in lectures recently has been... Well, can we talk?"

I finished my speech, delivered in the same semi-condescending tone folk use when reprimanding thirteen or fourteen-year-olds who try to experience adulthood too early. There was a grunt from the other side of the door, but Roy didn't respond. This time Lisa piped up.

"It's not just Rachael, Roy. Loads of your class have told me the stories you're writing are too much. People are on edge after the whole G-Block incident, you know?"

The response from the door's other side was clipped and impatient. "Not my problem. If they were happy to kiss my ass when it was mushy romance fuck-stories or... ha... 'deep' poetry, they should be happy to keep their lips on there when I'm trying to scare them."

The three of us jumped. We hadn't heard Roy's footsteps, so it took us all completely by surprise when his bedroom door swung inwards as soon as the '*m*' in '*them*' left his lips. He stood in the doorway, grinning at us. Under his bloodshot eyes were deep purple bags. The room beyond was dark save for the piercing glare of his laptop screen.

"What do you want?" His gaze darted between the three of us, although it hung around Lisa's nervous features a fraction longer than mine or Ted's. "You want me to stop? Write something different? Go back to making the girls Rick likes cross their legs? Huh?"

All three of us in the hallway took a step back, but it was Lisa that spoke. "No, Roy, it's just... look, that piece you read last week in the Travel Writing lecture, the one about..."

"The one about the blue desert, you mean? That I read about in—"

"Yes, that one," Lisa shuddered, cutting Roy off, "it freaks the fuck out of me, Roy, and pretty much everyone else in the class. I've been having nightmares about it. Rick's not wrong, a lot of the guys on your course have told me about some of the fucked-up stuff you've read out in other—"

"Look, if they don't want to listen, they can leave the room." Roy's brow furrowed. His face did have a dash of concern, but nowhere near enough to distil the clear anger. "I write what I want to write."

"Roy, a few months ago there was a bloodbath on our campus. You saw the photos like I did. Loads of people aren't OK. If you're not, you can let us know." Ted surprised both Lisa and me with this. He placed a hand on Roy's shoulder, which was quickly brushed aside.

"I'm fine. I'm just trying different stuff. As I said, I never asked them to listen. Makes no difference to me."

We stood blinking at the door after he slammed it for a good thirty seconds.

"Well," Ted eventually broke the silence, "I'd say that went well, don't you?"

The rest of the term continued in much the same way until we all went home for the summer. When we returned the following September, we were again living with Roy, although this time in our own rented flat above a small local shop. This had already been arranged months before Roy's strange turn of behavior. I found Lisa's protests annoying after a while, the constant messages in a private chat between the three of us. I got shity with her more than once during the last couple weeks of August.

"The agreement is already signed," my thumbs hammered, laying on the bed at my mum's place on one of the last nights I'd ever spend there, "there's nothing we can do about it now. Besides, he keeps himself in his room and he's got the money for rent. Is he really going to be any trouble?"

Roy didn't say much to us when he moved in his belongings. I was disappointed to see he still had that tired, wild-eyed look on his face. My prayers that some time back home with his people would reinvigorate him weren't answered. He had less with him than when he'd arrived at our old student flat the prior September. Some loose bedsheets, a bin bag full of clothes we could smell from the hallway, and a couple of boxes he'd scrawled "*RE-SEARCH*" on the side of in thick black marker. Definitely not enough for someone occupying a place long term. So yeah, we started on a worrying note, and it didn't get any less so as the weeks played on. It was during those three months between September and Christmas that life with Roy started taking a much steeper decline.

The first oddity was Roy's grades began to fall off. Way off. He went from getting high 90s to single digits and a lot of *See Me's*. I found this out vicariously, of course, through Lisa, who found out through Rachael (who still wasn't returning my messages). One time I'd managed to catch him on his daily journey from his room to the kitchen.

"Hey, buddy, you doing OK? Lisa said the feedback you've been getting from the lecturers isn't so good."

He didn't respond at first, but instead stood in the kitchen for a good minute staring at me. From the expression on his face, you'd think I'd just asked if I could fuck his dead mother. All I could think of was how awful he looked. The bags under his eyes had doubled in their depth and darkness. More blood vessels had joined the network around his pupils. Roy had always been thin, and a little on the pale side, but now he was gaunt. His pasty cheeks hung from his face, his features drooped and wax-like.

"I'm fine," he'd muttered, not really making eye contact. "I'm just not wasting my best stuff anymore. I'm working on something. Saving the good stuff for that."

"Ok, mate. Still, could you at least have a shower? I had a date the other night and she noticed the smell."

He shrugged. "Sure."

Roy didn't have a shower, or at least not one that I ever heard him take. The smell never left, but at least it never got worse either. It was a constant; a faint yet persistent whiff of gasoline and burned eggs that felt like it had sunk into the walls and carpet. I stopped trying to bring dates back to our place in the end. Ted and Lisa started dating about two months into that strange limbo period, so neither of them had the issue. Not that they didn't complain. More than once I'd catch both of them either hammering on Roy's door and yelling about the stench or marching up and down the shared living spaces, emptying cans of air freshener.

In addition to the smell and his grades, the other weirdness was Roy's following. He slowly started to gain it back, despite only delivering half-finished work to his once adoring public in the lecture halls. His new flock was different. They were odd, but not in the try-hard way the fawning goth chicks and sullen imitators of the previous year had been. The people that started knocking on our door, letting themselves in, and heading straight to Roy's room weren't even students. That was the only common thread between them, that they *didn't* attend our uni. Other than that, the selection process seemed totally random. There were men, women, some much older than us, and others young enough that we debated phoning the police (if we were somewhere in the States, where the age of consent is way higher, we would have done). I'll be honest,

I don't think it was anything sexual. Sometimes the younger ones turned up with parents; fathers or mothers, or both. They always had the same furtive expression, whether they were the homeless ones who smelled like piss, or the rich ones in crisp suits and ties. By the time December rolled around, Roy sometimes had as many as twelve or thirteen crammed into his tiny room at once.

I'd listen at the door during these nightly meetings. This is how I know there was nothing sexual going on, although this wasn't as much of a relief as you'd think. In the grand scheme of things, I don't think it would have made what happened *much* worse. I couldn't hear exactly what was said, but all I ever heard was talking. Roy talking. He'd talk for hours on end; I assume reading from whatever "*something*" he was working on. Judging by what happened the night before we once more returned home for a holiday break, I'd put money on my assumptions being right.

I heard Lisa's scream before I'd seen anything. I'd been in my room, getting a little stoned and playing Tekken after a long day learning about rivets and gears. I threw myself into the hall to see Lisa, standing in the doorway opposite mine, screaming so loud neighbors started banging on the walls. There was a man stood in front of her, facing away from me. It was one of Roy's followers, one of the well-off ones in the crisp suits. Lisa was looking up at him, her face covered in tears, screaming as loud as she could on every exhale. I found out why her screams couldn't stop when I put my hand on a crisp blue suit shoulder. When the man turned around to face me, I started screaming with her.

He'd taken out his eyes.

Wetness was running down his cheeks just like Lisa's, although *this* wetness was a dark red crimson. Eyelids flapped uselessly in front of gaping empty voids; voids that would have been pitch black were it not for the faint merlot hue of the flesh within. He was at least a foot taller than me, which did nothing to help the sudden onset of knee-buckling panic. The goatee on his otherwise smooth face was distended, stretched around something held beneath his pursed lips. Consciousness left me the moment they peeled apart.

Staring down at me from between his white teeth was a pair of socketless, blood-soaked eyeballs.

By the time I came to, the police were already poking around the flat. Ted and Lisa had hoisted me onto the couch after Ted, who was luckily drunk off his ass, smashed a bottle over the eye eater's head and phoned 999. I was offered an ambulance, but I declined. After hearing how Drunk Ted handled the situation, I felt much safer with him than I would have done at a hospital. Part of me wanted to move out after that. As you can imagine, part of me still wishes I had. As it was, I instead resolved that I wasn't going to let Roy or his disturbed followers ruin the first living space I'd ever picked out and signed a contract for. Over the Christmas break we all agreed that, once we returned, we were kicking Roy out.

Thing is, the police hadn't found anything they could use to arrest him. They had found a book, a manuscript draft which they'd confiscated but, again, couldn't find anything incriminating enough inside to warrant not returning it. One concerned police officer had told Lisa this via email. They'd warned her that, while there was nothing they could pin on Roy, that all three of us should be cautious. I'm sure the officer risked getting fired by saying this, but they'd very bluntly stated *"I almost guarantee I'm going to be called back to that flat soon, and I'm worried that next time the mutilation won't be self-inflicted. I can't tell you why, but this is just all wrong. Please, Ms Pearson, your boyfriend and your flat mate should find alternative accommodation as soon as possible."*

It was the book Roy was writing that worried them. I've since seen it of course, but when Lisa forwarded me on that initial email all I had to go by was the title:

"ha HA ha tHe children R bleEding (a housewife's tale'".

During those last three months, after we ignored the officer's advice and returned to the flat we shared with Roy, I'd come to know that book much, much better. It had clearly made an impression on some of the police officers because I noticed more than one Hi-Viz jacket knock on the door and lead themselves through to Roy's room. I'd hear Lisa crying about it at night, when I was too afraid of the low mumblings coming from the direction of Roy on the other side of the wall between our bedrooms to sleep. She was terrified, and I'll be honest, so was I.

Trying to kick Roy out hadn't gone well. We'd manage to keep ourselves composed for a full month of the new term before Lisa finally snapped. She marched down the hallway, banging on Roy's door with her fists.

"YOU COME OUT HERE RIGHT NOW ROY BARDIQUET, YOU SMELLY, CREEPY, BASTARD! I'VE FUCKING HAD ENOUGH! YOU'VE GOT TO FUCKING LEAVE NOW!"

Ted and I didn't have enough time to put down Tekken and head out into the hallway. By the time our PS4 controllers touched the ground, Lisa was backing into the living room, palms outstretched, pleading with the slowly advancing group of glazed eyed acolytes. The ten-or-so strong crowd was just as mismatched as ever. There was a pot-bellied policeman, a mother and teenage daughter with matching "*get me the manager*" haircuts, a clearly homeless man whose breath stank of White Lightning, a woman in a crisp grey suit with a big-name bank's *Hi My Name Is* badge still above her breast pocket. A normally unremarkable group of people, all rendered terrifying by the hateful expressions in their glassy eyes, and the short figure in the dark coat they parted to let through.

Roy was looking worse than ever. His skin was near translucent now. Dark blue veins crisscrossed his temples and the bags under his eyes. His eyes themselves were milky-red, more burst capillaries now than anything else. His thin lips were smirking at Lisa, but the rest of his thin milky features shared the hate of his followers.

"Oh, I'm leaving, am I, Lisa?" His words were slow, deliberate, the tone so measured and controlled it seemed like forming each syllable took conscious effort.

"Y-yes…" Lisa stammered, bumping into the kitchen table and yelping. "Yes, you've… you've got to get out… I'm sick of the smell and… and these… these freaks." She spat the last word, her anger somehow finding the strength to rise above her terror. The "*freaks*" found her defiance amusing. They began laughing in soft chuckles, each perfectly timed with Roy's own.

"Cute, Lisa. That's cute." His smirk grew, although it did falter when Ted stepped between them.

"Back off, Roy. I don't care how many of your sick little club you've got with you, if you lay a finger on her I'll fuck you up." I was still standing behind them, so I couldn't see his face, but the fury in Ted's roar was enough to make even me jump. That's why Roy's unflinching response shook me to my core.

"I'm already fucked up, Theodore. So are all of you. I'm just honest about it." He scanned the three of us with his sunken eyes. "I'm fond of two of you, so I'm going to ignore this transgression. Don't disturb me when I'm working again."

He and his followers shot Lisa one last disgusted look, then retreated down the dark hallway into Roy's bedroom. That night's wall-muffled sermon lasted well into the dawn hours. So did Lisa's sobs.

I didn't see Roy again until the night of the fire. I was still defiantly refusing to leave. Lisa had tried but, for some reason, Ted talked her out of it. She moved into his bedroom, leaving her old one as an empty space. As for Ted, he was still convinced he could end all of this at a moment's notice by giving Roy a black eye. I think he was just as scared as we were and found the macho fantasy comforting. I don't reckon any of us could have moved out though, not really. First because I doubt Roy would have let us, and second because the thought of leaving him and his followers to their own devices was somehow even worse than staying.

It became clear to me during that last month that I'd have to intervene. Even though I was terrified, I couldn't just let the situation develop. "*Evil triumphs when good men do nothing*", or whatever the quote is. It took me four weeks to build the courage to step up, but I knew I couldn't live with myself if... well, you'll see.

Roy's followers were up to something. That became apparent over the nights following the confrontation in the kitchen. I'd lay awake listening as the muffled sermons became intertwined with dull thuds and scrapes, banging and hammering, the grinding of saws on wood. After a week, the muted sounds of work started coming from Lisa's old bedroom, too. I didn't have many opportunities to talk to her about it, though. She rarely left Ted's room during those last weeks. Ted had a job tending a bar, and so would be out most evenings. He'd return after midnight, with the sounds of heavy activity always starting when he was out of the house or (as I could tell because of the thin walls) snoring. He was working the night Roy died, which I think is the only reason he was still around to knock those two pointless years off my sentence.

The first thing I noticed on the night of the fire was the stampeding of boots. I'd got used to hearing them traipsing up and down the hallway outside my room in the small hours. I learned to somehow sleep despite the heavy footsteps that grew louder as they approached the other side of my bedroom door, then remained silent until they'd clump back towards Roy's room when the sun rose. Listening to the heavy breathing of one of Roy's acolytes standing outside my door all night was old news by the night of the fire. Hearing the heavy thumps of the dozen-or-so pairs of feet leave the flat and slam the door behind them was new. I should have been relieved. I wasn't though. I still remembered the man with his eyes in his mouth. The police officer's warning was still in my memory, too. Wherever Roy's followers had gone, it couldn't have been to do anything good.

I assumed Roy had gone with them when I found his bedroom empty. A quick peek beyond my door showed me I wasn't being guarded for the first time in weeks. I did knock on Lisa's door, but there was no response. She was sleeping, I guessed. Must be, since I couldn't hear crying. I didn't have much reason to check Lisa's old room at that point. Instead, I'd tried Roy's door, tentative but hopeful I could catch him alone without his followers. I still thought I could get through to him. Just as Ted was holding onto the fantasy of control through masculine violence, I was still banking on the fact that Roy was my friend. My friend who was ill. My friend who was ill that could be reasoned with, got through to, helped.

When I learned the truth, I found out just how terrible a judge of character I'd been when I chose a friend in Roy. I also discovered my naïve ideas about salvation and healing were pitifully misguided. When I found the book on the desk of his empty room, I realized Roy didn't need a friend.

He needed an executioner.

The lump in my throat was already building when his bedroom door swung open. I'd only knocked it once, and not hard. The rickety wood moved almost of its own accord, like it was inviting me in. The room beyond was lit only by a small lamp on Roy's desk. I didn't notice that immediately, however. The first sensory feedback to hit me was from my nose. The stench of gasoline and burnt eggs was noxious. I had to raise my t-shirt over my nose, although it did little to smother the fumes. I headed over to the book on the desk because, in all honesty, I think that's what Roy wanted me to do. This was all part of his game, a game he'd intended to end some other way. At least, I hope what happened wasn't part of his plan. From what I read in my brief skim of the book though it wouldn't surprise me *at all* if his twisted genius had planned for me to do *everything* I did after I'd managed to stop vomiting. Fire included.

It was a printed volume, bound in a red cover, empty save for the title:

"*ha HA ha tHe children R bleEding (a housewife's tale*"

The font and odd typography were almost as disconcerting as the fact I had to open the front cover to confirm this was indeed the book written by R. Bardiquet. There is little more ominous than an authorless text. The inconsistencies with publishing norms were nothing compared to the contents though. I'm not going to go into details, because writing it out would just be recreating it. I only managed about five or six pages before my diaphragm contracted and the inside of my tee was filled with warm bile. I threw Roy's twisted book across the room, pulling off my shirt to wipe away my puke. I was jabbering incoherent nonsense, tears welling in my eyes. I don't have a word for my emotional state. Panicked? Terror-stricken? Unsane? None do justice to the depth of the fear that overtook me from reading those few pages.

What I *can* tell you about that book is it was a stream of untitled passages. Some poetry, others prose. They described the most abominable things you could… well, I don't want to say that you could imagine, because I genuinely don't believe you can. I hope you can't. Unspeakable acts, twisted creatures, horrifying landscapes. All were laid out in verse and text by Roy, with such clarity and poise they could not possibly have been purely from the imagination. This is when my resolve that I had to intervene solidified, in the moments I was wiping the last of the puke from my lips. I didn't want to know what the kind of people un-repulsed by this book are capable of. Roy on his own was, clearly, dangerous. A following devoted to whatever twisted message his magnum opus conveyed was unthinkable.

The open cardboard box I then noticed on Roy's bed, the one full of copies of the same scarlet volume I'd hurled against the wall, was the last straw. I'd never been happier that Ted had an affinity for Zippos. It meant that we had a few canisters of lighter fluid in one of the kitchen cupboards. Along with the half dozen bottles of vodka I found I had more than enough to do what I needed to. I was about to light the match I'd swiped from a drawer in Roy's desk and ignite his bedroom when I heard the whimpering.

"Lisa!"

I'd been so caught up in the terror-induced mad fervor that I'd completely forgotten about her. She hadn't made a sound up until that point, despite me yelling at the top of my lungs as I threw vodka and lighter fluid across every inch of Roy's floor and the hallway outside. I could still hear her pained moans when I, at last, managed to kick through the door to her and Ted's shared room. The cheap wood burst inwards to reveal a screaming Lisa nowhere in the room beyond. Her terrified shrieks weren't stopping though. It was then I realized they'd never been coming from her new bedroom. They were coming from her old one.

The door to Lisa's old bedroom, the one Roy's followers had been using, didn't need kicking. I didn't even need to knock. It creaked ajar as I walked towards it. The room beyond was unlit, but I knew Lisa was in there. Her screams grew noticeably louder the instant an inch of darkness was visible between door and frame.

The hallway light cast a long beam on the dark bedroom floor. It ended at Lisa's feet. Even with such low visibility, I knew straight away her screams were warranted. The light from the open doorway illuminated her feet, ankles, and up to her knees. She was unclothed, strapped with thick leather belts to a wooden *X*. Well, it wasn't an *X*, and it wasn't only made of wood, but that's the easiest way to describe it. I wouldn't see the full horror of the device until a few moments later when I switched the light on. By the time the majesty of the infernal contraption was revealed, though my attention was directed elsewhere, so my recollection of it is far from clear. What I *do* remember is that the heavy wooden cross had ornate diagrams carved on every inch of its surface. It was nailed into a rotating mass of cogs and wheels, all engraved with the same intricate and unnerving pictograms. These wheels were made from a range of materials; from iron and different grains of wood through to plastic, papier mâché, and (I hoped) animal bone.

As I said though, when I switched on the light, my attention wasn't on the wooden cross, its spinning wheels, or their arcane symbols. It was on Lisa.

"I CAN SEE YOU, OH GOD, RICK, I CAN SEE YOU. HOW CAN I SEE YOU, RICK?!"

I screamed the moment the light switch removed the blanket of darkness. I could now see the full extent of the contraption she was strapped to. It took up almost the whole room, connected to bubbling vats of god knows what, to pipes and valves that hissed reeking steam. The burnt-egg-and-gasoline smell was so thick that layers of phlegm built on each panicked breath. How I didn't pass out, I don't know. Well, I do. I think I was too scared of Lisa to pass out. My body simply could not allow itself to shut down and be vulnerable in the presence of her gaze.

She was strapped on the machine. Her eyes, the ones I remembered, were hidden behind a thick bandage wrapped tight around her head. I wept when I saw the two dark red patches above their location, my head filled with flashbacks to the man in the hallway.

"ICANSEEYOURICKICANSEEYOUHOWCANISEEYOU—"

I knew how she could see me, although I didn't have the words to explain it to her. To be fair to myself, even if I *did,* I had no remaining sanity with which to form them. Lisa was watching me with her new eyes. They lined every inch of her naked body. They were sewn on with crude stitches, lids and all, the surrounding skin removed from the faces of their original owners. The owners, I realized with a growing horror, were probably on the streets at that moment; their eyeless, hollow faces hidden beneath hoods and sunglasses as they distributed Roy's foul teachings to the unsuspecting world. That wasn't the worst part, though. The worst part was that the dozens of transplanted eyes were still blinking.

"RICK! RICKHOWCANISEEYOUWHATSHAPPENINGRICKI'MSCARED—"

Lisa was screaming rapid-fire pleas at me. She was struggling and tugging against the binds, pulling with such force that a deafening *crack* accompanied one of her wrists or ankles snapping. Fuck her ankles, though, and her wrists. As harsh as that sounds, she could have stabbed herself in the chest and I wouldn't have noticed. Not with… not with all those… those damn *eyes.*

I couldn't count how many there were. Transplanted gazes watched from her arms, legs, midriff, chest, back, neck, groin, hips, hands… everywhere. Registering that they were all staring at me, all blinking and tracking me around the room while Lisa continued to beg me to explain how her bound face wasn't blind, was enough for me to snap.

I hate myself for my cowardice, but I slammed the door shut. I tried to block out Lisa's wails as I lifted the match, my bottom lip trembling and vision swimming with tears.

"I told you I was working on something."

I turned, slowly. Roy was standing at the other end of the hallway. His pale hunched frame was all that stood between me, the kitchen, the living room, and (most importantly) the front door.

I tensed, ready to fight for my life. Then he did something that to this day still shocks me. He stood aside.

"Go ahead Rick." He was smiling at me. To my horror, it was the same warm smile he'd had during those first few months of our first year, before the incident which set this chain of events in motion. He continued, his overly measured words soft and reassuring in a way that sent a shiver down my spine. "I'm not going to try and stop you. This is always how your part in the story ends. Every time. The only thing that's different *this* time is the book. It wasn't what I was supposed to write. She found me though, she found me and *this* time I've written something totally... totally *new*."

To answer your question: no, I had and still have no fucking clue what he was raving about. Waiting around to find out wasn't going to happen, either. I didn't look behind me when I shut the door to the flat. Last I saw Roy he was sitting on a chair in the living room, chuckling softly to himself while the burnt-egg-and-gasoline smell was replaced by thick smoke and rising flames. I could hear Lisa's shrieks as I ran. I turned to allow myself a quick glance. My final glimpse was of neighbors stepping into their front gardens, smoke billowing from the windows above the shop, the shopkeeper below yelling frantically into his phone. None of that troubled me. The only concern I had in the last few moments I spent on that street was that, even above the screams of both Lisa and the neighbors, I could still hear Roy laughing.

I handed myself in to the police immediately. I didn't want Ted to get pinned for this, and after what I'd seen, normality was no longer an option. How could I settle into a job, a life, a family, when every time I closed my eyes, I could see a swarm of them on a naked woman's body staring back? Ted didn't deserve to have his life ruined, though. He'd already lost Lisa; he didn't deserve to lose himself too. That's also why I lied to him about what happened to Lisa. As far as Ted knows, Roy slit her throat. The police and jury didn't buy that, neither did the judge, but Ted did, and that's all I care about.

That's why I can finally write this down, get my story out into the world. Ted passed away yesterday. Tragic, but completely unrelated. Cancer. From what he'd told me during his visits over the years, he'd managed to move on. Settle down, have kids. I'm glad. It made it worth it in a way. If I hadn't acted when I did, it would have been Ted a few weeks later. Now there's no risk of him finding out the truth, I can be open, can tell the world the *real* side of my story.

The timing also isn't fully accidental, either. I've told a couple of the other inmates here my story. The true story. Usually, they laugh, say it's bullshit, but enjoy the "*good yarn*" nonetheless. Last week, though, one of the new guys didn't laugh. He grabbed me after, started whispering to me in hushed tones. You know Roy's book? The little red volume I thought I'd burned all known copies of? He'd seen it. I knew he wasn't lying too, because he was able to recite to me the exact same paragraphs I refused to write down earlier. If there are still copies out there, then burning Roy and Lisa alive was for nothing. My life behind bars was all for naught. I already know Roy brought more than one police officer into the fold. I don't know how deep this goes. Please warn everyone you know, tell them to stay away from any red book with an odd title, especially one called "ha HA ha tHe children R bleEding (a housewife's tale".

If any of your friends or family start acting strange, going to odd meetings in the dead of night they refuse to disclose details of, tell them my story. If they do anything other than laugh, run. Don't stop. They're already one of them. It's too late. I thought I'd kept you all safe from this. I fucked up. I'm sorry. I've used all of my accrued good-behavior internet privileges to get this warning out there. The night of the fire I did something unspeakable and threw my life away so that you could carry on living yours in safety. Get my message out. Please make my sacrifice worth it. Make sure nobody reads anything by Roy Bardiquet.

I just hope he's actually dead. It's getting harder to forget that they never found his body.

EDGAR HOGARTH

The following is a transcription of Edgar Hogarth's final patient interview. Edgar was interned at St Dionysius *for most of the 20th century, and the following was recorded three months before his passing in early 2001. The first I interviewed, the first I went into knowing that everything he said...*

Well, I'll let you determine. You have a right to know though. You all do. Geraldine was right about that, at least. His is a story much like every other resident of that ghastly place; that great rug under which we've swept so much over the decades. I thought we were doing good *work by hiding them away, but it's not made a difference.*

There will be a special place in hell reserved for us, for keeping the stories of Edgar and his like buried from the world. Buried from themselves, that we let them suffer the delusion of being "delusional". I am choosing to make his words public now because... well... it won't matter much soon, will it?

—Dr Dipesh Anand

[TRANSCRIPT STARTS. ALL WORDS UNLESS NOTED OTHERWISE ARE FROM EDGAR HOGARTH, IPSET WITNESS-CLASS POI #4820]

Do you ever daydream? Let your mind wander, go where it may as you trundle through life? I used to. I used to sit without tapping complex rhythms on my wrist to keep focused, would you believe? I could walk down a corridor without listing every detail, could sleep without being drugged into chemical unconsciousness.

I was not born this way. Despite what you've heard, my habits, quirks, and ticks aren't some mental impairment. I lived the first third of my life in complete normalcy. Nothing about my character was exceptional, nothing about my life unique. This was how I liked it. It took less than 24 hours for all that to change. I woke up a free man one day, the next a prisoner to a fear that at any moment I'd turn a corner without concentrating and end up…

[EDGAR PAUSES FOR 4:37 BEFORE CONTINUING]

The day in question was a Sunday. The Lord's day. The irony wasn't lost on me even during the weeks that followed, that confusing time when my darling Ava and Doctor Monterey tried to nurse me out of witless vacancy. It was sunny, too. Good weather always had a positive effect on my temperament. I remember because I was whistling throughout my walk from the village. It was an absent minded, improvised tune that became more disjointed and erratic the closer I got to…

[EDGAR PAUSES FOR 2:17]

Well, perhaps it would be better if I recounted from the beginning. Not for your sake, but mine. I find I must ease myself into thinking about it, lest the flashbacks return, and I suffer another attack of temporary insanity. I would like to get through a day *without* losing hours to one of my "troubled spells".

Like everything else in the *time before*, the morning of that Sunday was unremarkable. It hadn't yet been an hour since Pastor Henry had finished morning mass. The echoing clangs of the church bells thundered across the countryside, shaking birds from trees and babes from their slumber. The men of the village had gone to drink, the women to cook meals and wash children, the gaggle of old crones still lingered on the green discussing curtain-twitch gossip. My darling Ava had headed home to prepare lunch. My sister and her husband, both of whom I miss dearly, were joining us that afternoon. Ava had been excited; she'd found a new pork stock recipe in one of my mother's old almanacs. At least I think it was pork… although, looking back, it perhaps could have been beef. That's by the by though. The only reason it's even worth mentioning is that the dinner plans had me walking Penelope earlier than I usually would. This, in itself, was not an inconvenience. My jaunts around Farmer John's field with the young golden retriever were a welcome reprieve from the prying eyes and sanctimonious chitter-chatter of the village. The walks provided a chance to get lost in my thoughts, and a welcome chance at that.

The factory, the village, our friends and neighbors… all were noisy to be around, intrusive. No… only when walking Penelope could I turn away from the world for a while to reflect, muse, and ponder.

With news of war on the continent reaching our rural ears that morning, I had a great deal for my mind to untangle. I was more focused on thoughts of Germany than I was my route. As such, I can't tell you *when*, never mind give a specific *where*, I took a detour. I didn't notice we'd left the familiarity of the cabbages and scarecrows until Penelope began to whine. It took the high-pitched sounds of canine distress to pull me from my thoughts and realize the path we walked was not unfamiliar. Before she agreed to send me here, my darling Ava scoured Farmer John's fields and the surrounding lands. Unfortunately, she found no road or path matching the one I am about to describe. I swear to you though it was real…

[EDGAR PAUSES FOR 1:35. SOUND OF SOBBING PRESENT THROUGHOUT.]

It *is* real. I wish that *nothing* I am about to describe was factual, but the scars I acquired that day weren't only on my psyche. I walked away with wounds which *more than proved* my lucidity. It's just a shame the quacks and charlatans you've paraded in front of me over the years value their "books" and "science" more than sense and reason. Bastards.

[SOUND OF MAN SPITTING ON FLOOR.]

But yes, Penelope's whimpers struck through my absentmindedness like lightning. Despite the fact I was not sleeping, to say I awoke with a start (as though I had been roused from a deep slumber with a potful of boiled water to the face) would be an accurate observation. Her distress was contagious. I felt my stomach drop before my eyes had registered the alien nature of our surroundings. The scarecrows, miles of neglected fences, and plumes of smoke from hamlets scattered across the distant hills had vanished. All were absent from my view to the horizon in every direction (a phenomenon unheard of anywhere near the village). The fields surrounding the path weren't green anymore. They'd become a colour I did not recognize. I *would* describe it as a golden brown, were it not for the fact that the long reeds seemed to grow greyer the longer I gawped.

The shape of this landscape was also new. The countryside I knew was hilly, rolling, rough in depth and texture. Farmer John would often be heard complaining about his "*bloody legs, dammit*" after marching his flocks up and down the slopes all day. I'd spent many hours in *The Crow's Feet* listening to him rant at poor Susan the barmaid about how *"unfair it is that him upstairs saw fit to place so many buggering hills all over my bloody land"*. The *"him upstairs"* Farmer John regularly made crude reference to must have lacked inspiration when creating this new place. The sepia fields were flat, flat like the earth itself had been precisely measured and planned by an architect. From where we stood, all the way to the horizon, no elevation or decline could be observed. No distant mountains or bulging hillocks could be found no matter which way I frantically turned. The sea of reeds stretched further than I'd ever seen a landscape unfurl. The skyline was too far away, almost as though the earth I was standing on had no curve. It makes me uneasy picturing it in my head, even now.

Penelope hadn't stopped whimpering. The sound caused me no end of distress, and I have no shame in telling you that wanted nothing more than for her to stop that endless, grinding whine. Still, I didn't attempt to shush or scold her. I would have you call me anything but a hypocrite, and I too felt the fear. It was a deep dread; a primal foreboding from back when we walked as apes. I can't give the sensation a description that would do it justice. I feel it is an emotion you can only truly empathize with if you've experienced it for yourself. Both Penelope and I knew, knew with as much certainty as I knew the sun rose in the morning and set at night, that we were somewhere safe for no living thing.

My decision to turn and first walk at a brisk pace, then break out into a jog, then full-on sprint back the way we came wasn't conscious. My only thought was that I *had to* return to the village, that I *had to* leave this unfamiliar world as soon as possible. I think we'd been running at least two hours before I realized our predicament couldn't be solved by back-tracking and hope. Penelope and I only left the village some thirty minutes prior to losing ourselves in the endless fields of greying reeds. We should have found home on our marathon several times over. As it was, the unfamiliar dirt track always extended further than I could run, further than where the village should have been, stretching endlessly onward no matter how much my feet blistered, or my thighs burned. By the second hour of running, I had no choice but to collapse. I lay on my side in the dirt, tongue sticking to the roof of my mouth, each breath raw and painful. Penelope threw herself down next to me in a similar state, her rhythmic pants still spaced between whimpers.

It was at this point, when I was lying on the ground waiting for my screaming body to recover, that I noticed the sky.

[EDGAR PAUSES FOR 1:38]

Do you have a cigarette?

[INTERVIEWER INTERJECTS: Yes, of course. EDGAR PAUSES FOR 4:37. SOUND OF CIGARETTE BEING LIT AND SMOKED. EDGAR COUGHS.]

I'd been so absorbed by panic I hadn't paid the sky above much attention. The purple-orange hues had been hiding something, something I had to stare at for a good few minutes to uncover. Faint patterns, almost imperceptible, filled every inch of it. They weren't clouds though. They were ridges and bumps, bevels and impressions, chaotic patterns all somehow hewn from the colours of the horizon itself. A tapestried ceiling of unnatural intricacy, like the atmosphere had been carved into by some vast, otherworldly creature. I lay on my back and watched them march their slow march across the stratosphere. I tried to convince myself they were a trick of the light, or a solar phenomenon like the aurora borealis. I'm sure it's no surprise by now, but this did me no good. The longer I watched, the clearer the forms in the translucent entropy became. Within about thirty seconds I could make out individual shapes, shapes that it worried me to note were distinctly humanoid. By the time a minute had passed, I had no doubts. They were *people*.

Somehow my mind knew they *weren't* merely the illusion of people, or an impression or likeness of them, but *actual* people, people somehow trapped behind a veil that stretched the width and breadth of the heavens above me. I could make out the details with ease; flailing limbs, bodies writhing over one another, faces twisted and contorted in expressions of unimaginable pain…

[EDGAR PAUSES FOR 0:27]

I realize how much of a madman this makes me sound, hearing myself say it out loud. I wish I was. This is the thing, you see. I could hear them… I *can* hear them. Still. Every time I close my eyes without sedatives.

[EDGAR PAUSES FOR 1:28]

They were quiet at first, but the unholy choir was soon loud enough to dispel any myth of hallucination. It didn't take long for my ears to ring. I'm sure hadn't looked away, the drums would have burst. Such a sound I cannot put into words. Nor do I want to. I shudder contemplating its mere existence if I'm being brutally honest with you, and *it does exist*. The fact I was found with dried blood spreading from my ears in all directions is *proof*. This is what I mean about quacks and charlatans! If it was a hallucination from some flight of insanity why, when the screams return to my nightmares, does every physical examination show extensive and continuous damage to my inner ear the next morning?!

[INTERVIEWER INTERJECTS: Please calm down Edgar. EDGAR SIGHS AUDIBLY]

Anyway, it didn't take long for the dread to return. I'm not ashamed to admit I was in full blown hysterics by this point. But, even in my frantic state, I was able to work out that heading back to the village wasn't an option. Thankfully, that… that *noise* from above stopped the instant I looked away from the seething mass of bodies in the sky. Fear of its return kept my gaze anchored to the dirt beneath my feet. My ears throbbed as I walked. Penelope's whimpering, the crunch of dry earth, the rustling of a wind I couldn't feel through leaves of trees that weren't there… all seemed louder, piercing, uncomfortable even. Every sound, no matter how small, felt intrusive in the silent void left once the… once the *noise* had dissipated. I found myself almost tempted to look up again, just to fill that nauseating abyss. I forgot about the noise soon enough though.

[INTERVIEWER INTERJECTS: Why?]

Because I found the gate.

[EDGAR PAUSES FOR 5:59]

I'd barely been walking back on myself for a quarter hour when I bumped into it. Had I been looking forwards, I'd have seen it coming. As it was, the threat of catching an accidental glimpse of the mass of wraiths above meant I wasn't looking where I was going. I crashed into the bars at full speed, headfirst. The clang when I bounced off them echoed across the fields. Landing on my arse, I yelled, both from pain and surprise. It only took a few moments for my skull to throb, and I'm told the bruise on my brow was visible.

It was a metal gate, one of those wrought-iron things you usually find outside manor houses. Well, not iron, but it was wrought-*something*. The metal was polished. The bars gleamed, reflecting light from a sun or moon which did not exist outside of their mirror-like surfaces. I think I would have noticed the absence of both beforehand, but I'd been either unable or unwilling to process the information. There was no wall or fence to speak of. The gleaming frame stood connected to a single (equally gleaming) post, but other than that stood alone in the endless fields. It waited for me to stand and pat the dust and earth from my coat before swinging open. The movement was smooth. *Too* smooth; silent and fluid like no hinge I had seen before or, thankfully, since. I could feel myself trembling. My extremities were both numb and tingling, and were it not for her whimpers, I'd have been unaware of Penelope trying to bury her head in my knees. I only continued onward because I *knew* going back was futile. Every fiber of my being urged me not to walk through that gleaming archway, but what choice did I have?

The fact I encountered the gate going forwards a much shorter distance than I had retreated *wasn't* lost on me. I was too drunk on dread to heed it much mind, though. I think the tree was manipulating my emotions as well as my senses by that point. The fear had almost evolved into a desire… no, a *compulsion,* to continue (if only to get my inevitable fate over with). The dissonance was migraine-inducing. I was both being beckoned down that dirt track and repelled by the fear of meeting whatever waited at its end. I'd never been a believer in the supernatural. My weekly attendance of Pastor Henry's sermons had been, at best, an adherence to social norms. Truth be told, the belief part, the faith in the divine and all that, had always eluded me somewhat. It didn't now. For the first time in my life, my prayers, muttered hastily under my breath as I trudged on, were honest and heartfelt. I had long since abandoned any attempt to provide a rational explanation for my fate. Never one for nihilism, the only conclusion left to me at the time was that I had somehow fallen prey to a work of the Devil. Do I believe that now? I'm not so sure. Even Satan and Hell are part of God's design, but I cannot bring myself to believe that the being who created my darling Ava could also be responsible for what waited at the end of that dry dirt road.

[EDGAR PAUSES FOR 8:29]

Do you have another cigarette?

[SOUND OF CIGARETTE BEING LIT]

Actually, just leave the box.

[EDGAR PAUSES FOR 7:33. SOUND OF MAN SOBBING, SOUND OF CIGARETTE BEING SMOKED]

Sorry, Dr Anand.

[INTERVIEWER INTERJECTS: It's fine, Edgar. Please continue.]

The hill sneaked up on me. Seems illogical, but the phrasing is deliberate. I wish I could provide a more satisfactory explanation. It was always there… I just didn't know it was until it decided I needed to. In my memories, I can see it at the end of the path quite clearly, present from the moment I stepped through the gate. However, on the day it was as though it were behind a veil, or shimmer. Somehow it hid not just from my vision but my whole awareness, choosing to reveal itself without warning with a sudden enough drop of the curtain to give Penelope cause to bark. The hill emerged from the swaying monochrome reeds as though it were the head of some aberration from the ocean depths breaching the waves for air. A thing which had no right being on the surface yet was there anyway. It wasn't a large hill; the incline was short and shallow, the peak of the mound no further than 20 ft from the base. Yet, I still found myself having to squint to make out the form at the top.

It was a tree. One would think a tree was an instantly recognizable form, but there I was perplexed and baffled. I strained my eyes, fighting to decipher the silhouetted trunk and branches, almost as though they were words written in a language I only knew half the alphabet of. Unlike the mass of specters in the sky, the tree I couldn't look away from. Its shadowy branches ebbed and swayed on the winds I could hear but not feel, leaves that didn't exist rustling harshly. Penelope was barking non-stop, panicked yaps that echoed over the grating of the foliage. I told her to be quiet with a bark of my own. I don't know why. It was hypocritical of me when you consider all I wanted to do was scream. I loved that dog. It causes me no end of despair knowing that the last words she heard from her master were a harsh and unwarranted reprimand. She was still cowering at my heels as I walked around the circumference of the fat, gnarled trunk. She'd always been an obedient companion and so had somehow managed to find silence. I could feel her shaking though, the trembles so violent she nearly tripped me over on several occasions. I'm glad I didn't look down to meet her eye. This might seem an odd thing to say, but I have enough nightmares *without* adding what the terror in her canine face must have looked like.

Closer to the tree, I could make out details and features of the wood. Ridged bark, like an oak or pine, covered its surface, although the scales were thicker and darker than any species of tree I knew or now know of (and believe me, my research on the subject since that day has been extensive, despite the library here being woefully inadequate). Around the base of the trunk, where the jagged roots cut and thrust into dry dirt, there were bare patches where the thick scales had frayed or weathered away entirely. The exposed flesh was waxy. I use the word flesh because, whilst it definitely *was* wood, it looked more fibrous and malleable than it had any right being. I hope it was just a trick of my eyes, but it seemed like the bark shell contained a mass of human hair, matted tight and held together by the viscous sap. The smell was foul, too. It felt as though it were eating the skin from my nostrils. A munitions factory had recently opened near the village. Grenades. The lingering stench of the chlorine for the trenches is the closest comparison I have to the sap odour. Chlorine that had somehow gone rotten, if such a thing were even possible. I heard Penelope vomit, and to this day, thank the lord I'm not blessed with the sensitive nose of a canine. The burning, itchy vapours were repulsive enough to make me *almost* forget the dread. Nausea and disgust became the new reasons for the wrenching in my gut; my darling Ava's egg on toast breakfast threatening to return with each second spent inspecting the ochre liquid oozing from the fine strands. Thankfully, I never reached the point of actual sickness. Long before that moment came, I had found my way to the tree's other side. If you're up to date with my file, you'll understand why what I found rendered all other concerns moot.

 Only when viewed from the other side of the hill did the tree reveal its true form. The web of branches sprang from a thick appendage jutting out the reeking trunk. The majority stemmed from the bulbous knot where bark-covered limb and tree body connected, spreading in erratic patterns like veins on a tumour. The crook of the disjointed central limb stood a full 12 feet from the ground, bending overhead to form a half arch not visible from the gate. The tip was a fresh wound; a clean and precise slice that left more exposed sap-flesh. I did not have time to think much on this, however. What I found swinging on the end of the rope emerging from it required my full attention. I say that the rope emerged from the end of the branch, rather than was tied too or around it, because I could see no knots or binding of any kind. Even in my memories (and they are regrettably clear, perhaps even more so than my senses were as the event unfolded) I can't see how that damp, sticky twine held fast. It came forth from the sap and pus of the branch end, dangling from the clotted hairs as though it were fused to them… no, *made from them*. My instincts were telling me to run, trying to scream louder than the alien throbbing sensation that pulled me forwards. The reason my senses left me, the thing that caused me to ignore the dread and give in to the enticing beckons of those vascular branches, was the other end of the frayed cord.

It was wrapped around the neck of a child.

She was a scrap of a thing, filthy and naked. Couldn't have been older than 8 or 9. She was thrashing and struggling against the tree's grip, kicking out at the empty air as her tiny hands wrestled with the rope around her throat. It takes a man colder than I could comprehend to ignore a child in such distress; the bulbous, bulging veins in her eyes, the slickness of tears on reddened cheeks, the pleading screams through choked gasps. At the time, I did not understand why Penelope did not share my unignorable compulsion to save this child. The canine instead leapt between me and the struggling girl. I didn't scold her verbally for her barking this time. Instead, I just…

[EDGAR PAUSES FOR 4:43. SOUND OF ANOTHER CIGARETTE BEING LIT]

Sorry, I still carry so much guilt. I've always been a gentle man. Especially with animals. I even used to wince whenever I'd see a rider whip his horse! The thought that I… that the hands I used to have…

[EDGAR PAUSES FOR 6:29. SOUND OF A SINGLE SOB]

I can remember my knuckles stinging, her confused cry as she rolled sideways down the mound, the trail of wet redness and stray teeth left on the dirt. What I did was so against my base nature that it repulses me. In that moment, though, the only thing that I knew, the only thought that existed to me, was *"rescue the flailing innocent from the clutches of the noose"*. In all honesty, I think my fanatical devotion was so strong I would have done the same even if it were my darling Ava, such was the lure of the girl's distress. She tried to reach out to me as I approached. The weight of her skinny frame must have been too much for her other arm to bear alone. Her hand snapped back to pull at the mucus coated rope almost as soon as it thrust at me. I could feel why as I tried to lift her and remove the strangling pull of gravity.

The child, this wafer-thin thing caked in dirt and dried blood, weighed almost as much as I did. No mean feat. Even though old age and institutionalization haven't been kind to my waistline, I think we can *both* tell my history includes more than my share of fine ale and good living. My legs buckled under the unexpected strain, forcing me down onto one knee. I felt something besides fear. I was confused. It was this confusion, this shock from one too many inexplicable phenomena, that ironically gave me clarity to see through the urge to save this innocent creature and realize it was… well, the only word I have for it is *wrong*. The skin that wasn't obscured by mud or scab was too smooth, too flawless. The colouring was the tone of no known ethnicity; a canary yellow with a tinge of green so subtle one almost didn't notice it, as though an infected wound festered beneath every inch of translucent flesh. The girl's movement, the flailing and tugging, felt stiff and rehearsed. A performance. The chaos of a human soul clutching to life was not present… in fact, now the strange succubus effect had been broken, the struggles seemed almost lacklustre. The eyes were too disconcerting to ignore. With my new perspective, I realized that any contact her gaze had with my own was pure coincidence. Her pupils did not follow me as I fell. They remained locked on the space where I'd stood, staring into the too-distant horizon. Still, motionless, empty of any spark or brightness.

As though it had read my thoughts, the thing pretending to be a girl stopped moving. It didn't fall limp, but went stiff enough to convince any onlooker rigor mortis was beginning to set in. Each of its scrawny limbs shot straight down, going so rigid that the knees and elbows started bending in on themselves. I said something. I can't remember the exact words, but I do remember I screamed them. I also remember they were aimed at a God I knew was not present. The… the tree seemed to respond to this. Matted hair whipped through the air as the girl-thing's head snapped back, neck bent at an unnatural angle, throat now revealed. My screams grew louder. I was past the point of anything intelligible passing through my lips. My terror rendered coherent speech impossible.

The girl-thing's face, when lowered, had concealed organic features found on no human or creature of the land or sea. The rope was no rope at all. Muscular sinew attached the child lure to the branch, unwinding from an open orifice just above the centre of the collarbone. This wet hole leaked the same putrid sap as the tree, the strings of tendon emerging from it dripping as they split and circled to form the noose knot. A slit ran up the neck, all the way from the orifice to the base of the chin. There was a hard organic noise, not too dissimilar from wet wood being snapped in two. The vertical folds parted. Muscles writhed and bulged in the thing's throat, the jaw cracking in half and splaying itself. Bone was forced apart to allow this new opening to stretch to its full width, and I now knew why the gaze of the girl-thing was so lifeless. It looked upon me with its true eye for the first time. The yellow and vein covered orb sat where vocal chords should have been, pulsing in a socket formed from collar bone and broken jaw. Its pupil, a dinner plate sized circle black as gunpowder, bore through me, and I knew in that instant that I knelt before a being as malevolent as it was superior.

My screaming was continuous. I could hear it, the endless shrill distress, even over the thumping of blood in my ears. Intermittent flashes of pain leapt from my chest, my heart smashing into my rib cage. Stomach knotted into my diaphragm, lungs raw, I howled. Both from terror and agony. The sound reaching my ears, though loud, came as though from some miles away. My mind had removed itself from my senses by this point. I've met men who served in the war (the ones driven mad by the trenches) who understand what I mean by this. So far, they're the only ones. Shell shock, they call it. Stepping out of yourself, too overwhelmed by the horror of your surroundings to do anything but watch from afar. The sounds of a second organic crack reached me as bones shifted to make way for another inhuman orifice. This fresh divide had been obscured by the dirt and dry blood, the latter of which I realized I would soon add to. The edges of it puckered like a flower unveiling itself at dawn. The seam of the split undid itself slowly, separating the child body into two halves divided vertically from the base of the ribs down. The mustard gas smell was overpowering now. My eyes watered, and a felt a warm trickling from one of my nostrils. The distance between the segments grew wider as the putrid skin unzipped, the flesh of the lips curling outwards all the way. It was obvious they were lips because of what lay behind them.

Teeth. Rows and rows of teeth. Human molars to be specific, an army of them filling the unholy maw as though it belonged to a perverse species of shark. Where a spine should have dangled, a long tongue writhed and thrashed in the manner of an eel on the deck of a fisherman's boat. Fully unfurled, the spasming muscle ran to 6 feet in length at least. Ulcerations and abscesses covered its surface, saliva flying in all directions as it heaved and pulsated.

Elsewhere on the grotesque form, wet noises began to burst forth from the rope opening. The tendon connecting the thing to the tree started growing, revealing more of itself somehow. Thick wads of sap dripped down the cyclopean nightmare's cleaved torso from the sphincter at its throat. More and more sinew unfurled as the abomination lowered itself to my level.

I wanted to scrabble backwards. I wanted to run. I wanted to be back home, sat by the warm fire listening to my darling Ava recounting the village gossip of the day. I lacked the power to make any of this happen. All I could do was scream and raise my hands, watching as the thing descended upon me. The abdominal jaw was fully open; the concentric rows of molar poised beside me, ready to close. I could smell the burning of its breath, close enough for the repugnant tongue to prod and probe my colourless face. I lay there, helpless, hands above me in a futile gesture of self-preservation. The tree's eye drilled into me. Both It and I both knew I was doomed. Then, in the final moments when its tongue began to wrap around my left arm, a golden bolt struck the space between us.

Penelope smashed into the thing before I'd registered the sounds of her defiant barks. The tree and I had been too focused on each other to notice her bound back up the hill and leap, her thoughts only on the fact that her master was in danger. The wolf in her knew only one strategy. Go for the throat. Her jaws locked around the child-thing's eye, her body hanging between rows of teeth as she twisted and thrashed, determined not to stop until the threat to her world was dead. The abyssal creature and I moved in unison. For my part, I reached up to grab Penelope, my own thoughts now as much on keeping her safe from the nightmare as hers were on me. My fingers just about reached around her hind legs when the behemoth maw slammed shut.

The golden retriever howled. I joined her.

Penelope, along with my forearms and hands, were crushed to flatness before my brain could register the aberration had even moved. It took the warmth of flecks of blood splashing into my open mouth to notice that its mandibles were no longer apart. Only when I toppled onto my back was I aware of the sudden absence of feeling where my hands used to be. It was Penelope's scream, the piercing pain and confusion in that almost human sound, as her severed hind quarters landed at my feet that made everything fall into place. This new shock kick-started muscles previously paralyzed by incomprehensible terror. Somehow, I ran.

There was no pain from my severed wrists as I pelted down the hill. I flew through the gate. I could hear more organic sounds over my feet pounding the dirt, but I couldn't bring myself to look back to watch Penelope be consumed. I was beyond the ability to mourn her loss. The drive to keep running, to get as far away from the tree as possible, was too great. All I could do was run until the pain from open wounds and aching legs took over. I don't know how long I had been running before I collapsed, but it felt like hours. Maybe even days. The last thing I remember as fell to the earth, vision fading to black, is the sight of the hill, still mere feet behind me, the tree as close as it had ever been.

[EDGAR PAUSES FOR 5:32]

By the time I regained consciousness, the stumps where hands had once been were fully healed. My darling Ava said it had taken the village a whole night of searching to find me, and when they had I was face down in a ditch some twenty miles away babbling incoherent nonsense. I was covered in blood, both my own and Penelope's, but it didn't appear fresh despite my absence from the world I knew being brief. As you have probably guessed, it didn't take long from the first time I recounted my tale for the village to declare me mad. I was home for less than a month before they called your people, and you brought me to this… this shit hole.

[INTERVIEWER INTERJECTS: Relax, Edgar. I've read your file. Can you tell me about the eyewitness accounts?]

Of course I can! They never found any traces of Penelope. This fact, rather than lend credit to my story, only served to fuel the rumour that I had killed and eaten her. To this day I've yet to hear a reasonable explanation of *how* I managed to crush and remove both of my hands, nor why the blood on my clothing appeared weeks (maybe even months) old. I suppose people are so desperate to cling to their feeble notions of normalcy that they're willing to ignore the truth even when provided with hard evidence. Even my darling Ava, despite her claims to the contrary, looked upon me with that familiar combination of pity and disbelief I have grown used to seeing in other people's faces. A mental breakdown, they called it. A sudden madness. Were it not for one final detail I would *almost* believe them. For you see, when they found me, there was something wrapped around my arm. Some of them claimed it was the remains of a snake I'd bitten the head off of, others that it was the only remains of Penelope's entrails, more still that it was a dried vine or reed that proved I'd hidden her body in a river somewhere. All the rumours agreed on one thing, though, that the length of flesh was covered in ulcers and sores, and that it gave of the same reeking odour that you could smell by the munitions factory outside the village.

[EDGAR PAUSES FOR 2:38. SOUND OF CHAIR SCRAPING. INTERVIEWER INTERJECTS: Is that it, Edgar? You're sure there's nothing else you remember?]

Why?

[INTERVIEWER INTERJECTS: What if, hypothetically, I'd spoken to someone who'd witnessed the same thing you did?]

Then I'd say you spend too much time around nutters, Dr Anand. Thanks for lighting the cigarettes.

[END OF TRANSCRIPT]

DOROTHYRESCUE.MOV

OK so, I gotta get this off my chest, and you people seem as good as any. Not like I got a lotta options. I'm not exactly drowning in friends or family. Strangers will have to do.

So yeah, I gotta tell you about this video I found. I'll give you a bit of context to speed things up; I work for a social project in my town. Long story short, I get old laptops scrubbed and refurbished so they can get donated to schools, care homes, other social projects, wherever they need to go. Simple enough to understand, yeah? Cool. I don't wanna fuck around wasting time by giving you a load of details. I wanna get this done so I can shut off my damn laptop and get packing. I'm only doing this *now* so I can get shit down while everything is still fresh in my memory, you know?

Anyway, you can probably guess what happened, right? Laptop came in, weird ass video on it. Seems simple enough. You're probably thinking, "*Why are you bothering us with this, Ted? It's just a weird video, fuck off.*"

Well, I wouldn't be venting all this to damn strangers if it was *just* a weird fucking video, would I? In my line of work, I see *a lot* of weird videos. Do you know how many child molesters I've helped get sent to prison? Three. How many murderers? Seven. People leave a lot of dark fucking shit on old devices they throw out. I've been at this 10+ years, and this is the first video so weird I felt I had to tell someone, *anyone*, about it. Do the damn math.

Caught up? This was a *weird* video. Like, *I'm going to skip town tomorrow if I don't Alt+F4 from life first* level weird.

You're expecting the laptop itself was a bit off, right? That the password was 666, or that there was a message to me waiting on it, or the background was a picture of my cramped apartment? Nah. It was completely normal. It was waiting for me on the desk of my studio when I arrived at the center that morning. Babs muttered something about me being late as usual, but didn't say anything was off about this week's batch of virus riddled 00s machines.

The laptop with the video was on top of the pile, an old Dell running Windows XP. Black, shell chipped in places, sleek once but faded and beaten now. It had seen better decades, let alone days. In other words, nothing I would usually be posting about, right? I plugged it in and booted it up to find no password was needed to log in to the single account. Again, not unusual. Even the name of the previous owner's user account didn't raise suspicion. Chris, it said, below a picture of a gym-life looking guy in his late twenties.

Chris. I'm gonna be talking a lot about him in a minute, when we get to the damn video. Nearly there.

This is where the laptop did get a little peculiar. I logged into Chris' account to find the standard default Windows XP background; the rolling green hills and blue skies anyone that remembers the early-ish 00s is familiar with no doubt. That's not what made me cock an eyebrow and take a sip from my Mountain Dew. It was the desktop's contents. It was full, filled with copy after copy of the same .mov file.

dorothyrescue.mov

There were at least three dozen copies. I didn't count them. Nah, all I did was double click the copy in the top left, the original. I wanted to see what all the fuss was about. As I said right, I'd seen weird shit before. What was I gonna do, *not* play it? Worst-case scenario, I thought, was I would see some more gnarly shit that'd mean I had to call the cops. Big whoop. At least it'd make the week more interesting. That was only the worst-case scenario, too. My honest first guess was either a virus or that Chris was... how to put this tactfully... ill. Like, *in-the-head* ill. You got them sometimes too, machines that were a prop in a prolonged mental breakdown.

When the video started playing, my immediate reaction was one of disappointment. Nothing interesting, I thought, obviously some kind of student movie. Some Blair Witch/Paranormal activity knock off. The opening shot was of three people sitting around a wooden table in a dimly lit living room. They didn't introduce themselves, but luckily for you, I'm writing all this in hindsight so I can spill the beans.

The trio was composed of two women and a man. The man was Chris, though you've probably guessed that, right? He was different from his user photo though. Older, for starters, by a few years at least. Hair was notably thinner, and there were more than a few frown lines around his once borderline-handsome features. They weren't near-attractive anymore though. They were gaunt, stretched, had the same eye-bags and squint marks that… well, that a guy who spends his days in front of computer screens like I do have.

One of the two girls was in a similar state. Harriet, she was called. A wafer-thin thing that looked way too far from her last meal. I'd have thought they were both junkies were it not for the fact their skin was absent of any of the crust, scars, or scabs I knew came with prolonged substance abuse. You could tell from the first frame that Harriet was romantically attached to Chris/totally dependent on him. She was hanging off his arm, gazing up at him with her bloodshot eyes as he spoke into the camera. He spoke a lot, and fast, and it's been a few hours (and *a lot* of panicking) but I'll try and give you the most accurate rundown I can.

HARRIET: Is it on?
CHRIS: It's on, it's recording.
HARRIET: Do you think it'll work—
CHRIS: *Shh.*

Chris turns to the camera, ignoring the rake-thin woman clasping at his dirty shirt.

CHRIS: OK… if you're able to watch this, then part of our plan worked… we're going to be bringing this laptop with us so, if things *don't* go at least partly how we hoped, nobody will see this anyway—

REBECCA: Cut the shit Chris, I didn't fly down here so you could play paranormal YouTuber. Just light the fucking candle.

The other woman sitting at the table, Rebecca, was clearly the outsider of the group. Her face was full, rosy, the face of someone that enjoyed a world of home-cooked meals and hearty wholesome comforts. There wasn't the twinkling in her eyes you'd expect to see from such a life though. They were stern, cold, and never found their way to Chris or Harriet without filling with disdain first. This didn't seem to perturb Chris, and he ignored Rebecca just as he did the emaciated Harriet.

CHRIS: Last time we did this we opened a… nah, you'll see what we opened. We're going to do it again in a second. Just… look, they're still searching for Dorothy Raines. It's been years, but they ain't given up. We know where she is. The police, her family, will never find her. Even if we can't bring her back, hopefully if her family is watching this, can see it, it'll bring them a little closure, bring *you* a little closure.

Chris looked at me on the other side of the 4th wall, clearly anticipating I'd be someone other than a laptop fix-up guy working for an under-funded charity. The name Dorothy Raines rang a bell, and I remembered that there had been some news coverage of a Dorothy who vanished from her college apartment some years back. I couldn't recall much beyond that, but, then again, why would I? The news is obsessed with a new missing white girl every week. They all blend into one after a while.

On the screen, the wool sweater-wearing Rebecca rolled her eyes but didn't interrupt Chris. Her guilty swallow was so small it almost wasn't noticeable, but I picked up on it. Whatever the hell Chris was talking about, it wasn't a lie. The already-sick-of-Chris's-bullshit Rebecca wouldn't have been trying to hide obvious guilt if it was, right? As for Chris, he'd reached down under the table to pick up two objects. The first was an ugly candle. He placed it at the center of the table and all three on-screen noses wrinkled, all six eyes locked in the lumpy purple-grey wax and wide braided wick. It wasn't white like a normal candlewick, either. It was brown, sleek, shiny. Far too much like human hair for my liking, you know? It sent a shiver down my spine, let's put it that way. Still, though, at this point my thoughts were that Chris had just put a lot of effort into making his props. As much as I was a little unnerved, I wished I had popcorn.

"This might actually end up being a good movie." I muttered, leaning back in my chair.

On the screen, Chris had pulled out the second object from underneath the table. It was a book, a small black volume bound in what looked to be charred leather. Again a little shiver, again a sudden urge for movie snacks. Something about the book in Chris' hands was *off*, but I couldn't put my finger on what. Still can't, but the list of things I can't explain is now much longer, and weird pixels that are a little too good at pulling your attention are far lower down it. I want somebody to explain the fucking blue sand first for a start.

CHRIS: This book... ummm... no, I won't say its name, it—

REBECCA: For fuck sake, Chris, it's not going to kill them to know what it's called.

CHRIS: Cool, but do you want them to go looking for it?

REBECCA: *Silence.*

CHRIS: That's what I thought. Anyway, I found this book a few years ago, and in it are instructions on how to make... this.

He gestured toward the ugly candle with his free hand. Harriet, who was still clinging with white knuckles to Chris' shirt, let out a soft whimper.

CHRIS: This is an (*Arabic sounding word*). The shorthand version is it's a candle made from corpse wax, jizz—

HARRIET: Chris!

CHRIS: What, Harriet, it is! It's a candle made of corpse wax, *jizz,* hair, and placenta.

REBECCA: Jesus Christ, why did I get on that plane...

CHRIS: When you light it you can communicate with the dead. Or, at least, that's what we *thought* would happen. The *truth* is much worse.

He waved the book at the screen. The shivering in my spine returned, although now I wasn't so convinced this was just a movie. I know good actors make even the most unbelievable shit look convincing but, God damn, the guy "playing" Chris deserved an Oscar if this was all staged. That mix of fear, regret, guilt, anger, and disgust was far too specific for any actor to pull off.

CHRIS: You'll see what I mean, but when you light an (*Arabic sounding word*), you don't just talk to the dead; you go where they are. We lit one a few years back, the four of us, but Dorothy got stuck on the other side because Rebecca decided to use a martini blender instead of a mortar and pestle.

REBECCA: Fuck you, Chris.

CHRIS: Harriet and I have been studying this book since, and we *think* we've found a way to bring Dorothy back. Emphasis on *think.* It might not work.

REBECCA: I... we owe it to Dorothy to try though.

Chris nodded as Rebecca acknowledged the webcam in that dimly lit room, and by extension me, for the first time.

CHRIS: Exactly. If it works, then great, if not then... well, I think I speak for all of us when I say that this guilt isn't worth living with.

The two women stared at the table, their solemn faces all the indication I needed to prove Chris hadn't said anything untrue on their behalf. Harriet took the pause in his monologue as a cue. She unclasped her hand from his stained shirt and stood, walking off screen to a light switch somewhere out of shot of the webcam. There was a click, and every pixel plunged into fuzzy darkness.

This is where shit got *weird*-weird, right? Like, *I yelped and fell out of my chair* weird. Soon as the pixels faded to black, so did my studio. The strip of fluorescent lights flickered and died. Looking back now, that shoulda been my cue to bolt. Flickering lights that shut off when something spooky happens? That's a Grade A horror movie cliché red flag right there. But, as much as I vaguely registered the lights failing, I was far more interested in the choppy audio.

It was flickering, static. I caught the odd word or two, but nothing I could make sense of. The only voice speaking was Chris, that much I figured. What he was saying though I have no idea. Not sure I wanna know, either. By the time I'd pulled myself to my seat and banged the side of the screen a few times, it had cleared up a little. Not much mind, not enough. I could hear a buzzing warbled noise that sort of sounded like this Chris, but barely. I was on the verge of standing to try and fix the lights when I yelped again.

Chris' speech had been warped, crackled, and distorted, and *definitely* came from the speaker. The crystal-clear scrape of the lighter was right behind my left ear.

Luckily, I didn't fall out of my chair this time, but I did flail around in the darkness behind me. On the screen pixels had started shimmering back into life though, so I wasn't gonna waste long trying to fight shadow sounds conjured by my imagination (as I naively believed the lighter noise was). My jaw dropped as I stared at the laptop. All false ideas about student films and CGI now long gone.

The audio was still fucked, so I couldn't hear what was being said, but the trio was talking. No, not talking… yelling. Yelling and screaming. I could tell why they were so panicked straight away. Let's just say we're not in Kansas anymore, Toto. They looked as confused as I felt, and though I couldn't hear their words, I got the impression they'd expected to find something other than what they found.

One of them had lit the candle, because it sat flickering away on the middle of the table. The table which, coincidentally, was the only feature of the room they were in previously that remained.

Where the dimly lit room had once been was a wide, starless sky, with a horizon far too far away for any camera to find, whether on a shitty laptop or the Hubble telescope. Somehow I knew if I was there in person I couldn't have seen any farther than the potato camera on this beaten laptop, too. This horizon was far more distant than any you could find in a holiday brochure. Where the floor had once been was sand, thick deep-blue sand the color of tropical oceans. There were footprints in this sand; thousands of them, all heading in the same direction. Thankfully, the direction was *away* from the table. Not-so-thankfully, one of the women picked up the laptop so that I could follow Chris with his ugly candle as he headed the same way.

They trudged through the endless blue desert for a good two hours, led by the light of the corpse wax candle. I don't know which of the two women was carrying the laptop and webcam, but I caught the static-soaked hiss and spit of them frantically yelling every so often. I don't know why I didn't fast forward this bit. Something compelled me to sit and watch in real time, just in case I missed something, like the audio popping back in or the group changing direction. I began to shiver more as I watched, too. My dark studio grew slowly colder, the normally warm air icy and biting.

Again, massive red flag, right? Shoulda turned the damn thing off then and there. I *didn't* though, because I *couldn't*. Something about that grainy footage of those endless azure dunes, and the cracking and snarling audio distortion that played over it, had me encapsulated. My attention wasn't away from it long enough to connect the dots leading to *creepy video making room colder and turning lights off equals hella bad get the hell out of there right now*. Don't get me wrong, I *was* scared. With every minute that passed, I grew more and more unnerved, the knot in my gut I couldn't quite explain twisting tighter and tighter. I knew on some level that what I was experiencing *wasn't* good, and *definitely wasn't* going to end well. It didn't matter. Whether due to my own curiosity or because of some hypnotic effect of the footage, I sat nose inches from the screen for two solid hours. I didn't move from my spot until they found the island.

It was floating nearly half a mile above the sand. I don't have words for how big it was, nor can I explain how nobody inside the footage or watching in the present failed to notice it looming on the horizon before it was on top of us. Even though it was far too far from the light of the candle to make out clearly, I could tell what it was made of.

Flesh.

The unfathomably dark shadow the camera panned upwards to focus on writhed and pulsated in the sky. A perverse, living stormcloud; a continent-sized organic Zeppelin older than time itself. What slithers of light could ascend to that height were reflected in glistening sacs and bulging ligaments, town-sized bulbous cysts and tunnel-wide arteries. I could smell it too, somehow. No, not somehow. I *know* how. I could smell it because this fucking video was of somewhere never meant to be filmed.

I've had to come to terms with the sand, right? If the sand happened, then it's not a stretch to say that stench wasn't my imagination.

It was foul. I've smelled some foul shit in my time too but, God damn, this was like a porta john fulla roadkill left to bake in the sun for a month. I fully retched, although thankfully managed not to puke. My brain was waking up to the intense concentration of *"nope"* in the room by this point, and the first thoughts that I should maybe shut the laptop crossed my increasingly panicked mind. The screen had a few more gems to share before I finally screamed and threw it across the room though.

First was the hole.

The wide gulf in the azure dunes stretched almost as far from view as the impossible horizon itself. Like the island floating above, it seemed to ambush Chris and his party, appearing in his path as if from nowhere. Chris almost fell right into it, and I realized then that Rebecca had been carrying the laptop, because Harriet darted into the shot to grab Chris's shirt and stop the sudden void claiming him. I'm glad Rebecca didn't decide to aim the webcam down the hole. Seeing the look of terror on Chris's face after he caught a glimpse at the bottom was enough. Of all the things in the video, it's the hole my mind comes back to the most. Something about it is... *fuck*, I don't know how to describe it. When I picture it, I get this feeling, this dread, like I know I'm thinking about the absolute worst thing you could possibly think about. At the same time, though there is this sense of... destiny, I guess? Like I know I'm gonna end up there, in that hole, like I'm gonna find what waits at the bottom whether I like it or not.

Maybe that's what the bodies were about. There were millions of them throwing themselves into the pit. All those footprints had been leading in the same direction, right? Well, now you know where. Rebecca didn't move while Harriet helped Chris to his feet, so I had the pleasure of watching the alabaster figures hurling their twisted selves into the gaping void for nearly a minute. They'd parted like a biblical sea to allow the group passage, apparently. Like the hole, and the island, they were both impossible to ignore even from miles away, yet invisible until right on top of us... no, of *them,* on top of them! About 20 feet on either side of the trio the horde began, an endless stream of ghostly, misshapen people diving into the yawning gulf in the endless dunes. What made their mismatched features all the more terrifying was the fact that I could *hear* them.

Chris, Harriet, and Rebecca's words were still coming through cracked, distorted, unintelligible. The screams of the bodies falling into the pit weren't. They were coming through so clear I looked over my shoulder once or twice to make doubly sure none of the ivory abominations were in the room with me. The fanaticism with which they threw themselves was harrowing. You could hear it in their howls, see it in their contorted faces as they fell. Determination of levels hitherto unexperienced. The sea of writhing forms parted, forming a constant wary perimeter around the webcam when the trio composed themselves enough to start hiking along the rim of the pit. For a full ten minutes while the three trudged, I watched the endless cascade of pasty bodies tumbling to whatever horror awaited them in the depths. Countless trillions of them. It didn't take long for the deafening roar of their screams grew too much. That's when I had it *confirmed* that I was fully up the supernatural shit creek with no paddle and a hole in my canoe. I tried muting the footage. The little icon of a crossed-out speaker appeared, and the tinny popping of the trio's hidden conversation vanished.

The screaming waterfall of ivory bodies didn't though.

No matter how many times I hit that damn mute/unmute button, the endless shrieks and screeches of the suicidal tide continued echoing around my studio. I started sobbing. I was in full-blown panic mode by now, yeah? No shame there, pal, I bawled like a baby. My heart was clawing up out of my throat, my stomach dropping well below where my feet were. I didn't have a finger that wasn't numb, a limb that wasn't shaking.

Despite my terror, the video continued. It was the last part now, the part that's the reason I've decided to get the fuck out of Dodge.

Chris was still leading the women around the pit, lighting their way with his half-melted ugly candle. The sea of bodies hadn't waned in consistency or volume. How the group didn't spy *any* of the suicidal abominations before the island and pit materialized, I don't know. They were in an endless desert, yet even an infinite plane didn't feel large enough to contain the sheer number of malformed humanoid things martyring themselves to the void. I noticed the one that *wasn't* running at about the same time as Rebecca. I know this because the view went sideways the exact second I registered the woman in the dirty dress, the one sat facing away from the camera. Straight away it was obvious this girl wasn't like the tide of albino suicide. Her skin was pale, but human pale, not the pure white of a bleached bone. She had hair, short but still there. The clothes, despite being dirty, were the biggest giveaway though. And, of course, the fact she *wasn't* joining the gibbering creatures in their bid for oblivion.

Rebecca's feet ran past the screen as she raced to join Chris, Harriet, and the shaking figure. I caught a glimpse of their faces. They were smiling. Not for long though. As they approached the woman she stood, slowly, but didn't turn to face the webcam or the group. I caught a few of Chris' pop cracked words over the screams here. "*Dorothy*", "*sorry*", and "*rescue*". He put a hand on her shoulder, and she turned to face us.

I screamed. The woman who turned around wasn't a woman anymore. If it had once been this Dorothy, whatever happened since the trio left her in this place had robbed her of the humanity needed to claim that name.

Where this woman, this Dorothy's, face should have been was a hole. The gaping wound was ragged around the edges. Tatters of loose skin flapped and dangled at its rim, the length of which ran from chin to hairline, cheekbone to cheekbone. What was inside the abscess was far, far worse than the cavity itself though.

Inside the hole in Dorothy's face was… Nothing. Capital N Nothing. Not flesh, not a hollowed-out pit carved into gore and viscera, but Nothing. To call the emptiness in her face darkness, blackness, shadow, would be doing it a disservice. A defined universal absence, an absolute totality of non-being, non-existence; a glimpse into an abstract state of *not* that antithesized everything rational or sane. And, somehow, despite not having eyes, it was looking right at the camera. Right at *me*.

I screamed louder than I ever had done. The pops and cracks let me know the trio were doing the same in the footage. On screen, Rebecca was backing slowly away from the Walking Nothing that was once her Dorothy. Chris was reaching for the candle which, in his shock, he'd dropped. That was the mistake that cost Harriet her life.

She'd dropped to the floor just like the corpse wax candle. The whimpering heap she became was unable to resist as the Walking Nothing, that abyss on legs, stood over her, reaching down with two dainty hands. Chris stopped, jaw dropped, which was another costly mistake for Harriet. The Dorothy-thing lifted her with ease, pulling the sobbing girl's face towards the space where its own should have been. The closer Harriet got, the less distorted her whimpers and sobs became. I could hear her begging for mercy with the pin-drop clarity by the time her final moments came. I'm gonna have to drink *a lot* to forget them. Thank fuck they only lasted about half a minute.

As soon as their heads were level, the nothingness started creeping from Dorothy's face. The tendrils wrapped themselves around the trembling Harriet, obfuscating her from the webcam's eye. Harriet made a sound; a gargling howl I wish I didn't know humans could feel enough pain to make. The Walking Nothing only held Harriet for a few seconds. Felt like longer though. *Much* longer. My throat was ripped red raw from my own screams by the time it had finished.

I wish I could say that Harriet had stopped moving, that the Walking Nothing had suffocated her, and that she was at peace. I'd be lying though.

From the angle of the webcam, I couldn't see exactly what the Walking Nothing did to her. I saw the result though. I saw how Harriet lay face down in the sand for a while after being dropped. Saw how she pulled herself to her feet and turned to face not Chris, or Rebecca, or her attacker, but the laptop in the sand. To face *me*. She stared at me, and I saw straight away the dark lines around her face that matched the rim of the facial abyss on once-Dorothy. Tears were streaming down her cheeks; her bottom lip was trembling.

It was still trembling when one of her hands calmy pinched her nose and pulled. Her eyes, lips, nostrils, all continued twitching and moving as her face was removed from her head as though a carnival mask. The new abyss-headed monstrosity she'd become turned the sobbing face of Harriet over in its hands for a few seconds before discarding it into the pit like a frisbee.

That's when I'd had enough. Seeing two of those... those *things* staring directly at me like a fucking Zoom conversation tipped me over the edge. I could feel tears on my own cheeks as I slammed the screen shut, throwing the laptop against the opposite wall with a roar. The second plastic met drywall, my lights flickered back to life. You know the sand I kept mentioning? Well, here we are.

My studio was covered in a layer of rich blue sand. The azure grains coated every surface, no nook nor cranny was spared. I didn't hang around long enough to investigate further. The video itself had already sent me far, far over the line of thinking clearly, of being curious. Seeing the blue sand from the footage covering every inch of my workspace was a whole load of *nope* at a time when I was already way over my daily limit.

I'm sure Babs tried to stop me as I ran to my car. She'd been hammering on the door to my studio when I tumbled through it, covered head to toe in blue sand and tears. I wasn't in much of a state to register her presence though. How I managed to drive home without crashing, I don't know.

I don't expect you to believe me (as much as I want you to) because I wouldn't have. I need to tell *somebody,* you know? Before I go AWOL. My next step after this is to go off-grid. I don't care what you think; I *know* those Walking Voids were looking at me. Not at the camera, at *me.* If I could smell the stench of that damn island, if the fucking sand could... well, yeah, they could *definitely* see me. I don't want to know what would have happened if I'd watched until the end.

I'm not going to tell you where I'm going, for obvious reasons. I don't know who, or *what,* else might be reading this. I'm putting this out there in case copies of *dorothyrescue.mov* made it online. If you find one, DON'T watch it. Do not. I did, and now things I can't possibly understand know who I am. Know where I am. They're already after me.

I'm going to pack once I've posted this, then slip out the back window. I was gonna go out the front, you know? Leave like a normal person? I think the time for that has long passed though. I'm waiting for the right moment, then I'm getting the fuck out of here. Hopefully it comes soon. I've just got to wait for that impossibly pasty old man on the sidewalk to stop staring at me through my living room window.

The moment he stops pointing at me, I'm going to bolt. Wish me luck.

A CONVERSATION WITH ZEE

Geraldine.

    I'm not saying you're right. I don't know what's going on anymore though. I've always been aware that the Director held things back from us, but I read the files you leaked before Human Resources took them down. It's coming up to the date of the jump. I can't do this if it isn't... if he's... look, just in case... just in case Robert is wrong, here's something I think you should look at. You know him better than anyone. Just don't let me be making the wrong decision by sending this.
    00087 is a master of telesuggestive hypnosis, not to mention an emotional sadist. After some sleep, I managed to convince myself I'd been tricked by the three mouthed freak. The only reason I never uploaded the tape or transcript was embarrassment. It's been sitting in a USB on my desk for years. I thought it'd made it up, tried to play on my insecurities. Then I read your "report". We all did. Things are different now. If it's all true, if what the damn mime told me when I stopped the tape wasn't a load of shit just to get me riled up, then...
    I thought we were trying to save the world, to think we were actually... I'm scared, Geraldine. Everyone is. Even Dipesh is faltering. Wherever you are, I hope you're OK. I don't understand what you're doing or why but... just make it count, OK?

-L

The following is translated from French. Interviewer: LHG

Subject: Entity-00087.
BEGINNING OF TRANSCRIPT

LHG: Initial entity interview, designated entity Treble Zero Eighty Seven. Interviewer is Doctor Har—

00087: No.

LHG: No?

00087: I don't answer to a number.

LHG: It's just standard pro—

00087: No.

LHG: OK… well what do you answer to? Do you have a name?

00087: Yes.

LHG: Can you tell me?

00087: Yes.

LHG: What is it then?

00087: Ah, that's not what you asked. I *can* tell you, I *won't* though. If you *must* refer to me, I'll go by Zee.

LHG: OK then, Zee. Why won't you go by your *true* name? The file says your full title is Zara—

00087: Because I'm not an idiot. I know everything I say is going in a file to be poured over by your wise leader. This is all recorded. I'm over four centuries old, you sniveling quim. He won't break me so easily. Names are powerful things, so are voices. Who knows what he could do with both of mine in the same place?

LHG: By my "wise leader", I assume you mean Director—

00087 makes a noise of audible discomfort.

00087: Yes—*him*.

LHG: You're not the first sentient entity I've interviewed that's afraid of—

There is the sound of 00087's chains audibly rattling. Its next words come as a snarl.

00087: I'M NOT AFRAID. OF HIM OR ANYTHING ELSE.

00087 coughs, composing itself.

00087: I'm not afraid. I'm not. Just sensible.

LHG: But this is what I don't understand, Zee. Every entity I've interviewed seems… "sensible", about the Director. Not IPSET, just him.

00087: That's because IPSET is a joke. Do you *really* think I'd be sat here talking to *you* if this facility was run by a bunch of… ugh… *your kind*?

Sound of LHG swallowing.

00087: Oh my, you actually *do,* don't you? No dear, no. I'm here because I was stupid enough to get found by the man beyond all things. As soon as he goes away, I will too. He won't though, will he? That's the whole point.

LHG: My kind? What on Earth are you—

00087: Tell me, how many… what do you call us?

LHG: Entities.

00087: How many entities have you personally interviewed?

LHG: Seven.

00087: And how many were, in your professional opinion, such a risk that your little house of cards operation might not be able to stop them if they got out? How many were only really apprehended in the first place because of some deus ex machina miracle?

LHG: Seven.

00087: How many were you genuinely amazed hadn't already thrown off their chains to walk in the sun? How many would threaten to do all sorts of unspeakable things to you, would tease their way into your mind with unspeakable threats and abhorrent promises? How many were you *afraid of?*

LHG: Seven.

00087: How many were willing to discuss the director?

LHG does not respond.

00087: Well?

LHG: Zero.

00087: Do you ever wonder why?

Once more, LHG does not respond. There is the sound of 00087 chuckling. When he speaks again, it is in childish singsong.

00087: She doesn't know, she doesn't know, got her pen out ready to go, but the bitch still doesn't know.

There is an audible tremble in LHG's voice. The nervous clicking of a pen can be heard on the tape.

LHG: Know what, Zee? What don't I know?

00087: When I first emerged from the sea of guillotine-spilled blood, back when your countrymen shed the yolk of aristocratic indulgence off their back, I wandered sweet Paris doing all I knew how to: gorge myself in the decadent swill your foolish ape ancestors decided to become. It's what I'm *built* to do, see? To feed, to indulge. It's why I'm here. To keep the spirit of that moment living and preserved for the universe.

LHG: What does this have to do—

00087: It didn't take long for me to encounter… something *else*. Something entirely different from the warm trembling sacks I consumed. Before then there was only me and meat. After that encounter, I realized I was but one corner of an ecosystem as wide and deep as a thousand stretches of the universe.

LHG: What happened?

00087: Funny story really. I set about my usual routine, ready to ensnare my target, to keep my prize docile and tender. Instead of the man falling into a dribbling stupor, however, I was set upon by a swarm of miniature clockwork figures. They spewed from his distended jaw, launching themselves at me in a way no technology should have in the late 1700s. Of course I fought back, and it didn't take either of us to realize we were facing a fellow predator-in-arms. Combat gave way to conversation. I learned.

LHG: Learned what, Zee?

00087: Oh, many things. Things about the universe, and my place in it. Of time, of its scale and grandeur, how fate is inevitable but flexible. He was a traveler, you see, my new friend. I was lucky. My first encounter could have been with an insufferable idiot like the maggot baby. It wasn't though. It was with the traveler, and he'd seen much he was willing to share with something as like-mindedly curious and voraciously predatory as I. He explained to me the nature of what is, what isn't, and what shouldn't be but is anyway. I also learned that there's one thing, one single being that's beyond all others in *that* particular dissonant blasphemy, too. An, to use your parlance, "entity" my new friend from beyond the stars advised me to avoid above all others. A thing so powerful it could survive the end of the universe and remain to witness the cycle begin anew. The greatest aberration among aberrations, the tyrant king of the higher existential order on Earth.

LHG: You're referring to the man in charge?

00087 cackles.

00087: The—the man—oh, oh that's *good*. No, my pretty, you're a thousand leagues too shallow. I'm referring to what the things the man in charge fears fear themselves. What they *all* fear, those pompous pretender-gods in their pocket dimensions and secret realms. The one once-person they've known better than to cross since he watched the very first fish pull itself from the sea for the thousandth time.

LHG: And that person is?

00087: You know *exactly* who they are. Think about it, have you ever met anyone who was there with him at the beginning? When he founded this joke of an institute as a front for his own ends?

LHG: No, but that doesn't mean—

00087: And what about his name being in the *Black Book,* the only... ha... "human" mentioned as something other than an ingredient? Why all reports on his history are obfuscate from even the highest-ranking officers of this charlatan parade?

LHG: Confidentiality, obviously! And as for the *Taelim,* he founded us, that's just proof the work IPSET does is—

00087: Sure. Of *course* it is. And those skulking cold-blooded things that swim through the shit and offal under our cities carve his likeness in their temples because of sheer coincidence, I'll bet? He's not a man, my trembling flower. He's not a God, not a trespasser from the stars, he's not even whatever the hell I am. He's much, *much* worse.

LHG says nothing. There is the sound of 00087 laughing for almost two minutes.

00087: I love watching the colour drain from your face like that.

LHG: I... no, I trust the Director. We're saving the world. He's... he's *human,* for fuck's sake!

00087: Is he?

LHG: Yes!

00087: Maybe once, a lifetime of lifetimes ago. Think back to the quiet hours, after a few drinks in the staff lounge three floors above us. Yes, those evenings you're remembering right now, the many you've had over those long, harrowing years. How many inebriated colleagues have sworn to you they've *seen him die*?

LHG lapses back into silence.

00087: I'm a little fishie, my dear, a little fishie in a big old pond where we swim and laugh and feast on naïve little specs like your trembling self. Some of the fishies are big. Oh yes, my dear, they are, and do you know who one of the biggest, most twisted, most dangerous of them is?

LHG: I don't believe you.

00087: And I don't care. I'm not telling you to make you believe, I'm telling you because I like tasting the scent of your worried sweat on my tongues. So rich, so decadent. What I'd give to drink you, Le—

LHG: Enough, Zee, or I'll have you shipped off to the North Sea facility again. I'm sure the 00091 puppies miss their favorite chew toy.

00087 is silent.

LHG: That's what I thought. You may think *I'm* a joke, but I've read your file. Impossible to destroy isn't the same thing as impervious to pain. Here's one thing about the Director I *do* know: he signed off on as-we-see-fit captivity measures for you a while ago, didn't he? I must say, what you've gone through since makes for *real interesting* reading. It definitely gave me some ideas. Ideas you'd have to go along with if you're really that… um… *sensible*, about The Director.

00087 remains silent.

LHG: So, do we understand each other better now, Zee? I *know* you got my name by reading my thought patterns, so read them now to see if I'm bluffing. If you don't want to upset the Director, you have to not upset *me*. Like you said, you're a *small fishie*. I don't need to tell you that some of those *big fishies* I mentioned are just next door, do I? You carry on with the funny business and I'd be more than happy to arrange a play date. Am I clear?

00087 audibly gulps.

00087: Of course.

LHG: Now, tell me *everything* you know about Director Bramfield.

The audio becomes muffled, then abruptly halts.
END OF TRANSCRIPT

MISFORTUNE COOKIES

"Take two steps to the right."

That's what the fortune cookie said. You're confused, right? I was too. Confused as shit, at least I was until the morning after. It started making more sense over the next few days. Then it was confusing as hell again for a bit, but then it started re-making sense in a different way. A way that doesn't actually make any sense at all. The night I unfurled that first tiny scroll of faded papyrus though, my only response was "huh?"

The cookies came in matte black wrappers. They were also *delicious*. Emphasis necessary, because *God damn* these things were good. Nothing was on the packaging. I can't divulge ingredients. They tasted like… honey and salted caramel if the salt came from the seas of Atlantis, and the bees nested in the apiaries of Babylon. Not the usual brand Mr. Xing sent, but I hadn't ordered from Mr. Xing. Mr. Xing had gone out of business. For the first time in fifteen years, I had to get my chop suey somewhere new.

I decided to use the opportunity. I was going to try every Chinese food joint in Marathon County. A noble challenge, right? Bob Hastings: Marathon County's first Chinese food critic. Maybe even start a YouTube, I thought. Look, it was something to make the weeks go by a little easier. My life was… you know Milhouse's Dad in the Simpsons? I envied that guy. I made a spreadsheet for my little quest and everything. I'm old enough now that the chance for kids is probably behind me. Settling down into a meaningful marriage looks doubtful. You find the highlights where you can. Sue me.

Anyhow, I went for the first name on the list: *Asia House*. Uninventive name, but this is semi-rural Wisconsin. My expectations weren't high. Food was OK, but the cookies instantly derailed me from my spreadsheet-based culinary quest.

The moment the first crumb touched the tip of a tastebud, the world disappeared. I could feel warmth on my cheeks, but those cheeks were miles away. A chest heaving with sobs of unrestrained joy was a universe below me. My pokey Asylum Janitor budget trailer evaporated. I was floating somewhere. I couldn't make out the location, mainly because I couldn't see. Conan O'Brien's TV bullshit warbled into vapor. Nostrils full of Chinese food and body odor quietened themselves to stillness. Only one sense lived, and boy, was it ever alive.

I awoke from the taste coma after what felt like hours. In reality, I was "out" for the time it took for Conan to get a hollow laugh from his even hollower audience. It was upon awakening from my descent into the Babylonian honey dimension that I noticed my... ha... *fortune.*

"*Take two steps to the right.*"

After my brain settled down from the excitement of the trip, it decided to have a migraine. That meant I did too, so I found myself lying in the dark for the rest of the night trying not to puke. You know what I put the whole experience down to? Bad pork. As I drifted in and out of pained nausea sleep, I kept re-threading the fingers of my thoughts through the fortune. It wasn't intentional. The musings were aimless, driftwood, as though the 0.5x3 inch yellowed paper was a tapeworm wrapped tight around my cortex; bleeding itself drip by drip into that semi-lucid space between waking thoughts and the backward logic of dreams. *Definitely* bad pork.

This continued throughout the following morning, right up until the crossbow bolt. I was at the counter of the drug store. The migraine hadn't stopped, you know? Dollars ain't exactly flowing right now, so I'm far from stocked up on Aspirin. And yeah, Chinese food, tight budget, priorities, I know. Save it. Do you want to hear what happened when I took two steps to the right or not?

"*Take two steps to the right.*" I said it out loud as I did it. The tapeworm memory of the fortune had managed to drip back again. With my mind mulling the price of insulin these days, my body decided to take the instruction for a test drive.

Whoosh-THUNK

"Oh shit—"

"Darren, what the fuck?!"

"It just went off, man, it just went off!"

Behind me, a woman in the queue was screaming. I registered her before my brain did some backtracking and remembered the noise preceding her howls. *Whoosh-THUNK.* The dull thud of sharpened steel driving into plaster wall, muted by something dull, and wet, and living. Two male voices, both young, hungry, and out of their depth. That's when my brain checked in with my eyes. They showed it the pharmacist dangling from the stucco opposite by her crossbow bolt-pierced skull, and so my brain called my mouth and told it to start screaming too.

The sight of Mrs. Kravoplitz's eyeball dangling on her shattered cheek wasn't my *only* cause to scream. I was *also* screaming because of where I'd been standing before my body obeyed the fortune cookie demand.

I was stood right in front of Mrs. Kravoplitz.

For those of you that called it, refloppify your ego-boners. Implication here is pretty fucking obvious. If I'd been standing two steps to the left, the crossbow misfired by hapless armed robbers Darren Bulkins and Howie Groff would have found the back of my skull. Even Sheriff Harwurst pointed out how lucky I damn was to still be walking. I can still feel the whiffle of the bolt sailing past. The splash of Mrs. Kravoplitz's skull on my face is clearer though.

The cookie saved my life. I found the fortune under my bed/couch within ten seconds of returning to the trailer after giving my witness statement. Sure enough, there were the same words I was half convinced belonged to a bad pork-induced hallucination.

"Take two steps to the right."

I'll skip some nonsense for you. I thought I had some Chinese food guardian angel, yadda-schmadda, I ordered from *Asia House* every night for the next week. Ah, you're wondering about the bank balance, yeah? Cookie #2 dealt with that.

"Three up, two across."

I was at the gas station when my body and tongue worked that one out. They pointed at the scratch card on the Pyrex display; some $5 low-odds gamble. Three up and two across later, I was $500 richer. Not life-changing money, but enough to matter.

Of *course* I questioned it. I visited *Asia House*. They used the same brand of Fortune Cookies as Mr. Xing had. I know because the confused Cantonese-speaking man behind the counter kept throwing them at me once he'd had enough of my frantic babbling about acid trips, crossbows, and the Final Destination movies. I even tracked down their delivery guy, a stoner on a moped with the rather uninspired name Kyle. Kyle didn't have a clue what I was talking about either, but he did sell me some pot, so that trip wasn't wasted at least.

The cookies New Mr. Xing put into the bag were still there whenever Kyle left the bag outside my door. I asked Kyle to check. Only when I opened took the bag did the standard red and gold packaging became the matte black wrapping of my caramel-honey wisdom crackers. There was no explanation, I was just the luckiest man alive. About damn time, too. That's how it felt, and that's why I decided to be chill about the mystery. I'd been chosen for their blessing. That's all that mattered.

Ha! Oh, I'd been chosen alright. It was the blessing part I got laughably fucking wrong.

Cookie #7, a week later, was when the fortunes started to play their hand. So far, they'd led me to a few minor scratch card wins and two successful dates. I wanted more. I was awaiting the microscroll that unearthed a mansion, or a Mercedes. Again, derectify your mental chub-on. This *isn't* some greed undoes man, Monkey Paw, *"be careful what you wish for"* bullshit. I wish it *was*. I'd at least feel like I got what was coming to me if I'd earned my punishment. It's way more fucked, way less fair, and way, *way* less easy to explain.

"*Ah! Ow*—shit! What the fuck?!"

My expletives echoed down the St Dionysius corridor, prompting tuts from the cohort of flustered lab coats crowded around a cell door. Then they saw me, and their annoyance turned to concern, and then alarm. I was at work, tickling a hallway floor with my mop. It was when drowning in a daydream that the coils of prophetic suggestion once more ensnared my reflexes. The advice from the prior night's cookie had been simple:

"*Swat the fly.*"

Buzzing by my ear, a body long since needing no mental permission to act. My hand slammed into the fat, listless insect. I heard the crashing glass and saw the bloom of scarlet *before* I felt the pain or realized the fly had settled on a floor-ceiling mirror.

CRACK

"Fuck—*ah*—fuck!"

"Good lord, he's bleeding. Leona, call the medical bay, tell them one of the... the *janitorials* is coming."

I wanted to add a "you" to one of my "fucks" upon hearing the disdain in the word *janitorial*. My mouth couldn't find the motions though. With each progressive *fuck,* my shock/pain combo transformed into unsureness/panic. Why? Because I was still looking in what remained of the shattered mirror. My pale, sweating face was staring back at me. So was something else.

I only saw him because I was watching the reflection of the fly. You know, the one I'd half-shattered a mirror and opened my palm killing. The half-inch thing was very much dead; crushed remains upturned and twitching. The other side of the looking glass was a different story. The fly's still very much alive reflection was strutting across the fractured surface like it wasn't a mirror at all, but a window. Reflection-fly beat its legs against the glass, daring me to believe my eyes, taunting me into clutching at some false rationale. I blinked, and it was airborne. It flew into the mirror-corridor, right toward the crack-distorted reflection of my open mouth.

I was already confused as hell at the moment the weight of an invisible invertebrate force slammed into my uvula. I started choking. I couldn't scream when I felt the six legs scratching at the back of my throat. The blockage was too big. I watched the bulge travel down my reflected Adam's apple like I'd swallowed a damn mouse whole. My mind wheeled, flailing desperately for an explanation. I could see the dead fly on our side of the glass. It was still right where I'd smushed it. The fly that crawled across the shattered other side and into my reflection's gaping jaws had no real-life counterpart. I couldn't put this down to hallucination, either, because I could feel every writhing, twitching movement of it. The fly's journey through my esophagus was slow, torturous; agony both because of the repulsive context of the discomfort *and* the incomprehensibility of it.

However, the fly *wasn't* what had been watching me. It wasn't the reason I waved off the offer/insistence of medical attention and got back to my trailer as fast as weak legs and stiff pedals allow. It was when I bent forward to try and cough up the buzzing mass fuzzing its way toward my stomach that I saw what *else* looked back besides my purple-faced mirror self.

He was behind me. *Right* behind me, so close that my acknowledgment of his presence brought an awareness of a sticky breath across my back. Beyond the wet pants between my shoulder blades, he had no presence outside the mirror world, as a quick glance behind me confirmed. That's why the hot arrhythmic dampness did a balloon-animal number on my trembling gut.

He was short, short enough I'd missed his chitinous scalp scraping into view over my shoulders. If I hadn't bent forward to try and regurgitate the burrowing fly, I'd never have exposed him. A man… boy… *thing*. Skin bumped, rugged, bone-like. Black too, and not black as something comforting, like coal, midnight, or the shadows under your bed. His stiff epidermis was the negative-light blackness of unmapped ocean trenches, of undead stars in stellar gulfs, of the final sights seen when buried alive. His eyes, though, his eyes shone. Those blank, circular beacons. Those red orbs that burned brighter than a crematorium furnace, yet cast no shadows on his flat face. I didn't get a chance to see its mouth before the black spots of oxygen depletion clouded details. I didn't have to. I could *feel* him smiling.

I noped out so hard I wasn't aware of heading home until back at the trailer. I never found out how the docs at St Dionysius reacted to my screeching outburst. I'm sure Dr Anand and co. don't appreciate being flailed at like that. I'm guessing there's paperwork. A disciplinary awaits, I'll bet. I don't know. Haven't been back since.

I was rattled for many reasons, but mostly because I never managed to cough up the weight of the burrowing fly. On the ride back, I felt the light tickle of it drop into my stomach, quieting into a near-stillness I could *just about* ignore. It took effort not to think of the fat bluebottle gorging itself on my stomach contents. For hours I had waking nightmares of the mirror-fly perversely intruding upon my insides, more than once I had to slap myself back to the hear-and-now.

I tried to convince myself I'd misinterpreted the cookie message somehow, and forced the mirror fly out of mind. Last week had been the best in decades. I wasn't ready to give up my good fortune, I'd spent too long living with bad. It wouldn't be fair.

I didn't bother with the chop suey that night. Something about the smell of it put me off. It wasn't any different, but the usual MSG-fried noodle aroma didn't sit right. I went straight for the cookie. As usual, before reading the papyrus, I crammed the shattered cooking in my eager maw. I sank back into the bed/couch, ready to escape my troubles for a few moments in the honey abyss.

Straight away, I knew something was wrong.

When Conan's bullshit slowed into bass-note intangibility, it left no silence. I could *hear* something. A buzzing, low at first, but within a few pseudo-moments, it was at the forefront of my awareness; grabbing the sugar-rich bliss I'd expected and forcing it into a jarring, head-spinning dance. I returned to Earth not from a Nibbana of pure taste, but from living in the roar of a trillion of minuscule wings thrashing.

Migraine #8 was something else. Oh yeah, *they* hadn't stopped. This one was beyond the others though. It had me so close to attempting self-trepanning the drill bit was at my temple. I didn't fall asleep in the end, but passed out from pain. Whether asleep or awake, my aching mind kept repeating the same mantra:

"Eat it. Eat it all."

The following morning, a truck carrying processed sugar careened off the freeway and crashed into the gates and communal bathrooms of our trailer complex. A crowd had gathered round, jaws agape, ogling the scene with hungry eyes and hungrier smartphone cameras. Curiosity had me jostling to the front of the throng of neighbors. Migraine or not, the human inability to ignore tragic spectacle is unbreakable.

My reaction to the carnage was first to retch. My third reaction was also to retch, but *that* was because of my *second* reaction.

"Eat it. Eat it all."

The familiar pull, that epiphany-like tugging flowing from my gut to every nerve. My thoughts ran icy clear.

"No… not this… nothing good can happen if I… I won't!"

It was then I learned "following the cookies advice" had become "obeying the cookies demands" without me noticing. I didn't think I'd have to resist; I didn't know there was anything *to* resist. My compulsive stride toward the blood and septic water-soaked sugar hillock had me just as confused as the crowd. The first time I puked was from the smell of burst septic tank and the sight of disembowelled truck driver. The second time was because I realized I had no choice anymore.

"Eat it. Eat it all."

In front of me was a dune of sticky mulch already turning to oily syrup in the crashed engine leakage. Much of the ivory-white sugar was stained. Some patches were red, where the momentum of the crash carried the trucker's blood and offal out his windshield-sliced stomach. The rest of the trucker was laying some way away, body and head too separate to bother checking for a pulse, crows already circling above the Pinetree canopy. Patches closest to where the burst septic tank fountain rained were brown, muddy, reeking blobs of granular month-old chemical shit-water that grew until gravity had them snowballing down the sticky hills. At the base, all varieties of spoiled sugar met to form a sickly acrid puddle of eye-watering awfulness. Still gawping as much as the crowd, I watched myself scoop up a great wad of the thick, toxic, cess-jelly.

I looked down at the hot, dripping sludge in my cupped palms. Cries of *"what the fuck"* rang out from a food stamp crowd I'd last seen 50'000 miles ago. I fell through the tunnel vision, screaming as the compulsion to obey the cookie bent my elbows and raised my wrists. I could feel the heat of the blood and sunbaked septic fluids, the nostril-curling tang of freshly spilled gasoline, the gut-turning sickliness of the scent of pure sugar. Unable to stop myself, I buried my face in the steaming ooze.

Then I started eating.

I could hear barfing from every direction. I wished I could barf too, but my stomach wasn't mine anymore. I could taste all of it, every drop of blood, gas, septic tank hydroxide, and liquified human shit. The stench of each warm, moist handful was so powerful my nose burned. The gasoline and waste chemicals left ulcers as soon as they touched the soft tissue of my mouth. Somehow, the taste of every ingredient managed to remain distinct, palpable, and horrifying. I was weeping by the end of the ordeal three hours later when Sheriff Harwurst finally arrived and escorted me back to my trailer.

You might have seen the clips, those TOR-browsing wrong'n's among you. The guy in the faded Seinfeld tee? The one pleading directly into camera, bubbling piss-shit-blood-sugar at the corners of his mouth, rivers of it dribbling down his chin as he shoves fistful after fistful of it into his face? The clip called someonepleasestopme.webm? That's me. The cop is Sheriff Harwurst, and no, he never prosecuted me for the punch. He knows everyone who's no-one around here. *"This ain't like you, Bob Hastings,"* is a sentiment that spared me a fair bit of jail time.

He made sure I was settled before leaving. He's a decent guy, so he had me clean my mouth out with vodka, the closest thing to a sterilizer on hand. Put the blood-shit-gas-sugar-eating and violence down to the stress of the near-death experience with the crossbow bolt. Told my neighbor Sally Tully to keep an eye on me (which is 100% why *she* died, so I'm not taking the guilt there, that's on Harwurst).

The Sheriff departed when I was drifting into sleep on the bed/couch. The weight of exhaustion from the weeks again sinking me deeper into my dreams than my subconscious mind had ever dared delve.

My slumber was filled with visions of rolling seas. Not seas of water, not oceans of this earth at all. Seas of uncountable black bodies; a roiling mass of twitching insect life so vast it swallowed entire continents. I floated above it, clinging to a hand I couldn't see no matter how much I strained to look up. My dream self, who this far below the surface of lucidity had come full circle and felt more real than any waking self I'd ever been, could do nothing but stare below his dangling naked feet and listen.

The buzzing. The deafening barrage of an incomputable number of wings thrumming against an immeasurable count of hard, fat, rot-black bodies. A sound that raked nails across every nerve in my resolve. Sound isn't the word for it, but I don't have a better one. It was to hearing as the salted-caramel honey had been to taste. An all-encompassing purification of; a distilled sensation of being beyond mere experience. Time was no dimension here. For minutes/years/seconds/decades, I gazed into the frothing hive activity, listening to the swells and waves shriek their chitinous crescendo. As measures of non-time passed, the din got better at taking form. The noise found latches in my understanding around which it could bend itself into shapes, words, meaning. The "mindless noise" was anything but. It was a chant, a chorus, a mantra regurgitated over and over in endless praise by the filthy surf.

"A bride, a bride, a bride for the King of Flies!"

A perverse inversion of a monastic choir with more voices than there are numbers to count with. Once the words were clear, I became re-aware of the hand gripping mine. It was hard, clammy, and covered in coarse hairs. I looked up. The bulbous red orbs beamed back at me, the chitinous-yet-humanoid nakedness beneath twitching in what I knew to be anticipation. I could see everything now; the absence of a nose, the curled useless pairs of vestigial extra arms protruding from shallow armpits, the swinging barbed appendage between thick digitigrade legs. The mouth was the worst part. Hard flesh parted to reveal cracked, clearly human lips. They curled into a smile, narrow and small, but that carried jubilance beyond all reason, a euphoria that would break even the most devoted hedonist.

Then the rows of teeth parted. The last thing before waking up on my sticky carpet was the King of Flies mouth opening; his long tubular maxillae flopping from where a human tongue should be, the phlegmy slickness of it stroking across my face, of its length penetrating my unresisting mouth, following the mirror-fly's path toward my beckoning stomach…

It was Sally's frantic knocks that did it. I'd been asleep for over 24 hours, apparently. Despite falling into unconsciousness on the bed/couch, I found the waking world again on the floor. My mouth was full of something, something rotten and acrid. It was the remnants of week-old chop-suey from the trash.

"Bob? Bob, you in there?"

I gagged, pulling chunks of moldy pork and maggot-covered noodles from my stuffed cheeks with trembling fingers. At least, I did until I noticed the state of my hands. They were covered in something, a slick, ichorous substance that looked far too much like the residue left on my face, mouth, and throat in the nightmare's final moments.

"Fuck off… fuck off Sally."

"I fucking won't. Do you know how much shit Harwurst has threatened to unturn a blind eye to if he catches me using and you in here dead? I need to go find a fix, Bob, and I can't do that if I ain't confirmed you ain't dead."

"You can hear me, can't you, you stupid bitch?"

"Fuck you!"

The banging on the door continued. I pulled myself to my feet. That's when I noticed the first sign of wrongness, the initial clue I was in the endgame of whatever the cookies had planned. I screamed when I saw what waited on the counter.

"You're screaming now?! That's it, Bob, fuck your door!"

It was a fortune cookie. A black matte wrapped fortune cookie. No chop suey, no *Asia House* bag. Just the cookie. I'd opened it by the time Sally's boot made short work of the flimsy trailer door. Her sweaty palm was on my shoulder as I read the scroll within.

"Kiss her."

I was too weak to try and resist the tug this time. My body obeyed, the meaning clear and free of riddles. It was the least romantic kiss in human history. Both our eyes remained open, twin near-perfect circles of disbelief. Her lips were warm, the pressure of them forcing apart chaps and splits of my own. She didn't try to pull away, instead faltering her arms in mid-air. She *was* screaming though. It was hard to hear over the muted roar of wings, but she managed to get a few yells out.

The lurch of my diaphragm pinning itself to my ribs brought with it flashbacks to the rolling abyss of compound eyes and twitching insectoid limbs. I could feel them before she could hear them; the scritch-scratch of thousands of tiny legs crawling up my throat, past my probing tongue, and onward into their new vessel. I felt my neck bulge and stretch to accommodate for the tide. Pain and bewilderment had thick blobs of saltwater falling from my cheeks, but my rogue body pressed on with the embrace. The scream of wings was deafening even through inches of flesh and cartilage. Before long, Sally's neck was bulging too. She *was* trying to resist by that point; her frantic track-marked arms seemingly unable to decide between clawing at my back or her distended throat.

Nothing about Sally Tully's death was quick. It was slow, drawn-out, and excruciating to witness, let alone experience. It took about a minute for the volume of flies to rupture her stomach. A few more still for the blood to start pooling at her nostrils, tear ducts, and the crotch and seat of her dirty jeans. I could taste it too. A metallic tang gargling up from her throat, tangible even through the mouthfeel of the swarm. Then the fat bodies started crawling out of her ears, then out her nose, then from behind her eyes. My arms remained locked in place, holding her as captive to me as I was to the cookies, despite my inner monologue using every profanity to urge them into release.

Sally did get free eventually, but that's only because it's difficult to keep hold of somebody after they've exploded.

"A bride, a bride, a bride for the King of Flies!"

The chant reverberated up from my memory as the confetti-chunks of burst neighbor fell through the cloud of freed insects. The intense buzzing filling my trailer threatened every second to turn itself into words, to bring the harrowing mantra into reality.

"A bride, a bride, a bride for the King of Flies!"

I'd already started trying to put dots together. When I'd read the words *"Kiss Her"*. I'd thought... no, *hoped* that my part in all this was minor. Sally Tully, the bride of the Fly King, the main character in some eldritch game I was unfortunate enough to exist on the peripherals of. I'd fallen into something bigger than myself, but not focused on me. I'd experienced was chaff from whatever whirlwind of nightmares the universe had planned for Sally Tully. *Please* let that be the case.

Every one of those hopes was dashed when her trembling body could no longer contain the thick insectoid mass pushing her liquidated organs out of any available orifice.

"A bride, a bride, a bride for the King of Flies!"

I don't remember how long I screamed, but I know my throat was bleeding by the time I managed to stop. Remember the faint flickering of the mirror-fly in my stomach I said I could *almost* ignore? I couldn't anymore. It had been almost dormant since the mirror incident. Not now though. Now it was alive again, and its flickering, flitting, buzzing, or any synonym for winglike activity had long since been rendered inappropriate.

No. Now my lexicon needed new words. Words like writhing, wriggling, worming, digging.

A sharp stab of pain from my navel. I bent double on the floor-to-ceiling blanket of crawling chitinous bodies. My trailer was gone, buried beneath the roiling blanket. I was alone now with the swarm; sobbing and clutching my belly while the countless probing mouth-organs liquified and consumed every trace of Sally Tully. I won't lie to you, the churning eely discomfort forcing its way south toward my midriff meant I really didn't give a flying fuck about her anymore. I'd already realized her death was as senseless and wasteful as it seemed, that *she* was the innocent bystander I'd naively hoped I was.

"A bride, a bride, a bride for the King of Flies!"

The ringing buzz from the living carpet started making good on its threats of coherence. I felt my palms pressing into my ears, the pressure left on my skull by the lipless words somehow greater than that long narrowness undulated between my organs, moving and pushing them to the side as it approached its destination.

Through the white blinding flashes crisscrossing my vision, I kept coming back to those red orbs, that grotesquely human smile, a long cable salad of prehensile organic tubes flopping from between crooked, yellowing teeth.

I was still bent over double when I felt the coarse hairs on the back of my neck, the chitinous arms wrapping slowly around my shoulders. The horror was so great my eyes rolled back in their skull. I was babbling incoherent nonsense at the top of my lungs; my already long since broken psyche unable to process his emergence from reflections and dreams into cold hard reality. He was... *hugging* me, holding me from behind like a lover supporting a grieving spouse. The sticky panting was at my neck, moisture forming drops of foul-smelling condensation that rolled down my cheek. When he spoke, it was like having to endure a mealworm burrowing through my eardrum.

"Breathe, my bride... Breathe."

Cracked words, crooked words, words from a maxilla and mandible-filled mouth which had no right being able to form speech. I didn't have to have the meaning explained. The sharp kick at my groin was all the indication I needed. I'd never had kids of my own, but I understood the biology of childbirth, the mechanics of it. I think that made the situation worse, you know. Innocence would have stopped my brain from skipping ahead as it matched up the puzzle pieces.

"I... what... no! I can't have a—I'm a ma-*argh!*"

Another explosion of pain at my crotch was accompanied by a hot-breathed cooing at my ear.

"Shh my bride... shhh... you accepted this... you were ripe... ready... a willing mate... your body knows it... that's why it followed... why it obeyed..."

Fingers bristling with coarse hairs brushed my cheek. I didn't see how the King of Flies materialized from whatever hellish pseudo-reality he hails. It's possible he simply emerged from the throbbing molasses, the same thick rug of impenetrably black forms that swarmed over my groin and stomach as he said the word "obeyed". A swell of legs, thoraxes, and compound eyes washed over my lower body; digestive fluids piranha-schooling away my pants and boxers. I was beyond screaming now. This is a shame because if *any* sight so far warranted screaming, it was what waited beneath the melting denim and polyester.

"A bride, a bride, a bride for the King of Flies!"

A bulging, clearly defined bump wriggled inside my belly. Something as long as a football but half as wide; something ridged and writhing that pushed its way past my decoiled intestines to burrow down below my pelvic bone. I was on my backside, huffing like... well, we've all seen childbirth in movies, right?

A fresh kick, another push from beneath the flesh between my thighs. A sudden flash of odor let me know whatever was coming had forced the half-digested rotting Chinese food from my bowls. The living carpet squealed in collective grinding glee, fresh swells of hive activity lapping as my prolapsed and leaking colon.

I don't know which emotion was stronger; the seizure-inducing terror, or the coma-inducing pain. Razor wire snakes of it slithered across every muscle, all correlating at my groin. My eyes stopped rolling to gaze down in wide-eyed horror at the butchery playing out between my trembling, sweating thighs.

I'm not what you'd call endowed, but it's amazing how large a man looks when he's splayed inside out.

The final pushes made themselves known. As sharp and blinding as the other kicks had been, the pulsating thing hadn't even got started. The mound of soft tissue beyond my pubic bone protruded. Within moments, the nerve-rich flesh of the perineum had followed suit (which was *exactly* as painful as you're imagining). Inch by writhing inch, the bulge at my belly vanished, pulling the last of itself into the depths between my intestines.

"No... but no, please no, I'm—"

"Breathe... my bride... breathe..."

I don't know how I remained conscious when the mandibled head started pushing and chewing its way through my bladder. What little length I possessed ballooned for a few eternity-long moments, the spell only ending when a spurt of dark red almost-purple spat a full five feet from the tip. That's when the flesh gave. A banana-peel split of veiny skin pushed aside in nanoseconds; a dozen fresh rapid-fire stabbings slicing through my awareness as firm orbs and soft skin full of nerve endings were rent by the gnashing, biting pressure.

"Look... look, my bride..."

"*Ahhhhh! No—I can't—I won't—*"

"You're... crowning..."

His rusted words pulled my rolling eyes back between my legs. The scurrilous carpet of bodies was now playing midwife. The swarming flies moved like their ant cousins, using the bulk of their insurmountable number to form appendages. These twitching, shivering arms crashed into the burning carnage between my legs. I felt a pulling, an uncomfortable interior lurching as the chubby, ridged thrashing was extracted from my spread hips. The King of Flies told no lies. I *was* crowning. There was a head poking out from the gaping chasm where reproductive tissue once lay. I couldn't scream anymore. I'd fallen too far into the insanity caused by agony and incomprehensible circumstance. There was nothing but laughter now; a high-pitched cackling it frightens me to know came from my own throat. Once the quivering rug's prying fingers removed the wailing newborn, I gazed upon it for the first time, and the penny I can't actually explain finally dropped.

It was a maggot. A half foot long, beer can thick maggot. A maggot whose mandibled mouth contained tiny human teeth, and in whose six eye sockets sat sparkling sapien-blue irises. Irises I knew well; they were in every photo of me ever taken. A maggot that wailed with lungs and vocal cords, that made sounds any mammalian mother would recognize as infant distress.

The King of Flies stepped over me. He crouched, scooping up the wailing creature in his thick arms. I was still laughing. I laughed as I watched him cooing to it, hysterics still consuming me as his prehensile mouth-tube regurgitated black sludge into his offspring's waiting maw.

I couldn't think of it as *our* offspring. I wouldn't, and still can't. Not that first one, and not any of the ones that have and will follow.

The buzzing horde wasn't done with me, you see. Just as the tide has risen to lap at the prolapsed colon leakage, it now got to work removing the unnecessary remnants of my biological maleness. To my horror, what they revealed *wasn't* a cavernous flesh wound I'd have the mercy of bleeding out from.

New flesh lay beneath, flesh I knew was mine due to the pins-and-needles tickle of the swarm's infinite probing, suckling mouthparts. Not skin, nor was it chitin, either. It was a halfway: a rigid, muscular surface glistening with sweated mucus. At its center was a new opening, the orifice from which the King of Flies would reap his army of heirs. It was wide, leaking yellowish fluid. The stink rising from it matched exactly the fumes of the blood-shit-gasoline-sugar sludge it'd wolfed down the previous day. Even though it matched nothing I'd seen on a human, the area had a distinct sliced-papayaness to its shape. The folds and creases, although out of proportion, ran in approximation with a vague, perversely vulvaic anatomical sense I recognized.

My deranged cackling didn't stop as the probing horde suckled the last of the afterbirth from my grotesque new anatomy. It didn't falter when the King of Flies spread his entire seven-foot wingspan and howled in triumph, our—no, *his* spawn cradled in those muscular coarse haired arms. It only stopped when I coughed and looked down to see my human tongue limp and dead in my lap.

That was three days ago. I've born as many offspring for him since. My body isn't done changing, though into what I don't know. He isn't always here. The first time he left I pulled myself to the bed-couch, feeling around for my phone under the thrumming black mass that still coats every surface in the trailer. The pain continues to be insurmountable. That's what pushed me to make the climb, pulling my limp and now decaying legs behind me. I haven't tried phoning Sheriff Harwurst. No point. I can't speak with these tubes; the twelve-inch-long prehensile sucker-tendrils dangling from my aching jaw, too vast for me to close my mouth.

Since that tongue-shedding cough, there's not been a moment I feel like I'm not choking. Part of me is tempted to try removing my jaw, just to create some breathing room. Maybe that'll be the next thing to go?

Speaking of, that's why I've been writing this. The living carpet won't let me leave. The flies have sealed the door tight. Maybe Sheriff Harwurst will come poking around eventually, but I can't count on it. Marathon County is a strange place, and he's probably got his hands full with another case by now.

I think I'm beyond rescue. I'm not writing for salvation, but for meaning. This message is me using the last of Bob Hastings. I want you to remember he existed, you see. I can't find acceptance of this twisted fate without knowing someone, somewhere, remembers. Consider this his obituary, I guess.

I don't know where Bob Hastings went wrong. Maybe it was opening that first misfortune cookie. Maybe he opened the door to the realm of the King of Flies when he took that first bite. Maybe it was reading the fortune, or maybe he still had a chance right up until he took those fateful two steps to the right. Maybe something he did long before Mr Xing's closed its doors was the catalyst. Only the King of Flies knows, and his wet puckered lips are sealed.

What I do know is that I won't be Bob Hastings much longer. A few days, max. I was born Bob Hastings, but I'll die something else. One of the many brides of the King of Flies. So, so Bob

Hastings' selfish little life means something to someone, somewhere. Let me use the last of him to send out this warning:

Don't open, eat, or in any way engage with a matte black fortune cookie. The King of Flies is out there, and our family is always hungry to grow.

WHAT I FOUND IN FATHER'S BOX

I am writing to you as a man midway through an epiphany. Not the positive personal-growth kind of epiphany, either. The negative kind. The kind where you realize fate has you railroaded on a journey toward darker days than anyone could hope to endure.

Judging by what I've just read of the notes he'd kept in his study; I think things were much the same for Father. I think that's why he made the decision that led to all the somber guests consoling Mother downstairs. I'd always wanted to be in here, in his study, to see what he'd do in the hours shut away from the rest of us. I'd wanted it even more *after* I left home, to find out just what had grabbed his attention so tightly he could find no room for time with me, his only heir. I can't remember a time when I wasn't playing out the scene in my head, of opening that door for the first time, of finally stepping foot in this space so sacred and forbidden. I just never imagined I'd finally find my way in here because father decided to cease living.

Now that I finally know what occupied his time, I doubt there could ever have been alternative circumstances. Many peculiarities from my childhood seem far less peculiar in this new light. Why I was never allowed crayons, paints, chalks, or pencils. Why no photographs or paintings hung in the halls of the manor. Why my strict homeschool curriculum included no art lessons. Why I'd get the belt if I started doodling absentmindedly during handwriting practice…

I had a childhood full of *whys*. I've spent a few hours up here in Father's study. As much as I wish it wasn't so, I think I have found my *becauses*. The first were in the letter. He'd left it on the desk for me, lamp on, making sure it was the first thing my eyes were drawn to when I took my first ever steps into the once-forbidden room.

Charles,

I have instructed Winston to give you the keys to the study upon your arrival. My instructions were purposefully vague. As faithful as he has been, I do not feel it prudent to inform him of the full scale of what's occurred, will occur, and has been occurring for as long as the Bramfield bloodlines existed. However, he has served me a great many years and I trust he'll understand the implications of my request.

I anticipate my passing will be somewhat unexpected. One would be being disingenuous if one were to claim this isn't regrettable. Unfortunately, there are no alternatives. I do not have any conventional wisdom to pass on. As you will find, Charles, I have not been forthright with you regarding our lineage. I leave this letter as a final instruction. In my draw is a lockbox containing all you'll need to know for the coming years. I pray that what you find within doesn't break you, as it eventually broke me. I am not a man for apologies, Charles. I trust you can interpret my intent.

I hope you know me well enough to not mistake the vice of pride for lack of sentiment.

Father.

I'll skip the emotional unpacking. My father had made an exit from this world on his own terms and left little in the way of explanation. He'd left a body though, and arrangements that needed to be made, and a more-than-heartbroken widow behind him. He'd also left a son with a lifetime of open and now unanswerable questions. Our relationship was always strained, but only the most heartless of men would not be moved under such circumstances. However, I am not writing to you from a need to share that half hour I spent sobbing into my hands at his desk. My epiphany is not one of paternal understanding. I have no emotional reconciliation to capture for you. This isn't a happy tale of a man that gets to put decades of fatherly silence behind him. No. This is a tale of ancestral sins, an epiphany of bloodlines and misdeeds and intergenerational taint. It's the kind of epiphany that creates magnetism between power drills and frontal lobes; an epiphany I now have no choice but to endure because of what Father had in that damn box.

The unlocked container itself was... unremarkable. A beaten aluminum thing no wider, longer, or deeper than a cereal box. I managed to compose myself a little at this realization. I wondered if Father ever found out about the secret stash of Lucky Charms Winston had kept for me, and then realized that in a house ran as meticulously as Father's, the *"forbidden"* Saturday morning indulgence could have only come from father himself. A gesture of love so distant he'd deny all involvement. No use dwelling on the fact I hadn't figured this out until it was too late to thank him, though. The aluminum container was unmarked aside from a FAMILY HISTORY sticker, which must have been produced with the label maker in the same desk drawer. Inside the box, underneath some pens and a notepad, were two books. The first was a sketchbook, the second a thick scrapbook with frayed corners and a tea-stained cardboard cover. This thick volume of clippings, letters, photographs, and diagrams is what triggered my current existential crisis. I didn't open this book at first, though. No. Something about it put me off, had me subconsciously choosing to prolong my last few innocent minutes before inevitable exposure to its contents. First, I decided to look through the purple velvet-bound sketchbook. From the note on the inside cover, I knew who it belonged to. Father.

"My God, all of it is true. Winston, if you're reading this because something happened, please take care of Carole and Charles."

The ink of the message was faint, faded. I knew it must have been written *decades* ago. Never in living memory had I heard Father refer to me as anything other than *the boy* when parenting through his manservant. These were the words of a younger father, a father who hadn't yet put up every mental and emotional barrier at his disposal. I could feel a prickling at the corner of my eyes as I started down at the curl of the *C* in *Charles,* the tangible evidence of a time when he'd thought of me by name. As with the forbidden Lucky Charms memory, though, this wasn't an invitation to dwell in loss. The hubbub from the floors below was distant, but still present. Time wasn't a resource I could guarantee; my decades of absence from the family home didn't excuse me from hosting duties if the whole thing became too much for Mother. Besides, even if I did have the luxury of room for introspection, I still had no inclination to do so. Not over a small scrawl from before Father lost his familial instincts, at least. His sketches caught my attention with a much greater ravenous fever than any arrangements of words and letters could. Drawings, art, illustration, paintings. All were forbidden by my father. There was no greater blasphemy in his household than the creation of anything remotely visual. And yet, in my hands were pages and pages of his own works. Detailed, intricate, captivating. Not in a pleasing way, though. No. Father's pictures were captivating in the way that has viewers waking sweat-soaked and screaming in the middle of the night for years to come. From the very first image, I was wondering if maybe his barriers and walls hadn't been to keep me out, but to keep something terrible in...

The first was a portrait of a man with mouths for eyes. Dark and macabre, but not the kind of thing I chalked up to much beyond the product of a disturbed mind. A small note in the corner from Father informed me the haunting Giger-esque being from his nightmares was named Zarasashael. It was drawn in biro, probably the very same ballpoint pen he'd stored in the lockbox. The rendering was so realistic it could have been a photograph. Even the faintest folds and indents in the creature's skin had been captured; no inch of moist flesh didn't dance with faint light. I must admit, as harrowing as this... this *Zarasashael* was, I couldn't help but notice a flicker of pride in my chest. My initial reaction was nothing short of admiration, despite the abhorrence of the subject matter. I'd been amazed to learn that Father drew at all. That he even *could* draw, let alone draw *well*. No, not well. Amazingly. If such a thing were possible, *perfectly*. Whatever fondness I felt for this hidden side of him soon died, however. The sketches and portraits were good, but their... their *oddness* made it impossible to forget why I was viewing them. I couldn't forget Winston's recollection of Father in that tub, of the extension cord fizzing and spluttering on the murky surface, his blackened body dancing and shaking to the current still flowing through it. Father was a man who'd been pushed too far, and the parade of grotesque creations he'd had me carrying a growing weight in my gut; the weight of knowing my ignorance of his motives would probably be as short-lived as my admiration for his work. Something had driven him to become charred, damp remains, after all. I couldn't shake the feeling these images weren't a symptom of his decline. They were causal. This feeling grew as I turned the pages, along with a steady but nagging nausea. Despite the onslaught of Father's madness, my mind kept coming back to one thing, the inside-cover message he'd left for the Winston of the past.

"My God, all of it is true..."

When attached to those words, the steadily more horrific illustrations moved further from uncanny into dread inspiring. Father's skill somehow improved from the perfection of that first faded sketch, too. The dog-eared sketchbook must have accounted for *years* of work. How it fit so many pages between the beaten covers, I'll never know. As I turned through pages that must have accounted for years of work, I found his results growing even realer, more defined. Another thing I'll never know is how that's at all possible, given the photorealistic quantity of that tooth-eyed man on page one. I'm never picking up that book again, so I'm damned sure I'm not going to get a chance to study it further and find out. Even the least jarring of Father's imaginings were enough to make a second viewing possible only under duress.

Ten pages in, there was a two-page spread diagram of a creature Father had labelled as Thyrtherothax. He'd depicted the eight-limbed monstrosity bearing down on a man barely one-tenth its size. The lifelike quality of the details is utterly uncapturable with mere words. It shouldn't be possible. Not without a pencil sharpened to a point only one atom wide, at least. The light on the beast's invertebrate flesh seemed almost to glisten and shimmer, the faint creases and folds of its worming back almost rippling under my gaze. My breath caught in my throat when I first saw Father's rendition of those dead glassy eyes, of that human baby's face the size of a wrecking ball, and especially of the bus-sized maggot's body he'd drawn trailing into the inky dark behind it.

"God, all of it is true..."

A hundred pages later, Father had moved from abyssal creations like his Thyrtherothax and the mouth-eyed Zarasashael. He clearly had no shortage of inspiration, for as... imaginative, for lack of a better word, as the catalogue of abominations was, I never saw the same one twice. It would take what you'd think of as a "creative type" to come up with so many different twisted, snarling, near-indescribable beings. Father was many things. None of them were a synonym for creativity. Yet here his rolodex of haunting art was a living "fuck you" to the face of everything I thought I knew about him, each new demonic portrait a testament to how little I really understood who he was.

However, at some point in life he'd clearly got bored with (I naively hoped) making up nightmarish entities. Like I said, as the book progressed, he moved on to bigger, bolder works. By the middle of the pad, he had evolved into sketching vast, unnerving landscapes. Landscapes so real I'd get vertigo if I stared too long. My gut would lurch, a rushing tingling sensation growing behind the skin of my face, like my body was convinced it would fall into those worlds on the page created in ball-point by my stern, unimaginative, father. One was a cramped and cragged world of sharp, spiraling mountains; a range of drill-like Everests jostling for space under a starless sky, above chasms so deep a falling man plummets far below where one would reach the core of our Earth. I could make out things in the distance, standing behind and amongst the twisting rock pillars sprouting hairlike from each mountainside. They were tall things, slathering things, things like erect slugs with teeth so square Father must have measured each of the dozen 1mmx1mm white segments with a ruler and compass. The longer I looked, the more of the distant figures I noticed. I had to remind myself that figures in a drawing moving out from their caves to stare back at you was impossible. Almost as impossible as the fact I knew the alien sun they *didn't* writhe under was simultaneously blue and orange, despite father's drawings all being monochromatic. The simultaneous double-hue is a difficult phenomenon do describe. It's also one your brain blocks out if you try and think about it too long. Not a blend of colors. No. Their sun was both, at once, and my brain almost descended into migraine trying to decide the truth.

Another of his glimpses into inhospitable realms that stood out to me was the island in the blue desert, titled *The Core of G'ir'thyrx*. Again, don't ask me *how* I knew those black ink dunes were blue, but I did. The full technicolor memories I have when I think back to describe it are proof of this. I thought those rolling blue hills were an ocean at first, that is, until I realized the granular texture Father had chosen to shade them with wasn't accidental. How he found the time or patience to distinguish each of those countless trillions of grains I'll never know. The sands weren't the central focus of this piece, however. Father's muse here was clearly the continent-sized island that floated above the fields of dunes. He'd seen it with schizophrenic clarity in his mind's eye; the glistening rocks hewn from flesh, the skyscraper-tall tripods that marched along its surface, the great pillar of human corpses with the man in a cloud of shadow sat atop a throne at its peak. My father was not an imaginative man. His world was one of accounts, numbers, and trades. That's what made the cloud of solid ink around the throne, and the un-drawn figure I somehow knew waited within it, all the more terrifying.

"*All of it is true…*"

It was the last few dozen pages that prompted me to throw the sketchbook across the room and yell every profanity I knew. There was no admiration of artistic talent when viewing these. The only emotion in me other than sweaty-palmed dread was pity (although it was very, very short-lived). The final sketches, drawn in the years leading up to Father's decision to bathe with a toaster, judging by the freshness of the ink, were a testimony to the madness he'd suffered through in silence. For the first time, I started to feel guilt for the decades I'd spent in self-imposed exile from the family home. Perhaps if I'd still been around, if I hadn't been so distant. Mother wouldn't have known. She couldn't have. She was too busy with… well, let's just say tennis. I know my parents' version of love isn't exactly conventional. It's a contractual arrangement, and that's no secret. If father instructed her to leave him be, then be he was left. No one to intervene, nobody to rescue him from his self-imposed drift into lunacy. However, like every other emotion not adjacent to heart-smashing terror, my remorse died so quickly it was basically stillborn.

Father had clearly spent more of his time up here, with his drawings as I now knew, then I remembered in my adolescence. He'd have had to have done to find the time. The last quarter of the book was taken entirely by a single illustration, spanning sides and sides and sides of thick paper. So much ink had bled between the fibers that each page was heavy, bending, and fraying at the corners. In my mind's eye I could picture Father; hunched double over his desk in the dark, surrounded by hundreds of empty ballpoint pens, scratching away at the same inch of paper for hours and hours on end. The intricacy of the details was incredible. Not as incredible as the depth of the blackness though, of those parts of the image Father had made absolutely sure it was clear weren't touched by light. So much work had gone in that I couldn't imagine him having completed it in any timeframe shorter than two years. In the hands of any other artist, I doubt it would have been clear that those pen strokes were a multi-page portrait. Father wasn't any other artist, though. It was an image of a being, although how I knew this, I couldn't tell you. It had no form, per se. In my mind, I somehow knew that the reason Father had carried on this image for pages upon pages was that whatever this abyssal thing was, it was so vast as to render quantifying "form" as we understood it would be *impossible*. This was a thing beyond comprehension, a presence whose full image cannot be captured, viewed, or even speculated upon. Father had managed to transcribe a microscopic slither of its theoretical whole, and that infinitesimal glimpse alone was enough to break him completely. Break him through visualizing every other malevolence in his portfolio that he'd endured. From the first page, I knew that this was something pivoting on a new axis of otherworldliness. An entire additional dimension of incalculable existed on these pages. The only rational detail the human mind could grasp in Father's portrayal of this being were eyes.

He'd covered every single page in them.

I'll never be able to convey with words the pressure the seizes you upon realizing that such a thing could exist, even in the imagination. My train of thought as I picked apart understanding from the ink became a manifest cognitive presence; a conscious glob of intrusive urges jostling with my inner monologue for space in my head. A behemoth bodiless entity spanning entire solar systems constituted of nothing except stellar gases and star-sized eyes. Except... no, there *wasn't* a body to it. Father had blackened the spaces between those eyes for a reason. Any memories I have of an unknowable celestial anatomy within those solid inky plumes is my imagination, my mind playing tricks on me. They have to be. At least, that's what I keep telling myself. Father's art disturbed me by portraying more than should ever be possible with paper and a ballpoint pen. That last image, though... that last image that went on for pages, the one Father had labelled *Hahre*, was far beyond inexplicable. It was maddening. It was when the eyes started blinking back at me that I launched the book from my grasp.

I can still feel their gaze on me now, even though the book is closed and discarded in the corner next to a glass case of meaningless corporate awards and golfing trophies. I keep trying to convince myself it didn't happen. Pictures don't move, and they definitely don't observe you back. Father's message though…

"It is true..."

The epiphany I'm writing to you about began to form as I was reading through the second volume Father left me. I almost didn't open it. A large part of me wanted to close the metal box, lock the study door behind me, and never speak of this to anyone. Ever. Sadly, as I'm sure you would too, I had to know. It just took me a little while to pluck up both the courage and the steady handedness. It was several dozen deep breaths later that I placed the other book in the tin, the tea-stained scrapbook, in front of me. With one hand I opened it to the first page, my other poised with the pen and pad, ready to take notes. I knew the history of my maternal family well. Mother hailed from a wealthy line of entrepreneurs and financiers; old money whose blood and fortune could be traced back to the Hapsburgs. My paternal lineage, however, had always been a closely guarded secret. That's why I knew that when I saw the name Stuart Bramfield at the top of the first page, I had to start taking notes. Even then, I knew there was going to be a lot to emotionally unpack once I'd done reading. My head was already whirling, and I didn't want my clouded emotions to mean I missed out on some vital nugget of identity-affirming information. What I didn't realize was just how many of the emotions I'd have to unpack later would be unbridled terror.

I recognized the sullen man in the newspaper clipping instantly. That furrowed brow and thin face could only have belonged to my father's father. Stuart Bramfield, my long-lost paternal grandfather. How I wish he'd never been found, him and the others that came before. I was much happier when they'd remained lost. In the photo, he was standing next to a painting. Even though it was faded by time and blurred by 1930s camera quality, I shuddered when I saw it. It was the same figure from the first page of Father's sketchbook, the mouth-eyed Zarasashael character I'd mistakenly believed he'd created himself. What unsettled me so much about my grandfather's rendition was just how similar it was to the sketch. That, and how much more defined the painting was in the photo than the painter. There were no wrinkles or folds visible on Stuart Bramfield's beaming features. On Zarasashael, every brushstroke could be made out, as could each one of his minuscule razor-sharp eye teeth. The headline attached to the piece did little to ease my nerves:

MASS HYSTERIA AFTER LATE BRAMFIELD AUCTION

Father had included the article in its entirety. I'll have to paraphrase, but it's not a hard story to simplify. My Grandfather, Stuart Bramfield, was apparently a painter in high regard. After his death in 1939 (the year of Father's birth), his remaining unsold works were auctioned off to a collective of financially endowed admirers. Not a single piece was unsold. The mass hysteria in the headline refers to the fact that, the next morning, all 108 attendees, including the auctioneer, had taken their own lives. Though not without gouging out their own eyes first. I stared at the painting of the mouth-eyed man behind my grandfather. *Mass hysteria.* The portrait leered back at me through the photograph, daring me to believe the flimsy excuse.

"*My God, all of it is true…*"

Father had managed to collect similar clippings stretching back well into my grandfather's teenage years. The origins of our estate were becoming apparent, too. Bramfield Senior-Senior had been commissioned by almost every rich and powerful name of his era you could think of, judging by the photographs. He was smiling away in every monochrome image while his patrons stood in front of whatever warped (and inexplicably clear for sepia) canvas they'd acquired. The looks on their faces were… well, they were less than happy. If you've heard of a thousand-yard stare, you'll know what I'm talking about. An odd expression to see on faces like Calvin Coolidge, King Haakon VII of Norway, or Adolf Hitler's. Sadly, no explanation for how or why these meetings occurred was given. The photos stood alone, the only words coming from newspaper clippings detailing the trail of atrocities that followed the few posthumous auctions and exhibitions of Grandfather's works that occurred.

Eventually, the exploits of Stuart Bramfield and his resilience-shattering paintings gave way to clippings about *his* father, my Great-Grandfather Lionel Bramfield. Whereas Stuart had been the quasi-celebrity darling of the more macabre-inclined wealthy elites, Lionel Bramfield's "gifts" gained him no such acclaim. No. For Lionel, as I found via a letter from my Great-Grandmother, the artistic visual genius running in my veins brought nothing but a slow death in an asylum, ten years after Grandfather's birth in 1890.

Noted as dating from 1898, the letter from Carolina Boxstead reads:

"*Lionel,*

This is the last communication you shall receive. Despite my requests, you continue to persist in sending your letters. I have not read them, and I have not told little Stuart the truth about you. Nor shall I ever.

The days of wishing you'd see through your delusions are long behind me, Lionel. I have moved on, and taken up with another man, a widower with business interests in England. It is a convenient arrangement. Stuart and I will be sailing for Plymouth by the week's end. I have left no instructions on how to contact us with the asylum. This is the final farewell. Even if, by some miracle, you recover, don't come looking for us.

I can't close my eyes without seeing the girls, Lionel. I told you... no, begged you to put down those brushes. Those portraits had the devil in them, Lionel Bramfield, and you let him channel himself into them by your hand. I can't forgive you for that.

I don't blame Rosaline for what she did. I hope her soul has some rest. She didn't ask to stumble into your studio, to see that ghastly mural. You know I vomited twice when I saw it. I should never have let you convince me not to burn it.

She was just a maid, one of the common folk. She had not the education to comprehend what she saw; how could I lay the blame for her madness, or the actions that followed, with her? It wasn't her fault. It was yours.

There is no curse. Not that it matters anymore to me, but I hope for your own sake you one day can see that. No curse, just the darkness in your soul and the paints and brushes you use to free it.

Stuart is all I have left, Lionel. It wasn't only the girls that died that day, or Rosaline, but my love for you along with them.

Please, don't try to find us.

Carolina Boxstead."

Father has attached another, much older, newspaper clipping on the next page, describing the grizzly affair. It took place in 1891. Apparently, the maid of a wealthy Wisconsin family had gone mad, killing the landowners three young daughters before hanging herself. After that was a second clipping, this a writ of admission from "*The Saint Dionysius Asylum For The Irreversibly Mad*". Apparently, Carolina *nee* Boxstead wasn't the only person unsettled by Lionel's paintings. After she'd shown them to her brothers, the Boxstead boys had dragged Lionel to Saint Dionysius' themselves. Though not without losing an ear and several fingers between them. There were no examples of Lionel's work, but from the photographs of his son's exhibits and my father's sketches I could clearly imagine the horrors which led Rosaline the maid to butcher three innocent children and then herself.

"God, all of it is true…"

The next ancestor Father had uncovered was who I assume to be Lionel's father, Marcus Bramfield. There wasn't any clue as to how Father knew this man's name, as the only clippings under it were a series of ancient sepia tinplate photographs. I could tell instantly the grinning homesteader in the forest and log cabin was of my family tree, though; he had the thinness to his face and pointed chin characteristic of, apparently, all Bramfield men.

In each photo, "Marcus" stood, gap-toothed grin pulled ear to ear, in front of a painting. Each tied my stomach in a fresh knot, each knot a thousand times tighter than the last.

One was of Thyrtherothax, the baby-faced maggot thing of Father's own nightmares. In Marcus's depiction, the aberration was snatching up horses in its birdlike skeletal arms, stuffing them whole into its toothless maw. Another was a large portrait of a girl with no face; her jaw, brow, scalp, nose—all had been removed to reveal gore so lifelike, I could have sworn drips fell from her glistening cheeks when I was looking away. The final of the dozen-or-so tinplates was a landscape of a burning pyre. The rabid faces of the madmen dancing around it caused me to yelp when I first turned to that particular page. Their bright eyes bulged almost out of the photograph, the thick smell of smoke tricking itself into my mind with every second I spent looking at that sepia square. The worst part was that, after a few minutes, I had to convince myself I couldn't hear the child tied to a pole above the flames crying.

Each of Marcus Bramfield's paintings disgusted me more than I thought possible. For the first time in this ordeal, the fact I shared the name of these men repulsed me. My skin itched at the thought of the blood flowing through the veins beneath bearing any similarity. Marcus' works were just as detailed, realistic, photo-like as Father's sketches. However, attached to the wild-eyed and bestial leer of this new ancestor, they felt indescribably worse. Blasphemous, were I religious man. My revulsion took on life, nausea rising in my stomach. I recognized too many of those log cabin nightmares. I'd seen them in Father's sketchbook. The paintings in the tinplate photographs were far too small for him to copy with such accuracy and attention to detail, yet Father most certainly wasn't a man with an imagination. It didn't make sense.

"*All of it is true…*"

My epiphany was in full swing by the end of the final page. My awakening was crystallized by a letter; a crumpled note written in pencil, older even than the sepia tinplates of the ghoulish Marcus and his nightmarish paintings.

"*My Darling.*

You know I must leave you. We should never have disturbed the things in the forest. It is I that caught their attention, so it is I that should lead them away. I don't want you or the boy to suffer. He's started seeing the visions, too. They are there whenever I close my eyes. Ever since I touched that damned orange-blue light, all I can see are the same horrors and night-ghasts the boy draws. Don't ask me how, but they got him, too. Every Bramfield man, the thing said. Said we'd be… what was it… con-doo-wits, whatever that means. I don't know about all that, my darling. All I know is I got to get these heathen visions to stop. I can't have the boy growing up as some kind of freak. You saw what they did to the Injuns in the valley over a damn totem. What're they going to do when they see…

Look, I'm going to fix this. Even if it takes until the end of time, I'll make it right. I went back for that light, to see if I could find those damn things, get them to lift this… this curse, but they were gone. There are tracks leading into the forest, though. I'm going to start there, because I have to somewhere. There are things out there, my darling. I've seen them—I see them every night when I close my eyes. I can whittle them as though they were stood in front of me, lifelike and way better than anything I've carved (you know I've never been no damn good at it). And that light, that blue and orange light…

Don't you worry though. I'm going to find them and kill every last one of the bastards until they fix our damn boy. I can't come back until I sort this, no matter what I find. If I don't come back, please live your life. Your heart is too big to be filled by a dead man.

Eternally,
your Obadiah."

Father's warning rang over and over as I closed the book. It couldn't be true. There was *no such thing* as curses. Clearly, there was some kind of hereditary schizophrenia in the males of my line.

Yes, that had to be it. That was the only explanation, surely? I went to check the notes I thought I'd been taking as I read and screamed.

The notepad I'd been scribbling on had no notes. All the pages I distinctly remember filling with thoughts and questions on my complex paternal history were wordless. Despite all my memories to the contrary, my hand hadn't been writing.

It had been drawing.

I swore over and over, repeating every profanity I knew as I flicked through the images my ink-stained hand had rendered. They were, all of them, of eyes. The same eyes Father filled his last few months with meticulously sketching. The same eyes that blinked back at me when I screamed at them.

The wake downstairs is wrapping up. Winston will come to check on me soon, no doubt, or Mother. Thank God the estate is so vast. I think that's the only reason nobody heard the smashing glass, my cries and screams, or the banging as I slammed my guilty hand against the desk until it broke. I don't know how I'm going to explain this to them. They'll think I'm mad, that I've had a breakdown just like Father, have me committed to an asylum like Lionel Bramfield to save me from myself and the "insanity" waiting in my genes. I don't think it is madness, though. That notepad is still there, staring back at me from the floor, and the eyes are still blinking. I'm going to show them. So is Father's sketchbook, the one I managed to copy with unexplained muscle memory. I have to show them though, don't I? Otherwise, they won't believe me. I just hope they're made of stronger stuff than Lionel's maid. I don't know what to do. One day my hand will heal, and then how long do I have? I don't remember doing those drawings, but they are there. The thoughts racing through my mind are vivid and visual in a way they've never been. Every time I close my eyes, I am bombarded by a parade of nightmares. The Bramfield curse is real. There's no escaping it. This is my epiphany:

I can see why Father killed himself.

GREAT AUNT HORTENSIA

"Great-Aunt Hortensia is old money, Dani. If the seaside air and limey culture doesn't do it for you, think of the will. Nothing says best neph—I mean, best grandniece, ever, then flying halfway around the world to help the old coot sort through some old paintings, eh?"

That's the last thing Dad said to me before he slapped my back for good luck and sent me off on the red-eye from LAX to London Heathrow. The summer of 2020. The *worst* summer of my life. And, probably, the last. As the locals would say, cheers Dad. Prick. You can probably guess that I'm Dani. I'm in the UK, and I'm not happy about it. Well, that's an understatement. Fucking *(sorry)* pissed is what I am. Or I would be, if I wasn't so damn scared.

Heathrow and what I got to see of London were glamorous and exciting, like the England you see in Hugh Grant movies. Great-Aunt Hortensia doesn't live in London though. If she did, at least I'd have got to see some sights. No. To add insult to my no-doubt impending injuries, Great-Aunt Hortensia lives in Dovercourt. Heard of it? No? That's because nobody has. And now I'm going to die here. FML. So cliché, but Great-Aunt Hortensia herself was also unheard of in our house until we got the letter. Uncle Pete and Aunt Tiff got one too, so we knew it had to be legit. We asked Gramps, and he got that teary-eyed look before going off about some shindig back in the McCarthy days. Long story not short enough, after a few hours we found out I did indeed have a Great-Aunt Hortensia.

Gramps had only met her once. She was my Great-Great Aunt technically, but nobody has time for that many greats. Not to mention that Ol' G-G-Aunt H doesn't deserve *one* great, let alone two. From what Gramps recalled (which wasn't much), she was two things:
1. British
2. Rich

If you guessed it was fact number two that meant my dad wrote straight back to volunteer his youngest daughter for a summer across the Atlantic, you'd be correct. I can't remember exactly what the letter said. Basically, she was writing to her *"beloved relatives"* as she needed assistance in her twilight years. She had a *"sizeable estate of collected artworks and oddities"* which she wanted help *"making arrangements for with collectors before my time on this mortal plane draws to a close and I bid you a last adieu."* That last bit I remember very well. Such pretentious, much cringe. At the time, I thought it was because Great-Aunt Hortensia must be an eccentric British millionaire. During my UK summer, I grew to think she spoke and wrote like that because she was fucking *(sorry)* insane. After this morning though… Jesus, maybe that's just what *they* think people speak like?

Her quote-unquote mansion wasn't much to look at, either, but it at least matched its owner. The exterior walls were an off-yellow which may once have been vibrant, but after decades the relentless drizzling rain and frigid salt air had chipped and faded the paint on the wooden slats. The large building sagged in the middle, and it creaked and moaned on every breeze, no matter how slight. I gulped when I saw it. I was sure that the three stories with their single-pane painted-shut Victorian window frames and ancient ceramic pipes on every interior wall would collapse under their own weight before the summer's end. Turned out structural integrity was the *least* of my worries. I'm not currently biting my other hand, so I don't let out any noise because of a badly maintained house. Got to set the scene though, right?

Despite the dozens of staff that attended it, the mansion's interior was filthy. Dust and cobwebs had been left to take advantage of every available corner, crevice, and cranny. The floors, at least, were clean. Unlike everything else, they were well kept and scrubbed to immaculacy. It was the only activity I ever saw Great-Aunt Hortensia's workforce occupy themselves with, now that I think about it. Well, aside from cooking my two daily meals;

porridge for breakfast, and porridge with a satsuma on the side for dinner. I gave up complaining about this by day three. The servants never answered, and Boggis just got angry. You're wondering why I didn't complain to G-A-H, right? Well, that wasn't exactly an option.

I didn't actually *meet* my Great-Great Aunt until this morning, when Boggis (her housekeeper) told me I'd been summoned to the third floor. I can hear her stomping around upstairs while I'm writing this, bellowing at Boggis and her army of servants to *"find that filthy parasite runt if you don't want your eye jellies sucked out with a straw"*. I *would* have sympathy for her staff. Boggis may be a lumbering brute that smells like pickled eggs and is decades overdue for a dental visit, but having your eyes drunk by... whatever that thing is, sounds painful. However, I did say *would*. It's hard to care when you're hiding in an antique closet because their boss wants to do much, much worse to *you*. If you think working for Great-Aunt Hortensia is bad, Boggis, try being *related* to her.

Oh snap! You're probably itching to know *why* I'm in this closet, right?! Sorry, I can ramble sometimes. We'll get to it, but not before I explain exactly why the whole fucking (*sorry*) time here in England has been a nightmare-inducing shitshow (*sorry*). We've got a whole eight weeks of summer to cover before I tell you why I'm having to keep one hand over my mouth to muffle whimpers.

So anyway, the resentment set in roundabout the second the black cab dropped me off outside G-A-H's seaside mansion. Instead of getting ready for my first semester at Brown, I would be sorting through portraits of long-dead distant relatives and gazing out the window at murky grey waves. Well, that's what I thought I'd be sorting through. I'll admit, I was actually quite happy at first when Boggis showed me around *one of* the ground floor gallery rooms on my arrival. Yes, you read that right. Rooms. Plural. The faded easter-chick yellow mansion contained eight in total before you'd even touched a staircase. It was more gallery than anything else. Aside from a kitchen/dining space tucked at the back of the property, my lodgings in the basement, and Great-Aunt Hortensia's *"private wing"* in the attic, every square foot of floor space not in a bathroom was dedicated to displaying... well, I guess you *could* call it art. It was art in the way that raw footage of 9/11 could be classified as a documentary. All of G-A-H's quote-unquote *"pub-*

lic" collections were quote-unquote *normal* at least (more on that in a minute), but they were still disturbing.

Hortensia was an avid collector of what they call *"outsider"* art. This is why during my initial few weeks, I didn't find myself beset by *too much* boredom and lethargy. I used to *like* creepy shit (sorry) like that, you understand? I'd spent the plane journey imaging long weeks sorting through the kind of renaissance, true-to-life brushwork adorning the walls in shows like Downton Abbey. Dull, in other words. I was both shocked and relieved to find I couldn't have been more wrong. There were no drab oil landscapes or aging portraits of long-dead British aristocracy here. It was all dark and demented in a way my horror movie sensibilities found delectable.

At first, I thought the rooms of schizophrenia-induced paintings and grotesque sculptures in the ground floor galleries were pretty cool. No, not just pretty cool. They were *awesome*. Back home, I'd have happily paid entry to a gallery containing even a tenth of the bizarre oddities hung on Great Aunt Hortensia's walls. I'm not even that much of an art person, either. Movies are more my thing. I like to think of myself as cultured though, or at least I try to be. Enough of my friends have dragged me along to galleries and I make sure never to protest. Without blathering on about it too much, I'm not a *total* stranger to the art world. G-A-H's collection was *way* more interesting than anything any of my more pretentious-leaning friends had pulled me across town to view. Some of the works my great aunt owned were pretty notorious, too. I could see why the quote-unquote "public collections" cost about £2000 entry. I think she even has some of John Wayne Gacy's stuff down there, and a napkin doodle Charles Manson did in prison. Of course, the steep price never thinned the traipsing parade of viewers and ogglers. People paid more than I'd ever held at one time to see the macabre treasures, and until about the second week of summer, I felt kind of privileged to be able to study them at my leisure. Unfortunately, the endless chores Boggis had me doing soon wore off the intrigue. Even a Wayne-Gacy painting stops feeling deliciously decadent by the twentieth time you've polished and dusted the frame.

I would have got in touch with Dad, asked him to pull me out, said fuck (*sorry*) the damn will. I didn't come here to be a slave for some woman who refused to even come down from the attic to meet me, I'd have said. Again, *sooo* cliché, but there was no damn

WiFi or cell signal in the mansion. If you're wondering why I didn't just leave, and you're wondering whether or not I was even allowed to, then 10pts to Gryffindor. Every time I tried heading to the door, I'd feel Boggis' slimy paw on my shoulder. Even if I did manage to get out, where would I go? Keep walking until I found cell signal? The only way back to London was by train, and I'd be found at Dovercourt's rundown station long before the next salvation-on-rails arrived. I was isolated, trapped, and alone. But… well, I still held onto the thought that this was all only temporary, right? That it was just for the summer. It was easier to grit my teeth and get through it, I reasoned. Fantasize about beating the shit (sorry) out of Dad when I got home. I won't lie too, I *did* spend more than a few hours salivating over the many things I could do with my cut of the will.

So yeah, all in all I had plenty with which to bury my growing worry that Great-Aunt Hortensia was going to keep me here to join her army of thin, vacant-stared servants (the ones tearing through cupboards and looking around in crawl spaces for me as I write this). That's genuinely what I thought she wanted to do to me, that if my paranoid suspicions *did* turn out correct then joining her mindless entourage would be my fate. It would make sense, right? Creepy old lady pulls in distant relatives to turn them into gawping, slack-jawed zombies? If only that *was* what she had planned. That would have been way better than… well, I'm getting there. As for her servants, sadly, I don't think they were *ever* human in the first place. Fuck (*sorry*) knows what they are, but if they *were* once like you and I, then… well, my God. I don't want to know what a person goes through to become like that.

At the time I got quote-unquote *"promoted"* to the first floor, though, I didn't have any reason to be suspicious of them. I just thought their quiet, dejected demeanour was down to being overworked. Burnout, you know? Now I'm in the closet, now that I can hear them scuttling over the walls and ceilings outside, I'm starting to think the reason they never stopped working had nothing to do with toxic labor conditions. I'm starting to remember a lot about them I'd been trying my best to ignore. Stuff like the fact that the throng of gallery patrons seemed to instinctively give them a wide berth, or that their glazed eyes all pointed in different, seemingly random, directions. Then, of course, there's the waxy, greyish quality to their skin. All these little things I'd done my best to ignore, each of them a reason to kick myself for letting the thought of those distant relative death-dollars stop me running for my damn life. I couldn't ignore the obvious non-humanity of them by this morning. I'd spent too long in their shuffling, wordless company to fool myself any longer. Well, I *hope* they weren't human, at least. It's easier to imagine they're something else entirely, for my own sanity. The process that turns a person into something like that must be monstrous. Still, I think whatever Great-Aunt Hortensia has planned for *me* is much worse. I don't think Boggis would have looked so apologetic when he grabbed me otherwise.

I was moved to upstairs duties (as Boggis called it) on the Monday of my fourth week in Dovercourt. I was told it was because Boggis needed assistance up there but... well; I know better. It's because of the incident. This is when things went from weird-but-boring to weird-but-terrifying. The incident is how I found out I wasn't allowed to leave or talk to the patrons. By that point I'd started to crack a little, you see? A whole month of day in, day out chores, porridge, and serial killer paintings can do that to a girl. I was still trying to hold it together for those bereavement bucks, but something bumped me off the proverbial wagon. I can't even remember what, either. Ain't that a kicker? Anyhow, the incident. I tried escaping; you see. Twice, the first time by running for the front door, and the second by begging the patrons for rescue. Neither worked. The bruises from being Boggis-tackled when I tried the former faded weeks ago. The scars on my back start burning if I think about my punishment for the latter too long.

I knew better than to try and ask the patrons for help after the Monday I got those scars. They clearly didn't care. If they did, they'd have stopped Boggis going to town with his flail of rope and broken glass. I still can't help but wonder; was that a gallery installation he repurposed, or did he create the disciplinary weapon himself? Either way, seeing the guests fork over money for the privilege of watching me bleeding and crying on the floor eroded what faith I ever had in humanity. Especially when they started asking to pay to help him stitch up the wounds with fishing wire. That particular perversion only took their interest *after* Boggis' ham-fisted medical attention had me screaming again. Fuckers (*not sorry*).

The well-to-do visitors of the ground floor galleries paid handsomely to visit. They were the kind of folk you're probably imagining; slimy, off-putting, a little mouth-breathy, and grotesquely wealthy. Like the worst parts of an Anime convention gave up

Japan for Downton Abbey. The visitors to the members' only first-floor gallery were something else, though. Wrong in ways there are probably only words for in German. These were the collectors Great-Aunt Hortensia had written to us about. Both the first-floor patrons and the quote-unquote *"art"* they'd view/buy/sell were nearly as unsettling as Great-Aunt Hortensia herself. They went from unsettling to horrifying almost as quickly, too.

The first floor contained only two rooms aside from the landing. Apart from one of them (a small private gallery), the entire floor was cut off from access by all except Boggis. Until today I never saw what was on the rest of the floor, but my totally correct guess was that it was used for storage. The only reason I haven't gone poking around to investigate (other than memories of Boggis' glass shard whip) is that I've seen the things he brings out for the private gallery. The small glimpses I got of what must be hidden away behind that door were enough. As far as consumer experiences go, a private membership at Great Aunt Hortensia's came with perks. Not that I saw any of the private members make use of them. A shame too, because some of the decanters and bottles held liquids worth more than my Dad would have made in several lifetimes. I don't think the private members were interested in pleasantries, though. It didn't take me long at all to figure that the paid-up members of Hortensia's never visited Dovercourt for pleasure. Everything that happened once you'd reached the landing at the top of those rickety stairs was strictly business.

The first-floor patrons would wait on one of the two excessively comfy velvet chairs in front of the fireplace in the quote-unquote *"gallery"*. I say quote-unquote there because I rarely saw anything displayed there; only ever what the visiting patron was interested in buying (if they weren't there to sell). G-A-H's burly manservant would wheel whatever-it-was through from the storage. Boggis would then (to quote the locals again) bugger off, leaving me alone with the beads of sweat on my brow and whatever almost-person was making them fall that day. I won't lie to you. Some of them made me genuinely terrified that Boggis would return to find me in pieces, or worse. What terrified me more was that I didn't think he'd care. Thankfully, the private members had their own agendas, none of which involved taking advantage of an isolated, vulnerable young woman. Had I been left alone with the ground floor patrons, I think the outcome may have been different.

As mentioned though, the first-floor patrons didn't pay a standing sum for easy access to visceral thrills. There's no doubt in my mind that if I'd encountered some of them in a different context, I'd be unlikely to see another sunrise, but in the private gallery they all followed the same routine. They'd appraise the object or painting for about a half hour while I waited by the small bar to serve refreshments, if any asked. Then Boggis would return, and they'd discuss their quote-unquote *"business"*. I didn't pour a single drink the entire summer. None of the weirdos and freaks that rolled through asked, or even seemed to acknowledge I was there. I'm going to be honest; I think the only reason I got put on first-floor duty is that it's where Boggis spent the majority of his time. I think it was less about Boggis needing help, and more about orders from the attic to keep a closer eye on me…

Fuck (sorry), I'm getting side-tracked. All you need to know is that I got moved upstairs, and it was a whole new level of *"Jesus fucking Christ what the fuck is happening"* (sorry, sorry, sorry). There's no point speculating what Boggis' motives were, anyway. It doesn't matter anymore, does it? Whatever they were, they were sinister. That's been proved, and does anything else *really* matter?

The members in the upstairs gallery then. Like I said, were *wrong*-wrong. Not the sleazy kind of wrong of the ground-floor patrons. The collectors and dealers Boggis liaised with on Great-Aunt Hortensia's behalf were… well, they were the same kind of people as Great-Aunt Hortensia. Nightmares masquerading as humans.

Amongst the first few was a man in a 1950s style Private Eye trench coat. Except, no gumshoe in a movie I ever saw looked as tired and sleep deprived as he did. The bags under his eyes had bags, and they were full of bricks. None of the movie detectives had ears that leaked blood despite the rags stuffed in them or had perfect half-inch scars over every inch of visible skin. At least the item he purchased from Boggis wasn't distressing; it was just a beaten up, clearly used, Bluetooth speaker. Weird, definitely not worth the twenty grand the bleeding-eared detective dropped on it, but I'll level, I didn't care. Watching Insomniac Dick Tracy getting ripped off on a second-hand speaker was the *least* weird transaction I saw that week, and they only got weirder.

One time, I got to the first floor to see a series of paintings hung ready for sale. How *anyone* could paint that well, that accurately to life, I'll never know. I thought the damn things were photos at first. That's what made them so awful. The scenes they depicted were of, I'm guessing, various ritual sacrifices; an onslaught of paint and canvas suffering so vivid I broke down into floods of tears. Boggis had to slap me twice before I managed to compose myself. One of the pieces in particular, a large oil painting of some rabid pilgrim types dancing around a young child tied to a flaming witch-burning pyre, seared itself onto the backs of my eyelids for a week. I never saw any cash change hands for this collection; it was wrapped up and stuffed in a van by a few guys with New York accents. One disappeared into the bathroom and came back minus a hand, but with plenty of new tears. I still feel like puking a little when I picture how happy Boggis looked upon receiving that dripping paper bag.

Oh, and then there was the bug-eyed tweaker-looking couple, again American (from Florida, I'm guessing) who stank of homelessness and hard drug abuse. They exchanged a jar of blue sand for an ugly dark-purple candle that reeked of rotten meat; the former placed tenderly in Boggis' hands by the filthy woman of the pair, the latter rabidly snatched from his grasp by the trembling male. Once a man Boggis addressed simply as *"Mayor Jeffries"* paid for a box of old VHS tapes with several property deeds, and worryingly asked Boggis to thank Great-Aunt Hortensia for her business *again*. Tuesday once saw a bunch of government-spook-looking guys give over a briefcase of syringes full of yellow ooze, swapping them for a little red book. One of the g-men (well, g-women, technically) gave it a brief flick through, despite the thin-faced head of their group warning her not to. I'd already scrubbed my own blood out of those floorboards thanks to Boggis, so cleaning up hers didn't traumatize me as much as you'd think. Seeing a grown woman gouge her own eyes out with a ball-point pen, however, will have me in therapy for decades. Well, it *would* have done if I'd managed to make it out of here. Guess it's not something I've got to worry about now, right? Most disturbing was when a man whose face I physically can't remember showed up. This blur, this figure that I feel nauseous thinking about for too long, had an envelope containing (so they claimed) the coordinates of *"where they're keeping her damn God"*. Boggis nearly fainted when he heard this. He offered the swirling-faced stranger a large crate in exchange, a box so big he had to rope in four of the voiceless servants to carry it. I couldn't stop myself from sobbing when I heard the bangs and cries for help coming from inside. They sounded far too young for me to keep myself composed.

If you're wondering whether that got me another session with Boggis' favorite glass toy, congratulations, 10 more points to Gryffindor.

But yeah, this was how things went from week four onwards. As you can imagine, I was pretty fucking (*sorry*) broken by the time Boggis knocked on my door this morning to tell me I'd been summoned to the attic. I didn't really process what he'd said at first.

"The... the attic?"

Boggis rolled his bloodshot eyes at me, and I flinched out of Pavlovian reflex.

"Yes girl, the attic. Mistress Hortensia feels it's time to meet you in person. To... umm... thank you for your hard work this summer before you return to the colonies." Before he said those words, I'd never seen Boggis look at me with anything other than annoyance, disgust, or hatred. This was the first time he looked genuinely apologetic about my situation. It terrified me.

I had a lump in my throat all through breakfast (porridge, like every morning). For every minute of my cold shower, I was sobbing uncontrollably. I knew that whatever waited for me upstairs, it was worse than anything I'd seen so far, and I'd already seen far too much. The journey up the second flight of stairs was filled with internal debates about whether I could tackle Boggis. The seconds he spent unlocking the door were on whether taking another glass-shard lashing was worth buying me an extra few minutes. I've always been indecisive though, and that's why I heard the door clicking locked behind me before I'd registered that Boggis had pushed me through to the pitch-black room on the other side.

It was quiet in the gloom beyond. Even the distant rush of the grey Dovercourt waves was muted the moment Boggis shut me in the darkness. The only sensations in my ears were the ringing of near silence, the faint *thump-thump-thumping* of my heart against my ribcage, and the long low creaks of my weight on the floorboards as I crept. Unlike the other two stories, the floors in the attic were as dusty and neglected as the walls and ceilings. Despite an army of available scrubbers, it was obvious nobody had been up here to clean in years. Maybe even decades, if the must cloying scent of mould and damp was any indication.

"Ah… is that the runt?"

The voice was thick yet shrill, a high-pitched half-gargle that prompted the same physiological response as cutlery scratching on greasy plates. I heard the deep, ragged breaths that accompanied it when I was about halfway down the hallway. It spoke when I was only a few steps away. Those last few steps… well, they took Olympic endurance runner levels of willpower to take. If I could have headed in literally any other direction I would have, trust me. There were only two doors, you see. The one Boggis had shut behind me, and the one the gravelly words drifted from ahead. My legs felt like they were going to buckle, my breaths came through so shallow I was more lightheaded with every passing second. Despite my brain being so oxygen starved, unconsciousness loomed, despite the fact my free hand had to clench my chest tight lest I have a heart attack, my shaking grasp found the doorknob. I didn't have any other choice, did I?

All the breathing I could hear got louder as I turned the lump of rusted iron, both my shallow quivering pants and the booming wheezes beyond the red wooden door.

"Great… Great-Aunt Hortensia?"

My stammer was met with a hacking laugh from the rotund figure sat in the darkness across the room on the other. She was too entrenched in the shadows to make out anything beyond her silhouette. Not that this made her any less intimidating, I mention it only so you understand that even though my resolve was already basically snapped, the *worst* of her was yet to come. All I could tell at that point was that she was big in a way that usually requires medical intervention. Vast doesn't cover it. You ever seen *My 600lb Life*? Picture the largest three guests you've seen on that show, then smash them together. I'm all for #BodyPositivity, but there's limits, right? It's hard to be positive about a human body larger than most marine mammals.

"Ha… ha… runt, you still think? Amazing… the way you parasites cling to the lies is always… ha…" Quote-unquote *"Great-Aunt Hortensia"* let forth another rattling chuckle. I stood in the doorway, frozen in place. Every hair on my body was on end. I knew instantly that I *wasn't* just dealing with an insane, grotesquely obese aristocrat. On an instinctual level, I understood, even then, that something was *wrong* here, wrong in a way that folk can drive themselves into a nuthouse trying to understand.

"G-great... Great-Aunt Hortensia... I want... I want..." I could hear myself blubbering, pleading, even though the distant voice behind my eyes knew it was useless. "I want to go home... please..."

I could feel the warmth of tears on my face. They only grew heavier when the thing across the room started chuckling again. "Home... the runt wants to go home... ha... ha..."

There was a sound in the dark, like tongues smacking against unseen lips. This was accompanied by creaks and groans of leather and wood as Great-Aunt Hortensia adjusted her position, leaning forward.

"Well... we *all* want to go home, runt... I'll be able to soon... ha... but that's not something such a... pathetic... vermin could understand."

"Great-Aunt..."

A new sound growled from the spat from the darkness, somewhere between a snarl and a growl that had me doing a few involuntary Kegel exercises.

"Quiet your scum tongue, runt... it's been bad enough... listening to you skulking and whimpering these weeks... no matter... the shell will be worth it..."

There was a third sound in the dark, and as soon as it bounced through the blackness, I screamed so loudly dust fell from the distant rafters. It was a single click. The single click of a bedside lamp being turned on. A bedside lamp whose light gave me my first sanity-shattering view of Great-Aunt Hortensia.

A far as first impressions go... fuck (*not sorry*).

She had no eyes. I could see (pun not intended) why straight away. There wasn't room for any. Whatever she was, the vast folds containing her form clearly weren't vast enough. Her facial features were pressed and stretched across her bulbous head; both the empty sockets and the nostrils on her flattened nose revealed writhing, slug-like flesh underneath. This obviously not human anatomy was also visible at the multiple splits, tears, and lacerations that lined her bulging skin. The skin itself was grey, rotten. Maggots wriggled in and out of its waxy surface, and occasionally there'd be a sharp *crack* as one of the many flies buzzing around her got distracted and made a kamikaze run for the lamp on the rickety chairside table. My nostrils caught up eventually. If I wasn't so busy screaming, I would have barfed. The sickly-sweet aroma of decaying meat was overpowering. It sloshed around my lungs, pulling me further into nausea with every inter-scream inhale.

"Don't have strength... to empty you... but we have the serum... now... it's time... for us... to act..."

I screamed even louder when those sagging lips peeled back to reveal the writhing, cement-colored gums underneath. The teeth set into them were worse, though. I always thought Brits had bad teeth. It's the stereotype, right? Great-Aunt Hortensia didn't. Hers were *perfect*. I don't mean perfect like they were healthy and human; I meant they were perfect, like a God damn fucking (*sorry sorry sorry*) cartoon. Each was an exact square. Only on razor blades had I seen edges and corners as straight as on that dentistry. Detergent companies wish they could get whites as white as those teeth, too. They were dazzling, and not in an attractive way, in a way that helped my stomach leap the final few steps into nausea land. Don't ask me how, but I knew those teeth were the reason it didn't need the eyes of whoever's skin it was wearing. They, the teeth, were looking at me. It saw with them. I know this because I could *feel* the disgust emanating from them when I projectile vomited on the dusty floor.

"Ugh... parasites... disgusting... enough, runt... *give me... your skin.*"

I didn't stop to ask what she meant. I was already halfway back down the hallway by the time those teeth had parted. Though, for some stupid fucking (*so not sorry*) reason, I looked back over my shoulder before I tumbled through the door Boggis had just opened.

The cement gums had pushed outwards beyond the rotting lips. Because of their bulging a new split had formed, one that ran vertically down the center of Great-Aunt Hortensia's face. Maggots too slow to avoid the schism tumbled and plummeted off the razor-sharp teeth as her inner jaw began to protrude. I had just enough time to catch sight of the three glistening thick green tongues unfurl a full six feet from her distended gullet when I felt my shoulder slam into Boggis' chest. We tumbled down the stairs together. I somehow managed to avoid the syringe in his hand, but he didn't avoid my boot in his face. I'd love to say that was an awesome heroic moment, but the truth is, I was in full-on blind panic mode. I didn't register it was Boggis, or that he was holding a syringe full of the yellow stuff the G-men had deposited. All I knew was I had to run and, if running didn't work, kick, punch, and yell until it did again.

The servants weren't scrubbing the floor anymore. Do you remember when I said I don't think they were ever human? Well, this is when they decided to show it. When I flew around the corner into the second-floor landing, they were waiting for me at the foot of the stairs. Every pair of vacant, emaciated eyes stared up at me. A dozen or so of them, lips stretched tight against their mouths, every dead gaze locked on my trembling form. I started running again as soon as they made the noise. They started in unison. Not a human sound. It was mechanical, almost like one of those nuclear attack sirens played in reverse and at half speed. The noise itself wasn't why I ran to the only door I could see, though. It was because as they made it, they jumped onto the walls and started scrambling up them towards me.

Oh, and for those who have been paying attention to the layout of Great-Aunt Hortensia's mansion, yes, the only other door *was* to the second-floor gallery. That's how I found myself in this antique wooden cabinet in the storage room. I wasn't lying earlier when I said I'd not gone poking around in here. I've only run through it, sobbing and screaming. I can hear things though, things chittering and chattering in the dark space outside the safety of this cabinet. Things that sound like they might be even worse than whatever's pretending to be Great-Aunt Hortensia. Things that rattle the bars to their cages. Things that are screaming horrifying things about me into the dark. Things that somehow know my name.

I can hear Boggis opening the door to the storage room now, so I've got to wrap this up. I don't think I'm getting out of this. Well, no duh, but I didn't want you to think this had a happy ending. I've still got no signal. That's why I've written this on the notes app. If you found this cell phone, please find my family's contact details in it. Let them know what happened. Show them this. Let my dad know he's a greedy selfish prick and his greedy selfish prick ways got his daughter killed. Oh, and also please post this online somewhere, too. In case anyone else is experiencing something similar. They may find it helpful. Who knows, but it can't hurt to try, right?

Unless, that is, you found this outside of a sagging yellow wooden mansion in Dovercourt. If you did, don't bother with any of that, just run.

Final request, and this one is the most important. If you contact my family, and they tell you I'm not dead, send them this anyway. Tell them to get away as fast as they can. If I dropped my cell phone, there is no way I made it out of this shithole alive (*soooooo not sorry*).

SUBJECT: WTF

Director,

I'm snowed under at the moment, so I'll have to get to the point. Before you get too mad, the reason I'm snowed under is you. I'm not really that fussed about offending your sensibilities right now, just being honest. As you can probably guess from the subject line, WHAT THE FUCK, OBADIAH?! ARE YOU FUCKING MENTAL!

You can send Human Resources after me for my tone. Have them designate me as a compromised asset if you want. I'm more than past the point of caring. You've told me before that you admire me for speaking my mind, that you always have a soft spot for the ones who aren't intimidated by you. Well, Obadiah, get ready to respect me more than you ever have: you're a fucking idiot, an absolutely useless, short-sighted, paranoid, obsessive twat. You let damn Eastley wrap you around her little finger and she PLAYED YOU FOR A FOOL. I'm not even going to get into the resources we've wasted trying to track her down. She should have been designated comped a long time ago. She wasn't right since the Marathon County incident, and we both know it. I told you it was a bad idea to allow her family to remain with her in Wisconsin. I told you we didn't need her in London. I definitely told you this was going to come back to bite us in the ass.

But did you listen? No. You were too caught up in Event-HAHRE.

I've read the damn files, Obadiah. I can't believe how much you've rediverted into understanding that red book. It's not the damn Taealim. It's the ramblings of a goddamn mad man. Well-written ramblings, granted, but that's all it is. I've been the Senior Research Doctor at PLR for forty years, Obadiah. You know as well as I do that nobody knows Paranatural Literary Events or Entities like me. You want to know why that damn book has a trail of bloodshed behind it? Because you keep throwing lunatics in a cell with it and locking the damn door!

First, there was Dr Bridger. He was two years from retirement. He'd spent decades researching the Taealim. Do you know why he chewed open his own wrists? It wasn't because of "ha HA ha tHe children R bleEding (a housewife's tale". It was because the reality of his previous thirty years dawned on him, and his mind couldn't take it. It's fucking obvious, Obadiah. The fact you DOUBLED the budget on the Event-HAHRE project because of it is INSANE. I'm not even going to get into the shit with Dr Eastley. I know you always had a soft spot for her but, Jesus Christ Obadiah, how can you not see that she played you the whole time? She was broken from the start. Do you really think she's above pretending to be under the influence of a Literary Event just so you'd let your guard down? Those research assistants didn't have to die. Can you imagine how hard it was for me to watch the surveillance footage? I know things are done differently at the other facilities, but here in London, we're a family. I handpick every PLR recruit, as you know. I knew the owner of every pair of eyes she plucked out with that bionic arm of hers. They were my friends, Obadiah. You kept throwing them to her even though you couldn't see it was all a damn act.

And look where we are now; Dr Eastley is still evading you AND she's leaking the bloody IPSET database to the public! That's not why I think you must be fucking high though, director. It's because I've just finished reading the new Event-0003 policy.

What. The. Hell.

Need I remind you that we have a LITERAL ALIEN GOD in our captivity? For fucks sake, I can't believe I'm actually having to explain this to you, you were the one that captured the damn thing. Entity-E0003 activity has never been higher. Do you think that, just maybe, the fact that all the assets we used to have assigned to them are now on this ridiculous Event-HAHRE goose chase has SOMETHING to do with that? The other department leads and I have discussed this at length, Obadiah, and we've all reached the same conclusion. Hahre isn't real. They don't exist. Bardiquet was a lunatic, but that's it. We have the records. He wasn't under the radar, Obadiah. He was a troubled kid impacted by telesuggestive fallout from Event-0789. This is all clearly documented in the Event-HAHRE files. Why are we devoting ANY RESOURCES to this?!

As I said, Hahre ISN'T REAL. Bardiquet WASN'T a Prophet-Class POI. He's not fucking Jimmy. The book is harrowing, I'll give you that, but its effects AREN'T paranatural. You're dealing with the manifesto of a new Charles Manson, that's literally it. If it were ANYTHING ELSE, then why haven't there been any damn Event-0001 manifestations?! Usually, we can't sneeze in London without Entity-E0001 showing up. Not once during storage have any attempts been made by E0001 to obtain "ha HA ha tHe children R bleEding (a housewife's tale". Do you know why? Because it has no reason to, because Hahre isn't real.

Do you know what is real? Event-0003. Why in god's name would you give the Entity-E0003 matrioform access to Serum-8293B?! What could possibly be worth the E0003's lives being made that much easier?! They can assume new identities with zero genetic leftovers from the victim. No evidence, Obadiah. Over 89% of the E0003's we identified were found by trace DNA of the victim at suspected locations of an identity change. Serum-8293B breaks down everything that isn't skin down to a genetic level. No DNA left, Obadiah. The E0003's are basically invisible now. Do you know how fucking dangerous you've made them? We've lost track of the matrioform, too. Do you remember what happened when she was last unaccounted for? It's amazing the Chernobyl cover worked the first time. Do you really think we could keep blowing a nuclear reactor under wraps in the age of the internet?

So, to recap: because of a "prophecy" in a book written by a disturbed young adult, you've given a race of extraterrestrial predators that wear human skin the ability to liquidize our internal anatomy more-or-less at will. Half the time, we only get sightings reported because they're so sloppy. People notice when their wife or son has a damn open wound that won't heal. How the hell are we supposed to confirm sightings if their shell is completely intact?! They're going to wipe us out with our own goddam weapon! Synthesizing Serum-8293B took decades. All that work wasted. Because, surprise-surprise, with our attention on Event-HAHRE, Entity-0431 escaped. Do I need to remind you how many fucking researchers the damn Mime killed? How many terrified

IPSET staff died thinking their sacrifice was going to be worth something?

I've read the reports. We were THIS FUCKING CLOSE to formulating a version of Serum-8293B that reacted to Entity-E0003. THIS CLOSE to wiping them out. Instead, you go chasing some fairytale AND give them the keys to freely operate amongst us undetected?! And for what, ANOTHER copy of Bardiquet's damn book?! I'll ask again: ARE YOU FUCKING HIGH?!

What's more, you've done this trade at a time when we've received credible intelligence that THEY KNOW WHERE WE'RE KEEPING EVENT-0003! They're going to be coming for us, Obadiah. Coming for you most of all. You know better than anyone what will happen if they release Event-0003. Please, I am BEGGING you, stop chasing this Event-HAHRE nonsense. Hahre isn't real. Event-0003 is. Adjust your fucking priorities.

Apologies for the tone, but I am genuinely terrified, Obadiah. Dr Eastley wasn't the only one with a family. The longer we go on ploughing research into this fantasy apocalypse, the more we're sleepwalking into a real one.

Regards,
Dr Dipesh Anand
Department Lead, Paranatural Literary Research,
Institute of Paranatural Science, Events, and Technology

(Oh, and Dr Eastley, if it is you that's leaking all the emails and eyewitness account, I beg you to keep your grubby hands off of this one. I don't care what's going on between you and Obadiah, but if the public can see these, so can EVERYONE ELSE. Please don't fucking endanger all of us just because you have a petty grudge against the director.)

THE ZIT

The pimple stared at me. It was big, red, and angry. The biggest, reddest, and angriest zit I'd ever seen. I've seen hundreds, too. I belong to at least five different zits, spot, blister, and blackhead bursting group on Facebook.

"You've got a zit on your neck." I listened to my own voice, gaze not moving from the quivering, yellow-tipped mound.

"I know. It hurts a bit." Josh, my tinder date, reached over his shoulder in bed to rub the raised scarlet flesh.

"Can I... can I touch it?"

Josh paused for a moment. He was facing the bedroom wall. It was when he'd rolled over after we fucked that I noticed the zit. As he was turned away from me, I couldn't see him, but I could picture the confusion on his freckled face.

"Umm... no?" He eventually replied. "That's a bit of a weird thing to ask."

"Sorry."

We lay together in awkward post-coital silence for another few minutes. I couldn't look away from the pustule. It was the size of a £2 coin, with the yellowish-white head taking up most of its raised surface. I could imagine it on my own body; the tension of the skin around stretched taut, the burning pain from built up pus squeezing subdermal flesh every time I moved. Then I couldn't help but imagine the relief when I'd burst it. The flood of warmth and easing of pressure as the fluids drained, the sting as straw-coloured liquid ran through until blood bubbled to the surface. My fingers started to itch.

"Please?"

"What?"

"Please, can I touch your zit."

The mattress creaked. Josh sat up in my bed, balancing himself on his elbow. He turned to me, his brown eyes set behind narrow lids and a raised right eyebrow.

"Is this some kind of weird fetish?" He asked, a slight smirk on his lips. "Are you one of those nutters that get off on popping spots?"

"N-no!" I stammered, raising my hands in protest. "No, I'm not, honestly! It's not a sexual thing, I just… look, I find it therapeutic, OK? I see a zit and I just… I get these tingles until I see it popped. Then when I do… there's this… I don't know, sense of release? Like somebody cracked an egg on my head."

"Ohhhh!" Josh said, rolling his eyes. "So it's like an OCD, like ASMR but with touch sort of thing?"

I nodded, biting my lower lip and trying my best to do the big puppy dog eyes thing my older sister had taught me. The mattress creaked again as Josh lay back down, once again facing the wall.

"Fine." He called over his shoulder. "Touch it if you think it will help, but don't pop it. Please. It really does sting like a bitch."

"Why haven't you burst it?" I could feel my hands trembling as I reached towards the pulsing, pus-filled lump. My palms were sweating, breaths catching in my throat.

Josh yawned. "I prefer to let them go in their own time, you know? I don't want a scar."

He did have good skin. I'd thought that when we first sat down at Nando's earlier that evening. His neck didn't have the zit on it then. I know this because Josh had a very muscular neck, one that I'd enjoyed admiring the back of when he walked away to pay at the counter. It was blemish-less throughout our date, as was the rest of his skin. I'd enjoyed digging my nails into it when we got back to my flat. I was enjoying lightly brushing my fingertips across the quivering bump on it even more.

"*Ow*… see, I told you, it's sore." Josh said, with a sharp intake of breath.

"I'm not surprised. It's an angry one."

I traced my index finger across the red ringed yellow mound again. It shuddered under my touch, like jelly. Josh shivered.

"I'm… I'm not feeling so great when you do that… it's like there's a hook round my bladder or something…"

"Shh…"

I was entranced by the zit. My fingers ran delicate circles around the pulsing lump. I swallowed, my breath once more catching in my throat. All I could imagine was the sweet release Josh would feel after all that blood vessel blocking gunk was out of his skin.

"Ugh I'm serious... I don't feel..."

Josh was sounding groggy, slurring his words like he was drunk. I mean, he was, we *both* were, but he was starting to sound drunk-drunk. I didn't pay him much attention. All I could think of was how satisfying the solid mass would feel between my tingling fingertips; how much the tension in my chest would ease once I heard the faint *pft* of the skin between them breaking, of the hardness giving way as the zit spat pus and plasma.

I gazed longingly at the lump. The stretched pores on it were sweating. The trembling patch of flesh glistened in the glow of my dimmed bedroom light. I licked my lips. They were dry, unlike the tips of my fingers.

"Josh..." I said slowly, deliberate effort needed to form every word. "Josh... I've got to pop it Josh..."

"Prea... durn purr.."

Josh's slurs were inaudible. If I hadn't been so hypnotized by the writhing bump, I'd have called an ambulance straight away. His breathing was wrong, far too laboured and slow. His broad shoulders were starting to sag, too. The toned arms I'd very much enjoyed dragging my nails across were looking less defined.

I registered all of that, but only vaguely. I wasn't even thinking by that point; all I was aware of was the skin-crawling sensation I wouldn't stop feeling until that angry reservoir of pus was pacified. I gripped the grape-sized lump between my thumb and index finger. I gave a preliminary squeeze, a light compression just to gauge the level of resistance.

"*Grrrraaaarrrgggh!*"

I wasn't *so far* gone that I could ignore the obvious pain in Josh's gargled yell. This was when I first started getting a little nervous. This was a big zit after all. Bigger than any my ex used to let me pop. Or that I'd seen on my five Facebook groups. Unfortunately for both Josh and myself, I *was* too far gone to allow the sudden onset of nerves to stop me from giving another quick test-squeeze.

Pft.

A spiral of pure white pus no thicker than a pubic hair slithered out from one of the swollen pores. Josh didn't gargle this time. He was just panting softly, letting out the occasional whimper. My nerves weren't abating, but the crawling under my own skin did relent ever so slightly upon feeling Josh's break.

"Heh... see?" My laugh was weak, apologetic, like he'd walked in on me doing something the wrong kind of dirty. "It's... it's ready to be popped."

Before I could stop them, my fingers once more pressed together. The zit between them wriggled. A few more hair-thin pus branches bloomed on its surface.

"Ok... ok... now time for the big one."

I swallowed. I had to see this through now I'd started, as much as a turning in my gut was telling me to stop. Josh was still whimpering, shaking his head slowly. The muscles in his neck bulged and slid across each other in unusual ways, like they were too soft, which did nothing to help my trepidation. As I said though, I was too far in to back out now. It was time for the rip the plaster off quickly approach.

"OK Josh... you ready? Three... two..."

Beads of sweat were pouring off Josh's back. I could feel prickles of it on my forehead too, perfect accessories to those already on my trembling palms. I steadied myself on the bed with my off hand, sitting up and getting my left one in position around the pulsing zit.

"One!"

Pft-t-t-t-t

The solid lump between my fingers gave way. Josh let out another gargled howl, shaking in violent but oddly stiff spasms. A thick wad of white, greasy pus burst out from the open wound. It oozed from the gaping pore, pressing forth like modelling clay forced through a glory hole. Thin rivers of red leaked from the torn flesh around the pus-tube. I kept squeezing for a good minute, until the thick rope of cheese-like skin gunk was at least seven inches long.

"I'm sorry Josh, I'm sorry I'm sorry I'm sorry..."

I knew straight away I'd made a mistake. My immediate thought was that it was a cyst, or an insect bite. Something that needed actual medical attention with a scalpel and anesthetic, not the trembling hands of a nineteen year old girl from tinder. I could actually feel tears running down my cheeks. I had to keep going, though. Josh's pain wouldn't subside unless I finished the job.

The skin and muscles around the gushing zit started to dent, then eventually deflate. I was fully sobbing now. A full five minutes had passed, but the rope of pus just coiled higher and higher on the sheets below Josh' neck.

"Josh... Josh what the hell?!"

Josh couldn't respond. He just gagged and sputtered, nearly choking on his own labored breaths. I had to get this over with quick, get that zit emptied so I could get an ice pack on it. A shot of vodka in Josh too, by the looks of things.

"Josh, lay on your front, OK? I... I think I've got most of it... I just need to give it some oomph."

He was still spasming, but managed a jerky nod. At least, I hope that's what it was. I was glad I couldn't see his face; the guilt from hearing his whimpers and sobs was bad enough. I managed to pay more attention to how *wrong* his neck movements were this time. They were delayed, rubbery, not swinging on the sockets and joints I was used to. The skin around the gaping hole was also *wrong*. It flapped and folded far more than it should a, like it was stretched across a vast abscess rather than bone and muscle. I rolled him onto his front. The jerking spasms meant he couldn't do it himself. His muscles felt soft and flabby under my palms, not hard and flush-inducing like they had a few hours prior. I tried to ignore it. The panicking made that difficult though.

"Josh, I'm going to straddle you... again. Heh. Try... try and get a good angle to get the last of this out."

I laughed nervously at my own joke once more, swinging my leg over Josh's twitching body under the duvet. I sat down on his once rock-hard torso and screamed.

My ass plumped down not on bones and toned muscles, but on springs, fabric, bedcovers, and a few inches of flesh. The solid midriff beneath me held for a nanosecond before collapsing under my weight. My ears were assaulted by a nauseating, gut wrenching organic sound.

PFT-T-T-T-T-PFFFFF-TT-TT

You ever stamp on a Capri-Sun? Yeah...

The hole in the back of Josh's neck widened about five inches. The pus rope that ejaculated from the zit, with such force that drips of skin-gunk hit the ceiling, was as thick as my forearm. Even when the pressure resumed non-projectile levels, it didn't stop.

Josh's twitching hadn't either, but was much slower now. He also wasn't whimpering.

"Josh! Oh my god, Josh?! JOSH!"

I was blathering and blabbering, flapping my hands in the air as panic forced me to jump from the bed. As soon as I removed my weight from his torso, the zit stopped oozing. In my terrified clumsiness, however, I stepped on the duvet-mound where one of Josh's legs was. Once more, the limb beneath offered no resistance. It flattened beneath my foot and the bedclothes and, again, the hosepipe of pus on Josh's neck let out a brief lashing of fresh yellow-white rope.

What I saw when I ripped off the duvet made me need to stop and swallow down vomit. The only reason I didn't scream was because I couldn't with a throat full of regurgitated peri-peri chicken.

Every shred of tone and definition on Josh's gym-ripped body had gone. He was a lump, an orange spray-tanned skin sack straining to bursting point with a viscous yellow fluid. As I watched, horrified and still coughing back the urge to puke, the thick stuff where Josh's insides had once been oozed and shifted; settling to fill out the completely flat patches of empty skin where I'd sat and accidentally stepped.

"Josh… Josh no… Josh… Josh it'll be Ok Josh… I'll squeeze the last of it out and get an ice pack and you'll be fine."

Have you ever seen footage of the Kennedy assassination? After he was shot, his wife was (obviously) in a state of shock. The first thing she did was lean over to the back of the car to try and pick up the pieces of his skull. So they didn't get lost, so they could put them back. Shock makes people do funny stuff like that, makes them unable to comprehend the obvious futility of their situation.

I think I know how Kennedy's wife was feeling when she scraped those minced pieces of her husband's brain off their convertible. I'm sure it was pretty similar to how I felt when I stood at the foot of the bed and took one of Josh's squidgy feet in each hand.

"It's OK Josh, It's OK Josh, it's just a zit."

My vision swam with tears. My heart beat so violently it actually hurt, and although my diaphragm ached, I still couldn't breathe fast enough. I willed my numb, shaking hands into action, and squeezed Josh's toes into my fists.

They collapsed into empty flaps of sweaty sprayed-tanned skin with no resistance. A few freed toenails pinged off of the walls and carpet. I felt warm liquid gushing between my fingers.

"I'll get it all out Josh, it's… it's OK, Josh, I'll get it all out and I'll get you an ice pack."

I continued for hours, squeezing and flattening the gallons of pus out of the zit and any other orifice that leaked it. I was sobbing uncontrollably all the while, my inner voice somewhere far at the back of my mind, screaming at me to stop. I couldn't, though.

I couldn't stop as I massaged all the pus out of Josh's legs, flattening the folds of skin until every drop in his limbs leaked from his nail-less empty toes. I couldn't stop as I got a rolling pin and kneaded his torso like dough, smashing the white-yellow grease out of both ends of his gastrointestinal tract. I couldn't stop, even though my mouth was babbling *"no please don't"* over and over, when I grabbed his feet again and started curling him up like an empty tube of toothpaste.

Doing his head was the worst part.

His brown eyes were still moving slightly, still twinkling up at my tearful ones when I put the thick dictionary over them. There was no resistance from his skull when I put my whole weight on the book. I'm still trying to ignore the fact there were a lot of lumps of grey flesh mixed in with the rotten pale gunk that oozed out his ear holes.

"Well, Josh… heh… I did it…" I stood back after hours, staring at the completely flat and empty skin tightly folded into a neat bundle. "I did it… I got it all out."

Then I collapsed on the floor and screamed for an hour straight. After that? Well, that's when I started writing this.

He's on my pillow right now, rolled up like a sleeping bag. I've strapped a couple of belts round him, so he doesn't unfurl. I'm glad his flat, empty face doesn't have eyes. It would feel like it's staring at me if it did.

My room is covered in the foul-smelling pus. It's fucking everywhere. Guys, I'm frightened. I don't know what to do. Do I call an ambulance? The police? What the fuck could turn someone's insides to liquid like that?

For fuck's sakes, why did I have to pop that zit?

FATBERG

Do you know what a fatberg is? No? Then let me educate you. A fatberg is like an iceberg. Except instead of on fresh open seas, you find them in sewers and drains. Also, they're not made of ice. They're not only made of fat, either. I wouldn't be so bitter about my life if they were. Yeah. For the slow amongst you, my job is to go down into sewers and clear massive wads of congealed fryer fat, wet wipes, shit-filled nappies, bloated half-decomposed dead rats, and anything else disgusting that's too big for the drains to flush out. All of it held together by soaking up the constant flow of piss-and-shit water. Lovely.

    Today, me and Del, my piss-and-shit water wading comrade, cleared the biggest fatberg of our career. That's not why I'm writing to you lot, though. Nah. I'm here because what we found behind it was… well. That's just it. I have *no fucking idea*. Even if I did, it wouldn't help. Del would still be dead, and I'd still be bleeding out in my flat, praying that the ambulance arrives in time.

    Suffice to say, folks, I've had a bit of a day.

    We got the callout to Hampstead Heath about 14:17. Whole road full of drains had overflowed at once. Pure carnage on the street, the horrid stench of piss-and-shit water spread half a mile at least. We knew this was going to be a tough old boy to clear before we'd even geared up and climbed down into the dark for a poke around. Wading through the cramped moist tunnel only took about twenty minutes. Fatbergs aren't that hard to find anyway, but this one smelled so damn bad I could have sworn it was trying to be found, like it was summoning us deeper into the piss-and-shit water-soaked depths. We'd expected big, Del and me, but when we saw it both of us had to stop and take a second to process. Big wasn't the right word. Not even close.

"Blimey Rob, look at the fucking size of that bastard."

"We knew it was gonna be a big'n, mate."

"Oh, don't give me that shite, that's not a big'n, it's *the* big'n."

"Yeah, sure, I've seen bigger."

I hadn't seen bigger, and Del knew it. Me and him had worked the River Fleet for fifteen years. This monstrous hulking mass before us was at least four times as large as any we'd cleared down here before. Even the behemoth lump of shit, congealed fat, worms, and fast-food waste that built up after the 2012 Olympics was dwarfed by it. We'd known this new one was going to be big by the time we got down the ladder. The piss-and-shit water was up to our waists when it was normally only knee-high. All the evidence pointed to a big fucking blockage of "*oh for fuck's sake*" proportions. Even so, when we finally reached the Hampstead Heath-flooding mammoth fatberg we were both shocked at just how blocked the wide Victorian sewage tunnel actually was.

Here's the thing about the River Fleet—it's a *river*. Like an actual bona fide "*you could get a raft down it*" river. This is no ordinary sewage system, it's a bloody wonder of 19th-century architecture. You could easily run a train through parts of it. The centuries old brickwork was built over and around the already-existing river back in the days when it was above ground. Basically, the Fleet was nothing but a deluge of waste from London's slums; a constant piss-and-shit water current that rose up to claim whole roads and streets. Rather than kill the river in its infancy, Victorian Londoners decided to obey the will of the city, and so built the subterranean marvel of sanitation that is the River Fleet around the fledgling waste-creek. Regular pipes and drains invade sporadically along the cavernous brick walls, spewing forth a deluge of filth from most of London. All of it flows as the River Fleet, down the wide underground tunnel and back out into the world somewhere that it's not Del and Me's problem. Or it did, until this double-decker bus-sized fatberg blocked the whole damn thing.

"How in God's name are we gonna clear this bastard, Rob?"

I shrugged, waving my spade. "Same as we do all the others, I guess mate, hit it with this until it breaks up."

"Fucksakes, we're gonna be here all day."

We were indeed there all day. For six damn hours we were hacking away at the fat-and-shit-and-worms-and-rats boulder. My arms burned by the end of it, my lungs too. I thought I'd got used to the stench of the piss-and-shit water after fifteen years working in it, but God damn, the thick invisible fumes emanating from the carcass of suburban refuse felt like they were curdling in my lungs. Del and I both would have to take intermittent breaks to cough up thick wads of phlegm. They let a bloke from the telly down here once, to film a short bit about the Fleet and fatbergs for the news. He'd made a right pig's ear of it; flapping his arms around and making puke noises like a right tit while Del and I rolled our eyes in the background. We lost all right to laugh at him as the hours marched on. By the third or fourth, all resistance we'd built over the years to the piss-and-shit water was eroded. We were both like the man from the telly; coughing, spluttering, and fussing embarrassingly, and each adding to the muck whenever the backsplash of fecal sludge washed up to mouth-level. For a quarter of a day, the only sounds in the darkness were the thick squelches of shovels smacking into the wedge of fat, fast-food grease, unlucky worms, soiled nappies, and soaked up piss-and-shit water. Oh, and mine and Del's whimpers and retches, of course. I'm only admitting that part because I want you to appreciate just how huge and disgusting this fucking thing was. The biggest ever fatberg found weighed 90 tons and stretched down 84 meters of tunnel. This was twice that, easy. We made a good go of it, but in the end knew we'd have to deal with Davies chewing our ears out again over "wasted taxpayer pounds".

"We've gotta get some backup for this thing, Rob. We're never gonna clear it on our tod."

"Fucksakes… yeah, you're right. I'll give Davies a call, get him to send the boys down with the—"

"JESUS BLOODY CHRIST!"

Del yelled, cutting me off mid-sentence. He'd still been hacking away at the fatberg with his shovel while we talked. The last *squelch* had dislodged something from the wall of fat-and-shit-and-worms-and-rats. It fell into the waist-high sludge with a dull *plop*, submerging for a second before breaching the surface again to float with the lumps of broken-off fat and backlog of feces.

It was an arm. A pale, bloated, human arm.

I retched again. Del swore. For a few minutes we watched the severed limb bobbing in the piss-and-shit water, neither of us unable to do much but swear or puke. The beams from our helmet-torches eventually drifted from the floating limb to the wall of fat Del had dislodged it from. We both screamed when the lights found a dark red hole on the boulder's surface, the cascade of leaking scarlet where Del's shovel sliced the body buried within the fat-and-shit-and-worms-and-rats.

"What the fuck Del, what the fuck—"

"Rob, we've got to dig them out."

"Fuck that, we've got to phone the police—"

"Nah, we have to dig them out first!"

"Fuck that, they're already dead. Leave it to the—"

I was interrupted again, although this time not by Del. A long, low groan emanated from the fatberg. Its titanic mass shifted and rumbled, squeezing the one-armed body further out into the open. I felt my stomach trying to claw its way up out my throat. My legs turned to jelly, the pace of my breathing rising to jackhammer rapidity. Del seemed to take the noise as a sign. Be began hacking away at the clinging wall of fat and waste around the entombed body. For some stupid reason, call it loyalty or pride or blindly following Del's leadership, *I didn't* turn and run. Coughing and spluttering from the overpowering stench, I instead joined him. It wasn't the first body we'd found down in the Fleet. We'd never found more than one before, though. We'd definitely never found twelve.

"Fucking hell Del, we really need to phone the police."

"And what's gonna happen then, Rob mate? They're just gonna get us back down here to dig these poor bastards out, anyway."

"Yeah, but…"

"But what?! Some of them might still be alive! *Keep digging*!"

I wanted to argue, I *really* fucking did. I couldn't think of a reasonable counterpoint, though. Now, look, I get it. You're screaming at me right now *"there's obviously not going to be any left alive, phone the fucking police!"*. With the clarity of hindsight, yes, I see that. I wasn't exactly doing my best thinking at the time, though. That's why I didn't do what I should have done; slapped Del and dragged him back up to the surface and got the old bill. Instead, I leant on my shovel in silence, surrounded by the dozen bloated corpses we'd so far uncovered in the three hours since discovering the arm.

Del had tried to lay them together away from their tomb of congealed fat, but the natural flow of the Fleet kept bringing them back towards us. More than once I'd yelp from feeling a cold, wet scalp brush against my elbow. Now, obviously, I was traumatized. So was Del. I could tell by his wild eyes, from the fanaticism with which he hacked away chunks of fat to free the poor souls buried within. Anyone in their right mind would have phoned the police. But down there, in the pressing darkness and toxic piss-and-shit water fumes, you don't think straight. We were both in shock, no doubt about it. Del had lost the plot, but I'd lost it too. The mad leading the broken.

The corpses were naked. Men and women, none looked much older than me or Del (late 30s, for context). There were no kids, thank God, but the comfort this offered was little when up against the twisted, crushed screams the dozen faces we unearthed was locked in. We could tell how they died, too. Each had a perfect circle bored into the center of their forehead. The chunk of removed flesh and bone revealed inside the skull of each corpse a burned, shriveled brain. All of them had minor lacerations on their calves and ankles, not to mention obvious bruising from struggling against tight bindings (also at the wrists). Whatever happened to these people wasn't quick. There were too many signs of torture and neglect on their emaciated frames for that. Internal cranial combustion was clearly the cause of death, though.

Now look, yeah. I'm no forensics expert. Still, I could tell the bodies had died at different times. Each that we dug out, the fatberg looked less decomposed than the last. With growing horror, I realized that the further we dug into the mountain of congealed biowaste, the more recent the deaths of those we uncovered became. It was shortly after we exhumed the twelfth, that of an obese woman in her mid-twenties, that we stopped digging out burned-out corpses.

That's when Del found the hole.

We'd dug far enough into the congealed nightmare that the worms had given way to maggots, and the thick odor of the Fleet was tainted with the bowel-curdling tang of rotting flesh. Del had been trying to free a poor soul wedged feet up between the worn bricks and groaning fatberg when a stony crunching noise cut through the squelching of shovels and the gushing of piss-and-shit water. I turned to Del and the source of the crumbling sound, illuminating him with the beam of my helmet-torch. His spade was embedded in the brickwork deep enough that it could stand freely.

To the right of the shovel, made wider by tumbling bricks displaced by Del's wild swings, was a gaping hole in the slick, slimy wall. I knew that this was where our mammoth body-and-fat-and-maggot blockage had started. There was an arm poking from one edge of the hole, bobbing slightly on the surface of the water where the Fleet overspill lapped and trickled into the dark space within. As we watched, there was a loud *ker-plunk* of something on the other side falling and the piss-and-shit. Something heavy sounding, something big enough to conjure deep echoes from the hole, and a hair-raising re-awareness of the bodies in the fatberg from my mind.

"Del, we've got to get the police mate. This is getting fucking ridiculous now."

I couldn't push from my mind's eye the mental image of bodies being thrown down a deep pit, left there to rot until the weight of them collapsed the roof and wall of the adjacent sewage system. Nothing I did could stop me from imagining that web of decomposition sitting undisturbed for weeks, netting in the debris from the flowing piss-and-shit until it became the Titanic fatberg I wish we'd never tried to clear. My shallow breaths were riding on visions of plague pits or the mass graves of Auschwitz. My shock was evolving into a blind panic, fueled by murky imaginings of the kind of men capable of amassing this mass grave, and what they'd be capable of doing to those who unwittingly discovered it.

Del's shock had evolved into something else. He shared none of my trepidation. That wild look in his eyes, much to my horror, was closer to the men who went over the trenches before the order was given. The ones who respond to death by charging it head-on.

"Del, mate, please, we need to—"

"There's more of them in here Rob, I think I can hear people, I'm gonna go-*OW!*"

He never finished that sentence. There was an almost inaudible *fff-phut* sound from the darkness beyond Del when he got to the word "*go*". A sound not unlike a dart being blown through a metal pipe. When Del slapped his hand to his neck, taking it away to reveal a long slither of metal with grey pigeon feathers at one end, he confirmed that's exactly what the noise had come from.

"Rob... what..."

I lunged forward to catch Del just in time to stop him sinking beneath the surface into the piss-and-shit depths. He'd looked at the dart for a second, confused, before going pale and cross-eyed. I noticed the second *fff-phut* too late. By the time I registered the sharp stinging in my neck, my knees had already started to buckle. My clammy, rubbery arms released Del into the fecal churn, and my equally rubbery legs allowed the current to pull me under with him. I had just enough time to notice the glint of my helmet-torch reflected in a pair of beady eyes within the hole, before my nostrils filled with piss-and-shit, and I sank into unconsciousness.

When I awoke, I was in a darkness unpenetrated by helmet-torches. The sound of the gushing, gurgling fleet had gone, too. The stench remained, but it was much less pronounced, more distant. There was a mustiness to the air too, a cold cloying earthiness untainted by the metallic tints of London pollution. There were new sounds as well as smells. I knew I wasn't alone because I could hear female whimpering to my right, male muttering to my left. Unlaying them was an almost inaudible metallic clanking of chains, shifting as the people crammed either side of me moved and shifted.

We were pressed in tight. Whoever darted me had stripped me nude, and judging by the sensation of cold flesh pressing into my sides, so was everyone else in here. The woman to my right was shaking, sobbing, rattling the chains she must have had at her wrists and ankles (if her bindings were like my own). The heavy-set leatheriness to my left rocked backwards and forward with a slow rhythm, pushing and pulling me from the wall behind as he went. We were crammed in so densely that a wave of nausea washed over me, claustrophobia I'd never known before ensnaring my panicked thoughts. I couldn't move, could barely breathe. My muscles ached, diaphragm howling as I struggled to take in breath and cough up the last of the piss-and-shit water.

"Rob?! Rob mate, is that you?"

Del's voice echoed from somewhere a few feet in front of me. I continued spluttering up the last of the sewer water, unable to answer. The man to my right took it upon himself to reply to Del on my behalf.

"Shut up you fucking idiot, if you make too much noise they'll—"

The baritone didn't have to explain or elaborate on its warning. By the time the leathery man spoke up, it was already too late.

From somewhere in the darkness there was an earsplitting *thunk*, so loud that it rattled loose debris from the ceiling somewhere above me. The slamming sound was followed by grinding of hidden machinery, mechanisms so vast they caused the cold rock slabs beneath me to hum and vibrate. As the cramped holding cell filled with dim purple light, I realized the din was from an ancient stone door sliding open. When it ground to a halt with a final dust-raining crack, I knew exactly who the "they" in the baritone warning was.

They were standing in the doorway, lit by a glowing purple orb hanging from the ceiling outside our cell. My dread had taken the shape of evil men with horrifying plans until that moment. I screamed when awakened to the reality of just how wrong I'd been. These were no men, women, or any other variety of human.

Lizards. That's the closest thing I can provide as a frame of reference. Slick, black-scaled, bipedal lizards. There were three of them, each no taller than knee height. Their tails, legs, arms, and chests were all toned, although the structure of the muscles was all wrong to me, not how any humanoid anatomy I'd seen was constructed. Each carried a long staff with a sickle-shaped blade on the end. What clothing they did have took the shape of dark yellow sashes, slung shoulder-to-midriff and pinned with an ornate pendant cast from a pearlescent mottled blue metal.

They cast their gazes across us, each pair of green eyes flicking between the dozen prisoners in quick, dart-like motions as twitchy and sporadic as the tongues that would occasionally slather across their faces.

Del was crammed into the row of six naked prisoners opposite. His gaze met mine, and he nodded. What he thought he was affirming I'll never know. I wasn't thinking at all; all I could do was scream and whimper and beg to a God I didn't believe in as the Lizards walked purposefully toward me. Or, at least, that's where I thought they were heading. Instead, they stopped in front of the muttering baritone leatheriness to my left.

The trio of lizards spoke amongst themselves. My heart rate spiked once or twice when one of them would point at me, the other two scratching their chins as though appraising which of us would make the tastier meal. I'm not going to bother attempting to write the words they spoke. There's no way humans could pronounce them; every syllable and vowel was carved with vocal cords wholly different from our own. There were clicks, scrapes, the odd rattle, and occasionally dual-tone rumblings not too dissimilar from Mongolian throat singing. They spoke for about five minutes while we all cowered into the walls, terror on the face of every shackled man and woman. Well, all except two. Del still looked determined, wild-eyed, ready to step up and play the hero. The leathery man to my left just looked angry.

"DO IT!" He eventually spat, lunging up at our captors. "WHATEVER YOU'RE GOING TO DO FUCKING DO IT! YOU DRUG US, TAKE US FROM OUR HOMES, SO WHAT- EVER YOU'RE GOING To-*UHHHNN...*"

The leathery man's enraged baritone rant ended in a wet, gurgled groan. I felt the flecks of blood on my face before I'd even realized the sickle-tipped staff had moved. One of the green-eyed lizardmen, clearly frustrated by the interruption, lunged forward and swung its staff in a single fluid motion. The mottled blue-steel sickle swam through the man's neck like warm butter. The cut was so fluid his fat head didn't fly straight away. It waited on his neck for a few moments while the blood not displaced by the razor-sharp slice caught up with events and started to trickle down his neck. Then, slowly, the leathery head flopped forward, rolling down the man's fat belly and landing with a soft thud at his knees.

I understood the sounds coming from the lizards this time. They were laughing.

I wish the baritone man had stayed quiet. With him off the menu, I was, apparently, choice number one. When Del realized this, he stood up and volunteered himself as number two. The lizards shrugged and unhooked his chains from the wall as they had mine, ushering both of us out of the cell by prodding and jabbing our legs with their deadly curved blades. I hope Del didn't think I'd have done the same. I loved the guy like a brother, but he was clearly nuts. Even before we got to that... whatever that thing was, it was obvious these fucking lizards had us marked as the next bodies to add to their pit. Del was crazy, crazy and fearless, whereas I was nothing beyond terrified.

I remained so as our captors poked and prodded us through their labyrinthine maze of tunnels, all dimly lit by the strange purple orbs. We couldn't be too far below London, because from beyond the low ceiling above I could still hear the rumbling of distant traffic, and occasionally a whole passage would vibrate as a tube train thundered along overhead. The trio of lizards cutting and jabbing our ankles as we walked were three amongst dozens.

Bipedal reptiles of various shapes and sizes stood and watched us be paraded through the passages towards... no, I'll get to it in a second. I need to build myself up.

But yeah, there were a lot of lizards down there. Some of them were like our captors, yellow-sashed and armed with those deadly pearlescent sickle-spears. Others were brighter and slimmer, others still were fat, jaundiced, and more frog than lizard. All of them spoke in that same inimitable dialect, those weird fucking words we'll never be able to decipher.

As we drew closer to the chamber where... where Del died, I started to notice the hieroglyphs on the walls. The masonry down here wasn't in keeping with any subterranean London architecture I knew. Carved into the thick marble slabs, I'm assuming by the lizards themselves, were endless columns of pictograms depicting what must have been significant events from their history or religion, or maybe both.

Some blocks displayed hordes of inch-high lizards charging towards larger, human-looking figures brandishing spears. In others, the ancient humans and lizards appeared to be on the same side, throwing spears (both sickled and not) at an army of what looked like grey rectangles with teeth. Some were nonsensical. There was a faded one depicting a man in suspiciously modern clothing wearing a blank blue mask, for example, and several times a figure with a human ear for a face crossing a red and a black book across its chest. In another, there was a sort-of baby-faced slug thing that appeared to be trapped by some sickle-staff wearing lizards in a cave. A common motif on every wall was a large meteor crashing into a mountain, and a group of the yellowish frog-lizards carrying a blue and orange sort-of jagged Yin-Yang-ish symbol out of it.

I understood the significance of that last bit when we arrived at our destination. Whatever the ancient lizards had unearthed from the mountain, their ancestors were keeping it under London.

Del and I had been jabbed and scratched at the heels until we were standing in a vast chamber. Along the way, we'd been joined by a few more pairs of prisoners from other cells within the purple hieroglyph-lined maze. In the end, there was a group of eight of us, all shackled, naked, and (with the exception of Del), terrified.

The chamber we were taken to had such a high ceiling that the sockets from which the glowing purple orbs dangled were lost in shadow. I realized that the piss-and-shit water smell was complely gone here. In fact, the air had no scent at all really, to the point that the lack of nasal stimulation was both immediately noticeable and deeply concerning. Replacing smells and scents was a strange sensation that I struggle to put into words, like if electricity had an odor, one that scorched your nostrils and thinned your blood.

In terms of floor space, the chamber was the size of a football pitch, although most of this was taken up by the colossal obelisk in the room's center. This behemoth construction stood in the middle of a circle of six thick stone pillars that erupted from the marble mosaic floor until they too were lost in the darkness above. The ornate columns were lined with more hieroglyphs, although these were much more intricate than those on the walls of the tunnels the lizards had marched us through.

The pillar ring was some way away, so I couldn't really pick out many details of these new carvings. I wasn't paying them too much attention, though. Just being honest. I was far too awe-struck by the towering construct the circle of vertical marble contained; an obelisk, a vast irregular pyramid whose tip stopped just short of becoming lost in ceiling shadow. Save for an empty section about halfway up its face, it appeared to be constructed entirely from the same mottled blue-ish pearlescent metal as the lizard's sickle-tipped spears (the same ones that left a mess of cuts and scratches on my calves and ankles from our march through the tunnels). There were intricate circular patterns carved across every inch of the azure steel, and at various points, some of these circles were hollowed out to allow thick messes of cable to plummet from the hidden interior of the obelisk. These cables, some as thick as a drainpipe, dangled and trailed off into the banks of flashing and beeping machines lining the walls. There were more lizards here, the jaundiced frog-looking ones. They tended the thick cables and whirring machines, hundreds of bulging pairs of green eyes throwing disdainful gazes our way every time one of us would whimper or plead. There were a few of the besashed guard types too, although not as many as I'd have thought, given the obvious significance of this chamber and the obelisk it contained.

It was the hollowed-out middle of the obelisk which drew the most attention, however. When I caught sight of the car-sized glowing chunk of crystal suspended from bone, flesh, and sinew within the hole in the metal, my jaw dropped. It stayed dropped as I gazed dumbstruck at the dancing light across its surface. It was a color I've never seen, somehow orange and blue at the same time. I know that doesn't explain it at all, either. You try describing an entirely new color though. It's hard. We don't have the language. That's why I couldn't stop staring at the fucking thing.

Even though the crystalline lump was clearly mineral, it was beating almost imperceptibly in its fleshy bindings. As I stared, I realized this was where the electric "scent" was emanating from, as the coppery buzzing in my nostrils got more intense the longer I looked. Aside from the hollowed-out section containing the glowing, beating shard of blue-orange crystal, the only other feature of the obelisk was a distressingly not-lizard-sized chair. I gulped when I saw this, my mind flashing back to the circular boreholes and burned-out skulls of the corpses in the fatberg.

There were two more pillars on either side of the chamber's entrance, and it was to these that Del, myself, and the rest of the lizard's captives were hooked by the chains around our ankles. A new sound then entered the room, audible even above the muffled whimpers and sobs of us captives. It was squeaking. A slow, echoing squeak, like a shopping trolley wheel in need of oiling, or…

I blinked. The whimpers and sobs around me either died outright or transformed into confused mutters.

"Is that… is that a… *telly*?"

Del was right. It *was* a telly. One of those old boxy TVs with a glass screen that teachers used to wheel in when they couldn't be bothered to do any actual teaching. Two of the frog-lizards had pulled it out from behind one of the unfamiliar beeping, flashing machines around the obelisk. Another walked behind them, carrying an extension cord and a VHS tape. There was some untranslatable dialogue between the frog-lizards and our sickle-spear wielding guards. Then one of the fat yellow reptiles pushed the VHS into the slot of the player.

There was a ping, followed by a white dot appearing at the center of the screen. Audio too swam into my sensory range; the familiar faint hums and crackles I remembered from watching Disney and Star Wars tapes in my youth. The dot hovered in the middle of the glass for a few seconds before ballooning outward to fill the screen with a crackling static-tattered white background. A tinny, synthy jingle played as a single word rolled across the screen: IPSET.

I turned to meet Del's gaze. He shrugged at me from the other entrance pillar, letting me know the word IPSET meant as little to him as it did myself. We knew it was human in origin though, IPSET and the VHS tape, I mean. We knew because, as soon as the short polyphonic jingle finished, the screen wiped to a small Indian or possibly Pakistani looking bloke sat on a large leather chair in front of a stately fireplace.

"Ah, hello! I didn't see you there." He said, smiling over his circular glasses into the camera. "My name is Dr Anand, but you can call me Dipesh if that makes your transition easier."

From across the entranceway, I could see that Del looked as confused as I felt. I heard someone mutter *"what the fuck"* to my left, and to my right a woman was sobbing *"no, they're gonna make me a lab rat, they're gonna probe me"*. I understood her fear. The lab coat Dipesh was wearing, not to mention his Dr status, was doing a heck of a lot to ensure the terror I was shaken to my core by wasn't disrupted by the confusion caused by an out-of-place television. Oblivious to the concerns of his audience, Dipesh continued his spiel as the tape played on.

"If you're watching this, it means you've been hand-picked by the G'it'thexirian's to power the Great Cage. You're probably worried. Don't be! The only reason you were kidnapped is that we need to keep all of this super-secret. This is so super-secret that I don't even have clearance to know where you're watching this from. All the researchers and security we assign to aid the G'it'thexirian's are on duty until death, just so they can't accidentally give up the location. How crazy is that?!"

Photographs appeared next to Dipesh's head as he spoke. Photos of the chamber we were shackled to pillars in. It looked different, though. In the images there were humans, smiling men and women in lab coats stood amongst the jaundiced frog-lizards. Pictures of security guards with submachine guns grinning while they kneeled down next to yellow-sashed reptilians danced in front of our eyes, and though I looked around for one of these human guards, hoping I could somehow plead or bargain with one, there were none to be found. The only human beings were the naked, bleeding, terrified ones shackled to the pillars. Well, terrified with the exception of Del, of course. Mad bastard.

When the quick slideshow on the video finished, Dipesh continued chatting to us in his sing-song voice. "Now, you're probably wondering how you're going to contribute. That's a good question! Well, our friends the G'it'thexirian's have been protecting the planet from an extraterrestrial being called Entity Three, or Hhdufj to you, for billions of years, long before we humans ever walked the Earth. I know, impressive, right?"

My head was swimming. I was trying to understand what Dipesh was telling me, genuinely; I was. I just... I couldn't comprehend it. My mind wouldn't let me. My sanity wasn't robust enough to accept this. There wasn't a race of ancient, civilized reptiles that walked the Earth before humans. I knew that such things didn't exist. Yet, despite my mind's insistence that they were impossible, they'd captured me, anyway. I wasn't even going to begin to try and wrap my head around the other stuff. Let's deal with the lizards before we start trying to rationalize the fact that Dipesh casually dropped the fact that extraterrestrial beings, aka Goddamn fucking aliens, exist on us.

As for Dipesh, his smiling face in the video clearly had no cares for our quickly fracturing psyches. He continued on, grinning away as if he were recording a bit on the letter A for Sesame Street.

"You'd need to spend several decades studying Paranatural Theology to truly understand Hhdufj, but who has time for that, right? To give you the short-hand version, Hhdufj is an alien God. I know, scary stuff! But don't you worry, friend. Thanks to the ingenuity of the G'it'thexirian's and your heroic efforts, Hhdufj will never be free. Because trust me, none of us wants that!"

Hold on, I thought, did he say *"heroic efforts"*? No mate, no heroic efforts here. Not from Rob Sullivan. *"Heroic efforts"* was dangerously close to *"sacrifice"* in my book. My knees were wobbling again, weak. I didn't know where Dipesh was going with his speech, but I could already tell the destination was nowhere good.

"Hhdufj travelled here on a meteor, billions of years ago. Before we came along, the G'it'thexirian's would have to connect dinosaurs, mammals, and each other to keep Hhdufj imprisoned. Not convenient at all, right? Hooking up a T-Rex to the Great Cage must have been tricky when you're that tiny, aha! Thankfully, when we came along, everything changed. Inside you, yes, you watching this right now, is a battery of highly potent Paranatural energy. Here at IPSET, we refer to it as 'essence', but you can call it a soul or a spirit if that makes life easier. Are you ready to feel special, friend? Well, of all the beings in the universe, we humans have the most essence. That's right friend, you're a tiny, tiny battery, full of potential for utility."

I felt the color drain from my face. This part of Dipesh's ramblings, I understood. I'd seen the fucking Matrix, after all. I collapsed onto the floor, whimpering, as did a few others who'd clearly had the penny drop.

"That's where the Great Cage comes in. Since we emerged from our caves, the G'it'thexirian's have found powering the Great Cage way easier. Just one human gives the same power as a whole herd of brontosaurus, or an entire G'it'thexirian colony! Isn't science wonderful? That's where we come in. Because we here at IPSET would prefer not to lose the Earth to an extraterrestrial deity, we've been helping the G'it'thexirian's refine the process and keep things under wraps. Don't you worry, your suicide note is already in the mail to your family."

Del started yelling at this point, thrashing against his chains. He only stopped when one of the yellow-sashed guards thrust a sickle-tipped spear his way, hovering it above his throat. I didn't have a family really, my old mum died yonks back, and I'd never really settled with a missus. Del was different, though. Del had a bloody kid.

Fuck, Del had a bloody kid. Who's gonna tell Heather?

No, I can't think about that now. It's way out of my control. If that bloody ambulance doesn't get here soon, too, I think I'm going to have much bigger problems. In case you're wondering, no, I didn't get this gash in my leg because the lizards tried to turn me into a battery. I didn't even get it from the lizards. I'm going to get to that though, to those... those things, in a minute. I've got to tell you how Del died first.

Back then, Dipesh continued despite Del's brief commotion. "Now, as for you, you've got some veeery specific instructions. Once your body is connected, your essence will be transferred into the Great Cage battery. Don't worry about your physical form, the G'it'thexirian's will dispose of that on your behalf. To make your transition from matter to energy-based life easier, we've created a computer simulation that will create physical representations of you, your new home, the Great Cage, and Hhdufj. Sorry we couldn't make things more presentable; we were a little pressed for time. Also, please ignore the body of Dr Billings in the corner. He was one of the researchers that programmed the simulation and, well, after he died inside the original, his body seems to get copied across the duplicates. We're working on it but, for now, please do accept our sincerest apologies!"

We were all yelling now, shouting at our captors, screaming profanity or pleading for release. The cartoon illustrations Dipesh had spoken over made it very clear what his words meant. The panic those images caused, the mob terror inspired by the sequential explanation of having our souls ripped from our bodies, was palpable. Even Del was caught up in it. He was screaming and crying along with the rest of us, pulling at the hook holding his chains onto the pillar.

"Inside the Great Cage, you'll find a computer connected to a glass case. It's imperative that you do not smash the glass." One of the lizards had turned the volume on the telly up, muttering to itself as it did, so Dipesh could still be heard. "You can use the computer to send messages from the Great Cage to the IPSET database, and we'll try and assist whenever and wherever we can. You never know, we may figure out how to help one day! Sooner or later though, you will smash the glass. Hhdufj is crafty, he has lots of tricks, and you're only human! Don't worry, this is all part of the plan. Why do you think the Great Cage needs a steady supply of involunteers like yourself, aha?"

The yellow-sashed lizards had clearly had enough by this point. Two of them grabbed the woman next to me. She screamed, flailing and kicking against their thick oil-slick scales. It did no good. They didn't flinch, budge, even register her resistance as they pulled and prodded her along with their sick-tipped spears. We all knew where they were taking her. The chair, the horrifyingly human-sized chair, the one connected by thick wires to the flesh-and-metal obelisk, and by extension the glowing rock it held captive.

"So remember," Dipesh continued, his cheery tones projecting over the woman's screams, "once you're part of the Great Cage, hold off from smashing the glass as long as possible. We're not sure what will happen to you when you do, but we imagine it's not pleasant. Best to hold out as long as possible, eh? However, rest assured that the only freedom Hhdufj will find when he escapes your layer of the cage is the confines of the glass case in another layer of the cage. That's why we need so many of you."

The lizard guards had bolted the crying, naked woman to the chair. From behind one of the beeping machines at its base, two of the frog-lizards emerged. They were carrying another thick table.

At its tip was a blue-metal instrument; a three-pronged claw with a hand-crank jutting out to one side. There was a hollow cylinder suspended between the three prongs, the edges of which were razor-thin and serrated.

"So go now, and prepare for your existence to have new meaning, friend. You have been chosen to have something most do not. Purpose. Remember, just because you're insignificant doesn't mean your death has to be."

The woman's cries didn't stop while the yellow-sashed reptilian guards scampered up the side of the stone chair to hold her head still. The tears continued flowing freely when the fat yellow ones followed and used the prongs to position the device at her forehead. My own tears started when one of the jaundiced frog-lizards started turning the hand-crank.

If I do survive tonight, I hope I can get the sound of that first wet squelching crack out of my head. Something tells me I won't, though.

It was audible even over the beeping machines and sobbing captives, the unmistakable crunching of steel grinding through skin, muscle, and bone. When the woman's eyes slowly rose and saw the loose disc of bone hanging by a thread of skin from her forehead, left in place after the crank-operating lizard had reversed the trepanning tool with a quick reverse spin of the lever, she howled. Not screamed, not wailed, *howled*. Like a fucking beast, like a cornered animal. I didn't know people could make sounds that primal. The only mercy was that she wasn't conscious enough to process the reality of feeling air on her exposed brain for long.

Something shot from the center of the retracted drill-cylinder; something fleshy, purple, and writhing. It attached itself to the gaping hole in the woman's forehead. In a moment she stopped screaming, and a moment later the rest of us started.

You ever seen a film where someone gets the electric chair? You know where they're all shaking and spasming, rocking like a one-man earthquake from all the volts going through them? This was nothing like that. There was no shaking, no tremors or twitches.

First was her jaw. It jutted out so far, I thought the damn thing was gonna fall off. Her nostrils flared, eyes rolling back in her skull so far small rivulets of blood trickled from the corners of her eyelids. Then they came from her ears, then her nostrils. Then the veins across her entire body pulsed and bubbled under her skin.

Then the blood from her nose, ears, and eyes was bubbling too, and the steam was pouring from her ears. I screamed louder than I ever have done as I watched the flesh of her eyeballs bubble and blister, the skin where her boiling blood fell cracking and splitting. This continued for a full five minutes when, without warning, she fell still.

For a second, there was silence. Then, from the center of the obelisk, a long, low rumbling emerged. It started small, quickly rising into an angry crescendo that shook loose a light rain of dust from the hidden ceiling so far above us. The machines lining the walls wheezed and blipped louder than they ever had. The cable attached to the woman glowed a brilliant red, the organic purple appendage connecting it to her forehead writhing and bulging. The air was permeated by a strange sucking sound; sort of organic but at the same time tinged with undertones of, for lack of a better word, lightning. Once the cable-sucker was satisfied it retracted back into the blue-steel implement. The red glow of the cable died, and the rumbling from the obelisk resumed near-inaudible levels. All four lizards clambered down from the chair, leaving the woman to slump forward, a thick trail of steaming black sludge leaking from the gaping, blistered, and empty hole in her skull.

"YOU BASTARDS!" Del roared, pulling harder than ever against his chains, "YOU FUCKING BASTARDS YOU FUCKING TRY THAT WITH ME I'LL KILL YOU, YOU HEAR ME?! I'LL FUCKING—"

Del was interrupted not by a sound, but by light. More specifically, by light leaving. Without warning, the purple orbs hanging from the ceiling went out. The chamber was plunged into near-total darkness, lit only by the faint dials and displays of the strange machines, and the disconcerting orange-blue glow from the rumbling crystal boulder. I may not have understood the lizard's words as they started yelling at each other, but I understood the tones. Confusion, worry, concern. Whatever they'd expected to happen when they dragged us down here to the obelisk, this wasn't part of it. In the glow, I caught sight of the largest of the yellow-sashed guards barking untranslatable orders at his shorter comrades. The jaundiced frog-lizards were scurrying more frantically around their beeping machines than they'd been doing, more haphazardly, clumsily.

I heard Del yell something, but his words were drowned out by the deep, booming explosions now coming from the tunnel behind us.

The chamber shook. Cascading debris bounced and clattered off the marble mosaic floor. This rumbling was different to that emanated from the obelisk. It was coming from behind us, from deep within the labyrinthine passages we'd been marched through. The lizards were trying to yell to each other over the din, the panic in their words obvious even though I couldn't understand them. In what little light was afforded by the glowing rock and the beeping machines I could make out Del. He was furiously yanking and pulling at the hook holding him to the pillar, taking full advantage of the booming distraction.

The purple orbs above flickered once or twice but didn't return to life. The booms from behind continued for a full two minutes, by the end of which the yellow-sashed guards stood with their sickle-tipped spears raised and pointed at the entranceway. New sounds were rising from the tunnels now, in the fleeting silences between the explosions. The first was accompanied by a smell, the distant rushing (and pungent stench) of the piss-and-shit water. Screams were an additional undertone too, echoing reptilian ones from vocal cords far different than ours. There were human screams in the chamber too, of course. All seven of us naked remaining prisoners were yelling in terror and copying Del's chain, pulling by this point. However, this wasn't exactly fucking surprising. The fact that something in those tunnels was making the things that made us scream in turn though, that created an additional layer of panic in all of us, including Del.

I don't know what happened first; Del and his screaming entourage pulling their hook free from the towering column, or the section of machine-covered wall behind them exploding. The clank of the metal hook falling to the marble mosaic floor happened more-or-less at the exact same time as the dozen-or-so whirring machines flew from the cavernous wall. If it wasn't for the pillar to shield him, I'm sure Del would have died there and then, flattened like four of our eight yellow-sashed guards by a blue-steel projectile. My hands flew to my ears to shield them from the deafening roar of the blast. It didn't do any bloody good. The ringing started straight away, pain shooting from my eardrums through my clenched jaw and screwed eyes. I found myself hugging the rumbling floor, whimpering, face covered in tears as all around me were human and non-human screams, flying blue-steel shrapnel, and the faint-but-there warble of the glowing rock.

My vision swam. Something inside me, some crucial resilience necessary to stay awake and trying, snapped. I was in a terror-wrought daze, slipping in and out of awareness while my brain scrabbled to find something concrete to latch on to. I opened my eyes at one point to see Del standing over me. When I opened them again, he was wrestling the sickle-tipped spear out of one of the panicking lizard's arms. On the third moment of lucidity, he was pulling me to my feet, his legs and waist covered in thick dark purple ooze. He was mouthing things at me, but I couldn't hear them. The other prisoners were either whimpering on the floor, helping each other out of chains, or taking advantage of our distracted captors. I couldn't hear it above the all-empowering tinnitus, but I could smell the river of piss-and-shit water cascading from the smoking hole in the wall.

In the delirious shock, my first thought was terrorists. The timing was too good for gas pipes bursting, natural disasters, or a mechanical fault, so it had to be terrorists. Terrorists use bombs, bombs cause explosions. Unlike everything else so far, it made sense. The lizards in the chamber were shrieking now; those yellow-sashed guards not being overpowered by inspired prisoners, who were pointing at the hole. Their jaundiced frog-looking counterparts were all sobbing, whimpering, yelling untranslatable prayers at the shadowed ceiling.

I knew it *wasn't* terrorists when the blue-orange boulder's humming started growing, like it knew what was coming. When the new thing, the freshest nightmare in this day of them, stepped out of the hole, my fears were confirmed.

Terrorists. Ha. I should be so bloody lucky.

"HELLO UNDER-PARASITES... ha... WE'RE HERE TO TAKE BACK GOD!"

Its yell boomed over both reptilian and sapien screams, crystalline humming, and the rumbling of crumbling masonry from above. It was a deep voice, ragged, like a man that'd lived through centuries trying to talk while gargling broken glass. Definitely not the kind of voice you expect to hear coming from a teenage girl, which is why I started sobbing when I looked up and realized the voice which had somehow cut through the ringing in my ears belonged to one.

She stood at the lip of the new hole, illuminated by the growing blue-orange glow of the trapped rock which was now trembling in her presence. The girl couldn't have been older than 19. Her blonde curls fell to her shoulders, and the makeup on her face was chipped, smudged, cracking like it had been applied weeks ago. There was a faint greyness to her skin, a slight waxy sheen visible only because of how the blue-orange shimmer danced just-too-brightly on her exposed form. I can't express enough how almost unnoticeable this all was, though. One of those people you don't realize is from the wrong side of the uncanny valley until it's already far too late. Seriously, if she hadn't been naked and booming cracked threats from an explosion hole, I wouldn't have looked at her twice. Hell, if it wasn't for the voice and what lay waiting between her lips, the short young woman would have been the least threatening thing I'd seen all day.

Nothing can drive something from the bottom to the top of that list like what she did once she'd finished laughing though.

I noticed the teeth first. They were white, not like American TV advert white, but like pure light of a dying star white. White so bright it's blinding to your mind's eye as well as your real ones. The angles of them were wrong too, but only because they were so right. Right angles, exact ones, in all the right places, each unsettlingly perfect square nestled right up against its neighbors, two parallel lines running right along the edge of each ruler-straight row. Nothing living has teeth that perfect, I'm bloody sure of that. Fuck what I saw. Those damn teeth were so straight the dissonance over whether or not I was looking at CGI still makes me want to puke. I did in the chamber, all over me and Del. He was dragging me toward the entranceway, still yelling stuff like "come on Rob" and "we've got to fucking move". I was too transfixed by the girl, though, too busy looking over my shoulder at those nauseatingly not-crooked teeth, to not trip and stumble over us both.

Her lips were pulled back further now. I could make out cement-grey gums. They wriggled and writhed, juxtaposing the relative stillness of her other features. I only had a second or two to contemplate this observation, however. That's when she started the damn howl.

Everyone dropped to their knees again to cover their ears, homo-sapiens and nightmare reptilians alike. The howl didn't make a ringing in my ears as much as a tingling; an unpleasant buzzing sensation that swelled until it rattled my teeth and shook my jaw. It was both high pitched and low, a consistent whine that occupied only the extreme ends of my hearing range. Monotonous, unwavering, a sound I'd sweet came from a machine were it not from the fact I could see her screeching jaw extending until it stretched at least three feet from her neck, the chest below rattling with the effort.

The purpose of the howl made itself clear pretty damn quickly. It was a call to arms.

Dozens of them poured from the hole. I thought it was a single being at first, a tide of cement-colored gelatin gushing forth from the wound in the architecture. It was when the blob started splitting into individual chunks, and when those chunks peeled back their own lips to reveal rows of the same impossible teeth, that I realized I wasn't looking at a thing, but a swarm. A writhing sea of boneless bodies that had travelled through London's sewer lines, pressed together so tightly it was impossible to tell where one mound of glistening slug-like flesh ended and the next began.

As soon as the "girl's" howl stopped, Del was pulling me back on my feet. We were at the entranceway by the time the first of the grinning grey chunks had slithered their way to our group. They'd shifted and reformed as they'd glided across the marble and beeping machines, stretching and straightening in rippling waves until each stood easily 9 feet tall. No longer grinning puddles, as the swarm bore down on us it became not an ooze but a forest of quivering concrete-toned flesh columns, each with twin rows of too-perfect teeth. Del was brandishing his stolen sickle staff in their direction, yelling every profanity in the blue-collar handbook, while he tugged me once more to my feet. I couldn't move; my legs were numb, chest straight-jacket tight, gaze unable to turn away from the sobbing man and the grinning grey pillar of flesh towering above him.

The thing had parted its twin rows of maddening teeth. From the wide gullet beyond came a fresh noxious odor, one far too similar to the stench of the corpses we'd freed from the fatberg what felt like several lifetimes ago. Following the rancid pungence came three long tendrils. These limbs, which I can only describe as somewhere between a plant stem and a squid tentacle, rapidly flexed themselves out of the slug-things slavering maw. They reached easily ten feet long in a few seconds, whipping and lashing through the air so fast they became little more than mucus flicking green blurs.

"Rob, come on mate, we've got to fucking move!"

Del's words were falling on deaf ears. I was entranced by the scene before me, paralyzed by a shock-born curiosity that locked my limbs and caused a warmth to trickle down my left thigh.

I felt his arm slam into my chest, wrapping around me so hard it knocked the breath from my lungs. The same instant, the green blurs found the sobbing man at the base of the quivering gelatinous cylinder. Del lifted me as the man was lifted by the tendrils. However, unlike him, I was merely half pulled, half carried into the shadowy tunnels. The man wasn't so lucky. I registered his high-pitched shriek before I realized his legs were far too far away from his torso. One limb was in the thing's throat before the blood and entrails had splashed onto the marble mosaic tiles. The man was still screaming as his head and torso were stuffed between those square teeth, and carried on doing so through far too many of the wet organic crunches that followed.

Del had had enough by this point, I think. My view turned sideways as he hoisted me onto his shoulder, lifting my feet from the ground and sprinting with me across his back into the darkness. I had one final glimpse of the chamber. Man and lizard being torn apart like wet tissue paper by the canopy of tendrils above the glistening grey forest of grinning flesh columns, the shaking blue-orange rock in its blue-steel Great Cage, all of it is still burned onto the back of my eyelids. None of it remains clearer than the uncanny valley girl though, marching above the carnage on three impossibly long mouth tendrils towards the obelisk, her petite body dangling rubbery and limp as her tripod of tongues strode over the forest toward her imprisoned "god".

Fucking hell. Dipesh had said it, she'd said it: *Alien God.* Then that would make her, make them... *Jesus Christ...* no, it's too much. I've lost too much blood to get sidetracked by that, and there's still no sign of that damn ambulance...

Anyway, we'll get to that, to how I got the gaping bite wound in my calf that's currently pissing out the last few pints of hemoglobin I got in me. I don't quite remember how long Del carried me through the tunnels. My thoughts were a blur. I kept thinking back to the hieroglyphs Del was running us past, now hidden in the absence of the purple light fixtures. My mind's eye would linger on the grey rectangles with teeth, of the men and lizards throwing their spears, fighting back the tide. Those hieroglyphs had been carved a while ago. That was obvious even to me from the level of weathering and fade of the paint. These lizard-people, the ones that had captured us, clearly weren't their fierce ancestors. But neither were we.

All around, I could hear the sounds of similar massacres echoing from hidden avenues and passageways heading off from our unlit tunnel. The gunfire of the men and women in Dipesh's video presentation was nowhere to be found. Neither were untranslatable but just about jist-understandable whoops and hollers of reptilian victory. There were just screams, cries, wails.

The occasional distant boom as a fresh wave of grinning grey death burst forth from another adjacent sewer line. I didn't understand the words our captors were screaming as they died, but I could feel their terror. Despite everything, every echoed rip or wet crunch of rent and chewed flesh still sent a pang of horrified empathy through me. Some of those reptilian screams lacked the edge of adulthood. Del and I weren't caught between two sides in a war; we were collateral damage in an ethnic cleansing. Except, instead of oppressive and subjugated cultural groups, it was things from my nightmares being slaughtered by things so disturbing; I doubt I'll ever sleep again, even if that fucking ambulance does eventually show up.

By some miracle, Del managed to carry us through the widest of the tunnels unscathed. At some point he'd dropped his sickle-tipped spear, I imagine so he could sling me fully across his back, so he didn't fall over as he ran. I was too dazed to register that Del was following the smell. By the time he'd got us to what he was looking for I was aware of it, the familiar way it curled my nostrils and turned my stomach, but I hadn't been with it enough to notice how it grew in intensity with each corner Del turned. It wasn't the stench of the piss-and-shit water. *That* particular odor was everywhere. The explosions had come from adjacent sewer lines after all, so the gelatinous horde wasn't the only thing that came pouring from the holes in the walls. No. This smell was the sickly-sweet rancid tang of rotting flesh. *Human* flesh.

Del, that clear-headed iron-willed son of a bitch, had found the damn pit where the lizards had been dumping the shells left over by their Great Cage. He'd found the fucking fatberg. He'd found freedom.

The landing was soft, although it's best for all of us if we don't think too long about why. Suffice to say that by the time we emerged from the drain cover onto the dark London street, both of us felt the need to puke on the pavement. The piss-and-shit smell of the River Fleet had been almost comforting as we sprinted away from the fatberg, hole, and the twisted things we'd unearthed within it. Almost.

"Rob... what the fuck..."

Del stood, panting, holding himself up against a lamppost. I was knelt on the floor, wiping my mouth after having decorated the pavement with what little remained of my lunch.

"I dunno Del mate, I fucking dunno... I wanna go home... fuck... fuck all of this..."

"Yeah... yeah, let's get back to the bloody van..."

Despite our shock, I think we were both acutely aware that we were naked and covered in almost every bodily fluid you can think of. We scurried over to the van as quickly as we could, and I can't express enough the relief I felt that it was still exactly where we'd left it all those hours ago. Relief almost as great as the plummeting dread when we heard the voices of the two men standing behind it.

"You see, it holds the shell together, kills the bacteria in it, purges the blood... they can't tell us apart from themselves, even if the shell is old. Holds its form too, no more sagging into useless lumps after a few months. *Ha!* And to think they'd intended to use it as a weapon against us. That's what *he* wanted to do to us, you know, turn us to mulch from the inside out, get it into us somehow using the Old Runt's flies, of all things. The gall of the Arch-Parasite, I tell you, to think that they could ever understand us enough to—"

"But why did she give it to you, Boggis? Why didn't the Matrioform bless all of us with—"

"For the same reason she saw fit to bless me with a name, you quimbling nothing. Because I can do their voices. We're this close, and she doesn't want one of you clumsy oafs mucking it up for us now. Remember your place."

I recognized the first voice. Well, *almost* recognized. It was different in a way I don't have words for, but that caused my stomach to drop several feet below my body. It was Davies, the man Del and I spent most mornings being lectured to about budgets and tax-payer pounds by. As we crept around the side of the van to peer around one of the open doors, we could see him clearly, standing a few feet away from us, facing the distant end of the street. Standing next to him, facing the same direction, was a... how shall we say it... *rotund* bloke. This second man's skin was waxy, grey, too tight where it should be loose and too loose where it should stretch across non-existent muscles. Davies himself had a touch of the same, I noticed, but it was almost imperceptible. It also definitely hadn't been present on his overly maintained features that morning, when he'd chewed us out about whatever we'd fucked up the previous day.

The other man's voice was most definitely *not* human. It was so far away from human, and so close to the glass-laced rasping roar of the girl in the chamber, that I let out the whimper that alerted them to our presence.

"Ah… hello runts." Davies had whipped around, and I instantly knew that the thing the other man had called Boggis most definitely was *not* Davies. Although, only because I'd spent every morning for the last ten years looking at Davies' angry features. If it wasn't for that and the fact he'd peeled back his lips to reveal two rows of impossibly square teeth, I'd never have guessed Davie's was probably laying in his office right now; skinless and (hopefully) dead. The *"Boggis"* was right—it *was* good at doing our voices.

As for the large guy with the inhuman voice, it was obvious from the get-go that he hadn't been human for some time. His grey bloated face was lined with cracks and fractures, the crusted splits revealing the writhing slug-flesh within the stolen skin. The eye that wasn't missing bulged and rolled in its puckered socket, never pointing or focusing on anything in particular, as dead and useless as the rotting human flesh holding it in place. The other socket, the empty one, held nothing but a drooping bulge of the same glistening grey gelatin that slathered around his… its own gnashing rows of square enamel.

"There you go, nameless one." Davies/Boggis said, smirking at Del and I as we cowered back behind the van door. "A pair of frightened runts. What fortuitous circumstance, you can get yourself a new shell *and* prove yourself to the great Hhdufj on the day of its emergence."

This is where I have to stop for a moment, because what I'm about to relay does genuinely bring me shame. But, since that ambulance still hasn't arrived and I probably won't be here when/if it does, I need to get it off my chest. I'm sorry, Del. I was panicking; I was terrified, you'd seemed so, so strong, throughout all of this. I don't know what my terror driven mind thought was going to happen. That you'd fight them? That you'd overpower them and save the day? Fucking hell… look, if it's any consolation, what I did don't exactly save my neck. All it did was prolong my death. At least you got to go quickly, mate.

Ok, here goes… I pushed Del into them.

I'd love to tell you it was an accident, or a reflex, but that's a lie. All I was thinking about was saving my own neck. The three tendrils from Davies/Boggis mouth were already extended by the time Del crashed at his feet. I didn't stay long enough to watch what happened, but I heard the screams, the wet organic crunches and thuds, the cracking and squelching of bone and fresh getting mangled between angular teeth. I heard all of this as I fumbled at the handle of the driver's seat door, moaning, sobbing, and wailing as I did so.

I felt the teeth clamp onto my leg while I was trying to climb up into the seat. The pain was instant, electric. It jolted up through my left leg and straight to my spine, from where it was blasted across to every single nerve ending I had. I howled, although the spasm of my limbs worked in my favor. My arms tightened, pulling me into the driver's seat of the van. Although, not all of me. A sizeable chunk of my left leg remained, hanging from the square teeth of the grinning slug-flesh puddle that had oozed from under the van.

I don't think I've ever driven so fast in my life. My left leg was useless, and I'd already lost enough blood to make remaining conscious a challenge. I think adrenaline was what kept me going, but even that's wearing off now. I don't remember much between slamming the van door, getting my keys from the glovebox, starting the engine, unlocking the front door to my flat, and collapsing on the floor here. God, if… fuck, who're we kidding, that ambulance ain't coming. There's going to be a lot of unpaid speeding tickets, let's put it that way.

The pain from my leg is fucking unbearable. That's why I've been writing this. To distract myself, to try and stay conscious. Guess it doesn't matter now. I'll be heading down to hell soon no doubt, after what I did to Del. Christ, I'm going to die a fucking Judas. What a time to realize you're a scumbag.

Look, let me do at least one small thing before I bleed out, before I go. Try and kindle a little flicker of redemption. Let me warn you, all of you. There are things out there, things beneath us, and amongst us. You need to get armed, get ready. I was just a normal guy, having a normal day. I'm in Britain for fuck's sake, I don't even own a gun. In no way was I prepared for this shit, and neither were the god-knows how many people dead in that fatberg pit, or lost to a thing walking around in their skin, or hooked up to a brain-melting obelisk by now-absent government scientists…

I don't know what I stumbled into, or what the fuck just happened, but I get the feeling I might be clocking out just before shit really hits the fan. So yeah, let me use my last moments to do something not selfish for fucking once. Let me warn you so your ignorance doesn't kill you as ours did us. Start getting ready to defend yourself, because none of us is as safe as we think. Any of us could find ourselves part of some messed-up thing far beyond our comprehension. We're never safe. I didn't do anything to deserve this, neither did Del. All we did was go to work. And yet, here I am, bleeding out on my floor, guilt-ridden over the death of my only real friend, and hoping a bunch of strangers believe my ramblings about alien gods and lizard-people living under London's sewage system.

Still, even if you don't believe me, at least you know what a fucking fatberg is now.

R-SQUAD

I threw the quiet kid's lunch in the trash a lot, and I survived a school shooting *before* they were a regular thing. This is a story about both of those things. Well, sort of. Couple of disclaimers before we start though, yeah?

ONE: I know about the stereotypes, but the kid that decided to bring an assault rifle to school *wasn't* the quiet one. This ain't your typical local news special about me being nice to the bullied kid, meaning he decided not to pull the trigger when I was in the crosshairs. I fucking wish.

TWO: This took place in the '90s, a little while after Columbine. This is important because, even though he wanted to shoot me in the fucking head, I want you to get *why* Ricky Hitch did what he did. School was harsh back then, man, in a *different* way. Having *"retard"* yelled at you every time you walked down the corridor should have made *more* of us snap, TBH.

That's disclaimer **THREE**, so's you know. Ricky (the shooter), Glen (the quiet kid, get to him in a sec), and I were in the remedial class. Class R, which everyone from principal to pupil thought of as meaning R as in… well, the other word, *not* remedial.

I was part of R-squad because of what I later learned to be undiagnosed dyslexia. Oh, in case you're wondering, I'm using a dictation app. Not just because of the dyslexia either, but I haven't told you about Glen yet, so I'd be getting way *way* ahead of myself if I start babbling about losing my hands. We will get there though! Patience.

Ricky was one of R-squad because of... well, whatever the fuck it was, it meant he had an explosive temper. Could have been bipolar, Tourette's might also have been part of it, who knows. I *do* know he didn't come from what you'd call a "*good*" home. His clothes were far too hand-me-down and unwashed for that. He turned up with far too many black eyes. Like I said, this was the '90s. You think the system doesn't give a shit now? Woo boy... But yeah, Ricky definitely wasn't a quiet kid. He was loud, man, real fucking loud.

We heard him over the *dakka-dakka-dakka* of the rifle as he made his way through the two classrooms before the "*Retard Box*" (according to graffiti on the door under the *Class-R* sign). He was yelling "*who's the fucking retard now?!*" and "*could a fucking spastic do this?!*".

After the incident, I learned his aim was so off, he only managed to kill 7 out of the 40-or-so non Class R kids, but he got both the teachers. Shit, saying *only* makes it sound callous. Look, those classrooms were small, OK? Pokey, crammed. Not designed for 20+ kids in each. If you'd seen them, you'd know it's stupid lucky the body count wasn't higher. This was before active shooter drills were a thing. Everyone just cowered in the corner or ducked behind desks. These days it's a worry on every kid's mind, but even *after* Columbine, most back then didn't think school shooters were something that happened outside of the TV.

He'd started his spree at 09:05. Being the third classroom of the ground floor corridor, Class R was the #3 on his list. There were 12 of us in total, with a range of complex needs (many of which would receive specialist education outside the regular school system these days). You can imagine the howls, the tears, the sobbing and shrieking and overstimulated yells by the time the heavy door to the corridor swung open. Ricky stood in the doorway, tears streaming down his face, thick jaw clenched. He had a black eye again, split lip. There was blood on his white polo shirt, but it had soaked and faded into the fabric, far too coagulated to be fresh.

So, this is where you get an advantage by viewing events from over 20 years in the future. If you're wondering whether Ricky snapped and killed his fist-happy drink-loving abusive stepdad before taking his gun and heading out to school, you're 100% correct. The local news didn't shut up about that particular aspect of the whole thing for *weeks*.

"Richard! What in God's name are you doing! Put down that gun this inst—"

Props to Mr. Galgreach, our teacher, because he didn't die a coward. His response to seeing one of his students blood-covered and wielding a rifle was to discipline them. Sadly, for Mr. Galgreach, courage was no shield that day. Ricky didn't give him a chance to finish his sentence. Without the buffer of thick concrete walls, the *dakka-dakka-dakka* of the M16 was louder than anything I'd heard before. My parents were liberals, very anti-gun. I'd never heard one fire in-person before. I could smell the urine leaking from a fair few of the Class-R kids' pants. I'm going to be honest, if I hadn't gone before the first bell, I'd have been one of them. That sleek black tube in Ricky's hands roared like some beast from the darkest circles; snarling and whining and clicking as it spat hot death, an image made all the clearer by the metallic sulphur smell emanating from each ear-splitting shot. Movies never prepare you for that, the loudness of it. The ringing those explosive cracks leave in your ears is all-consuming.

Well, almost all-consuming. I think it would have been if it weren't for the sight of Mr. Galgreach's head exploding like a watermelon dropped from a skyscraper. You could tell Ricky had a special kind of hatred reserved for the cold and chastising Mr. Galgreach. He didn't miss a shot.

The screaming didn't stop until Ricky fired a few more shots into the ceiling. Still, all that managed to do was quieten Class-R's fear into sobs and whimpers. Every single one of the R-squad kids had either pissed their pants or would do once their bladders filled enough. Myself included. My teacher's body was slumped over his desk, basically minus a head. I might have hated him too, but are you kidding? I was fucking terrified. The looks on every face showed me the other kids were in the same state.

Well, all of them apart from Glen.

Yeah, you thought I'd forgotten about him? No. I was waiting for this point in my recollection because it's the easiest way to showcase why Glen was in Class R, what made Glen… well, what made him Glen. Glen was, for lack of a better term, a blank slate. Until that day, he was the definition of an IRL NPC. He'd walk to where he was supposed to go, say nothing, stare blankly into space until the bell went, then go to his next place. Nobody ever saw him eat, drink, or use the bathroom. He never reacted to anything, either.

Oh, and I mean *anything*.

Here's a list of a few things I'd seen happen to Glen that didn't make him so much as blink:
- Mr. Galgreach throwing a board eraser at him.
- Getting hit by a flying chair during one of Ricky's outbursts.
- One of the other Class-R kids rubbing stool on his face.
- A group of jocks taking it in turns to smack him in the head with lunch trays.
- Etc.

You get the point. Glen was unphasable to the point that trying to phase him was a pastime of the worst of the mainstream school population. You'll also probably have picked up on the stool bit. This is fundamental to understanding why Ricky snapped, I think. On top of everything else, being more-or-less neurotypical and having to share a cramped space with kids that have advanced neurological conditions and needs grates you down. When me, Ricky (on his good days), and the kids with conditions like Asperger's or Tourette's would talk about it over lunch, we'd call it *"Jack Nicholson Syndrome"*. You know, after *Cuckoo's Nest*. It wasn't the stool smearing kids' fault, either. These days they'd be getting the specialist education and care they need, instead of being left to the cruel temper of men like Mr. Galgreach. Not to mention the other kids. Ricky used to show up to school with black eyes, but I'd often leave with them from trying to stop some prick in a varsity jacket tripping up Tina (the cerebral palsy kid), or telling them to leave Josh the fuck alone (Downs Syndrome). They may not have been what I'd call friends, but in the tribal world of '90s high school R-Squad were still my people, you know?

I'm going to skip over some deliberately repressed memories here. Things went bad. *Real* bad. Ricky, it turned out, had pent up a lot of anger in a specific area. A lot of unresolved Jack Nicholson Syndrome. He turned it towards… Fuck, how to put this? Any feelings of comradeship I felt towards the other kids in R-squad *weren't* shared by Ricky.

We'll fast forward, for my sake, more than yours. When regular service resumes, it's just me and Glen left. My ears are ringing, chest boa constrictor tight, cheeks wet with tears, breath rapid and full of *"please please please Ricky please don't"*. My eyes are locked on a smoking, oily black tube hovering inches from my face. The spot on my forehead directly in front of the barrel is tingling and tense, like the lump of eager metal at the other end is pulling me toward it. Ricky's face is also tear-stained, although his breathing is calm and measured.

"I have to, Harvey." Ricky says, squinting down the sights. "They're gonna talk about me on the news, and I don't want them saying I had a soft spot for anyone. The only way they'll pay is if they know they broke me *so hard* even my friends got it."

Panic is a weird thing, right? You get weird thoughts. Genuinely, in that moment, my horror at realising I was probably going to die was replaced with warmth at hearing Ricky thought of me as a friend. Odd, ain't it?

This is where I think my past kindness towards Glen genuinely saved my life. See, Josh and Tina weren't the only kids I'd have to look out for in the lunch hall. As I said, nobody ever saw Glen eat. School had a policy, though. Every kid *had* to get a meal. Nobody gave a rat's ass if they ate it, sure, but part of the corporate-sponsored lunch menu bullshit was that no child went hungry (what they're getting full on didn't matter so much). This meant that every lunch period Glen would be sitting with a tray of Sloppy Joes or Sawdust Lasagne just begging to get thrown over him. So, what did I do? Well, for years I'd helped Glen out by making sure I took his unwanted meals to the trash before the varsity jacket kids could get to them. A small thing, sure, but apparently the only small act of kindness Glen had ever known. It was enough to make him step in front of the gun, at least.

"What the fuck?" Ricky's grip on this death-dealing metal tube relaxed a little in surprise. He raised an eyebrow as Glen stepped forward, as surprised as I was to see the mute, non-responsive boy put himself between the oily barrel and my trembling face.

"What is this, Glen? What the fuck?" Ricky repeated, swallowing. "You want to die first, is that it? Or what, do you love him, do you? Some kind of fa—"

"Lunch… helped…"

Even Ricky yelped in surprise when we heard Glen speak for the first time. Two words, but that was more than enough to know that whatever was going on with Glen had nothing to do with educational needs. That voice… that voice wasn't… well, it matched what happened in about two minutes when Ricky unloaded nearly a whole clip into Glen's face. How to describe it…

OK, so imagine if glass could talk, right? If it could scrape and crack and squeak shards across one another in a way that made sounds human ears could understand. Chandelier dialect, the language of broken bottles. If you can imagine that, you can imagine Glen's voice. If you can't then gee, fuck, I don't know what to tell you. Just imagine a weird voice, I guess? Two words were all it took for both of us to start doubting if the quiet kid was a kid at all. Envision something strange-sounding enough to prompt that reaction.

"What... what the fuck..." The barrel was trembling because Ricky was trembling, trembling more than he had done at any point during his summary execution of the kids he blamed for his social ostracism. "Don't... don't you fucking talk again Glen, you fucking... you fucking hear me?"

My heart smashed into my ribs as Glen turned to look down at me. I was crouched on the floor, trembling in a puddle of my own fear (my bladder had refilled somewhere along the way, just to drain itself in terror, I think). Outside I could hear sirens, screams, the tinny warble of a cop yelling at the building through a megaphone. I didn't really take much of it in, though. I was too awe and horror-struck by Glen's wide, nightmare-inducing grin. A grin made all the more sanity shattering by two things; that it was the first expression I'd ever seen on his blank features, and that he'd rotated his head nearly 180 degrees to flash it down at me.

"Cover... face..."

I did as instructed. Those words, like windowpanes smashing, were too jarring for me to do anything *but* obey. My palms had just about reached my chin when Ricky's reaction to them kicked in.

Dakka-dakka-dakka-dakka-dakka-dakka-clickclickclickclick

Every last slug found its way into the back of Glen's broken-neck-backward head. The dull thuds of hot brass smashing through skull and grey matter, however, never came. Instead, each deafening gunfire crack was met with a soft crunching, a low rumble of squeaks and scritches akin to a drunk street magician walking across a bed of broken bottles.

My hands were over my eyes for most of what happened next, but I did catch a few details between my screw-eyed screams. Ricky was screaming, too. Much louder than I was. As for Glen... well, Glen disintegrated.

The second the last bullet found its way into his head, Glen shattered into thousands of floating shards of... well, Glen. The outsides of these shards were the flesh, hair, clothes that'd been standing before us. Their undersides, though, their undersides were a reflected mirror-coated brilliance. No blood, no organs or bones or gore or viscera, just a sparkling diamond wondrousness whose beauty managed to make me forget my fear for a few glorious nanoseconds. The air seemed still as Ricky and I listened to the tinkling of wasted bullets plummeting to the floor. The shards didn't fall, though. They expanded outwards in a dazzling explosion before stopping without warning, hanging mid-air in a slow orbit around something equally as graceful and world-redefining.

Light reflected in the floating Glen shards came from a glowing orb hanging in the air where his stomach would have... *should* have been. It was white, and bright enough to have made me cover my eyes if I hadn't been already. I could feel the heat coming off it on the back of my hands, like a tiny sun contained in a schoolyard abattoir. Between clammy fingers, I caught sight of Ricky reaching out to it. I kept them closed when I heard the clatter of his rifle on the ground. I couldn't help but open them a crack when I heard him scream again. Though. Mainly. This was because the burning sensation on my knuckles vanished.

Ricky was standing in the eye of a storm of circling Glen shards. He was floating a few feet off the ground. The orb was gone, yet somehow the bright glare from it on the classroom around us remained. That was of little interest to me, though. All my focus was on Ricky; every ounce of force in the fresh wave of dread that washed over me came from him and him alone.

Though this time, it *wasn't* because he was pointing a gun at me.

He was screaming, but the screams were coming through gargled, strangled, like someone was holding a piano wire tight around his neck. The arm he'd used to touch the orb was swollen and burned. It blistered and bulged as I watched, melon-sized tumors began to bubble from muscles under the surface. Ricky howled as his fingers grew fat and webbed, the nails at the end of each popping free as the digits became too bulbous to hold them. The limb swelled until the width matched the length, and distinguishing appendage from torso became impossible. His other arm soon followed, and not long after, his screams of agony were met with the ripping of denim and nylon. Ricky managed a final howl before the lumps of new flesh pooling from his brow swallowed his mouth. I peered through my fingers, paralyzed and wailing, as

Ricky ballooned until he was a spinning orb of twitching, pulsing meat. His surface wriggled and writhed, bending and flexing until perfectly smooth. He hovered for a few moments; a perfect untarnished globe of sweating skin. Then, above the background notes of sirens and megaphones, a sound. Dull, moist, slurping. An opening appeared on one side of the orb, something like an eyelid crossed with a sphincter. The puckered rim lips unfurled, revealing Ricky's slick, mucus-covered face. He opened his eyes, staring down at me, and screamed once more.

"Harvey, please, it hurts, help me, Harv—"

He was cut off by something wet, slimy and organic pushing its way out his mouth. I recognised the long glistening things in a heartbeat. They were fingers. *Ricky's* fingers. The eyes on Ricky's face grew wider, somehow *more* fear-filled as the fingers, hands, and eventually arms pushed their way out of his mouth. It wasn't a smooth transition. Tears were streaming down his cheeks as they split, and there was an audible *snap* when his nose buckled and broke. Both cheeks tore, and the pattern of his wincing let me know he felt every single one of those teeth dislodge. I don't know if it even *was* Ricky by that point, though. What emerged from Ricky's mouth, what crushed his jaw and made his eyes bulge and pop from their sockets, was the arms, head, and chest of Ricky. *Another* Ricky.

He... it... no, he managed to pull himself out of the hovering sphere all the way to his midriff before the cycle renewed. "Please Harvey, please, Harvey, it hurts so much, I'm so sorry Harvey, please—"

Once more, his sentence was interrupted. This time it was from fingers poking up through his ribcage. He roared as the nails broke through the skin. It was seeing yet another Ricky, this one blood-covered, crack open the former's ribs to try and free itself that things finally became too much for me. I think I'd done well to hold out until then, to be fair. Before I knew what was really happening, I slipped into unconsciousness.

When I awoke, I was in a hospital bed. The first thing I registered was pain. Pain from thousands of cuts across my front, like I'd stood brave and shirtless against a storm of broken glass. According to the doctor who brought me up to speed, my hands got the worst of it. Apparently, I was lucky they were covering my face, or I'd have been even *more* disfigured from the... ha... "smashing window". But yeah, they had to amputate those, apparently. I'm going to be honest; life hasn't really given me a chance to emotionally deal with that yet. I've never not had problems bigger than being a double amputee.

You know who was in the bed next to me, staring at the wall and saying nothing? Fucking Glen. He was, much to the doctor and police's confusion, unscathed. They also had bigger problems though, like the fact that Ricky was... double ha... "an armed fugitive."

Obviously, they never found the flesh orb. They found Glen sitting at his desk, the carnage Ricky left behind, me cut-up and out cold, and a classroom with walls were covered floor-to-ceiling in deep scratches. The window wasn't even broken for fuck's sake...

Anyway, I'm not going to get myself worked up about *that* again. The sheer dumbfuckery of the establishment *isn't* why I'm dictating the day that, to quote the Fresh Prince, my life got flipped turned upside down. Except, instead of Bel-Air, I got Glen.

He hasn't left me alone. Ever. Not a single day has gone by since that I've not woken up to look out my window and see him staring up at me. I've tried calling the police so many times, but I'm always told they're "too busy" or that I'm imagining things. I get the same reaction from my parents too, come to think of it, and from every friend or partner that eerie fuck has managed to ruin my relationship with. It's almost like I'm the only person who thinks his behavior is fucking creepy as hell. Like he's got some kind of effect on people, like he can make sure nobody in my life disturbs our... whatever the fuck he thinks this is.

The police weren't even bothered when he started letting himself into my damn house. This over a decade after Ricky's shooting spree, too. When I was a grown ass man. They just kept telling me someone with my physical impairments should be happy to have a helpful friend. Never mind the obvious ableism, they literally told me not to worry about coming home to find Glen, my damn stalker since damned high school, sat on my couch. I've fucking had enough.

I've tried talking to him over the years. It's been many, so you can probably guess that I gave up screaming at him to leave, begging him, pleading with him, way back. I've tried asking him what he is more than once, tried to put some understanding behind what the fuck happened that day. I've asked what he did to Ricky, what the floating shards were about, what happened to the glowing orb, all of it. The response? Nothing. He remains Glen; blank and unresponsive as the day I met him. *Exactly* as the day I met him. He hasn't aged since then, not that anybody will listen to me about that either.

He's still sat there now, not moving, saying nothing. That's why I'm posting this, to test a theory. I'm hoping I'm wrong, and that *one* of you will actually think his behavior isn't normal. Maybe it only works with people I know in person. I'll be honest, I've always been too scared to follow through with publishing this. I've written drafts before, but I've never taken the plunge and posted.

Why?

Because Glen's face never changes, his eyes never move from the wall, unless I'm doing one thing. That one thing? Trying to tell people online about him. His blank expression goes when I do that. He looks at me then. He's looking at me now, staring at me from across the room as my finger hovers over the "submit" button.

I've never seen him look so angry before.

NORMAL PEOPLE NEED NOT APPLY

He calls me his masterpiece. '*From Man, the Machine.*' That's what the plaque says. I can't see it, but he's told me that's my "title". All I can see is the screen and the onlookers on the other side of the glass. Looking at both is still disorienting. I'm not used to my eyes being so far apart and don't reckon I ever will be. Also, I miss blinking. A lot.

His name is Tobias Keinseele. There are two things you need to know about him. One, he's an artist. Two, he's completely fucking insane.

You'd recognize him if you saw him straight away, that mirror-surfaced glass eye is hard to miss. Chances are you won't see him, though, not unless you're down on your luck. If you *have* already heard of him, and are alive to read this, then fuck you. Why? Because it means you're one of the oily leeches on the other side of the glass. One of the ones gawping at me, the ones rich and wealthy enough to know about Tobias Keinseele and his gallery of anatomical defiance. I've recognized *dozens* of them. So many of the faces I saw in the papers and on TV have seen me, too. I doubt they think of me as a "me" anymore though, if they ever did see us dregs, drifters, and junkies as people, that is. Hell, Tobias's gallery is probably the only time folk like that acknowledge folk like me exist at all.

That's how I met him, you see. I needed money for a fix. The ad in the paper was simple enough. "*Artist looking for models with unusual histories, cash-in-hand, address below*". Did I question the danger of that vagueness? No. My junk-focused mind only noticed those three little words: cash-in-hand.

It took me nearly an hour walking deep into the sprawling industrial district to find the place. By this point in my addict journey, I was used to walking until my feet bled to get a fix. I was already imagining the prick of the needle and rush of euphoria when my shaking finger pressed on the buzzer of the large, derelict warehouse. Normal people, people that don't wake up in gutters, would have been suspicious of the near-abandoned industrial estate. Folk like yourselves would probably have turned around and looked for safer ways to make some scratch. I'm not... I *wasn't* folk like yourselves, though. At the time, this ominous cube of brick-and-mortar with its boarded windows and distance from the safety of civilization was no different from any building I woke up in. That's probably why Tobias was so eager to meet me. I wouldn't be missed. The voice that answered the intercom also would have made you flee, I bet. Not me though. I'd spent too many decades destroying my mind to pick up the obvious sinister honeytrap tones in that high-pitched crooning.

"Yeeeeessss?" It was Tobias that answered, not that I knew it then. At the time, all I registered was that it was a German-tinged voice, male but cracking and splitting in pitch at odd points. "Can I help you?"

"Advert... model..." I managed. My throat hurt, and I realized it had been almost two days since I'd spoken to anyone with more than a grunt. If I had legs, I'd kick myself for taking my vocal cords for granted.

Tobias either didn't notice or didn't care about my near-broken speech patterns. His response was ecstatic. "Ahhhh—wonderful! I'll buzz you in, please head straight up the stairs".

There was only one other door leading from the stairwell on the other side, and this was at the top of five flights of stairs. I was wheezing by the time I reached the top, out of breath. I could walk for miles on the promise of a fix, but stairs were a different story. I almost fell through the door at the top. I had to bend over for a few moments, wheezing and breathing in deep gulps of dusty air to catch my breath.

That's what made it so easy for him to crack the baseball bat over the back of my head.

***

I was more than used to coming around in strange places without remembering how I'd got there. I was also used to the numbness in my extremities (one of the first things I registered on waking aside from the throbbing pain behind my eyes). It wasn't until my wits swam into focus enough to register the mirror-eyed man standing a few feet in front of me that I started to worry.

"Ahhh..." he crooned, "good, you're finally awake. I was worried that I'd overdone it. That would have been veeeeeeeeery disappointing."

I started to gather more of my cognition. I realized I'd gone a while without a fix, because my heart was pounding somewhere that felt too far away. My eyes stung, and I knew that if I could feel my arms and legs, they'd be sweat-covered and jittery.

"How... how long... what?" My voice coming through weak, feeble, and distant.

Tobias tutted, waggling a finger. "Now please, don't try speaking just yet. You need to be calm, calm and collected. Everything will make sense once I've given you the tour." He clapped his hands, rubbing them together and beaming.

"Tour... what..."

"Shhh... you must save your strength. We have not one moment to waste." He strode out of view, and with a growing alarm, I found I couldn't turn my head to follow. I couldn't even move my eyes. I stared straight ahead, unable to do anything else, eyeballs itching as the room that had been around the mauve-suited, one-eyed man swam into focus.

It *wasn't* the room at the top of the stairs. That room had been dark, dusty, lit only by what daylight managed to fight through a row of windows along the top of one wall. The room I was in when I came to had no windows and was better lit (but not much). The slight increase in light came from two naked bulbs hanging on frayed wires; flickering things that cast a pathetic yellow gleam across the tiled walls and floor. There was also less dust in the air, but the smell of anaesthetic and coal fumes that replaced it was far from welcome. I'm assuming it was still in the warehouse, that *I'm* still in the warehouse, but I have no way to prove this. It looked less abandoned, less forgotten than the warehouse (although again, not much), but this offered no comfort. It's hard to find *any* comfort in *anything* when you wake up in a filthy, blood-spattered surgical theatre. Especially one with a forge, anvil, welder, and smelting equipment clearly visible in one corner. Especially-especially when in the opposite corner there's a large canvas and steel-frame laundry bin filled with bulges that leak a dark red through the fabric. Especially-especially-especially when you recognize one of the feet poking out the top of said gore-filled bag...

The hammering of my ventricles intensified, made worse by the fact that my panicking body could not find lungs with which to take frantic, shallow breaths. I couldn't feel my chest at all. To my increasing terror, I still couldn't feel much of anything, and what I could feel felt wrong, twisted, out of place. My feet were still absent, but my tingling fingers weren't where I remembered them ever being. My twisting gut rumbled from somewhere behind my face, which itself was totally numb save for the acute pricking of my dry eyes. I *still* couldn't blink, either, couldn't look anywhere but directly ahead. When I screamed, the sound echoed from elsewhere, away from the spot my frightened mind was used to hearing that howl from. And the ears I heard with? Tinny, ringing, and again totally absent from my perception of physical sensation. I would have tried to struggle, but I couldn't find any muscles to struggle with. All I could do was scream.

"Stop that." The mirror-eyed Tobias was in my field of view once more. This time his expression was furious, his Germanic crooning laced with razor-wire. "Stop that caterwauling immediately. I don't want to have to silence you; it will ruin the effect."

I stopped screaming, but not entirely because of his threat. It was because of the reflection that I caught in his mirrored chrome left eye. What I saw rendered me too confused, too horrified to do anything, even scream. I suspect that if Tobias hadn't taken chemical measures to prevent it, I would have lost consciousness once more. It was only a glimpse, and a distorted, confused one at that, but it was enough for me to instantly understand the severity, and futility, of my situation. I should have seen my face looking back at me in the reflection of that eye.

I didn't.

"Where's my... where's my..." I heard my voice drifting from way off, despite feeling nothing from any mouth, jaw, teeth, or throat.

"All in good time, my little prize." Tobias sounded jovial as he fiddled and clanked with something behind me. My vision juddered and then, without warning, I swiveled 180 degrees.

At the time, I figured Tobias had me strapped into some kind of wheelchair. Again, there was panic-inducing cognitive dissonance, this time at the absence of inertia or jolting sensation as he pushed me through the thick double doors.

The hallway beyond was pitch black. I only knew it was a hallway because of the brief glimpse I got of the long red carpet trailing off into the shadows before the doors slammed behind us. My eyes registered nothing in this new place. My ears were a different story. From wherever they were, they picked up tinny whimpers, muffled metallic sobs, and faint organic grinding coming from deep in the darkness. My gut, one of only two organs I could still feel, twisted itself into an even tighter knot. My heart threatened to bruise itself from how hard it was hammering against my (I naively thought at the time) ribs. Both sensations intensified from the feeling of the wind against my naked corneas; the realization that Tobias was wheeling me *toward* those haunting grunts, moans, and wet crunches. I didn't know we'd stopped moving until my ears picked up the click of a light switch and my vision was flooded with the white light of a strip bulb hanging in a small alcove. Tobias had placed me directly facing the indent in the wall, so that my immobile eyes could take in the collection of framed paintings it contained.

"These, my little prize, are the Bramfield paintings. These were my muse, my catalyst, my spark, what started me on my journey toward here, toward now, toward you."

If I weren't already terrified of the consequences of crossing that sickly crooning, I would have screamed again. Compared to what I was about to witness, these paintings were, well, tame. Had they been the last stop on Tobias' gallery tour, I'd have been numb to them, as numb to them as I was most of my worryingly-still-unresponsive body. I didn't fully realize what was happening yet though, and without the wider context, those paintings were enough to send the two organs I could still feel into convulsions.

They were, without a doubt, painted by somebody who had seen hell. Nobody could paint things that detailed, that monstrously, hideously intricate unless they'd seen them firsthand.

"Beautiful, aren't they?" The venomous crooning said, sighing. "When I first saw them as a child, I knew that Bramfield he, he had something. Something different, something none of these other pretenders with their 'outsider art' could ever capture. Something raw, something real."

I was naïvely grateful that Tobias didn't have me linger in front of the paintings for long. He was far too eager to show me his own work to let me study the paintings of his self-appointed teacher, his horrific muse, for more than a few minutes. Obscenity took on new meaning for me over the seconds I gazed into those brush strokes. Despite never being religious, the only word I have for what the artist did with oil colors and canvas is blasphemy. Blasphemy not against any god, but against life itself.

There was a vast landscape of a gigantic baby's head. It had no body, unless you can call a fleshy, glistening maggot's tail a body, but it did have limbs. Eight of them, in fact; brittle raking arms that sprouted from asymmetrical pustule-coated lumps behind either ear. Its eyes were cold beyond reason; a deadness in them returned my gaze in a way no brush should have been able to capture.

Another was a smaller portrait of a man with mouths for eyes. Something about his moist glistening skin, his pallid, phlegm-coated lips, his hideous wide grin triggered a deep fear in me far worse than his mismatched facial anatomy, though. This one disturbs me in retrospect, mostly because of how much it directly inspired the first of Tobias' own pieces. On my first (and thankfully only) viewing, it disturbed me mostly because of the laughter I had to convince myself I couldn't hear when I focused on it.

Finally, there was that damn throne. It's the one thing in all of Bramfield's work that disturbs me as much as the art of Tobias which it inspired (well, almost). It was the smallest of all the framed canvases, yet it held my attention the longest. It was a throne of corpses. Thousands of them. All photorealistic, the twisted screams of pain and agony on each face reminiscent of any captured image of a mass grave after a human atrocity. Every single one told a story of agony, of suffering beyond all comprehension or reason. At the top of the corpse pyre, sitting at the peak of the pile of naked bodies almost too high above for the artist to render, was a figure in a cloud of dark mist. I've never been more thankful for anything than I am for the fact the painter, this Bramfield, wasn't close enough to make out any details of their form. I am writing to you at a time when I've seen more nightmares than any person should have in an even marginally fair world. Despite *everything* I have seen since, the memory of that figure on its throne of wailing death still *terrifies* me.

As I said though, Tobias didn't give me much time to wallow in Bramfield's oil-and-canvas terror. He had terrors of his own to share, and his enthusiasm to do so was palpable.

"Brilliant, aren't they? Unrivaled, some say. Me though? No. *Rivaled* in my book. Very much rivaled. Beaten. By me, of course, as you'll soon see, my little prize."

There was another click, and we were once more in the inky, sightless darkness. Once more a stinging breeze whistled on my naked eyes, and once more too did the grunts, snarls, thunks and wails grow louder. My gut had never been tighter. The dull, groggy fog of recent unconsciousness had fully died now. I could feel my wrists, palms, fingers, but nothing of the rest of my arms. My legs, face, and almost the entirety of the rest of me was still gone, still so numb that I couldn't even feel pins and needles. I wanted to cry, to break down into terrified sobs, to call for my mom, but no tears came.

When the light clicked again, and the first of the alcoves containing Tobias' own work revealed itself, I couldn't help but scream. My shrill terror bounced down the darkness, rattling both the horrors they contained and the captor pushing me toward them. I didn't care. Threats be damned. The sight of those three tortured, twisted souls was too much for me to hold my emotions back.

"Please, my precious prize, I don't want to have to ask a third time, stay *silent.* Your screams are ruining the mood, the *majesty.* This is the dry run for you, for my, for *our adoring* public." This word *silent* was accompanied by a metallic clang that rattled my vision. My far-too-distant wails tempered off into near muteness. Inside my mind, the screaming was loud though, relentless. How I had the comprehension to follow Tobias' spiel, I still don't know.

"Good, thank you. Now as I was saying, yes... Bramfield, well, Bramfield was limited in his vision. Paint, *ha,* so quaint. Too quaint, too pedestrian. True art needs to have layers, *dimensions.*"

I could barely hear him. My vision swam, my gut desperately trying to find and a diaphragm to throw itself against so I could puke. In this alcove was a sculpture, a sculpture that moved, and moaned, and whimpered.

"Yes, you see, I chose sculpture as my calling, my outlet. Capturing brilliance, capturing genius, requires depth, mass, *motion.*

How could I choose any medium *other* than flesh and steel, hmm? Exactly, one could not."

In front of us, suspended from the alcove walls by thick chains, was a rusted circular metal platform about twice the width of a drain cover. From its underside sprouted a thick cone of cogs, gears, valves, and pistons. They hummed and spat and whirred and hissed, shaking the heavy corroded disk so much that the rattling of the chains could be heard even over the din of machinery.

So too could the drooling moans of the three poor souls fused to the other side.

How they were still living, I could not fathom. I still can't, as is the case for every single one of Tobias' waking nightmares. I have never wanted anything as much as I wanted to shut my eyes at that moment. If you'd have given me a choice between continuing to look or shooting myself, my finger would have been squeezing the trigger before you'd finished your sentence.

The pride in the crooning behind me made me somehow even sicker. "As you can see, I experimented with *homage* in my early work, with tribute, with imitation. *Pathetic,* in other words. This piece here, '*An ode to Zarasashael*', is the only one of my early pieces worth the power keeping it alive, and even then, only barely. Very gauche, a tad… *melodramatic?* Is that the word? Ah well. What is the past but a slideshow of embarrassment?"

It was obvious what the mirror-eyed maniac meant when referencing imitation. These poor once-people had been arranged to as best resemble the mouth-eyed man in Bramfield's painting as Tobias possibly could.

None of them had any tissue remaining below the chest, although only the central figure retained their entire set of ribs. This pitiful creature was the most intact of the three, and the only one connected to the rusty disk, which to my horror I quickly realized from the scars and burned tissue it had been welded to. The armless torso was writhing on the brown-orange surface, pulling at the various hooks and bolts melted into its flesh to hold it in place. I was again acutely aware of the numbness in my own arms at the sight of the gnarled, scarred stumps at the creature's shoulders. Sadly, and twisted and nightmarish as these observations were, the heads of the three unfortunate souls left little room in my shattering psyche for much else.

"I had to remove *a lot* of cranial matter to get the facial position right. I don't know if they're conscious anymore, not really.

Probably better for them that way, though, right? Ha!" The oddly-pitched laugh would have sent a shiver down my spine if I could feel the damn thing. Again, it was horrifically obvious what he meant.

He'd removed the eyes, brow, and nose of each of his trio of victims. More or less the entire upper halves of their heads were gone. Jagged trails of scar tissue ran along the seams where he'd attached them to each other, fusing the remaining two once-people to the armless torso. He'd positioned them back-to-back, so that their jaws jutted out like thick horns as the amalgamated aberration's new brow. Upside-down mouths twitching and drooled where the eyes of the disk-torso should have been, their throats bulging at unsurvivable angles on either side of its neck. The three slavering half-skulls met at the center of the sculpture's perverse 'face'. Where they connected sat a sack of membranous skin stuffed to the point of translucency, revealing a mess of pulsing, grey brain matter within.

The two peripheral figures were somehow even less intact than the pillar torso. Aside from their twisted necks and halved faces, all that remained of them were internal organs hanging in sagging, goiter-like bulges the size of basketballs. These trembling lumps protruded tumor-like from underneath each of the central figures' armpits, and it was impossible to tell where the raw flesh of one body ended and the next began. The quivering organ-buboes were further connected to the central torso by exposed veins, arteries, and gastrointestinal tubes, merging every biological system of the heaving bodies into a single organic mass.

"Keeping them alive was tricky, my little prize. This is actually the *third* iteration of the piece, but here it is, still breathing all these decades later. Marvellous, no? I'm particularly proud of the mechanisms here, even if they are somewhat crude by my current standards. That cone is full of prototypes for gizmos and doodads I still use today. Still, you'll find that out shortly, won't you? Onwards!"

The seconds between his final word and the click of the alcove lights vanishing felt far too long. I had far too much time watching that misshapen, mangled thing that had once been three writhing and thrashing on its humming baseplate. I could still see it when the darkness washed once more over us.

I felt the tiniest flutter of relief when it became clear Tobias didn't intend to show me his entire gallery. We walked through the dark for at least fifteen minutes, the ebb and sway of the stinging wind on the flesh of my eyes informing me when we turned corners in the sightless labyrinth. Tobias was chattering along the entire time, but I'll be damned if I could remember what he said now. I wasn't paying much attention. My thoughts were wrapped in the plummeting realization that I was well and truly fucked.

It's no secret that I hadn't made the best decisions in life. Truth is, I was probably only a few years from dead. Some part of me, though, some small part, had always believed I'd sober up and turn my life around at the 11th hour. How long I'd been unconscious for after Tobias hit me with the bat I didn't know, but it was long enough that my last fix was well and truly flushed from my system. I was soberer than I'd been in years. Even then, the irony that I'd found lucidity at the moment shit turned far too late was starting to tear me apart.

My inner lamenting was interrupted here and there by dread-stoking noises from the unseen alcoves we passed. Some were barely audible grunts and slavering, similar to those made by the tri-mouthed living bust. The deeper into the darkness Tobias took me, the more grotesquely human the sounds became. Grunts became whimpers, slavering evolved into sobs. Once or twice, I could hear a rasping *"help…"* or *"please… please kill me…"*.

Tobias chattered and crooned over the growing racket. I lost count of the number of distinct voices (for lack of a better term). By the time there was another click and my naked eyes once more found light, we must have passed dozens of alcoves, at least. I doubt I'd be sane enough to write this if he'd insisted on showing me all of them.

"Ah, my little prize, I was *particularly* excited about showing you this one. It's called *'What thoughts bloom on yonder breeze'*. I know what you're thinking. I was going through a pretentious, yes, *pretentious* phase when it came to titles. The work though? It's one of my *best*, my little prize, almost as good as… well, you shall see."

I still can't fathom how a mind as sadistic and twisted as Tobias Keinseele's defines 'good' when it comes to his art. It took my eyes a little while to adjust to the sudden flash of light, but as my vision de-blurred, I could feel a fresh wave of terror building in my misplaced gut. Once more, my heart smashed into its surroundings, and though I could feel my hands, I couldn't move them to clutch my chest and steady it. I now know why, of course, but back then, the reminder of my paralysis only served to intensify the renewed panic born from the sight of Tobias' second exhibited work.

There was nothing suspended from the brickwork wall of the alcove this time. This second piece stood freely on the grimy cracked tiles. The inorganic components consisted of two television-sized cast-iron drums welded together at an acute angle. From the thin wedge between them rose two thick steel poles. These had been bent and twisted in a spiral, and they almost resembled an abstract tornado or whirlpool that nearly reached the lofty ceiling. The boxes at the cable-spiral's base hummed in a similar fashion to the cone hanging from the base of the last sculpture. This vibration ran along the twisted rods, sending cracking blue sparks across the surface of the thing wedged tight between them.

This was the part that had my stomach looking for a diaphragm again, the flesh component of Tobias' chosen medium.

I'm guessing that it must have been a person once. Though how long ago I couldn't say. At first, I only knew it was human in origin because of the tufts of grey hair and occasional teeth, finger, and toenail clusters dotted sporadically across its undulating surface.

"I was going through a radical experimental phase here, my little prize. Experimenting with diseases, pathogens, cancers. This one was a foray into unchecked growth, into cellular chaos, a mirror of inhumane humanity we've allowed our society's reflection to become. Pah, as I said, pretentious. The form though, my prize, the *form* is my master crafted gift to you, to me, to *us*. Feast your eyes on it and weep as I do." Tobias was indeed weeping; I could hear it in his words. I would have been too, although for entirely different reasons.

The 'form' Tobias was so proud of, his 'gift', was a potato-shaped lump of flesh about 10 feet long. It was suspended in the air somehow, rotating slowly as it floated between the steel spirals, riding the crackling faint blue bolts of lightning that jumped from their humming surface. As the thrashing lump turned in place, a few gnarled facial features came into view on its surface. A bloodshot eye near its base, a swollen mouth at its middle, cauliflower ear and a second eye closer to its top. The only thing that stopped me screaming when that bloodshot gaze locked on mine was the morbid curiosity driving me to hear Tobias' explanation, his excuse, for the abomination before me.

"This one, my little prize, is still conscious."

It was at this moment the twisted, swollen mouth on the thing's surface wrenched itself open and screeched at us. Flecks of phlegm burst from between cracked, brown teeth. Never before had I heard so much rage, so much anger, so much hatred poured into any sound made by a human mouth. It was like no roar I could ever imagine a human capable of making. It *was* human, though. Of that, I was certain, no matter how much I wish I wasn't. I had no bones I could feel, but if I did, the obvious still-human-ness of that otherwise unworldly shrieking would have chilled me to them.

Tobias allowed the mouth on the behemoth tumor to carry on shrieking and screaming its unchecked hatred at me until the gnarled features orbited once more from view. I could hear him tittering to himself as it roared, laughing at the white-hot rage in those bulging bloodshot eyes. I could do nothing but wilt under the force of that fury. It was clear the fact I wasn't in any way responsible didn't matter one bit to the person that was now this disgusting, heaving mass. The consciousness behind those misshapen eyes was so far into the realms of suffering, it could feel nothing but hatred for *anyone* that didn't share in its pain.

"You see, my little prize, it was this piece, the reaction of the model here, that made me realize what my clay *emotionally* became was far more important than what it *physically* became. This lump here, the cancerous nothing, has created beauty from the most base, the most ugly, the most disgustingly passionate depths of the human spectrum. It was upon seeing this recently and finishing the *last* piece I want to show you, that… well, you'll see. I'm so excited, my little prize, I honestly *can't wait.*"

We reached the final alcove of our tour after another half hour of walking in total blackness. Tobias must have had the maze engraved in his memory, either that or his mirror-eye could see in the dark, because not once did he get lost or bump into a hidden wall. The sounds from the unlit alcoves reached further and further into my nightmares for inspiration. The whimpers and moans grew to eerie levels of quiet. Soon they became less pained, more subdued. Sobs soon became unintelligible, gibbering, insane ramblings and twisted mutters which rose from the dark spaces where whimpers of fear once came.

If I could feel my spine, it would have tingled. My absent toes would have curled. I had to convince myself I couldn't hear a machine gun paced *tink-tink-tink-tink* of flesh against glass that perfectly aligned with my heartbeat. I think I'd have started pleading with Tobias if I hadn't spent the prior few years high off my ass. I started pleading with myself instead, begging myself to let this be some kind of trip, some withdrawal-induced fever dream. Part of me thought I'd died, that I'd OD'd, and this place was hell.

Fuck, maybe it is. I can't think of many other places you'd see the kind of fucking thing that was in front of me when the final set of alcove lights went up.

It had once been at least six people, judging by the number of mouths. I didn't have time to count the eyes, though, and there could very well have been more than a dozen. It was impossible to count the rest of the pieces, but there was definitely more than enough on display to account for six people. *At least* six.

This alcove was larger than the others, wide enough to account for about three of the previous ones and then some. The entire space was taken up by a vast canvas stretched taut end-to-end. I could tell straight away what it was made of. There was still blood pumping through the veins in it, obvious scarring marks identical to those on the merged faces of Tobias' first sculpture.

The six mouths were arranged at the center of the room-sized skin canvas, scar-fused into it. The galaxy of eyes spiraled from them, and the sea of blinking gazes was itself surrounded by a fractal ring of twitching ears.

"Marvellous isn't it, my little prize? This one I call '*From the Machine, Man*'. Keeping this piece breathing, why… well, I'm a miracle worker. A true miracle worker. Look at those lungs, though, my little prize. Look at those hearts still beat-beat-beating. They're one now, all those minds. One in body and soul. *That* was the message of this piece, that we are all separated only by the physical constraints of our shells."

I stared (what else could I do) as Tobias rambled on about his masterwork. I was beyond processing any of what he was saying by this point, really. I wasn't afraid, terrified, horrified, panicking. None of the synonyms I have for fear cover the levels of it I felt at that moment. If they could move, my eyes would have rolled back in their sockets. The *tink-tink-tink-tink* that ran in time with my thrashing heartbeat was too loud to ignore now, as was once more the acute awareness that I still couldn't find lungs to draw labored breaths from.

The vast canvas was moving. It was pulsing, stretching, heaving as the galaxy of exposed organs spasmed and squeezed. Every part of the people Tobias had used was on display. Hearts, livers, lungs, intestines, brains, bladders, nothing save for bone and muscle, had gone to waste. Every exposed organ was fused to the skin-canvas, and with each beat of the strategically-placed hearts, I could see dark fluids rushing in and out of each of them. They were all, beyond any sense of reason or sanity, still alive.

It was when the nexus of eyes stopped rolling chameleon-like to fixate on me that my screams started. When the six mouths on the canvas opened and spoke in unison with a chorus of male and female voices, Tobias had to *finally* make good on his threats to silence me.

"What is this?" the tapestry groaned, every one of its dozen eyes honed on my immobile ones. "What has he brought us? What has he made? What is… oh… *oh…*"

What the mouths on the canvas did next, the sound the mouths made when the eyes had finally taken in my entire form, still haunts me.

They started laughing. A horrid laugh, a crooked tittering, a harsh, disjointed guffaw that almost drowned out my now-unrestrained howls of pure panic. I didn't have long to scream, though. As I said, Tobias made good on his earlier threats. There was a metallic scraping accompanied by the briefest screech of speaker feedback, like an aux jack being pulled from a cheap guitar amp. The second it hit my hearing, the sounds of my screams left. All I could hear now was the cackles of the living canvas and the all too clear *tink-tink-tink-tink* of vascular muscle on glass.

"You forced my hand, my little prize." Tobias had to yell to be heard over the hysterics of the flesh wall. "So, I'm sorry, but *no voice for you*. Not that it matters much; we're near the end, our destination, the finale, *home*. I'm so… well, gosh, I'm just so excited, my little prize. *So* excited."

We weren't gliding through the dark for long on this final journey. We'd also run out of unseen alcoves, although the near-silence was hardly a comfort. Tobias wasn't jabbering to himself anymore, either. The only sounds I could hear from his direction were his echoing footsteps and breaths. The latter were coming through fast, ragged. His anticipation was palpable. It radiated from him; a razor-wire eagerness only found elsewhere in nature, riding the lungs of half-starved predators before a kill.

I couldn't feel my breaths. I couldn't feel anything at all except the stinging of my eyes, the knotting of my gut, and the *tink-tink-tink-tink* of my heart against what I prayed were my ribs. Inside my mind, I rolled and roiled in the blind terror that rose the moment Tobias, for lack of a better word, 'disconnected' my voice. The acute awareness of every missing sensation magnified a thousand-fold in that moment. An uncountable number of worst-case scenarios flashed past my mind's eye, each more hellish and resolve-breaking than the last.

When Tobias clicked on his final light switch, it took me less than half a second to realize that, hellish as they'd been, none of my predictions were as bad as the reality that awaited me.

"So, with my last piece, *'From the Machine, Man'*, I was experimenting with unity, my little prize. Yes, the *form* is impressive, but the *mind*, the one from the many, is the *real* piece. A super-sentience, a hyper-resilient collective consciousness that can peer into the void of cognitive infinity without breaking."

Without warning, he launched himself back into my field of view, grin stretching ear-to-ear, white bulb reflection and childlike glee sparkling in both his organic and metallic eyes.

"And you, my little prize, are to be its antithesis, its polar negative, my response to my own creation. With them I expressed concepts of unity and togetherness. With you, I shall explore the uttermost depths of isolation." His face was inches from my naked pupils. Once more I found what parts of me that could were balking at the lack of a visible face in the reflection on his mirrored eye. "Welcome, my little prize... no, my little *masterpiece,* to the beginning of your contribution to history."

He stepped aside to reveal the alcove that would be my tomb, and for the first time, the full horror of my fate dawned on me.

The alcove was a large glass case. Inside it was an elaborate network of devices and machinery that included a keyboard, screen, and computer tower. They weren't what made me wish I still had lungs to scream. What did that was the hands positioned on wires at the keyboard, ready to type.

I didn't want to believe it, but there they were, connected by wires painfully screwed and mashed into still exposed bones. I tried to flex my still tingling fingers, urging the digits in the case to remain still.

They didn't.

My hands were behind the glass, hooked up to a janky iron box with a radio antenna sticking out the top. I watched them flex and wriggle at my command, I could feel the keyboard beneath my fingertips. My gut was once more trying to find a diaphragm. Not just because of the hands, either. The brain floating in the small steel bar spiral was equally responsible.

"Yes, you see that? That's you, where you *actually* are now." Tobias opened the case and poked the floating brain with his little finger. In an instant, every shred of my awareness became white-hot pain. I was blind, deaf, totally unable to register any physical sensation except agony. The moment Tobias removed the digit, the burning ceased. He cocked an eyebrow, his point proved. "Wireless signal transmission, my little *modular* masterpiece. Observe."

And this is when the last of my remaining sanity broke. Tobias reaches down and picked up one of my eyes. My vision split, the view from my left still fixed on my twitching hands in the case. From my right everything became a blur.

"Observe, my little masterpiece, observe. From man, the machine."

Tobias hadn't been pushing a wheelchair. He'd been pushing a wheeled surgical trolley, the kind used to transport tools. On it was... were the last remaining parts of... of *me*. Each was connected to a small black box, exactly like the one wired to my hands, bent radio antennae and all. My heart was *tink-tink-tink-tinking* in a glass jar, hung from a rusted metal plate where a lid should be. I could see my stomach and intestines in a similar, albeit slightly larger, vessel. It was the eyes that were the worst part, though. The last thing I remember before I finally won the war for unconsciousness was Tobias holding them to face each other.

They were each stretched across a brass ring no wider than a tennis ball. They, too, were connected to small cast-iron boxes with bent antennas to beam signals to and from my floating brain. Thin hooks had been fed through the raw flesh of my eyeballs, the orbs stretched so much to fit the rig that my pupils were flat, distorted, goat-like.

If I had a mouth, I would have never stopped screaming. Sadly, Tobias had ensured I'd never scream again.

The last thing he did before switching off the alcove light and leaving me in my tomb was to arrange the small black boxes and jars I'd become. One eye forever faces the screen. It is this, he's told me, that's the *real* art. With nothing to do *but* type, my remotely operated hands have been letting out a crescendo of… well, of exactly the kind of mad ramblings you'd expect someone in my position to write. My words are projected on the alcove wall behind my case, and the many visitors to Tobias' gallery do *so* love to titter and chuckle at them.

My other eye is facing them, you see. Tobias *wants* me to see how the patrons react to my descent into madness.

That was five years ago. Five years I have been here, unable to do anything except type jabbering lunacy in the hopes that one of the rich, powerful, and publicly known patrons has a pang of guilt and shuts off the machines somehow keeping me alive. I'd given up hope. That is, until the power surge.

It happened this morning. Small, almost too small to notice, but enough to cause the aging desktop tower in my case to restart. For the first time in five years, I *wasn't* staring at an infinitely scrolling blank page. I was looking at a desktop display, a desktop display with an internet browser icon clearly in reach.

I'm not trying to reach all of you. Most of you, I imagine, are upstanding folk who wouldn't take vague cash-in-hand modeling work. Most of you aren't desperate enough to need to venture into abandoned industrial estates to do whatever is necessary for a scrap of cash.

Those of you that are though, please, heed my warning. If you see an ad like the one I answered, don't follow it up. Do literally *anything* else. I don't care how hungry you are, how bad you want that fix, or how angry the landlord is getting. *Nothing* is worth this.

I have to wrap this up. I can hear Tobias coming back through the tiny mics in my eye boxes. Please, please, *please* don't answer his ad. Five years is a *long time*. He's made many more creations in that time, and never seems to have a shortage of 'models' to work with. Don't let yourself become the next one.

DISTEMPORAL ASSETS

Let's not fuck around. You want me to get to the point, right? This works for me, because I don't have long before the government spooks figure out which car I'm hiding under. I won't bother telling you how I graduated from Oxford, about my decades of success as a field archaeologist, or how I was pulled out of my previous dig salvaging the Baniyam Buddha's in Afghanistan when the US & co withdrew. All you need to know is I came back to America with them, and that's how I found myself about 50 miles southwest of Las Vegas staring at a pearlescent metal hatch.

"Blimey Freddy, you weren't kidding." I whistled, scratching the mole on my chin, staring at the mottled blue-steel column protruding from orange earth at the bottom of the 30 foot pit. Even though I was used to the baking sun from my time in Hazarajat highlands, the shade and coolness of the pit were welcome by the time Freddy and I had climbed down there.

"I told you," Freddy said, taking off his battered trucker cap to scratch his balding head, "it's a goddamn flying saucer."

"I don't know about an alien spacecraft, but it's definitely older than any metal construction buried here has any right being." Leona stood, brushing the dust off her knees, and turned away from the oil barrel-size column with its wheel-lock hatch roof. She greeted me with a warm hug, Freddy a nod. This was unsurprising. Leona and I had been undergraduates together at Oxford. Leona and Freddy had only met the day before, when her current university had called her about the phone call they'd received from him the day before that. She'd called me when she arrived, because I'd called her the previous week to let her know I was safely out of

Afghanistan. I'd agreed to join because of how Freddy found the hatch. Or, more accurately, why he'd been digging up the remote stretch of the desert he'd somehow come to own. He'd told Leona's university, who told Leona, who told me, that he'd found a treasure map.

Managed to keep up so far? Good.

Freddy owned a house on the same land as the pit we were standing in. While renovating the remote property, he'd found the map and coordinates hidden under some floorboards. Three days later, he'd rented a bulldozer and started going to town. That's when he found the hatch. He'd told the university he'd found a UFO. The university told Leona she still owed them for the prescription opioid addiction they kept hushed up. She told me a lot of swearwords in French. I told her I'd get the next plane ticket from Wisconsin once I was done being processed at Fort McCoy.

Confusing, right? Sorry. All you need to know is that everyone was where they were when Scott, who none of us knew, removed his headphones and turned off the metal detector he'd been waving around.

"It's definitely not a saucer," he said, scratching his goatee. "wherever this leads, it goes off in one direction. No signal round any edges of the pit except where you're stood. If it is a ship, this is at the nose." He gestured with a thumb over his shoulder to the hatch, his words intercut with the smack of chewing gum.

"So, like a pirate ship?" Freddy asked, raising a pudgy eyebrow at the news the thing buried on his land *wasn't* a UFO just like the one his grandpappy was there when they found at Roswell.

"More like a submarine, I'll bet. That is, if it is a ship. It's probably just a bunker left here by some prepper during the cold war."

"A bunker that's over 5000 years old?" Leona had her hands on her hips, greying-haired face incredulous. "I've seen a lot of buried metal. I don't know what this thing is made of, but it looks like steel. Do you know how long steel takes to rust? When it's buried somewhere as dry as the desert? *Seigneur, sauve-moi de cet imbécile.*"

I couldn't see Scott's eyes behind the sunglasses, but I know they looked sheepish. It had been decades since I'd made the impatient Leona swear in her native tongue, but I still remembered the experience. I felt for Scott. If he was here and Leona was here, it meant he was Leona's assistant. That meant he was an undergrad. If there was one thing Leona couldn't stand even when she was one herself, it was undergrads. Fortunately for Scott (and for you, if you're bored of a middle-aged man getting nostalgic for a former flame), we weren't in the awkward silence long.

The shrill hiss was deafening as soon as it started.

"Oh, hell no." Freddy reached a pudgy arm into a duffel bag at the base of the pit's ladder. When he stood back up, the meaty limb was holding a shotgun. Before we three academics could register what was going on, Freddy had the barrel pointed at the corroded pearlescent steel column.

"*Oh oui bien sûr, un bunker de la guerre froide. Putains d'étudiants.*" Leona threw herself to the pit's edge, yelling, grabbing Scott by the arm and taking him with her as she went. They fell to the ground just in time to avoid being blasted by the thick vapor projected from three-fifths of the hatch's rim. Had Freddy and I stood a fraction to the right, we'd have had to do the same. I ducked anyway though, only because the sudden high-pitched gaseous whistling triggered the attuned fight-or-flight response I'd honed back in Afghanistan.

It wasn't until I looked up that I realized how lucky Scott was that Leona had developed the same reflexes during the time with me she'd spent there, living under the constant threat of rockets, grenades, and gunfire. The flat almost-ring of steam reached all the way to the walls of the pit. Once it subsided after a few seconds of whistling, the densely packed sand and rock wasn't sand and rock anymore. It was glass. Sparkling, slightly glowing, still cooling, glass.

"Thanks, professor," Scott mumbled, pulling himself to his feet once the hatch stopped shrieking. The sheepish look I imagined behind those dark sunglasses had only gotten worse.

"Never mention it." Leona was already on her feet, once again brushing dust from her khakis. She turned to Freddy. "Monsieur Frederick, please put down the gun."

Freddy spat on the orange Earth. "The hell I will. I ain't about to let myself get et'n by some space monster."

"*Mon dieu, qu'est-ce qu'il y a avec les hommes et les armes…* Monsieur Frederick please, whatever we're dealing with here, I don't think it's a—"

THUNK

Only Freddy didn't throw himself back to the pit floor. He raised the shotgun, aiming down the sights at the turning rusted wheel on the center of the hatch. Leona, Scott, and I could only look up at the corroded steel column, mouths agape, as the wheel lock unscrewed. It turned for thirty long seconds, unseen gears and cogs grinding for the first time in, according to Leona's assessment, millennia.

Leona wasn't protesting anymore. She'd run out of words, French or English. She was staring with wide eyes at the hatch just like the men of the pit, too shocked to speak. She didn't even have words when there was a second loud *THUNK* followed by the long, groaning creak of scraping hinges. The fiery archaeology professor was silent even as the rusted circular plate started to lift itself ajar. She didn't *need* words when it clanged fully open with a last energetic swing, though. None of us did. We were too busy screaming.

That's when I learned Freddy wasn't a man who messed around. I heard the click of him readying his weapon the instant the two sets of rubber-covered fingers appeared at the rim of the hatch. He grunted in unison with the top of a helmeted head emerging. He'd already fired before I got a chance to take in any details of the figure pulling itself out the hole.

"*QU'EST-CE QUE AU NOM DE DIEU EST MAUVAIS AVEC VOUS, VOUS FOU PUTAIN D'AMÉRICAIN!*"

We three unarmed pit dwellers screamed again. We heard the distant metallic *thump* of the headless body hitting the bottom of the shaft within the hatch, but not before we had time to wipe blood and shattered helmet from our shocked faces.

"SEE," Freddy yelled with a grin, staring around at the mess of bone, glass, gore, and plastic on the opposite wall, "I TOLD you nerds it was a UFO, I TOLD you there'd be a space monster."

"*Ugh...* this blood tastes real human for a space monster..." Scott was still laying on the floor, spitting dramatically and wiping flecks of splatter from his goatee. "What? I'm just saying what we're all thinking." He added, when he saw Leona and I's horrified expressions. I couldn't argue with him, though.

If you're screaming while in the presence of someone getting shot with a shotgun at point-blank range, chances are you're going to get some blood in your mouth. I recognized the coppery tang on my tongue, just like Scott had. I also couldn't shake the knowledge that the chances of an alien having fingers and hands shaped exactly like a human being were astronomically slim.

We couldn't stop Freddy going down the hole, though we did try. We followed him, of course. Leona and I weren't about to let whatever lay inside this… whatever it was, be claimed by a redneck with a bloodlust for aliens. Scott came too, but he didn't have a choice, because when he protested Leona swore at him in French, and that was the end of that.

We were descending the ladder for two full minutes before we reached the bottom.

"Good thing I packed flashlights, eh?"

Sure enough, Freddy had three battery-powered torches in the duffle bag he'd slung over his shoulder before climbing into the hatch. This was indeed a good thing, too, because the space at the bottom was pitched black aside from the thin rays of Nevada sun able to find their way this far down the hole. Scott vomited when they clicked into life, and even Freddy let out a "*Jesus*" followed by a sharp intake of breath.

The figure Freddy shot had broken several limbs as it tumbled, and a fair few more when it landed. There was more than one sharp bone poking through its dark rubber suit. It didn't have a head, because as you'll recall Freddy had eviscerated its head with buckshot. What remained of the lower jaw, neck, and base of the skull was surrounded by the remnants of a helmet made from some kind of composite plastic or fiberglass. The headgear's interior was lined with a lime green gel, and various pipes and frayed wires ran from the lining into a thick tube. The socket where this tube would have connected had been lost to Freddy's shotgun, but the scuba-like tank full of fluids on the figure's back with a shotgun-severed cable trailing from it allowed me to paint a rough picture. One I'd confirm in a few moments once we started exploring the rest of the ship. What shocked me most about the figure, what caused me to yell and Leona to clasp a pair of hands to her mouth, was the name badge on the headless, distressingly human, female corpse's chest:

IPSET: Dr Harper-Girard.

"A name, you know?" Freddy asked, poking the body with his gun.

"*Mine.*" Leona and I replied in unison, shooting each other an awkward glance immediately after. Freddy looked confused.

"Well, mine is Harper, hers is Girard," I explained. "Surely the university sent some paperwork?"

He shrugged. "They mighta done, but I'll be honest; the wife checks the mail. I just knew they were sending some science folk to poke around and sign the bit of paper that said I'd found a boner-fi-dee UFO."

Leona rolled her eyes before turning to me. "What do you think it means? What's IPSET? I'm frightened, Robert."

"I know," I replied, "me too."

"I recognize those hips, they're—"

"I know." I shot her a glare. I couldn't bear to hear out loud the observation we'd both made. I recognized those hips too; I'd spent a whole evening staring at them on a dancefloor many decades ago. On the first night, our friendship gained the suffix *"with benefits."*

We both tried to ignore our growing fears as we poked around the ship's entrance. The word IPSET meant nothing to me at the time. It wasn't until my torch illuminated some signage on the rusted wall spelling out *Institute of Paranatural Science, Events, and Technology* that I even knew it was an acronym. Other than this revelatory nugget of information, the room was pretty barren save for a rack containing another suit of the same kind the now-deceased Dr Harper-Girard had been wearing. Scott had been right; the hatch was indeed at the nose of the ship. The room was a sharp triangle shape, with the suit storage set into the thin wall at one end. The wider one at the other was featureless save for a door and keypad. It was a kind of fingerprint scanner. The screen was still half-illuminated, despite the rust and chipped paint of the walls and floor grates. A small LED flashed red when Freddy and Scott pressed their thumbs on the surface. With a faint *BEEP* it turned green for Leona, prompting a gulp from us both. Her hand found its way into mine when the steel door hissed and slid open; something that hadn't happened for a long time.

"Holy shit," Freddy yelled, when we'd collectively had enough time to try and make sense of the room beyond, "you still don't think this is a UFO?"

"No," Scott replied, voice weak and quiet, "no, I think you're right. This is a UFO."

Leona and I exchanged a sidelong glance when we took our first steps across the threshold. A UFO with signs on the wall in plain English? Aliens with names like Dr Harper-Girard? *Cultivez un cerveau*, as Leona would say. I didn't say anything out loud because I didn't have a better explanation, but I knew straight away whatever we'd found here wasn't extraterrestrial. It wasn't until we got to the final room at the other end of the ship that the horrifying truth revealed itself, but even before this, I knew we weren't in a UFO. For one thing, it wasn't flying. For another, as mentioned, the chances of an alien race idiosyncratically having our exact body shape and writing in an Earth language were… well, they were about as mathematically close to impossible as it's possible to be. It goes without saying that none of my knowledge of ancient civilizations was helpful. I'd stopped relying on prior experience the moment I saw the hatch. In this region of North America, you expect to be excavating lost Gosiute and Panamint holy sites, not ancient steel vessels that are somehow both rusted and more technologically advanced than anything you've ever seen. Still, despite our trepidation and the layer of mixed sweat between our palms, Leona and I followed Scott and Freddy across the threshold.

The middle section of the ship was mostly used as some kind of storage bay, from the looks of things. This much we could work out. It doesn't take a genius to recognize stacked crates (no matter how unfamiliar the plastic-like material they're made from looks). We were walking between shelves of these dark red boxes for about five minutes when we emerged in the clearing. Despite being nearly five minutes' walk away from the nose of the ship, we'd spied this space from back at the doorway. It was clearly visible from wherever you stood in the girthy storage hold, mainly because of the dancing and swirling lights above it on the distant ceiling. As I said, we were walking towards it for a full five minutes. A much longer time than it seems when you've got the luxury of reading it in a sentence. Plenty of chronological space for my evermore panicking mind to wrap itself tightly around the inexplicableness of my situation. So lost was I in my growing worry that the shelves of red crates giving way to the clearing almost took me by surprise. The jolting feeling of near shock was short-lived, though. What we found in the clearing meant *almost*-surprise gave way to *actual*-disconcertion real damn quickly.

The heart of the ship was unlike any engine I've seen. Our torches were unnecessary. The hundreds of clear tubes sprouting from the floor-to-ceiling vat that made up the bulk of it were filled with a luminescent green liquid. It cast the engine in an emerald glow, carving out against the shadows with eerie chlorophyllic highlights an array of components and mechanisms whose purposes I couldn't fathom. I could guess the purpose of the bulbous dome set into the base of the vat, though. You don't need a doctorate in esoteric engineering to work out the meaning of *POWER LEVEL—2%*. It was a battery. And, thanks to a glass viewing port on the dome's face, I could see from where the ship drew its power. I could see it, but I'm not sure I could believe it. I'm still not sure I want to.

There was a man inside, a man wearing a mottled blue mask of the same pearlescent metal as the hatch in the pit (although without the rust or corrosion). A man suspended in clear, bubbling fluid; his frame connected to the engine by the similar glowing tubes to those running from it itself into hidden ducts in the ship's ceiling. A man that, as we could hear even through the thick glass and blue-steel mask, was screaming.

I couldn't tell you how old he was. That's why all four of us started yelling along with him. His age kept changing. He was… flickering, phasing in and out of existence every few seconds at completely random intervals as we watched. When we arrived, his frail frame was ancient; wizened and wrinkled and thin. Then he'd flickered like his body was disrupted by static on an old television set. When he emerged, he was middle-aged, only a year or so younger than Leona and me. After the next flicker, he was a baby, then in his twenties, then a toddler, then on the cusp of puberty. The only thing about him which remained constant was the shrieking, gurgling pain his lungs managed to project even through the viscous liquid and solid material of his waking tomb.

"My God…" Freddy was so taken aback he actually lowered the barrel of his shotgun. Scott was somewhere off in the shadows, being sick again. I know the eyes behind those glasses weren't sheepish anymore, unless Scott sobbed and blubbered when he was embarrassed.

Leona's grip on my hand tightened. *"Mon Dieu, Robert. We have to help that poor soul. Aide-moi à trouver une porte!"*

"I don't think there *is* a door," I replied, mouth dry, "don't touch it, we don't know what it is."

I pulled her back towards me, stopping her from rushing to the shrieking man/boy/baby with tubes painfully fused to his back. Aside from the pearlescent blue-steel mask, the thick wad of crudely grafted cables was the only thing in the battery tank that didn't shimmer or flicker. Just the poor man/boy/baby and his wretched, twisted body.

Unfortunately, I wasn't close enough to intercept Freddy.

"Son of a bitch. We've got to get him out of there!" Before any of us could stop him, Freddy had dropped the shotgun and was feeling around the rim of the viewing glass for a mechanism to open it. He was hammering on the flashing *POWER LEVEL—2%* screen when the alarm started going off.

"ALERT! NON-CLASSIFIED PERSONNEL DETECTED! MISSION COMPROMISED! FLUSHING REMAINING DISTEMPORAL ASSETS! FLUSHING NON-CLASSIFIED PERSONNEL! ALERT! NON-CLASSIFIED…"

The darkness around us was pierced now by red as well as emerald light. A shrill ringing blasted from hidden klaxons, competing with the repeating security message to see which could deafen us first. Scott had to stop puking to ram his fingers in his ears. I felt Leona's grip leave mine, though I'm not sure who let go of who. From somewhere up ahead in the depths of the ship we hadn't yet explored, I could hear a man's screams even above the din. Because of what happened to Freddy and Scott he wasn't screaming alone for long. As soon as the message had repeated itself twice, dozens of needle-thin hooks on string-like steel cable shot up from the floor around both of them. Each man yelled as the miniature barbed grapples found purchase on their skin. My ears screamed when I had to take my hands off them, but if I hadn't, I couldn't have held Leona back when the cables retracted. The look on Freddy's face when the dozens of hooks snapped back into the floor will be with me until I die. I'll never forget his screams as the barbs took lumps of his flesh with them. What will haunt me more is Scott's tears, the way I could see him mouthing for his mum even after one of the pneumatic micro harpoons tore his bottom lip clean from his face, leaving teeth, gums, and jawbone exposed for display.

The second wave of hooks followed the first, and just as quickly flayed whole sections of Freddy and Scott. By the time the rapid-fire onslaught of barbs and cable was finished I was sobbing, backed into a corner, with Leona trying her hardest to bury herself forever in my chest. The ship's defense mechanism worked through both of them like a school of piranha; turning them from men, to a cloud of red mist, to slack-jawed glistening skeletons in a few short minutes. The hooks didn't stop there, though. They continued shooting and digging, slicing and crushing bones until nothing at all remained of the Americans in our party.

"NON-CLASSIFIED PERSONNEL FLUSHED. REMAINING DISTEMPORAL ASSETS FLUSHED. MISSION COMPROMISED. BREACH REPORT FILED. CONTEMPORARY IPSET PICKUP INITIATED. NON-CLASSIFIED PERSONNEL..."

This new message repeated as loudly as the first, but at least the alarm had stopped. Neither of us was in much of a state to appreciate that, though. I was too busy crying like a bullied child, Leona was too busy jabbering nonsense in French. For Lord knows how many minutes we sat alone in the scarlet-lime tinted shadows, each doing our best to gulp down enough stale oxygen to prevent passing out. Somehow, one of us managed to compose themselves, and then the other. I don't know which was which. I *do* know it was Leona that pointed out the scream from deeper in the ship. She was the one who wanted... no, *demanded* that we find out who it came from. She was the one that needed answers; that had to know why a woman with both our names lay dead and headless at the foot of the shaft. She was the one that couldn't leave well enough alone. *I* was the one who wanted to run and never come back.

She was the one who won that argument.

So, it was we who found ourselves, after another five minutes, walking between more rows of dark red crates, at a second door. I think, somehow, I knew even then what would happen when I put my thumb to it, because I didn't jump as much as Leona did. I can't feign total bravery, though. It was still enough to make me yelp, enough to raise hairs on my arms and twist knots in my bowels. The sight of that door hissing open for my thumb filled me with dread and horror, second only to that spawned by the contents of the room beyond. It was a bedroom. A poorly lit, but remarkably clean and not rusted, bedroom. There was a double bed against one wall, a desk, and a small, tiled section in one corner with a curtain to hide a combination shower/toilet/sink space. It was a bedroom that had been lived in, too. There were pens on the desk, and a notepad, and a half-eaten sandwich free of mold. There was a red book face down on one pillow, and a cup of still-steaming coffee on one of the bedside tables, even a microwave set into one wall. There were photographs next to the microwave, held on with plastic magnets to a bulky metal box, which I assume was a fridge.

I recognized the people in those photos, even though the faces were older than I was used to. So did Leona. She knew the woman with hair slightly greyer than her own standing with a team of scientists in one, just as much as she knew the same even greyer woman in a modest wedding dress smiling with a man familiar to both of us another. This was in a lot of the photos, almost always with her. I knew his hairline, even if there was less of it. I knew the mole on his chin, too. The man and woman in images would have been enough to prompt Leona and me to turn and run from the ship as fast as we could. We did run, but not *just* because of how familiar-yet-unfamiliar the couple was. We ran because, at the opposite end of the room, were two glowing-green pods. Both had Dr Harper-Girard above them on steel plaques. One was empty, a trail of glistening footprints leading from it to the shower/toilet space, to the fridge area, then the microwave, desk, and out the door.

The other had a man in it. A man wearing a rubber suit with an IPSET: Dr Harper-Girard badge. A man with thick black sludge pumping into him through the tube set into his mouth. Even though his eyes were crossed, even though there was blood pouring from his nostrils and tar-like slime pooling at his chin, I knew his face as well as I knew my own.

Because, despite a few more wrinkles and a little more male pattern baldness, it was.

We'd been running so hard and fast that both of us had to stop and retch when we found ourselves back in the pit. I do remember that it was me who took Leona's hand the second time. Seeing my dead self in some kind of stasis pod broke me. I think it was also the final piece of the *"who was the Dr Harper-Girard Freddy shot"* puzzle. This snapped Leona too, I think, because she didn't resist. She didn't stop to ask me why or swear in French. She just ran with me.

She ran with me all the way to the hire car. She ran with me all the way to the airport, on the flight back to London, to my old home. She's been running with me since the IPSET spooks showed up outside our house, even though we changed our names and went to great lengths to burn every paper trail. She was running with me all the way until early this morning, when they finally got her. We'd been moving around the UK for the last four years. We thought we'd be safe somewhere as remote and forgotten as Dovercourt. We were wrong. They're nearly at the car I'm hiding under now. They've been chasing me on foot across Essex County all day. It's nearly midnight. I'm tired. Part of me thinks I should give myself in. I won't though.

They keep saying they just want to talk, to ask a couple of questions about what we'd seen in Nevada. They keep telling me that Leona is safe. I believe them, but I'm still not going. I know that once I do, everything will be fine, and somehow in a few years, I'll find myself agreeing to be frozen in that damn time machine. Someone, probably Leona, will convince me that if we can set the awakening date just a little earlier, we'll be able to change things this time around.

There'll be some reason we had to go back too, of course. Some apocalyptic event so disturbing, so horrific, that decent people like Leona and I will agree to travel in a time machine powered by a temporally displaced human in an arcane mask.

That's why I'm hiding under the car. Destiny has called me, but I don't want to answer. I don't want to join IPSET. I don't want to save the world. I already tried, and I already failed. The version of me that got out from under the car is dead, filled with black sludge somewhere and rotting in a stasis chamber underneath the Nevada desert. I know it won't be any different when it's my turn.

If you're reading this, please, somehow, volunteer yourself. I know one of you will be crazy enough to want to try this suicide mission in my place. I know there'll be plenty of you who hate your own mundane lives enough to pick apart the IPSET puzzle, to give your life purpose by sacrificing it to prevent whatever this Armageddon is. You might hate your life enough to want that. I don't. I've only got a few decades left before I'm officially old. I wanted to spend them with Leona. Just not like this. I don't want to die as a *"distemporal asset"*. I don't want to spend my last seconds with a toxic purge fluid being flushed through my system, choking and in agony because my younger self allows Freddy to set off a security failsafe. I don't want to kiss Leona goodbye in the future, knowing what happens when she opens the hatch in the past. Our future selves weren't *that much* older than us. We'd finally found each other after all these decades. We deserve more time. It's not fair.

I'm a coward, and I'm not ashamed of that. I don't want to die like my future self; cold and alone, outside of my own present. I refuse for that to be my destiny. I'm not a martyr, or a savior, or some kind of chrononaut. I'm just a guy. A scared, helpless guy, hiding under a car.

Please, someone else, step up and be the tragic hero of this story. I never asked to discover my future self in a time machine at an archaeological dig.

THE EVIDENCE

I knew when I married him that Don was a good man, but not a smart one. That's partly why I loved him. It's also why he was such a good fit for the Marathon County Sheriff's Department. Kind-hearted, followed orders; too happy obeying to ask questions. Exactly what you want in a cop.

I fell in love with Don for a lot of reasons. He always stood up straight, always showered twice a day, ironed every damn shirt he wore. He was a proud man, and it was those little things he was proud of that I found so damn adorable. Gentle, too. Never raised a hand to anyone unless he absolutely had to. What didn't matter to me was that Don had never been the sharpest knife in the rack. I always knew Don wasn't smart. I didn't think he was stupid. I learned how wrong I was when he came home one night with that damn statue.

When I asked him why on Earth he'd bring evidence from a crime scene home in the first place, he told me he didn't know. I was sympathetic at first; you know? Not angry, not *terrified* like I am now. I thought he'd been unable to part with it because of some kind of post-traumatic stress. Like I said, my Don was kind-hearted. "*Soft*" was the word my father, who definitely *isn't* kind-hearted, used. That's another part of what made Don such a good cop in these parts, though. You needed softness when settling violent disputes between drunk couples or picking up strung-out tweakers from the curb all day, especially when every perp knew you since you were knee-high to a grasshopper.

Marathon County *ain't* the kind of place where nights like the one he found the statue happened.

It was a triple homicide. Don had dealt with his share of murders, but never a multiple body count. I saw how rattled he was as soon as he damn near fell through the door. I'd been married to him for eight years, dating for six before that. High school sweethearts, that old chestnut. In none of those 14 journeys round the sun had I ever seen my man so pale, so shaking, so distraught. You know them photos of the WW1 soldiers with the thousand-yard stare? Yeah, if you do, you've seen the look my Don had on his face that night. He didn't say anything to me the entire evening. He sat down, put the statue on the table, downed a glass of water, then went to bed. Not one single word in my direction. Didn't even meet my damn gaze. I didn't find out from Don what happened but from his boss, Sheriff Harwurst, an old family friend (as most folk round here are).

Harwurst painted a grim picture over the landline. Don had answered a call about a domestic disturbance from one of the other apartments in that complex. He'd arrived to find the door to the crime scene, apartment 19, hanging from its hinges. You could smell the blood in the hallways, apparently, but did Don stop and call for backup? No, he didn't. Not my Don. Daddy called him soft, but Daddy was an idiot. Don was kind, warm, had no roughness to his edges. What he didn't lack, though, was balls.

That's another reason I loved him—he had (metaphorically speaking) the biggest cannons I'd ever known to a man to swing. A gentle, fearless giant. So yeah, I had no reason to doubt Harwurst's recount of Don running *into* the apartment, firearm raised, ready to save a life, end one, or probably both. Harwurst didn't arrive until later, after Don didn't radio back. They sent the whole armed unit. They feared the worst, but what they got was… well, it was worse than any worst folk round here usually imagine.

Don hadn't answered because he was curled in the fetal position in one corner of the studio apartment. I'd never seen Don cry; men round these parts *don't,* generally speaking. I didn't believe that part of Harwurst's story until he described the carnage he found Don amongst.

As I said, it was a triple homicide. Don't ask me who done it because they still ain't caught the sick sonofabitch. The victims were all male, all tweakers too, most likely given the neighborhood Don found them in. Finding three bodies would have shit anyone up, and that's the truth, but Don was a cop. Three bodies in and of themselves ain't usually enough to rattle cops, especially ones with a few years under his belt like he had.

No, it *wasn't* finding three bodies that rocked my husband worse than I'd ever seen. It's what had been done to them *before* they died.

The sick bastard who killed them had made some… alterations. That's how Harwurst described it to me before I'd sworn at him so much; he gave up being coy about details. I must admit, I *still* regret browbeating him into the full truth. He's a good man, and by the time I put down the phone, I realized he hadn't been trying to withhold anything from me as some kind of commentary on the emotional fragility of my gender. He didn't want to talk it out in full because he was shit-ass scared, too.

It was impossible to identify the victims for a simple reason. They'd had their faces removed. The killer had stripped back the flesh until nothing but bone and muscle remained. They'd been thorough too; tongues, jaws, teeth, eyes, noses. Almost everything that wasn't the skull itself had been carved off. The wounds weren't clean either. They were jagged, ripped, the kind of wounds made slowly and painfully by a blade far too blunt for butchery.

Harwurst's vivid description of the meatless skulls was in itself enough to buckle my knees so badly I had to sit down. His recollection didn't stop there, though.

The faceless corpses had been positioned kneeling in a circle, facing inwards. At its center was a compost-heap of scraps of skin, bone, muscle, teeth, hair, eyes… all the offshoots and trimmings leftover post-mutilation. Other parts had been removed too. Every finger and toenail had been pulled out, hamstrings had gouged out and discarded to keep them immobile. There were also gaping holes between each of their legs. You don't need schooling in Criminology to figure the message behind leaving your man as anatomically endowed as a Ken doll. The swollen bruising around the castration wounds meant they'd been made when they were alive by Harwurst's reckoning. He also reckoned the horizontal gashes across each of their stomachs weren't made post-mortem, either. "*Disemboweled*" ain't a word I ever expected to hear in Marathon County, not on our side of the TV screen at least. The offcuts and offal from every wound and opening had been added to the mound of gore. I nearly puked when Harwurst told me there was enough of it stacked up to reach his waist.

The walls of the studio apartment were caked in blood. Every bit of furniture was smashed, most thrown across the room, judging from the dents and holes in the cheap plaster walls. A CD player had been left on, playing Gustav Holst's *Mars* on repeat (which Harwurst sheepishly admitted he had to cross-reference to the track number against the list on the CD case to figure). They'd found Don curled in a ball amongst the carnage, sobbing at the incomprehensible violence and destruction around him.

Harwurst sent him straight back to the station to shower and head home. That's why he was calling to check in. The sheriff *didn't* know about the statue. I figured at the time it would be best to keep it that way.

Christ, maybe Don wasn't the *only* idiot in this house…

We didn't talk about the statue until the next morning. I didn't even register it that first night. My husband had come home traumatized by an event so horrific I was traumatized just from listening to someone recount the traumatic details. That's three levels of trauma I was dealing with; trauma cubed. Excuse me for caring more about my man's emotional well-being than some trinket he stole.

I fell asleep holding Don while listening to him quietly sob. It was the first and only time I'd ever been the big spoon. He wasn't in my arms when I awoke. I found him downstairs, sitting at the kitchen table, staring at the statue. *That's* when I noticed it properly for the first time.

It was placed atop the mound of viscera when Don found it. It was made of a material that resembled jade, if jade was the bright orange of magma. It didn't feel like jade to the touch, either. Despite looking smooth and polished it felt… rough? Rough doesn't feel like quite the right word, though. Charged is more appropriate, almost like it *felt* how battery acid *tastes*.

The statue was of two men standing back-to-back. They were, to put it delicately, *huge*. They were a level of swollen that nobody could argue was healthy, attractive, or in any way a shape that human beings were meant to be. Their stomachs sagged to their knees; ankles folded around feet so tumor-like that the stubby toes poking from beneath them were barely visible. There was no part of them that didn't sag, bulge, or droop, and all of it had been captured in hideously accurate detail by the sculptor. Every pore was visible, every hair-thin wrinkle and fold of skin plain to see. If the subject matter wasn't so damn unsettling, I'd have said it was one of the best bits of art I'd ever seen.

The sculptor hadn't given the orange-jade men faces. They had heads, sure, but both were depicted wearing tight bags or sacks that obscured their features. What *wasn't* obscured were the painfully tight-looking lengths of barbed wire wrapped around the bags. Just looking at it made my face itch, my insides queasy.

As I said, Don was staring at it when I found him downstairs. I asked him about it, and he said he didn't know why he picked it up. Shock, he reckoned. He couldn't stop thinking about it last night, he told me. The statue, not the… the incident. At the time, I figured the statue fixation was some kind of coping mechanism. I know better now.

I was gentle the first time I told him to take it back to the station. Reminded him kindly that having it was *technically* illegal, but given the circumstances, Sheriff Harwurst was sure to look the other way. Don agreed to take it back later that day, and after he went down to the station to file his report of the previous night's incident, he was calmer.

For the rest of that first week, I genuinely believed that was the last I'd see of it. Then the weekend came.

Don and I had a Friday Night Date Night agreement that was sacrosanct. Had been since high school. I'd given him a fair bit of slack during that first week. He was despondent, withdrawn, distant. Again, I put it down to the trauma. It's the *exact reason* I picked his favorite restaurant, *Mac's Steak & Brat Smack-Down Buffet*, for our meal. To cheer him up, and because he knew I hate *Mac's Steak & Brat Smack-Down Buffet* with a passion.

You can imagine my anger when I was left waiting there like a jilted high school kid for three hours.

I was willing to look past a lot, but failing to follow Friday Night Date Night tradition wasn't on that list. Don was supposed to meet me straight from work, as he did every week. I'm sure you can also imagine how much calling to find he *wasn't there* further stoked my it. The final nail in my rage coffin was where I eventually *did* find him. More specifically, what I found him with.

He was sitting at his desk in his study. You can probably already guess what I caught him doing. Staring at that damn statue.

Don didn't jump, didn't flinch, didn't even blink when I threw open the door. It took a good ten minutes of me yelling at him for him to mumble an apology. No amount of berating could conjure an explanation for why he'd not gone to work that day, or where he'd gone after I heard him leave the house that morning. I gave up digging for a reason why he still had the statue after an hour or two.

I felt bad after my outburst. Don had gone through a lot, and when I calmed down, I rationalized that I'd probably been unrealistic in my expectations of how quickly he'd bounce back. I apologized, and he agreed to return that statue and speak to Harwurst about some time off. I watched him take it with him in the car the next morning, just to be sure.

Again, I thought that was the last I'd see of it.

Don was still withdrawn and sullen for the next few weeks, but I started to show flashes of his former self here and there. He didn't miss Friday Night Date Night again, that's for damn certain. I'm not a snoop either, and I always liked to give Don his privacy, but I have to admit I did search his study once or twice when he was at work during that first week. Just to make sure he'd *actually* made good on his promise.

By the time the night of the incident was almost a month behind us, I'd almost thought we were getting back to normality. That's when I got the second call from Harwurst.

Don hadn't returned to work since his week of recuperative leave. At first, I argued. I saw him leave the house every morning, I said, uniform and badge ready in his bag. It was when Harwurst started mentioning how easy it was to lose said badge that I stopped playing incredulous wife and started listening proper. I didn't ask about the statue, both because I didn't want to get Don fired, and because I already knew the answer.

When Don got back from "work" I was midway through tearing his study apart. He tried playing dumb at first, until I mentioned the call from Harwurst. He broke down at that, and confessed at least to his lies about his whereabouts. I took what he said then as the truth. I still feel like a fool about that.

He told me he'd been in bars, drinking. That he couldn't forget about the incident. That's why he was so tired all the time, he told me, so withdrawn, so unfocused. I also bought the lie about him throwing the statue in a river. Well, no, I'm not giving myself enough credit there. I *didn't* believe him. I just *wanted* to. So much so that I made the unconscious decision to just leave it, to live in the fantasy land where my brave husband was a recovering alcoholic cop despite never smelling of booze or spending a dime.

It only took two nights for that fantasy to come crumbling down.

I was woken by a crash outside our window. Nothing major you understand, probably just raccoons or the wind knocking some dead foliage our way. It was realizing that Don wasn't lying next to me that got my feed out of bed and treading as quiet as possible round the house. I heard him before I saw him, and because of that, I managed to see him without seeing me. I don't know what would have happened if he had. I don't think I'd still be alive to write this, that's for damn certain.

He was standing in the downstairs bathroom, facing the mirror. It was the look in his eyes that made tears instantly fall from my own, that clasped my hand to my mouth to stifle a terrified whimper. I'd never seen that look on my Don's face. I'd never seen it on *anyone's*.

Evil. It's not a word I ever thought I'd find myself using in seriousness, or outside of church. It's the only one I have, though.

Don never smiled with his teeth. His reflection was grinning so wide I could see all of them, even the molars. His normally narrow eyes were stretched to perfect bulging circles. Ventricles and veins pulsed on their surface, and his left eyelid twitched without warning in an erratic, arrhythmic pattern. His nostrils were flared almost to the point of being level with his cheekbones, brows raised until it crushed his forehead against his hairline. The muscles and folds of the version of my Don in that reflection were stretched back so far that, if I couldn't see the back of his head from my perch on the first-floor landing, I'd have sworn someone was holding him upright by the scalp.

He was talking to himself, repeating a single word over and over. "Perfection". It's a word I'm all too familiar with now, but that night it raised nothing but terrified confusion. He was dragging his razor across the mirror, like he was trying to shave the face on the other side of it. Over and over, he dragged the blades across the glass. The squeaks and scrapes set my teeth on edge and the vertebrae of my spine shuddered.

I couldn't stand to watch for more than a few minutes. As I said, the only word I had, I *have,* is evil. It wasn't light that danced in those bulging eyes. It wasn't the happy spark and joy I'd fallen in love with. What twinkled in Don's eyes the night was a cold, dead lust, a lifeless urge for things too foul for me or you to comprehend. A small part of me wishes I'd been carrying my phone, that I'd taken a photo. Unless you saw those eyes for yourself, the above probably doesn't make sense. In fact, I kind of hope it doesn't. If it does, and you've seen eyes like my... like Don's, then your life is already, or about to be, as fucked as mine.

I couldn't sleep that night. When Don eventually came back to bed a few hours later, I just lay trembling in the dark, waiting until his snoring started to burst into stifled sobs. I left him a note when he went out the next morning. Told him he needed to sort his shit out, and that I was going to stay with my sister to clear my head. I couldn't tell him the *real* reason I wanted to get out of there, that I couldn't close my eyes without seeing a version of his face so terrifying it made the thought of being around him induce a panic attack.

A week went by before I started to get worried about the fact he hadn't called. After a while, I started to think that I'd maybe been half asleep when I saw him, or that I'd dreamt it (God, I wish that were the fucking case). Once more my negativity turned inward, and I started beating myself up over my "overreaction". Don was unwell, and I'd abandoned him, I told myself. I was a terrible wife. I'd left him alone when he needed me most.

My sister didn't share my view. She had made me promise not to go back to him groveling, not to make the first move, not to be the one that reaches out to break the ice. I broke that promise on the Saturday morning by phoning Don; and broke it again when I went home upon the call going straight to voicemail.

It had been a week since I'd last stood in my living room. Looking at the state of it, Don had abandoned it himself not long after. The whole house was trashed. Every piece of furniture had been pulled apart, or thrown across the room, or in some cases taken to with a sledgehammer by the looks of things. There were splatterings of blood here and there, pools of it forming around sharp metal edges and splintered wood where he'd pulled furniture and appliances apart with his bare hands. My tears started silently falling almost the exact moment I crossed the threshold into our once-beautiful home. I couldn't allow myself to believe my Don, my gentle caring Don, was capable of this level of wanton destruction, this carnage. I *wouldn't* believe it.

I had to tip-toe over broken glass, wood, and plaster in almost every room. A thick cloud of dust sprang from wherever my foot fell, and there wasn't a single room that didn't stink of urine, rotting food, or both. He'd done that too, you see. He'd done it on our upturned couch, on the inside of our beaten-in fridge, and in the drawer where I kept our wedding photos. My tears weren't silent as the mental images grew more and more vivid. Each room gave enough new evidence for my imagination to make an ever-clearer montage of Don, with his bulging eyes and tooth-filled grin, ripping apart the life we'd built together in the most destructive, most barbaric way he possibly could.

This was *not* my Don. It couldn't be. But it was.

It was his study that broke me. When I found it, I could do nothing but fall to my knees and weep. Unlike the rest of the house, the study was more or less intact. In here, it seemed Don had decided to create rather than destroy. He'd built himself an effigy on his desk, a crude replica of two large, back-to-back figures I recognized immediately. I can't bring myself to write what he made them out of. My Don might be… well, he might be the reason all this happened, but I care enough for my memory of him that I *won't* conjure the mental image of him using his bare hands to make a sculpture out of… well, out of the *other* kind of body waste.

I could smell it as soon as I reached the upper floor landing. It wasn't the disgustingness of it that pushed the last of my composure from me. No. It was the mental image of my once-proud Don, of the bestial, primal, horrific thing he'd become. It was the thought of the man I admired above all others broken, wretched, and weak. Despite my terror and anger at our destroyed home, all I wanted to do was help him.

I was about to phone the only person I could think of, Harwurst, when something on Don's desk made me pause. It was a receipt for a storage unit on the edge of town. I knew the address; a friend of ours kept some of her ex-husband's stuff there after a messy divorce. I shouldn't have listened to my gut. It was my gut that told me *not* to phone Harwurst. It was my gut that told me to put my phone away, to go downstairs, and get back in the car. It was my gut that convinced me I could help Don, that I could get through to him, and that once I found him at the storage unit, we'd reconcile and he'd get better, that all this could be put behind us.

If anyone tells you to always trust your gut, don't listen to them.

It was easy to find which of the few dozen storage units Don had rented. It was late by the time I arrived, and it was the only one in the lot with a light on. Even if it hadn't been, the wiry old man in the booth was more than happy to throw the spare set of keys at me once I explained who I was. *"That creepy damn guy with the bulging fucking eyes"* had come to visit his unit a few days back, and none of the booth attendants had seen him leave. When I questioned why the police hadn't been called already, the man in the booth scratched his chin, looking sheepish. They were scared of him, too scared to phone the cops. Seems ridiculous, right? It wouldn't if you'd seen his face in the mirror that night like I had. To me, the attendants' fear made *perfect* sense. I asked when the creepy guy, Don, first took out rental on the unit. The wiry man told me it had been a few weeks prior, coinciding with the day Don had thrown the damn statue in the river.

Obviously, I was putting the dots together in my head. I'd blinded myself to a lot that I should have seen coming, but I wasn't foolish enough to *still* believe *that* lie. As much as it made my stomach plummet, I knew that when I found Don the orange-jade effigy would be with him. I thanked the wiry attendant before heading in the direction of Don's unit. The man in the booth seemed sympathetic. He let me know gently but firmly that if I wasn't back in an hour, he would phone the police. Said he couldn't rest with my death on his conscience, no matter how scared of *"that creepy fucking tweaker"* he was. I didn't argue.

Don's unit, Unit 19, was at the very edge of the lot. I couldn't hear anything except for the distant groan of traffic and the faint crinkle of a chain-link fence catching the wind as I approached. It was a cold night. This wasn't unusual with it being November, but for some reason, I became acutely aware of it in the near-silence. I could feel, hear, and see my rapid, shallow breaths. I managed to get at least six into each footstep, the fog of my lung's warmth billowing from my lips. The handle to the door of Unit 19 was cold too, but much colder than the air. It was the kind of frigid that meant it almost burned to the touch. If my fingers weren't already trembling when they wrapped around it, they would have been by the time I'd finished turning.

The units themselves were quite spacious as far as storage units go. Each had two rooms; a short hallway where one entered, and accessible via an inner door at the hallway's other end was the storage area. The storage area had a rolling garage door to allow goods in and out, of course, but this could only be opened from the inside.

It was for the inner door that I needed the key. The walk from the outside door to the other end of the hallway was one of the longest of my life. Mainly because, in here, I could hear Don.

He was bawling. Not crying, not sobbing, bawling. Like a toddler that had lost its parents, and not in the "*at the grocery store*" way. It was completely unrestrained in a way that I don't think I've *ever* heard an adult, man or woman, shed tears. It was a sound of pure despair; one you don't realize you're glad you've never heard until you do. The emotions that swelled in my chest when I heard it were as strong as they were complex. Sympathy, fear, disgust, care. The need to save and the need to flee started an intense battle within me the moment those sniveling wails hit my eardrums.

Don's choking moans made the writing on the walls a hundred times more unsettling too. I'll tell you that for nothing.

It must have taken him days. The same word across every inch of brick, over and over and over. You can probably guess the word already. Perfection. What that word meant to Don, I wouldn't know until the inner door to the storage area creaked open. I had to get there first. Even though the hallway was only about 10 feet in length, this was still a challenge. The cries and retches echoing off the dark bricks made putting one foot in front of the other a conscious effort. My mind wouldn't let me do anything but fixate on Don's reflection in the mirror; those eyes filled with their cold, dead lust. With every foot the distance between the second door and I shrank, the pictures behind my eyes grew more vivid. Over and over, my sadistic conscience replayed the reel of Don smashing our possessions, of him urinating on our wedding album, of him tearing apart our house until his hands bled. Tears were streaming down my face, each one for the proud man I'd never known not to stand fully straight, and for the sniveling hunched creature I feared he'd become.

After the key clicked in the lock, and the door to the storage area swung open, I knew straight away that the levels of terror in my anticipation were nowhere near enough.

The smell hit me in the face like a sack full of drowned rats. I actually took a step back, gagging and trying to pull my shirt up over my mouth to cover my nostrils. It was the same stenches Don had left in the house but magnified a thousand-fold. There were new layers to it here, though, layers of mold, of decay, of rotting meat. There was no light on the other side. Light from the grimy bulb in the hallway barely made it half a foot before the shadows consumed it. The stench wasn't the only thing to assault me from the shadows, though. With it came the flies.

There were *dozens* of them, *hundreds*. If it hadn't been for Don's crying, I'd probably have heard their collective buzzing from the hall. I screamed, violently fanning my arms in front of me to stop any of the fat black buzzing lumps from finding their way into my mouth or nostrils. My anticipation was now a full-blown dread. Every artery thrummed from the sheer force of my frightened pulse. Fast, deep gulps oversaturated my brain with oxygen. Black spots started tickling the corners of my vision. Consciousness threatened to leave. My knees were midway to buckling when a realization slammed a fresh load of adrenaline through my veins.

The moment I'd screamed, Don had stopped.

I called out his name, but there was no answer. I could hear him in the darkness. He was standing somewhere on the other side of the room. His breaths were slow, heavy, and ragged enough to hear even over the horde of insects I'd freed when I opened the door. When he didn't answer a further two times, I found my fingers tightening around my phone. Not to find help, but to find light. My palms were sweating so much that I nearly dropped the damn thing as I swiped my passcode onto the screen. My trembling index digit missed the button for the flashlight twice before finding it.

The *real* screaming, the screaming that meant my ears were ringing for a solid week after that night, started as soon as it did.

The first thing the beam of phone light revealed was the floor. The concrete was caked in both the bodily excretions the stench led me to expect, *and* large patches of dark red crust I recognized but really didn't want to. There were glistening chunks strewn across the floor, chunks of greying-brown that wriggled with maggots. Some of the chunks had hair, others had fingernails. One had a dead, glassy eye.

In the center of the room was the damn statue. The floor beneath it was clear, immaculate even. Don had taken great care to ensure that none of his mess, the destruction left in the wake of the man he'd become, touched it. I would have picked the damn thing up and smashed it right then, but I had another priority. Even though I knew I'd find them here, the two orange figures weren't who I came for.

Don was standing at the other end of the room, facing the wall. The light crept up his naked, trembling body. Every inch climbed revealed a fresh wave of dread. My Don, who'd showered twice daily and took great pride in his self-maintenance, was caked in every substance spattering the floor. My beautiful Don, who'd never let himself slouch even an inch, was now hunched over on a bent and crooked spine. My darling Don, covered head-to-toe in deep pus-filled scratches, burns, and blisters. The full image of the back of his naked body was too much. I yelled something. I forget what. What I said isn't important. What's important is the sound of words coming from my own mouth startled me. Startled me so much that I dropped the damn phone.

I was only in the dark for a few seconds. I'd dropped to my knees to search around in the muck almost before I'd heard the clattering squelch of it hitting the floor. I found it in no time at all, pulling myself to my feet and pointing the light once more in front of me.

Straight into a pair of bulging dead eyes and a grin that showed every tooth.

Somehow, I *didn't* repeat my clumsy mistake when I fell over backward. The phone stayed in my hand; the horror-revealing beam of light locked on the monstrous figure that was once my husband. Even hunched and crooked, he towered over me. The look in his eyes let me know what I needed to; that it was over, that it had been the moment he was unlucky enough to be the cop who answered the call to that damn apartment. I remember begging him to get it over with, for him to kill me and end this nightmare. He didn't say anything back. He just stood there, naked and caked in depravity, grinning down at me with that… that *evil* face. I wish I could say that it wasn't Don but… but it was. Something in me knew that my Don, my beautiful Don, wasn't trapped by that face. It was his, no less so than the soft little half-smile I fell in love with. He wasn't possessed; he hadn't been taken over or inhabited by some demonic entity. This was him now. This was my Don. This was what he'd become, what he always would be.

In my mind's eye, I could see him pouncing. I tensed, ready to fight him off as he tried to tear me apart with his bare hands. The moment never came. Twisted as it sounds, part of me *still* wishes it had, all these years later. What he did instead was far, far worse.

With a single fluid motion, Don reached with both hands and grabbed the back of his head. Grinning down at me, left eye twitching, he muttered one, single word.

"Perfection."

Then he pulled.

My screaming had been caught in my throat while I was down on the floor with the dried blood, urine, and feces. It found its way back out as Don's muscular forearms wrenched his scalp. Even though my lungs were hitting decibels they never had, I could still hear the tearing. It started at his neck; a thin line of scarlet born on the bulge of his throat that flashed up to his jawline within a fraction of a fraction of a second. The wet crackling snaps of flesh prizing itself apart grew louder the further Don's arms stretched from his skull. His scalp, hair, and face went with them. I retched at the sight of his eyes rolling back in their sockets, vanishing from view as the face around them when limp and sagged. Within a few seconds, he'd dragged the skin of his head and clean off, sliding it from bone and muscle as easily as removing a hood.

Exposed teeth, bulging lidless eyes, gaping open nostrils. None of the nightmare-inducing anatomical horrors I'd expected were waiting for me under the facial skin Don tossed over his shoulder like a wet paper towel. This next part I know sounds impossible and is the *exact reason* I've spent the last five years in *St Dionysus' Home for the Incurably Mad*. This scrap of paper might be the only chance I get to tell my story, though, and I'm *not* going to leave anything out.

Underneath Don's freshly removed face were two heads where one should have been. Two squashed heads that writhed and undulated to separate themselves and inflate to their full size. Two heads wrapped tight in orange plastic bags; bags kept in place by constricting lengths of rusted barbed wire…

I was already running to the door by that point, although my feet found it difficult to find purchase with the muck all over the floor. More than once, I fell over in those few seconds before I finally found the hall. I got far too many glimpses of those two… those two… *things,* clawing their way out of Don's body. Somehow, he didn't buckle until the very end. The two barbed wired crowned lumps clawed and fought their way from his neck, both against Don's flesh and each other. His chest and torso bulged and stretched as they pulled more of themselves from whatever hell they'd risen from. I heard ribs crack as one of the orange-headed twins wrenched an arm free. The back of my neck felt warm wetness as the other one punched through Don's stomach with a gnarled foot.

I shouldn't have done it, but I couldn't stop myself from taking one last, mortified look over my shoulder before I started running until they found me on the freeway three days later with bleeding feet.

The two figures from the statue were standing above their likeness. Don was... gone. Completely eviscerated. I don't know how, and I don't know why, but they'd used him as some kind of portal or opening or gateway. I'd love to think that wasn't what he wanted, but... I still remember that face. His face. I think that was his plan all along. The moment he found that statue, it had its hold on him, and I think this was always his endgame. The two men he'd birthed into the world with his madness would have dwarfed him. Each was easily over 7 feet tall, and nearly as wide. Even over the stench left by Don's activities, I could smell the rancid mucus that covered them, the acrid ammonia burning that oozed from them with each of their labored, bag-covered breaths.

As I said, I *wish* I'd never looked back. Now every time I shut my eyes, the first thing I see is that image, of them standing there in the blood and shit and piss, of one of them raising their tumorous hand and pointing at me...

The next few years are a blur. By the time the waking nightmares started to subside I'd already been here at *St Dionysus* for several years. I'd apparently been pretty... difficult, let's say, during my time here. It's taken another few years for them to trust me with a pen. I've bribed one of the orderlies. He's going to get this out there, type it up and put it online. Everyone thinks that *I* killed Don, and all those people. I was too out of it to give my side of the story. I *need* to tell my side. I *need* people to know, need *you* to know, what really happened.

I don't want to say what I bribed him with. I don't have much, you can use your imagination. Please make it worth it. I need the world to know. Not just because I'm innocent, but because those... those things... well, they're still out there. They have been all this time. If they could corrupt someone like my Don, make him become... make him do... *none* of you are safe. None of you.

I hope the orderly makes good on his end of the bargain. I hope you get to read this. I was going to tell you my name but there's no point. You don't believe me anyway, do you? I'll know my stories out there, and that's enough. I hope you get to read this because, one day, you might find a statue of two back-to-back men that feels like battery acid tastes. You might feel tempted to take that statue, to keep it.

Please, even if you don't believe me now, when you find that statue leave it be. Walk away from it. Pretend you never saw it and live your life. And if you see the two men with their bags and barbed wire… well, I'm sorry, but it's probably already too late.

DON'T LAUGH

I was attacked by a butt vampire. Don't stop reading. I *know*. Ridiculous. But if you've got a better name for the thing that ate my date an hour ago, I'd love to hear it. Mainly because that means you might know how to kill it. This would be useful information, because the damn thing followed me home. As I said, it's a butt-vampire. I literally cannot think of another name for it.

It stopped Benji and I when we were walking back from the restaurant. In case you were wondering; Italian, and delicious. It was our third date, which meant *you-know-what*. I was excited. It had been 7 months since I last had *you-know-what*. I needed it. It's still been 7 months, except now I'm covered in Benji's bodily fluids. Not the good kind of bodily fluids I wanted to be covered in tonight, either. We were walking together hand in hand. He was failing at telling jokes; I was pretending to laugh at them. It was late; the street was empty. That's what made it so easy to hear the tinkling.

"Hold on a second, Clara. Do you hear that?"

"Is that… wind chimes?"

It *was* wind chimes. They were coming from a side alley up ahead. From the kind of pokey space between two abandoned buildings you *definitely* don't walk down alone at night. Or during the day, but that's mainly because the piss smell was so bad my nose was wrinkling even from a good 10 feet away.

It *definitely wasn't* the kind of alley you heard wind chimes coming from. Nothing good came from alleys like that, even if the low tinkling was soothing (in a honeytrap kind of way). I tugged on Benji's hand, but I don't think he was as resistant to it as me.

I'll never know, because we'd only been listening to it for about ten seconds when the mime stepped out of the alley.

You can imagine a stereotypical street mime here, the French type from cartoons, because that's exactly how the heavy-set smiling man was dressed. Beret, striped shirt, white gloves, black slacks made of a non-descript inky fabric, the works. Well, *almost* the works. He was wearing large, square sunglasses in addition to the traditional ensemble. They didn't clash as much with the beret as you'd think. My grip on Benji's hand went cracked-knuckle tight the instant the black-and-white stripes bounded from the alleyway.

"Benji… let's go. It's late."

"Hold on a minute. It's street art."

"At eleven-thirty at night? *In Wisconsin?*"

"Yeah. Do you know what kind of street art happens in weird places late at night? The *cool* kind."

For a smart guy, Benji was dumb at a moment when dumb was stupid, and stupid meant deadly. It wasn't the "cool kind" of street art. I knew that straight away, mainly because the wind chime tinkling followed the Mime out of the shadows even though he wasn't holding any fucking wind chimes.

"Benji…"

"*Shh.*"

At the time, I was angry. I let go of his hand, slapping his arm, my brow suddenly furrowed. A snap decision was made that there would be no *you-know-what* that night. Although, apparently, not just by me.

I think the Mime knew it had Benji in its trance. It turned its smiling face towards me briefly, shrugged, then focused all of its attention on my date. A few loud *cracks* permeated the air as it flexed its neck, its press-lipped grin wide and brimming with a hungry malice. I couldn't tell you what I thought was going to happen. What I can tell you is that I'd never have put money on the Mime doing what it did next.

It danced. The strangest dance I've ever seen. Every limb moved in fluid arcs that felt both random and meticulously planned. White-gloved fingers juddered and twitched, twisting themselves into arthritic poses to the hidden beat of a silent melody. The honeytrap hypnosis intensified with every precise sway of the Mime's hips and pop-lock snap of its wrists. Even I was entranced by this point. My feet found roots in the cracked pavement, holding me in place as the black-and-white stripes weaved and gyrated in Benji's direction. The world seemed to slow around it. Sounds elongated and warped; the distant traffic noise stretching and deepening, retreating further to the edge of my hearing. Color drained from everything except the Mime. Even though he himself was monotone, my brain started to register all the colors possible in those horizontal stripes on his shirt. My eyes still reported the same monochromatic aesthetic, but my emotions fluttered as though I was face-to-face with a Rainbow.

"*Pretty...*"

I heard the words leave my lips, like I was seven again and had just discovered a pearl at the beach. Benji was gawping at the Mime, slack-jawed, a trickle of drool running from one corner of his mouth. Without warning, the Mime stopped wriggling. It was about three feet away from Benji when it halted and turned in one fluid movement. Before I could really make sense of what was happening, the Mime dropped his trousers.

The spell was broken instantly. For me, at least. Colors returned to their proper place; sounds remembered how they should assemble themselves in my ears. I stifled a scream.

There, on the Mime's pale ass cheeks, were a pair of red, glaring eyes. They blinked and rolled in their sockets. Sockets which were, exactly as you're imagining, each planted squarely in the center of a flabby lump of butt flesh. You're laughing right now, aren't you? I'm not going to tell you to go fuck yourself for that, even though you're going to feel *reeeal* bad about it when you find out what happened to Benji. But, yeah, I can't really chastise you too much. Initially, I did find it a little funny too. It's a funny mental image. After the shock wore off, I even let out a nervous little laugh (emphasis on little). Benji didn't, though. Benji was still drooling.

I screamed *for real* when the Mime bent over forwards. It wasn't funny anymore then. There was a wet *plop* when his palms hit the pavement. His butt-head reared up, the Mime stretching his knees and standing on tippy-toes until the anger-filled red eyes were level with Benji's naval. I grabbed Benji's hand again, tried pulling him away, tried running one last time, but it was no good. My legs didn't answer to me anymore, and it was clear Benji wasn't going to answer to anyone.

"Benji... Benji, we've got to run!"

I screamed again when the Mime looked over his shoulder and snarled at me. *"Calme-toi, salope. Le directeur nous entendra."*

His words were as thin, taunting, and French as his face. So terrified was I that, without thinking or even understanding, I obeyed the command. My hand slapped itself to my mouth. Fat blobs of saltwater cascaded from my eyes, rolling over my trembling fingers and falling with dull splats on the asphalt, pooling next to my date's saliva. Benji's vacant eyes were still fixed on those furious pupils on the Mime's gluteus maximus. Drool was still slithering from one corner of his mouth. He was smiling.

"Hur… hur… funny man."

The handsome idiot was swaying back and forth ever so slightly. His clammy palm didn't respond to mine trying to grab and pull it. That's why, when those ass-cheeks clapped themselves apart, he didn't react. I did. My feet were still glued to paving slabs, so I didn't fall so much as bend over backward at the knees. I was still screaming, and now I was far too horrified by the Mime's rear to pay any attention to the French expletives snarling from his face. Something shot out from between those cheeks. Something long, phlegm-coated, and undulating. Something that looked almost like a length of lower intestine, if lower intestines were lined with thousands of needle teeth. The spell on Benji was broken the moment it latched onto his belly. Unfortunately, it was far too late.

"Hurrr-OUCH—Clara what the fu-*OH MY GOD!*"

He was screaming by the time the sphincterous tube began pulsing and heaving. I could tell Benji's feet were just as rooted as mine. He didn't fall when he passed out, but curled in on himself; a shivering man-mushroom hunched down before those glaring red eyes. Slipping into unconsciousness meant his screaming stopped pretty quickly. Mine didn't. I was screaming throughout the long minutes as the toothy intestinal trunk sucked and squeezed at Benji's naval. It would whiplash violently every few seconds, each spasm accompanied by a low squelching rumble from his innards. Fountains of deep red splashed from his nostrils on every movement. Before long, great bubbling gulps of blood were coming from his mouth too; the sucking, slurping leech appendage mulching and squeezing his insides until the watery paste started to leak from every available orifice. My high-pitched shrieks were uninterrupted for every second of Benji getting smaller and smaller, continuous and unabating as I watched the Mime's belly swell and stretch. The horizontal stripes warped and distended as the gut ballooned. Even above my screaming and the wet crunches, I could *still* hear the wind chimes. The tinkling had reached crescendo, a white-noise tinnitus roar that oozed and ebbed with the monochromatic technicolor stripes.

"*Oh c'est bien. Tellement faim. Trop longtemps sans nourriture.*" The Mime's French rambling took on nauseating undertones as Benji deflated. It spoke with the kind of heavy breathlessness I'd planned to be panting with myself (before my romantic evening turned into a horrific nightmare, that is). I watched, half-hypnotized and unable to intervene as lumps of Benji moved down the long tube; squeezed and squelched down the muscular passage, the bumps marching along its length like unattended infants in the belly of an anaconda. My screaming had devolved into sob-peppered panicked gibberish by the time the Mime was finished. There was a final loud slurp. A prolonged, low, wet noise that echoed down the street of empty car showrooms and closed stores. With one movement, the Mime's trunk hoovered up the last of Benji's empty skin, swallowing the final remnants of my date up into its bowels.

I was babbling in tongues when the Mime pulled up his pants. The one final glance I caught of those red rear-facing eyes will be burned into my retina for decades, I'm sure. It's the way they were rolling back, the obvious look of euphoria, of ecstasy, of *satisfaction* in them. As mind-snapping as Benji's death was to witness, knowing his end had brought that... that *thing* so much pleasure made my revulsion a billion times stronger. I'd been nauseous *before* noticing it. How I wasn't immediately puking when I did, I'll never know. Go me, I guess. My panicked gibberish didn't stop when he sat down on the sidewalk opposite me, patting his distended, swollen belly.

"*Désolé. Je ne joue pas normalement avec ma nourriture. D'habitude, j'aime attendre que tu sois seul. Mais ce salaud de Bramfield m'a affamé pendant des mois. Je ne peux pas me permettre d'être sélectif.*"

Then the Mime did something horrifying. He *smiled* at me. It was then I noticed the other inconsistency, the unsettling aspect of his face I'd been too entranced by the wind chimes and subsequent date-munching to register. His teeth *weren't* teeth. They were nubs of hardened sinew on a muscular membrane, one that stretched between his lips, folding out of sight when his jaw wasn't open. But, if he had no throat, how was he…

My question was answered when he removed his sunglasses. I didn't have screams left in me anymore. That's why I could hear the wet grinding from his belly, a soft whirring just like a blender (if you'd made a blender out of bones and wrapped it in rotting flesh). What made me retch wasn't the sound, though. It was what lay behind the Mime's tinted lenses. Because, you see, he didn't have eyes in those sockets. He had mouths. Two puckered, anus-sized mouths, complete with eyelid-thin lips and baby-small teeth. The Mime belched. A horrific smell of burning hair wafted up from the twin ocular throats. Once more I was fighting back nausea, and once more it was inspired by disgust more than fear. Then, without warning, he vomited.

It started at his neck. The last time I'd had *you-know-what* was with Dean Harwurst. Dean was into British nature documentaries, and once we'd watched one on Bullfrogs. You ever seen a bullfrog stretch out its throat to intimidate predators? Imagine that, but on a French street mime. The bleached skin of his thick neck ballooned, newly acquired potbelly shrinking with more jaw-clenching wet squelches as his head inflated. As for the Mimes' jaw, it simply bent to accommodate the swelling neck and lower face. It flexed itself to make room with an elasticity no bone should possess. The membrane between lips was fully visible, the cartilage pseudo-teeth spread further and further apart. Beneath the thin skin I could see a yellowish-white liquid churning, filling the empty cavity between the Mime's displaced ears.

I had just enough time to register all that when he heaved.

The eye-mouths opened. Twin torrents of pus-colored sludge gushed from the lips on either side of his nose. The flood was hot, steam cascaded from it, the splashes that lapped across my screaming form burned like fresh coffee. The hurling continued for a full minute. Doesn't seem like much, but when you're on the other end of the equivalent of a person being fed through a wood chipper, it's an eternity. Far too much time to pass between the torrent starting and the bullfrog neck returning to normal proportions after the mime finished dousing me in the bloodless, liquidized remains of Benji.

The purging part of his horrifying bulimic feeding must have broken the spell on my feet, because I found that I was running down the road. So was the Mime. He was banging on the windows of my car while I was fumbling for the keys, screaming at me in French from alternating eye-mouths. I reversed over him, but it did no good. So distracted was I by the sight of him running after my beat-up Ford Escort faster than any man should that I almost crashed into a tree.

But of course, the Mime isn't a man, is he? He's a butt-vampire.

What else would you call it?

It hypnotized us, as a vampire would. It's pale and pasty, like a vampire is. It killed Benji by draining all his blood, which is what vampires are stereotypically known for. The fact it has a backward digestive system and mouths for fucking eyes is irrelevant; facts are facts, it ticks the vampire boxes.

That's why I've barricaded myself inside my apartment. The damn thing followed me home. I knew I shouldn't have moved so close to downtown. I could walk the distance in less than half an hour. Me, with my feeble and not-really-that-fast human legs. I had barely five minutes to drag the refrigerator in front of the door before I heard shrill French expletives coming from the parking lot outside.

That's the thing, you see. I live in one of those units where there are no inside hallways. Every front door opens to the outside world. If the butt-vampire is indeed a vampire and not a butt-something-much-worse, I'll be safe when the sun rises. If not, then... well, I'm fucked, aren't I? That's why I'm writing this, which I'm trying to get my story out there. If you've come across a butt-vampire before, and it's not a vampire, please let me know. I've been sharpening a stake on the off chance it's one of those vampires that sunlight only slows down but doesn't kill. I just thank God I live in the kind of neighborhood where the crime is bad enough for barred windows and doors that don't fuck about.

So yeah, a butt-vampire ate my date. It's outside my apartment right now, shrieking at me to open up. It'll be dawn in an hour and if it's not gone by then, I'm going to have to deal with it. Anyone got some good tips on how?

SPONTANEOUS HUMAN MALNUTRITION

When the time comes, don't believe your local news. I don't care what the doctors, teachers, police, my parents, or anyone else in this backward-ass town says. There's *no such thing* as Spontaneous Human Malnutrition.

Fuck, you probably haven't even heard of it. Well, no, of course you haven't heard of it. It's *not fucking real.* Spontaneous Human Malnutrition. SHM. Those three letters didn't just ruin my last year of middle school. They've ruined my damn life.

It's like every adult in town has gone mad. People don't just… they don't…

Fuck. Fuckety fucksticks. How to even begin?

It started during the Covid lockdowns. It wasn't until the fifth or sixth case that the local news started putting the pieces together. That's three weeks after Grant and I started our investigation, *bee tee dubz*. We knew something was up from the third victim. Why? Because the third victim was Doug's Mom.

Doug is (or was) the third member of our cafeteria-loser Musketeers set-up. When his mom… when whatever SMH *actually is* happened to her, she was in the background of our weekly D&D Zoom session. Doug was shaking dice and praying to the nerd gods for a critical when a weird noise came from his audio. It was barely half a second long, almost too quick to notice, but it was *loud.* Like, real fucking loud. So loud that Doug jumped a few inches in his seat and dropped the dice.

Grant and I never found out if Doug hit that crit. His blonde bowl-cut whipped away from the screen before we heard the clattering of dice on polished wood. Me and Grant didn't really care too much about killing cave trolls anymore, though. Both of us were glued to the scene playing out in Doug's kitchen.

The noise had come from Doug's Mom. She'd stumbled into view, clutching the kitchen sink. She was vibrating. Not trembling, not shaking, *vibrating*. The motion didn't seem to be coming from any of her muscles. It was rapid jolting like that caused by pneumatic tools rather than fits and convulsions. She'd fallen to the floor by the time Doug reached her, totally rigid and still juddering so fast that her form on my screen was barely more than a blur. From the angle, I couldn't see too much of what was going on. I saw Doug reach down to touch her, heard him yelp in pain, started yelling along with him when he recoiled and held up the stumps where his fingers had been. My speakers screeched at the moment he made contact; a horrible shrill grinding with a wet edge, the exact same noise Freddy Gruber's elbow made when he accidentally leant on a power-sander in wood shop back in 6th grade.

Doug had no colour left in his face. He wasn't aware of Grant and I yelling to him through our webcams, either. His Mom's ankles were still vibrating, the pace now so rapid that a cloud of sawdust started billowing from the floorboards beneath her. We were all screaming, Grant and I in terror, Doug from terror and blinding agony. Before any of us could find the scrap of calm needed to dial 911, Doug's mum let out a violent spasm.

Then, with no warning, she fell still.

The last frames of the Zoom call were Doug, standing over his mom's still and smoking body, pleading with her to wake up. I liked Doug's Mom. She was like an aunt to me. I'm glad I didn't have to see any more of her post-SHM than those thin, nearly-fleshless ankles. I hadn't seen what SHM did to a person in full yet. I wouldn't have to wait long. Within a week, it'd be on the front page of both the local Tribune *and* Herald. At the time, though all I could do was sit in lockdown isolation and ruminate, robbing myself of sleep for days trying to make any kind of sense out of what the fuck I'd just seen.

That was my first brush with SHM. We were locked down, so I couldn't get to Doug. By the time the Covid quarantines finished, he'd been sent off to some institution. That's how Grant and I knew we had to keep our fucking mouths shut. Doug didn't, you see. He was *very* vocal about what he saw, and *even more vocal* about how Spontaneous Human Malnutrition was a load of bullshit. Doug knew he was being lied to, and so did we. We didn't have the anger of losing our fucking Mom to drive us though. I think that's why Doug took a different approach. He didn't think sleuthing would get him anywhere. Answers need to be taken, not found, he'd said. We tried to stop him, but once he got the idea to set fire to a police station in his head, there was no getting it out.

Yeah, 2020 was definitely one of *those* years for me.

Anyway, as I said, Doug's Mom was the third victim, and it wasn't until the fifth or sixth that the media started connecting dots. There was nothing about the vibrating, of course. *That* seemed to be being kept deliberately under wraps. What led local newscasters to connect the occurrences was the apparent containment within our town, and the… how shall I put this… *unique* state the victims are found in.

It's from the victims that the SHM lie was created. *You* won't find any info on it. I know this because I'm not stupid. One of the *first things* I did when the disappearances started was liaise with my out-of-town contacts. The ONLY SHM info online is on the web pages of local schools, hospitals, community centers etc. Try and access any of these from an IP outside the county? 404'd my friends. Try and get around that with a VPN? SWAT time. Only took two reports of *that* in our paranormal investigation Discord for Grant and me to realize we were completely fucking alone. Everyone wants to help until helping means an armed unit at the door.

But what is the SHM lie? The clue is in the name.

Spontaneous, because it happens suddenly and without any prior warning. There's no rhyme or reason to *who* gets picked, or when. The oldest victim was in their 80s, the youngest was young enough that there are too many first graders around here familiar with funerals. Some go in their sleep, others (like Doug's Mom) when they're hum-drumming through their daily grind. There's no sign it's coming either. Well, that we knew of, at least. It wasn't like any of the victims were around to recount what they experienced in the lead-up. Whatever happens, it happens suddenly. Nobody reported feeling unwell prior to getting SHM'd. They're fine one second, buzzing so hard they're dangerous to touch the next.

The *Human* part is obvious. It's the *M* in SHM, the *Malnutrition*, that's the biggest part of the lie.

A local doctor coined the term based on the state victims were left in after the deadly super-convulsions. No matter their size beforehand, every SHM victim came out the other end looking... well, malnourished. *Extremely* malnourished. The kind of malnourished that the term *"0% body fat"* was made for. They showed a couple photos on the news and in the papers, like I said, pictures that all came with a disclaimer that sensitive viewers would find them distressing. Apparently, we're *all* sensitive viewers when it comes to SHM. Even the local news anchors. It's a shame actually that the internet blacklisting means the clip of *76News* host Chip Dallas bursting into tears live on-air won't make it to YouTube. Despite the grim context, it's still pretty funny to see such a corny POS lose their shit so bad.

We didn't think it was funny at the time, though, of course. Took a few days of emotional distance before we found enough teenage edginess to force a laugh at his blubbering. Mainly because it meant we both had to lie about the fact that we'd been crying too.

It's the eyes that do it. Nothing prepares you for them, even in a photograph.

When you hear about something called Spontaneous Human Malnutrition, you expect to see ribcages. You expect to see bones and joints sticking out at odd angles, draped in a sheet-thin layer of near translucent skin that leaves nothing of the anatomy within to imagination. As harrowing as seeing those peeled-back lips, those teeth sticking up jagged and crooked from shriveled gums, can be, you're not blindsided by them. The sight of their distended bellies is haunting, sure, but if you've ever seen what *normal* malnutrition looks like, then you're not in unfamiliar territory. The severity of it will take you back, no doubt. Being able to see every crease and fold of a person's lower intestine is jarring, even if you're given a heads up, after all. Despite your shock, though, these things *won't* create any kind of cognitive dissonance for you. They're about on-par with what your brain will conjure when you read the phrase *"died of starvation"*.

The eyes though? No amount of disclaimers or trigger warnings could prep you enough for the eyes.

First thing off was the look of the face surrounding them. Every single SHM victim I've seen had the same expression. Terror, complete and utter terror. *All of them* died screaming. The eyeballs themselves are far, far worse, though. Unnatural. No disease can do that, and I know because Grant and I researched it for weeks. It doesn't matter what color your eyes are before SMH. When you come out the other end of it, they'll be black. Not black like coal or like ink or shadow, black like the darkest reaches of deep space. The kind of black that absorbs all light, so nothing twinkles or shimmers in them. You've seen a shark's eyes, right? Imagine them but a thousand times darker. *That's* why everyone watching Chip Dallas' 76News special on the mysterious new disease that had so far taken six people was crying, screaming, or laughing uncontrollably.

Not everyone lapped up the disease lie, though. It's a small town, but it's not *that* small. We've got two high schools. Grant and I were far from the only ones who saw Spontaneous Human Malnutrition for the bullshit it was. You know what they say about the truth, though. A lie can hold it down and beat the shit out of it before it even knows it's in a fight.

Doug was the first non-believer to get, as we were told, "*sent away*". He'd tried to burn down a police station, though. When they took him, we weren't at all surprised. It wasn't until Brian Jarrick's quote-unquote "*suicide*" that Grant and I realized just how far the mayor/police/government/military/whoever was prepared to go to keep everything covered up.

It was six months after the first SHM case, so that's about 102 confirmed deaths for context. At the regular nightly vigils, the townsfolk would say nothing with their lips but *everything* with their furtive glances and nervous floor fixations. Brian Jarrick is… *was*, a local podcaster. Before SHM he'd talked mainly about nature trails in the closest national park, or shows that were coming through one of the three theatres we boasted. As the SHM epidemic unfolded, this all changed. Brian saw through the bullshit, too, and he was *very* vocal about it. He had the balls to ask the questions on his podcast. Grant and I would only whisper to each other in our quiet corner of the cafeteria.

- If it's a disease, then where's the CDC?
- Why hasn't this gained national/international attention?
- What kind of disease turns your eyes like that?
- Where does all the body mass they've lost go?
- How can they vibrate so fast it sands down wood, but they remain physically unscathed?

- Why hasn't it spread outside the boundaries of our town?
- Why aren't the death certificates public?

Brian became a firebrand, a preacher voicing the doubts we all shared, the questions so many of us had, but were all too afraid to ask. He'd known they were coming for him, too. You can probably guess the story. Night before his suicide he abjectly stated that he would *under no circumstances* commit suicide. When the first guy to point this out on Facebook was reported dead an hour later, the message became pretty clear. After that, pretty much every public doubter and worried citizen kept their mouths shut.

Grant and I didn't accept it, though. We *couldn't*. It *wasn't* a disease. We didn't know *what* it was, but we knew that there was no such fucking thing as Spontaneous Human Malnutrition. We were being lied to, and unless we could figure out why, we wouldn't be safe. We both begged our respective parents to move out of town, of course, but you can imagine how that went down. Grant's Dad told him to "stop being a pussy", mine sat me down and gave me a lecture on the "importance of not running from your problems". Both of them, and our moms, brought into the SHM lie. I'm not going to lie, so heavy was my sense of helplessness that I cried myself to sleep most nights after that one. If it weren't for Grant, the sense of isolation, that feeling of being the only sane one in the nuthouse, would have broken me.

But Grant's not me. He's made of tougher stuff. Whereas I retreated into existential despair, Grant decided Brian Jarrick's death was the catalyst to get up and get shit done. That's why he was the one that managed to gather the puzzle pieces and put them together. It took him a little while, though. A few months and several dozen more bodies happened before the morning he arrived at my door with a cardboard box full of laptops. I still remember his expression as clear as day. He was the phrase "I've done it" personified, but where his wide grin wore the phrase triumphantly, his eyes bore it with guilt, shame, and fear.

He made me help him carry the box up to my room to dump the dozen-or-so old laptops onto my bed. I had to run through every variation of "what the fuck" that I knew before he spewed a rambling, near-breathless explanation.

He'd started with the footage recorded from our DnD session. He'd been planning to keep it a surprise, but he'd been recording them to put together an animated highlight reel for Doug's birthday. I was a little annoyed at the invasion of privacy at first, but more irate that Grant had kept this SHM clue from me. After a brief and admittedly genuine apology, Grant opened up one of the laptops. He pulled a USB drive out of his pocket and plugged it in. When I asked why he hadn't just used my PC if he had the clip on a thumb drive, he muttered something about not wanting to buy me a new monitor. I understood exactly what he meant once he'd played me the clip.

This probably is no shock to any of you, but the three-minute snippet was of the end of our final DnD session. It was the video of Doug's Mom dying. It wasn't raw footage, though. Grant had edited it. Specifically, he'd slowed it down to a tenth of the original speed. The three-minute clip represented only about twenty seconds of real-time footage. It was enough. Grant had found all we needed to *prove* SHM was a hokum made-up bullshit disease to cover up something else happening.

Despite what you're thinking, it didn't feel like a victory. I've never felt worse about being proved right. The "something else" was so far outside the realms of my explanation that trying to understand what I was watching literally gave me a migraine. All I remember thinking when the clip finished was that I'd give *anything* to wake up in a reality where I'd been wrong.

Once more, I was watching Doug standing over his mom in his kitchen. He was moving at super-slow speeds, as to be expected. She *wasn't*. She was still shaking, but it was *shaking* now, *not* blur-inducing vibrations. Her speed was still faster than it should have been, but thanks to Grant's editing, we could see what she was actually doing down there. She was writhing, kicking, flexing every joint in her body with jolting spasms that bent them into contortionist-like angles. To my disgust, I realized that what I'd thought was the natural crack and pop of slowed audio was *actually* the snapping and crunching of bones and cartilage. More than once, she'd twist into a position that showed more than just her ankles. We saw her legs, saw the flesh on them shrink away in a matter of seconds. We'd catch glimpses of her hands, of the skin around her digits vacuum-sealing the bones so tightly that fingernails splintered and cracked. Only once did we see her face. It was one time too many.

She'd spasmed forward, folding inward without warning until her temples touched her toes. Her eyes were… they were burning. Bright green flames poured from her sockets, the black orbs at their center bubbling and sputtering with intense heat. The skin of her face was pulled so tight that pulsing veins around her eyes seemed to dance and writhe above the skin. She was screaming, too. Screaming with such force that the windpipe in her shrinking neck bulged and her wilting tonsils bled. Her jaw was open long past that point that it should have dislocated. That's when I realized what the weird audio spike had been when I'd seen the footage months earlier, when it was live and at normal speed.

It was Doug's Mom screams, sped up so fast they sounded like microphone feedback.

With the footage slowed down, it was *clearly* audible. Garbled and distorted, sure, but there was no mistaking the stretched, tinny shrieks cascading from the laptop speaker. It wasn't a scream of fear, but of pain. Unrestrained, unreserved agony. It was when Doug started to bend over in super-slow motion that my stomach dropped. I remembered his fingers, the power-sander sound that reminded me of Freddy Gruber's elbow in 6th grade.

With the footage slowed, Doug's attempts to save his mother sounded *nothing* like a power sander. It sounded like lightning. The moment the tips of his fingers were within six-or-so inches off the top of her head, there was an almighty *crack*, a booming thunder so loud that the speakers screamed for a few seconds before falling silent. Twin streams of emerald flame leaped from Doug's Mom's boiling, hissing eyes the moment the hardware-killing noise hit. The green fire wrapped around Doug's slow-motion fingers. The moment they made contact, the flesh of his digits curled and split, falling away in fluttering shreds that cascaded back towards his Mom's black hole eyes. Within a few seconds, there was nothing left but bone, and below long that too was lost in the bubbling voids.

Doug had pulled his hand away quickly, so I knew he didn't lose more than a few fingers. Still, the tension caused by watching him (from our slowed perspective) holding his hand in that acid-like green burning had me grinding my teeth so hard that I lost a filling. The relief I felt when he finally pulled his hand away was short-lived, however. The worst of Grant's discovery was yet to come. That's the moment that *they* arrived.

I can't describe them to you because I've not actually seen them. Neither has Grant. That's the thing though, you *can't*. The way you can't see them, though? That I can describe real fucking clear, even though thinking about it too long makes me so queasy that I nearly puke.

I didn't notice them at first. They started small, three clusters of fuzzy darkness hovering at Doug's feet. Within a few frames, though, they were as tall as his knees and wider as he was. In other words, impossible to ignore. The panic riding my breathing grew louder and louder as the three beings unfurled. Once materialized at their full height, they were easily 9 feet tall, the very peaks of the conical heads brushing the ceiling of Doug's Mom's lofty rustic kitchen. At first, I thought they were dark, shadowy, the same intense blackness that... haha... "SHM" left the eyes of every single victim. That's when Grant reached forward, paused the video, and minimized the window. I stared at the generic desktop wallpaper, my jaw falling open and closed. I sputtered, trying to get words out. All my mouth could find was shrill, nonsensical gibberish.

The three figures were still there. The pixels of their forms weren't displaying darkness. They were dead.

I peered down to look closer. Sure enough, the backlight of the screen was completely gone where the figures stood. The pixels at the edges of the silhouettes, the ones that should have been displaying the clear blues and greens of a rolling hill, flickered and glitched. They cycled through every color visible to the naked eye (not to mention some that shouldn't have been, although *please* don't ask me to elaborate on this because if I think about it too much it literally triggers an epileptic fit, no teenage hyperbole).

It was at this point that Grant started frantically booting up the rest of the laptops. On the screens of every single one were three identical clusters of dead pixels outlined by a maddening razor-thin spectrum of maddening color. Whatever these things were, capturing their likeness and displaying it digitally was too much for manmade electronics. Grant proved this by showing me his phone, which he'd used to film one of the laptops while it played the video. There, on his home screen, were three miniature clusters of lightless pixels with conical heads. Figures that aligned perfectly with the aforementioned video when he tapped it open with his thumb a few seconds later.

I was babbling and shaking by this point. There were more than a few tears; let's put it that way. Grant wasn't done yet though. The clip still wasn't finished.

The last twenty seconds of the clip were of the three figures towering over Doug. They didn't move, but I could tell they must have been doing *something* behind their shroud of pixel death. I know for two reasons. I'll get through the *least* harrowing of them first, because, for the second, I need to build myself up a little. The first reason I knew the conical-headed giants were there for a reason was Doug's Mom. She was convulsing more violently than ever. Her spasms were rocketing her from the floor so hard that she seemed almost to be floating toward the three dark masses. Well, perhaps pulled toward them is more appropriate. Pulled by her bubbling, boiling, black-hole eyes.

The green flames had once more leaped from them. This time, though, there were three tendrils of fire, and thankfully, none of them found Doug. Instead, they snaked their way through the air until they each found a mass of pixel death. The flames disappeared behind their respective voids, and to my growing horror, I realized they were at the *exact height* one would expect to find on a 9 foot conical headed being, a mouth. The arcs of green fire kept Doug's Mom and the dead pixel figures connected until almost the very end of the clip. Her convulsions grew more violent and contorting than ever. Her skin rippled as the final ounces of fat, muscle, and mass were sucked into those void-filled orbs to be burned into green flames. Every vein on her face bulged to a bursting point. Her mouth twisted into a teeth-baring grimace from which streaks of foam oozed. Doug stood above his mom, still slow-motion and oblivious, as the three towering beings around him consumed her until she was little more than an abyss-eyed skeleton draped in papery skin.

As I said though, that was the *first* of the two reasons I knew those beings must have been doing something beneath those lifeless pixels. The *second* one, the one that's kept me up for however many nights have passed since that morning, was much worse.

I could *hear* them.

Not through the speaker. The speaker was dead, busted. This was made all too apparent by the fact that Doug's Mom's electric-chair convulsions and screaming from burning eyes had been inaudible since Doug made the mistake of trying to touch her. No. I could hear them in the room. From all around me, their hollow tones echoed and bounced off every wall. I yelled, whipping around in every direction, adrenaline shooting through every blood vessel. Grant was crying now, crying and mouthing *"I'm sorry"* over and over like a twisted mantra. It wasn't just the fact that I could hear them which made me throw the laptop out the damn window. It was what I could hear them doing, too.

They were laughing. All three of them were locked in high-pitched, chittering hysterics. The kind of laughter you imagine a spider makes before it injects its cocooned prey with chemicals that turn them into liquid mulch. Every barked *ha* screeched through my eardrums, twisting my spine and setting off every nervous tic I never knew I had.

I shouted at Grant for about a half hour once I was satisfied the laptop hadn't survived the fall. He took it like a champ, and when I'd finally calmed down, he showed me the bloodied knuckles he'd obtained when he put his fist through drywall after watching it the first time. The fear it created... was *beyond* rationality. Hearing that laughter set off something deep within me, a set of emotions long dormant thanks to the comfortable safety of modern life. Once upon a time, human beings *needed* that mix of aggression and panic. They needed it because, if they *didn't* have it, they'd never be able to fight their way out of the corners the beings that live in shadows could back them into. I know those feelings now, although *every single part* of me wishes that I didn't.

It was after I apologized for losing my cool, and Grant began to talk about our options for what to do next, that our phones rang. I felt the little composure I'd managed to build since the laptop went flying ebb away in an instant. There was no number, but instead of "caller not recognized" or "withheld number", the writing on the screen showed two simple, spirit-crushing words.

"humAn phone"

I looked up at Grant, tears once more falling down my cheeks. He was in the same state. He nodded at me, and I gulped, resigning myself to whatever happened next. We both clicked the green icon to accept the call. A single voice answered, and once more it came not from our phones but from every square inch of space around us. It was a single voice, whining and high-pitched. The syllables sounded not like organic speech, but like someone had stretched and manipulated audio of billions of people screaming until it became coherent language. Again, only two words, but they were enough for both Grant and I to get on our bikes and cycle as far away from my house as we possibly could.

"hellO boys."

My folks were the ones who reported us missing. They found us hiding in our shack in the woods, that one we'd naïvely believed our parents didn't know about. It was when we started to explain *why* we ran that shit went sideways fast.

We'd expected the cops not to believe us. We never thought they'd place us under house arrest and cut both our houses off from the internet. We were both dumbfounded when they confiscated our phones and told us every device we owned was getting taken in for evidence. We were *real fucking surprised* when one of the cops punched Grant in the face and told us, in no uncertain terms, that just because we were kids didn't mean we wouldn't get, and I quote, "dealt with".

When I found out about the bribe money to keep shtum I don't know what I felt more; shocked at how much it was, or disgusted that my parents accepted it. They don't believe me, by the way. They're pissed that we tried to leave town at, and again I quote, but from my dad now, "*a time when the community needs to come together and not do anything to rock the boat.*"

That was a week ago. I haven't slept since. I also haven't heard from Grant. I've been watching the news though. 17 more have gone in the last five days. 17 more people burned away and consumed by… by whatever those things are. And our police, at the very least, are in on it. Keeping it covered up… not *just* keeping it covered up, *allowing* it to happen. I *know* it runs deeper, though. It *has* to. Why else would those scientists in hazmat suits keep showing up outside my house at night? Why else would a black van be parked across the street morning, noon, and night? Why fucking else would three police officers resign due citing "a conflict of conscience" and die under "mysterious" circumstances the night afterward?

Whatever's happening in my town, it's big, and it's being kept quiet. Not only kept quiet, it's being *allowed* to happen. I stole my dad's work phone to post this. I'm hoping that it gets out there, that it makes it past the blacklist they've got in place. That's part of the reason I've omitted the name of where I actually live; they'll no doubt have scrapers mining every search engine for it. I mean fuck, it probably won't work, but I'm plum out of ideas and, honestly, *way beyond* desperate by this point.

This isn't a "send help now" post, because the "help" is half the fucking problem. This is so you can be on the alert. If you get wind of *anything* that sounds even *remotely* like SHM, skip town. Leave. Especially if you live in a pokey little cult-like "quiet town" like mine. I don't care what you think of your neighbors. Forget everything you know about your friends, your family. When shit hits the fan, they *will* play along with the lie.

As I said, this doesn't seem to have spread beyond the town limits so far. Whatever those beings are, they've picked here as their hunting ground. They could move, though, or there could be more of them. Who knows how many ghost towns and dwindling populations are actually whole communities being deliberately fed to these things?! The US is a BIG place. You really think anyone would notice if Podunkville in Shit-Heap County vanished slowly over a few years?

That's what's happening here, and nobody around me is trying to stop it. My parents, the news, the police, the mayor, everyone with any kind of authority are doing what they can to make sure we sit tight and let it happen. There's no such thing as Spontaneous Human Malnutrition. There never has been and there never will be, but because the idiots around me refuse to stop insisting otherwise, I'm going to get consumed by…

No. Fuck it. Fuck the house arrest. I can't stay here. Those things know who I am, know where I am. They'll be coming for me sooner or later. House arrest be damned. I've got nowhere to go but, Jesus Christ, that footage. Dying alone and starving in the forest would be much better than… than that.

Dad, if you're reading this, I'm sorry. I don't want to know what it feels like to have eyes that burn like dying suns. I'm not going out the way Doug's Mom did, the way I know you're hiding from me that Grant already has done. I can't take this madness anymore Dad. You know I'm right about all this. I am sorry, I truly am, but you and I both need to accept that it's *not my fault* you decided to fall down this rabbit hole.

As for the rest of you, wish me luck. You might see me cycling through your town one day. Who knows. I'm posting this then hitting the road. It's about an hour's journey between my house and the edge of town. If I push it, I can make it before my dad or the cops realize what I've done. I'm taking a risk by posting this I know, but that's the thing. There's always a chance those things might reach me first. Hell, they might even be reading this now. They've already proved they can mess with our phones. It wouldn't be a stretch if they were watching me type this right…

No. Can't think like that. Got to focus, got to remember that as risky as leaving is, the risk of staying is always higher. It's a certainty. I'm going to be keeping my head down, so you won't hear from me again, but keep your fingers crossed for me. Please.

Oh, and remember, if and when your local Chip Dallas facsimile starts telling you not to worry about a mysterious new disease called Spontaneous Human Malnutrition, don't believe a word they say. It doesn't exist, and you have every reason to panic.

RE: YOUR RESIGNATION

Dear Dr Eastley,

I'm afraid to say I was disappointed, but unsurprised, to receive your letter of resignation. As you know, we take the emotional well-being of our research teams very seriously at IPSET.

However, I want you to know that the threats you made, both legal and otherwise, prompted us to take recourse. I felt it would be prudent to remind you of a few truths. As much as I accept that I am the, as you put it, *"bastard that dragged* (you) *into all this shit"*, it would be wise to remember the reality of the events you rather childishly refuse to accept responsibility for.

Firstly, your enlistment with IPSET. Nobody forced your hand to sign the contract. Yes, I do accept that under the circumstances, you were somewhat incentivized to do so. However, as you frequently pointed out in your letter, "(you) *would rather die than work another day for* (us) *freaks"*. I'd like to remind you that when given the freedom to choose between death and IPSET, you chose IPSET. We cannot be held responsible for you feeling you made the wrong decision after the fact.

Secondly, your tenure in the nursery of the North Sea Facility. As per procedure, you were given a full brief of the acidity of the larval-stage Entity-0090 secretions. I have seen the safety video myself. Human Resources could not have been clearer about the need to maintain a 19 foot radius at all times. I don't care how often you repeated yourself in your letter, but *"*(we) *didn't tell* (you) *they could fucking talk"* isn't an excuse. I have seen the footage of the incident. I do accept that your injuries looked painful. However, IPSET holds no responsibility for your inability to resist telesuggestive speech patterns.

You'd seen photographs of Entity-0090 in your orientation. Despite your youth back then, the way you panicked was, in no uncertain terms, unprofessional. Your wailing and shrieks overexcited several larval-stage Entity-0090 specimens. Yes, I understand that "(you) *watched* (your) *fucking flesh melt until* (you) *had a fucking bone hand that* (you) *had to snap off* (yourself)". Need I remind you though that Security Sergeant Wilson's husband had to bury a box of melted flesh that, even though we took great lengths to seal the shoebox-sized coffin, carried a distinct aroma of dead fish? My ability to sympathize with your amputation is limited given this context.

Besides, as I'm sure you don't need reminding, the bionic arm we provided as a replacement is more than suitable. As unpleasant as the installation surgery may have been, I'm sure a woman of your intellect understands the necessity for the recipient to be conscious when augmenting the nervous system with advanced wetworks. At least, I'd hoped a woman of your intellect would understand. I would be lying, Dr Eastley, if your expansive letter didn't make me question my own judgement.

The third example you cited, that of your family, infuriated me. I'll be honest, Dr Eastley, I struggle to comprehend where you found the nerve to level such a charge against IPSET, myself, or anybody at the Marathon County Facility. I found the gall you showed in doing so, to be totally blunt, offensive.

You were fully aware of Event-0216 when you **volunteered to study it**. I emphasize this because you seem to have completely forgotten that it was **you who requested your family be transferred with you to the Marathon County Facility**. It was a testament to your abilities that IPSET Human Resources went to such great lengths to accommodate your requests. I see now that this was a wasted, and unappreciated, investment of time and finance.

As I recall, you were incredibly excited about the discovery of Entity-E0216. The blame cannot be placed on myself or IPSET for what transpired over the six months after your first contact. IPSET contamination protocols are specific and thorough for a reason. I have reviewed the security footage, and upon exiting the test chamber, you very clearly **did not** remain in the decontamination chamber for the mandated 120 minutes. 118 minutes 27 seconds isn't two hours. I am aware of your repeated reports of *"that snively bastard* Harper-Girard*"*. These accusations were found to have no merit. The Entity-E0216 breach was found by IPSET HR to have been caused by lax adherence to policy, not sabotage. As director, I stand by the findings of that investigation. The blame for what happened to your family lies with you, not Dr Harper-Girard.

I was under the impression this matter was put to bed after the hearing. It truly saddens me that this wasn't the case, Geraldine.

IPSET cannot be held responsible for the E0216 crustaceospores being small enough to fit through the air vent in your, quite frankly, more than comfortable on-site accommodation. It is no fault of ours that your husband and two children slept through the infection process. We were not aware the E0216 spores secreted anesthetic from their exoskeletons (although the observation has proved helpful in future research, so at least their deaths weren't in vain, eh?)

I'll be completely honest, even *I* found the footage of the emergence terrifying. Not as much as when I was there. It was quite an experience watching the surveillance video back before I wrote this, watching us both screaming in the lab while security took down Gregory. Sorry, that was callous; it wasn't Gregory. It was the Entity-E0216 that Gregory had become. Suffice to say though, the fatal shot clearly occurs *after* full transformation had occurred. We did not *"murder* (your) *fucking husband"*, we put down the monstrosity your negligent attitude to Health & Safety policy allowed him to become.

I was fond of your family, Dr Eastley. It pains me to believe that you're deluded enough to think I hold any responsibility for your children and husband becoming... well, you know what they became. I'm looking at the photos as I write this; little Tiffany's spine stretching, the new legs shredding out the skin of her back. It's the still from the moment her eyes fell out that disturbs me the most, Geraldine. They still have their old skin, you know, in the lab. I know you're aware of the E0216 corpses they left behind; you were on the team that dissected young Steven's after all. I didn't know if you knew about the skin though, the human skin I mean, the skin they'd shed.

Do you remember that night, Geraldine? I'm sure you do. We're long-lived, but we're not indestructible. Gregory and your children are even less so. Do you remember the months they spent in the infirmary? Do you remember how I'd visit them as though they were my own? I was just as horrified as you when their faces started elongating. The mandibles that mangled and pushed their jaws out of the way brought tears to *both* of our eyes, Dr Eastley, not just yours.

I'm sure you remember how we ran through the Marathon County Facility when they started chasing us. Goddammit, Geraldine, very few times have I actually been scared, but knowing those E0216 monstrosities, with their centipede bodies and fresh-rending face claws, were once little Steven and Tiffany still gives me nightmares. I was there holding your hand in the North Sea Infirmary when Gregory was caught up in whatever project I had him on. They were my godchildren, Dr Eastley. Even though I've seen my fair share of both, that title still holds emotional significance to me.

I am trying to keep this letter professional, despite you not having shown me the same courtesy, but fuck you for placing your family's death on me. I was crying at the funeral too, Geraldine. You know full well that **everything** we do at IPSET has meaning, no matter how much it upsets us. I don't recall you protesting when we were both cowering in a corner listening to your infected children getting gunned down in the corridor.

This is where I'd also like to remind you that, for a *"twisted heartless fucking immortal sociopath"*, I took your requests for compassionate leave incredibly seriously. You were the first IPSET employee to receive a sick day; did you know that? That was specifically because of my intervention. HR wanted you labelled as a compromised asset. Perhaps I made a mistake in overruling them.

This is why your letter disappointed me, Dr Eastley. I'd grown fond of you, not just as a colleague, but as a friend. Very rarely has this happened during my long, long career. It brought me no pleasure at all to read your take on your time with the PLR team.

If you'll recall, you **begged** me to be transferred to Paranatural Literary Research. I warned you, and I know you remember that. I made it very clear that, just because you'd be working with books rather than bioentities, you weren't any safer (emotionally or physically). I find it genuinely shocking that you've managed to omit the fact I denied your request **seven times** before agreeing to have you transferred to the London Facility. You were a key asset in the bioentity team, Dr Eastley. Moving you in with the page-turners was done at great expense to IPSET's long-term strategy.

It's insulting that you think "(I) *put* (you) *on Event-HAHRE as a twisted fucking punishment*". I put you on Event-HAHRE because you were the most valuable fucking asset in PLR as soon as you touched down in the UK.

Do you think Dr Anand could have deciphered that damn book? Or that idiot Boxstead? Three of the teams that brought it in gouged out their damn eyeballs within a week. Four more had to be terminated when they tried to resign and join that damn cult you identified. You were the only person on Event-HAHRE who wasn't broken by that little red book. It even broke Dr Bridger, and he was reassigned to HAHRE after three decades of studying a copy of *The Taealim Alrajul Al'akhir*.

Think about that, Geraldine. Dr Bridger spent thirty years working with a multidimensional, sentient, endlessly self-writing literary event-entity that was actively trying to kill him. Before he retired from the field, the man rescued five agents from an Entity-E0879 pocket dimension. He was as tough as they come. He'd had *The Taealim* project since the '90s and hadn't broken, Event-HAHRE managed it in a damn afternoon. I didn't exactly have many options.

Look, Geraldine, as upset with you as I am, I can't help but stop once again to thank you for what you achieved during your time on the Event-HAHRE team. That's partly why I don't accept your accusations re how you lost your arm. You're one of the most teleresistant assets we have. Our understanding of Event-HAHRE has grown exponentially, and I'll be the first to admit we knew next to nothing before you were reassigned to PLR. Given what you uncovered, we would have been in serious trouble if we'd let it slip through the net. Jesus, even I'm scared of the damn thing, and I've been in the Over-Library and communed with the Listener. Sorry, that's Entity-E0001 to you.

The point is, I want you to understand something. I am truly sincere when I say I regret your tenure in PLR ending the way it did. One of the few criticisms I do accept is that "(I) *could have fucking done fucking something to fucking pull* (you) *out of there.*" This I do apologize for. However, given what we were learning of Event-HAHRE, I will not apologize for keeping my most valuable asset on the project.

I'll be blunt Geraldine. Those researchers you killed? They meant nothing to me. Nothing. Given the scope of threat Event-HAHRE represents, I'd satiate your bloodlust with a million more if it meant keeping you in the room with that damn book. Let's be honest, ripping out their eyes to stop yourself from going blind is the first time you've ever needed research assistants, anyway. I did not "*make* (you) *eat their damn eyes*". The book made you do that. I just refused to open the door. I still would. If I had, you'd never have slipped into that trance, and we'd never have learned about the mask.

Their lives were a minor inconvenience. Your sanity, however, was a great loss. I did not inject you with the immortality serum only to lose your mind to madness. However, as long as your instability doesn't interrupt your work on Event-HAHRE, it may not be too much of a setback. There is a great deal to uncover in that book. I'm sure we'd get a good few centuries out of you before I'd have to allow HR to designate you a compromised asset. I'm sure they'll be thrilled when the day comes.

So, in short, I am writing to you to respectfully decline your resignation. I don't know where you are, or how you escaped, but we will find you. Accessing the database to copy everything was smart, I'll give you that. Emailing a resignation letter to me to gloat about your plans to leak the files you've stolen was, however, stupid. It was perhaps the most disappointing thing in your thirty-page letter, Dr Eastley.

I was like a father to you, Geraldine. I was there at your wedding, deep in the bowels of the North Sea facility. Sending IPSET security to collect you, knowing how rough they can be, genuinely broke my heart. We cracked your location in about thirty minutes. Technology was always Gregory's forte, wasn't it? Maybe if it was you that we lost to Entity-E0216 I'd be worried right now, instead of just heartbroken.

Keep on the move all you want, Geraldine. We'll find you sooner or later. Or, you know, you could voluntarily return? Either way, IPSET cannot afford delays to the Event-HAHRE project. You'll be back in your cell by the end of the month, just to forewarn you. How much violence occurs between then and now is your call.

Oh, and don't be stupid and post this on the internet somewhere like you did with that fisherman's crayon letter. Yes, I know it was you that leaked the Entity-0090 nursery breach account. I'm already upset with you Dr Eastley. Don't make me angry with you, too.

Warmest regards,
Dr Obadiah Bramfield, Director.
The Institute of Paranatural Science, Events, and Technology.

WHAT TO TELL 'EM WHEN THEY ASK

I want to start by saying this: I *wasn't* a gangster. I don't like the word. Didn't then, still don't. I was a businessman. My business just happened to be crime.

Here's the thing though, right? I've been a straight goer for thirty years now. The old bill never managed to nick me, to catch me on the job and send me down. I got out as soon as I had enough scratch to fly off to Ibiza and stay low. That's where I'm writing to you from, my sunny bungalow while Wife #5 makes Martinis and I enjoy a Mediterranean breeze I don't deserve.

She barely speaks a word of the Queen's. I'm not too good at Spanish, neither. There's something I've wanted to get off my chest for a few years. Due to… well, the doctor advised yesterday that I cancel any long-term plans. If I don't share this now, I won't get another chance. Bless Wife #5, but she ain't the ear I need on this one. I need someone who'll understand my words. *All* my words. I'm still wanted back home, and I don't know who in the old crowd is trustworthy these days or even still breathing, so you lot will have to do.

Now, I got up to a lot of things back in the day. More'n one fella caught a slug in the chops to pay for the years of paradise I've enjoyed. Am I guilty? Nah. That's not what this is about. I never done someone that weren't holding a shooter or a blade themselves. This ain't a remorseful confession because I don't have any. It was what it was, which was business.

This ain't about what I *did* but what I *saw*, and how I learned I'd never come close to the depravity of what *real* evil is. A single night, halfway through my stint as Bethnal Green's Billy Big Bollocks, the *only* night I *wasn't* the most dangerous thing in the room.

The year was 1976. I don't remember what month, but I know it was winter because I was freezing my tits off. I had three of the lads with me; Big Steve, Nicky the Shimmy-Shaker, and Screwloose. Big Steve's name was ironic. He was a little fella, barely over 5 feet, but he had a mean kick and wasn't afraid to kneecap anyone dumb enough to cross me. Gangling, awkward Nicky was known as the Shimmy-Shaker because of the way he'd bump and fumble into oblivious tourists and walk away with their wallet/jewelry/etc. Young Nicky was good in a scrap, and of all the firm he was the one whose loyalty I never questioned. As for Screwloose... well, you only get a name like Screwloose one way, and that's why he only came out on jobs like this one. The big jobs, the ones where you know it's going to get bloody.

Only the four of us knew the job was a job. Or so we thought. Turned out the six fellas from the Turkish gang setting up on my turf had a job of their own. It was supposed to be a meet, a negotiation. I'm a sly bastard, and I'd intended to negotiate by way of Screwloose' sawn-off shotgun named Elvis. The Turkish fellas were also sly bastards, and they'd had the same idea. So yeah, we'd gone down to that warehouse to ambush a bunch of mugs who were there to ambush us themselves.

Both sides had agreed to the warehouse because it was the kind of place you had meetings like this. Quiet, remote, far away from prying eyes and listening ears. Slap bang in the middle of an abandoned industrial estate, easily a few miles across. Perfect for business of the criminal variety. Chosen by me because I knew it was too isolated for gunshots to be overheard, accepted by the Turks for (I now realize) exactly the same reason.

Now, seems quite dramatic, don't it? Thing is, in my line of work that should have been any other night. That was a standard blooming Tuesday for me. Why else do you think I kept a guy named Screwloose on the firm? In the back of your mind, you're *always* prepared for a job to go south. We learned as soon as we opened the warehouse door that our idea of south was nowhere near southern enough.

What we found wasn't a job that had just gone bloody south, it had gone Scott's lost bloody expedition Antarctic south. Remember how I said Big Steve was my go-to guy for shattering kneecaps? Yeah, the bastard wasn't exactly squeamish. The aftermath of what must've gone down just before we arrived had him chucking up pie and mash. Young Nicky started sobbing. Wasn't a good look, that. Kind of thing that would have got him a slap on any other night. Thing is, given what we were staring at, I understood. If I wasn't pushing 40 at the time and hardened to the world, I'd probably have done the same. Even Screwloose muttered a *"Jesus bleeding Christ"* under his breath.

We'd been expecting six Turkish fellas. We'd expected them to be breathing. We found two, and they weren't.

"Bloody hell Archie, what d'you fink 'appened 'ere?" Big Steve said after he'd pulled himself up from painting the floor. "This weren't no argy-bargy Arch, this weren't no ruck."

"Don't ya think I can't see that, Steve mate? Course this weren't no bloody fight. Look at the bloke at the bloody table; he's missing the back of his bonce! What d'you think coulda done that?" I raised an eyebrow at Big Steve. He was pale, and though he did his best to hide it, I could see the tremble in his fingers.

"A shooter Arch, a big one." This time it was Screwloose speaking. His knuckles were tight around the outline of Elvis, his own big shooter, tucked inside his trench coat.

"Right you are Screwloose, exactly. Only thing what coulda done him in like that is a shooter, a *big* bloody shooter."

"And what about the other fella, Archie?" This was Nicky the Shimmy-Shaker, quiet and sniffling.

"The other? Well bugger me sideways Nicky, I have no bloody idea. I do know this whole mess leaves a big bloody question, though."

"What's that Arch?" Screwl once more. No tremble here, just that usual cold edge.

"Simple Screwloose, me' ol' chum. The question this raises is *who the fuck has balls so big they think they can get away with this Jack the Ripper shit on MY BLOODY TURF?!"* The anger in my raised voice bounced off the warehouse walls.

Was I *actually* angry? Of course I was. Showing it was a choice, though. I wasn't *only* angry. Anger wasn't even most of what I was. I had to inflate my own rage to put on the face-saving bravado I needed. I couldn't let the lads see what *else* I felt, the emotion that outweighed my ire tenfold. For the first time since I was a nipper on my first job, I was afraid. I don't care how tough or big you are, I'm as hard as they come, mate. Didn't matter. Nobody could have walked into that carnage without feeling their gut drop through a trapdoor.

'hoM swEt Hom'

The words were daubed on the wall behind Mr Blown-Out Bonce. Each letter was as tall as Big Steve, easily. It was obvious what they'd been painted with. I'll give you a clue; it's dark red and bloomin' difficult to clean out a carpet. I ain't talking about wine or tomato sauce neither.

The poor bloke with exposed brain matter was slumped forward on a table. There was an empty chair opposite him set up for the meet that never happened. If I'd have lifted his head, he'd have been Erdem Akbas, my counterpart in the Turkish firm. Well, what was left of his face would've been Erdem Akbas. The suit was too nice for the almost-headless corpse to belong to anyone else. So was the chrome-plated pistol he'd been midway through drawing when he'd gained a new orifice. His grip was still tight around the handle, the flashy shooter hanging halfway out the holster.

It wasn't him that turned my stomach, though. The *other* bloke did that, the one whose blood was used to paint the crudely spelled message on the decaying brickwork. We knew the blood hadn't come from Erdem. Erdem's was pooling all over the table, dripping a little over one edge, but hadn't traveled far from his head wound. The blood used as ink could only have come from the poor bastard scattered in about a dozen pieces. If I didn't know any better, I'd say he'd been blown up. I *did* know better, though. A few summers prior, we'd moved some hand grenades for a less-than-patriotic business associate in Northern Ireland. I had a guy on my crew we used to call Handsy Eddy. I didn't after the grenade job. I'll let your imagination do the rest, yeah?

The unnamed Turkish footman (aka Goon #1) in the warehouse hadn't been anywhere near an explosion. We'd had to scrape Handsy Eddy's remains off the walls after the accident. Aside from the crimson writing, the walls of the warehouse were... well, they weren't *clean,* but there was nothing on them besides London soot and grime. Plus, the bits of Handsy Eddy we buried were ragged and burned. There were no scorch marks on any of the chunks of flesh strewn about the meeting space. No fabric melted to the skin. The cheap suit the poor bastard had been wearing was in tatters, spread everywhere like polyester confetti. The pieces of the Turkish footman weren't ragged, neither. He'd been taken apart evenly, been segmented, split. The precision where torso had been torn from limbs was almost surgical.

I wasn't a stranger to what a man's insides looked like. I'd even seen my own more than once, before I learned never to take your eye off a man with a shiv. I'd never seen *anything* like this. None of us had, not even Screwloose. A thigh here, a calf somewhere way over there, fingers flung about the place, guts and gizzards splayed out in a heap. The only part that *hadn't* been discarded was the poor bastard's head. Whoever done this has driven the biggest iron spike I've ever bloody seen through the Turkish footman's face. The sick bastard had nailed the severed head to the wall, hanging it like a pride-of-place hunting trophy above the message.

In my time, I done a lot of bad things, things any straight goer would recoil at. I don't lose no sleep over it. I was a criminal, but that didn't mean I was unethical. I *wasn't* a gangster; I was a businessman. I had *rules*. Three things that *never* got moved on my turf: gear, nonce material, and people. Other than that, anything was fair game for me, especially violence, extortion, torture, murder, etc. However, no matter how much I wanted them dead, my vendetta against the Turks was business. No part of me thought any of them deserved anything close to what they'd been given.

I don't know how long we stood in that warehouse doorway before Screwloose walked in to get a closer look. Crazy bastard didn't bother to step around the eviscerated remains, just plowed straight through till he was underneath the crudely written message.

"This is a bloody mess, Arch." He eventually said. "'Scuse my French, but fucking 'ell. This weren't no job mate; this was a bleedin' animal what done this."

I followed Screwloose to gaze up at the mounted head. It was harder to mask my worry this close, especially with Screwloose visibly shaken. Big Steve was my go-to chap for cracking kneecaps. I called Screwloose when kneecaps weren't enough. He was a few years older than I was, old enough to have held a rifle during the last few years of the War. He'd done and seen some things out there in France. Things that made taking a power drill to a man's Achilles tendon or closing a vice around their family jewels no big ask.

When we heard the scream from deeper in the warehouse, I was almost glad for the distraction. Almost.

"Wh-wh-what the 'ell was that?!" Nicky's hand was tightening around the crowbar tucked into his trouser leg.

Big Steve already had a switchblade in one hand and his token hammer in the other. "I reckon that's where we'll find the sick bastard that did this."

My own fingers were already finding the snub-nosed .44 holstered at my right hip. "Steve's right Nicky, whoever done this can't have got far."

"Blood's not even dried yet." Screwloose murmured, scratching one of the glistening letters with a dirty fingernail.

"Right, exactly," I nodded again, the break in tension making it easier to rally both myself and the boys, "some prick thinks he can play Yorkshire Ripper in *my* backyard. We ain't bloody having it lads, alright? Never mind the Turks, let's find this rat before it flees the nest. We need to send a message."

"What message is that, Arch?"

"The message is simple, Nicky; the only person that gets to decide who dies on Archie Stenworth's bloody patch is *Archie bloody Stenworth!*"

There's something about yelling your own name that fills you with confidence. When your name has clout, at least. Reminding myself that I *was* Archie bloody Stenworth, the People's Guv'na of Bethnal Green, shook me out of my dread. Gave me that fire back, you know? Whoever'd done this was a sick, twisted pervert, I reasoned, but that's all. Even if this one had a knife and shooter, even if he managed to get the drop on Erdem Akbas and his boys, he was still just one more sick bastard hiding in the grass on my turf. We knew how to deal with them. Whether they got their kicks from kids, corpses, animals, or whatever *this* was, the solution was always the same, and it *always* worked.

This was the rationale that gave me the strength to lead the boys into the shadowy depths between the rows of shelving. Even Nicky the Shimmy-Shaker managed to pull himself together at the sight of me charging in the direction of screaming, shooter in hand and fury in my eyes. My bravado wasn't false now. You didn't get far in my line of work without learning to snuff your fear. I was Archie bloody Stenworth, and I was ready to go and do what Archie bloody Stenworth did.

So yeah, my fearlessness was genuine for all of about three minutes. Maintaining it became an effort again the moment we found the hole.

It was in the furthest corner of the warehouse, hidden where the shadows cast by flickering strip-bulbs curled and ebbed at their thickest. A gaping cavity in the solid concrete, twice as wide as a tube tunnel and descending at a sharp angle into much purer darkness than the cloying kind within which we stood.

"Reckon that's where we'll find 'em." Screwloose said, once more fingering Elvis through his thick leather coat.

"Yeah," I agreed, fighting the urge to gulp, "I reckon you're right, Screwloose. What gave it away mate, was it that dead bastard over there, that one up there, or the fucking screaming?" I paused. "Excuse my French lads, sorry."

I don't want to teach you how to suck eggs; you *know* the screams were coming from the hole. Of course they bloody were. I'm not going to insult you by pointing that out like it's some big surprise. If we'd found that hole and the screaming *weren't* coming from it I'd have been a bit flummoxed. Finding the hole *was* a shock, though. Nothing I knew of could drill a hole that big and precise through concrete, especially not in the few days since we was last at this warehouse (when a scream-filled void in the floor definitely *wasn't* a bleedin' fixture).

Hole-induced shock alone wasn't what knocked the wind I'd only just found out my sails. It was finding Turkish Goons #2 and #3 along with it that gave me a tight chest and breathing I had to consciously keep steady.

These new poor dead bastards were dressed in the same cheap polyester. Goon #2 was hanging over the lip at the other side of the hole, and was mostly intact. Apart from the gaping chasm in his chest, none of him was missing that I could see. That statement became less true with every second that passed though, as chunks of his exposed entrails would lose the will to remain attached, falling and landing with a wet thud somewhere in the depths. Aside from being on his belly, the wound was identical to what remained of Erdem Akbas' head. The kind of frayed, torn, ragged evisceration left over when you find yourself on the receiving end of two chambers of buckshot. Thing is, though, a belly is a lot bigger than a head. The two halves of Turkish Goon #3 were held together by exposed spinal cord and a half dozen brave strands of sinew and other ligature. A sawn-off can take a decent chunk of a man, but

I'd never seen one that could near tear someone in half (even point-blank). There was no blood spray where the poor bastard lay, either. Either he'd been shot by the biggest bloody shooter in Bethnal Green and then moved, or he was never shot at all.

Goon #2 was the lucky one. Goon #3... well, Jesus bloody Christ, I can't even *think* about the state of him without a stiff drink in my hand.

Somehow, the poor mug was still alive. I say somehow because up until that night I'd assumed having most of your skin removed was fatal. The skinless man was coughing and spitting up blood from his perch on a girder some 45 feet above the hole. Crude rods had been jammed through his back to fix him sitting upright, their gnarled ends emerging at either shoulder blade to like rusted wings. His flayed hide was spread behind him like a cape hanging from the protruding rebars. Lidless eyes darted between us, exposed ribs rising and falling. I think we were all glad for the screams coming from the hole; they meant we couldn't hear his gargling chokes as tried to lean down and extend a skinless hand, to attempt to beg for help. His jaw flapped open and closed, teeth without lips locked forever in an impossibly wide grin that juxtaposed the terrified madness in his gaze.

"Should we get him down, Arch?!" Big Steve was yelling, both to be heard over the screams and because... well, bloody hell, you read what I just wrote, yeah?

"Bugger that!" The brick was flying through the air before I realized Screwloose had picked it up and lobbed it. We'd moved hand grenades in the past, but Screwloose was the only bloke on the firm who'd actually used one (apart from Handsy Eddy, of course). His throwing arm hadn't lost its aim or power since he'd been a young lad trudging through the gutted remains of Nazi-occupied France. The snap of Goon #3's neck could be heard even over the wails from the hole. The grey grime-coated chunk of loose architecture connected squarely with bony chin, sending a rain of shattered cartilage and loose marrow below. The force carried the projectile through, taking most of the exposed face with it, leaving the head lolling between rod-pierced shoulder blades on a broken, twitching spine. The flayed man hung still, limp, his only motion a slight sway on the thick spikes shoved both through him and (somehow) the solid steel girder he sat on.

"What do we do, Arch, we gonna get the rest of the lads?!" I could almost feel Nicky's disappointment when I shook my head.

"Nah, we sort this out now. The vermin what done this doesn't leave this warehouse, you got it?"

The boys nodded. Screwloose with enthusiasm, Big Steve gravely, and Nicky the Shimmy-Shaker like he'd love to do literally *anything* else. I think if it'd been any other mug asking him to stay, he'd have told them to jog on. So would Steve and Screwloose. I'm not any mug though, am I? I'm Archie bloody Stenworth. Of *course* they followed me down into that bloody hole.

Did I *want* to go down there? Course I bloody didn't. Thing is, you can't be the Billy Big Bollocks of Bethnal Green if any bastard gets ideas in their head about your bollocks not being that big after all. The thought of going *into* that hole, *toward* those screams, made my bowels twist into balloon animals. The thought of showing weakness twisted them worse. There wouldn't be much weight to the name Archie Stenworth if word got around that Archie Stenworth was scared of going down a hole because he saw a little blood (as the rumor mill would report). Jesus, if only I'd known.

This was the '70s, remember. No mobiles. We didn't even have a torch with us. Didn't think we'd need one, see? The '70s it meant something else, too. All four of us smoked. We all had zippo lighters in our back pockets, so we at least had *some* light as we ventured deeper. Not enough to provide any comfort, mind. The slither of illumination we could muster was scarce, flickering, and prone to snuffing out. Not what you want when your only guide is the disembodied screams echoing around you.

The angle of the decline made the first few minutes a descent. Before long, though, the tunnel leveled out, meaning we could walk instead of half-sliding on our backsides. At no point did the screaming we followed falter. It always sounded just around the next corner, forever a fraction of an inch beyond where the darkness swallowed our feeble orange flamelight. With every yard I slid or step I took, I felt a little less like Archie bloody Stenworth. By the time we reached the point where the tunnel widened into a larger cavern, I was barely Archie at all. In my mind, I was little Archibald again, afraid and jumping at every creak and chitter in the shadows as I ran from the kitchen door to the outhouse at the back of me' Mum's garden on a cold winter's night. I was still managing to hide it from the lads, but the illusion was paper-thin. We were easily a mile underground. The concrete had given way to rubble and drainpipes until they too vanished. The space we were in bore no signs of civilization, no signs of the London we'd left behind. I was Archie bloody Stenworth, the Billy Big Bollocks of Bethnal Green. This far beneath my brick-and-mortar kingdom, my bollocks felt smaller than they ever had.

"Jesus bloody Christ, Arch, look at this place. We must be the first people to have been down here since—"

"About an hour ago." Screwloose cut Big Steve off mid-sentence, pointing at the corpse on the ground. We'd found Goon #4. He was in a heap a little ways into the cavern. He wasn't *laying* in a heap, mind. For him to be laying down, he'd have had to have been in one piece. Goon #4, much like the far-too-young Goon #1 back in the warehouse, was in many.

"How the—how the bloody hell did he cut him up so fast?!"

"Don't think about it, yeah? It won't matter how he done it by morning because the bastard'll be dead. You hear me, Steve mate? Dead. Doesn't matter how good a butcher the sick twat what done this would make, yeah? He picked the wrong bloody borough to try this shit in."

"But Arch, mate, this is bloody madness. I know we ain't exactly soft but—"

"Enough!" I rounded on Big Steve, mustering whatever was left of Archie bloody Stenworth to bully my go-to kneecapper into a fearlessness I myself could no longer show. Big Steve gulped, nodding. He wasn't going to run, but I knew he was only staying for the same reason I led us down here in the first place. To save face.

I turned, holding up my zippo in a futile attempt to pierce more of the shadows. That was when Screwloose said three words that twisted every nerve into a tighter knot than I'd ever thought possible.

"Arch, where's Nicky?"

"What?" I looked behind me back at the lads. There was Big Steve, staring at the floor as he recomposed himself. There was Screwloose, Elvis gripped in the hand that wasn't holding his own lighter. Nicky the Shimmy-Shaker? He was nowhere.

"Nicky!" My yells bounced off unseen cavern walls. "Nicky! Bloody hell Nicky, where are ya?!"

I had to ignore the smirk Screwloose didn't quite manage to hide. There was a waver in my voice, small but noticeable enough. This must have been the point that I'd forgotten all about being

Archie bloody Stenworth, because I didn't care. All I wanted to do was find Nicky and get out. Sod being the Billy Big Bollocks, I thought. Goon #4 wasn't the source of the screams. They were still going on, still toying with us by being always just out of reach. Except in the wide cavern, outside the narrowing winding tunnels, they felt to be coming from everywhere. Like the flames of our lighters had made a bubble, a bubble that outside of which was nothing save shadows and screams. A bubble that could pop at any moment.

Before I knew what was happening, I was on my knees. This was the '70s. I didn't know what panic attacks were; barely anyone back then did. Mental health ain't a taboo these days, though, and I've read enough about them to know that a panic attack is exactly what I was having. Me, Archie bloody Stenworth. Not a good look, that.

"Arch? Guv'ner?" Screwloose was standing above me. I remember the glee twinkling in his eyes; it was clear even through the blur at the edges of my vision. I couldn't focus on it, though. My brain was overloaded by sensation; by my heart slamming into my ribs, by my breaths coming too fast and shallow to deliver the air I needed, by pressure at my temples and the ringing in my ears along with it. I couldn't distinguish where the sounds of the screaming ended and the sight of the shadows began. Everything from the frigid air on my face to the wrenching guilt at losing Nicky merged into one massive, overpowering, all-consuming dread.

To my surprise, it was Big Steve that brought me back.

"Snap out of it Arch, we need to find Nicky." I'd never been so happy to feel the sting of a slap on my cheek. When my breathing was slow, and I was "aware" again, I was looking up at Big Steve. He was holding out the same hand he'd caught me across the chops with, his expression terrified but understanding. I'll tell you what, if Big Steve made it out of that cave, he'd have got a promotion. He pulled me to my feet so I could dust myself off.

"Sorry lads, don't know what came over me." I coughed. "Nicky was with us when we came out the tunnel, weren't he?"

"Yeah, he was." Big Steve replied. "Right behind me and Screwloose. Could still hear him trying not to cry over the—"

WHAM!

Even Screwloose jumped when the heavy object landed between the three of us. The wet slam as it connected with the churned earth was so loud we all fell backward, pushed by the shockwave of the impact. As a reflex, my eyes closed. That meant I couldn't see the warm liquid that carried on the pressurized air, the wetness that splattered across my face. I didn't have to. Enough drops found my open mouth. I knew that metallic tang immediately.

It was Big Steve that opened his eyes first. "JESUS BLOODY CHRIST NICKY!"

My own eyes snapped open. In less than a heartbeat, I was back on my feet, yelling at the folded heap of snapped limbs and twisted joints laying at them. Again, I didn't come here to insult your intelligence. You know I recognized that face. Even though the jaw had been carved in, the nostrils wrenched open, and the eyelids sliced off, it's obvious to anyone with half a brain cell in their noggin whose mangled corpse was staring back up at me, dead-eyed and mid-scream. All I could think about was how I would break the news to his poor mum.

"Nicky... what the bloody actual hell!" Screwloose didn't sound afraid. He sounded furious, which, for a man like Screwloose, was probably the same thing. He lifted his lighter as high as he could. Big Steve and I followed suit, all three of us straining to see just how in the actual Christ Nicky had managed to fall from the stalactites hidden so far above.

That's when we saw it for the first time.

Thanks to Elvis, we only caught a glimpse. Unfortunately, the moment we spotted it, Screwloose squeezed his trigger finger. The half-second we had was enough to make out a pair of vast, circular surfaces peering down from the shadows. Orbs that barely reflected the lighter light, only catching enough of the flicker for them to let us know we were being toyed with.

"Bloody hell, Screwloose! How you gonna hit it from that far with a bloody buckshot?!"

He didn't answer. He was already sprinting into the dark in the direction the eyes had vanished. Don't ask me why, but Big Steve and I followed. I regret that Big Steve never made it out, and poor young Nicky, of course. I never could find it in myself to give a monkey's about Screwloose though. We'd been running after him for about five minutes when the light from his Zippo vanished. Big Steve and I stood; our own bubble of light now pathetically small.

"Arch?"

"What?"

"You notice that?"

"What, Screwloose fucking vanishing?!"

"Yeah, that too, but Arch, the screaming's stopped."

I blinked, then paid better attention to my ears. Sure enough, the always-distant screaming we'd been following had ceased. There was no sound, save the thumping of blood rushing through my eardrums with every heartbeat. Except, after a few moments, I realized that wasn't *all* I could hear. There was another sound, deep and low and faint. A sound coming from above, like something large, wet, and organic being dragged down a rough cavern wall. I turned to ask Steve if heard it too, but the words caught in my throat. He was white. Not a single ounce of pigmentation remained on his clammy, tear-streaked face. That's not what left me speechless, though. What left me speechless was his trembling, extended finger.

He was pointing at something behind me.

Every shred of sense I possessed protested as I turned. It was the slowest quarter-second I've ever experienced. By the end of it, I was openly screaming for the first time since my ol' dad chased me around the house with a belt. There, dangling upside-down a few short inches from the tip of my nose, was Screwloose. There was no blood in his usually ruddy face. I expect that's because it was all leaking from the stumps where his arms used to be. His eyes rolled back in his skull for a few seconds before locking onto mine. "Not… fair… was… my turn…"

He managed to cough out the words. I'll never forget the anger in his eyes, the fury that he'd never got his chance to be top dog. His rage lasted right until he went cross-eyed. I let out a nervous laugh at first. His grimace turned into a drooling, childish smile that I found contagious in my panic. I couldn't stop myself from letting out a nervous chuckle.

"Screwloose are you… are you OK mate?"

I was in shock. My mind couldn't take it; it had forced the screaming voice behind my eyes which understood what was happening into silence. That's why I was so bemused when the tip of the blade pushed itself through Screwloose's forehead. Its emergence was slow, wet, accompanied a harrowing slurping, suckling sound. It forced its way through skull and grey matter, entering the back of Screwloose's head, not stopping until blood-soaked steel protruded from the other side. The blade was wide, too. A machete-sized thing. By the time it had pushed through, everything from brow to crown was split perfectly down the middle. I don't know if Screwloose *actually* hung there for a few minutes, or if it just felt that way. I *do* know that when the blade rose without warning my bemusement was officially over. I was screaming once more, unashamedly and without restraint. No need to mask it now, because so was Big Steve.

As for Screwloose, it would be hard for him to spread dissent now he'd been split in two. The vast rusted cleaver swam through his throat, chest, stomach. With a single motion, it cleaved the dangling man in half, sliding up his form, slicing without resistance. That's when I realized what had been holding Screwloose aloft. My knees grew weak as my gaze followed the path of the blade to Screwloose's ankles. My cries were coming through as a word now, *No,* over and over and over again the word *No* as loud as I could muster. My eyes could see it, but no part of me could believe it.

Around Screwloose's ankles were a pair of hands. The biggest I'd ever seen. Thin fingers as long as broom handles curled across his legs, wrinkled leather palms the size of dinner plates crushing one calf each. Then, from behind the two pieces of Screwloose, the third arm rose, the one holding a rusted machete both as long as a man and sharp as razor wire. I had just enough wherewithal to notice a sticky peeling noise. Unfortunately, I didn't have enough to realize what it meant. Before I could will myself into doing anything other than yell *No,* the arms holding the halves of Screwloose pulled apart.

We were still screaming when the butchered segments were thrown into opposite ends of the darkness, tossed outside our light bubble with such force that our cries didn't mask the loud snaps and cracks of bone. I didn't look behind me to see where they'd landed. I couldn't look anywhere except straight up. Neither could Big Steve. I couldn't even form a *No* anymore. All I could do was create noise, project untainted terror and hope my legs would take over and carry me back to safer, saner pastures.

"sorry about the mess. i wasn't expecting visitors." It wasn't me or Big Steve that spoke. The raspy, monotonous, child-like words came from the waking nightmare lowering itself into the flame light.

The thing was hanging from the stalactites by threads of glistening mucus as thick as a telephone pole. The fat bulbous body was the length and depth of a double-decker bus. The closest thing

I can compare it to is a maggot, or the swollen egg-spewing abdomen of an externally pregnant queen ant. At the other end of the behemoth larval form, directly above us, were eight arms. Each was twice as long as I was tall, but so thin as to appear brittle (if they hadn't just demonstrated their monstrous strength, that is). The trio of limbs that finished Screwloose were part of a cluster of four sprouting from a pulsing tumour-like growth. The thing had one of these bulges protruding from behind each ear, the talon-fingered arms framing its vast head like mandibles made of avian legs by an insane taxidermist. The fourth arm on that side held a huge burlap sack; dark, fly-covered, and dripping black ichor. On its opposite flank, it held nothing save for a man in a cheap polyester suit. Not that it mattered anymore, but we'd found Goon #5.

Goon #5… bugger me…

Goon #5's low-price suit was more-or-less intact. Only the back of his jacket and orange shirt had been torn open. So had his spinal cord. Once more, the thing had opted for a clinical cut instead of ragged buckshot-mimicking wounds. Goon #5's back had been sliced vertically, skin and muscles peeled back to reveal a column of vertebrae. The interlocking bones of his spine had been cracked open like yellowed ivory clams. Goon #5's weblike cranial nerves were exposed to the open air, dry and twitching with the spinal fluid they needed completely drained. This unnatural cavity ran from Goon #5's lower lumbar all the way up to the base of his skull. A portion of this too had been cracked open; a swollen welt of undulating brain tissue bulged from between perfectly-sawn fragments of cranium.

Goon #5 twitched and moaned in the thing's arms, suspended by talon-like digits grasping his head, neck, and groin. The fourth hand was running an index finger up and down the perimeter of the wound. It moved gracefully, like a dying man stroking their beloved's cheek for the final time.

"i didn't *want* visitors. You're a bad landlord mr stenworth."

Hearing my name crushed my lungs and kick-started a wave of diaphragmatic spasms. My gaze moved from the groaning Turkish footman to the face at the center of the arms. It was human in shape, but no bloody human has a head the size of a van. I wish that's where the details I have to share ended. A van-sized human head would've been bad enough, right? I should be so lucky. This thing, the thing that had massacred some of the hardest men in London, had the face of a baby. A colossal, slime-coated baby.

Its pudgy cheeks and beef-joint button nose were pale, translucent, and beset by a network of varicose veins. The fat lips were caked in all shades of red, both bright wet crimsons and dark crusted purples. A trail of drool dangled from one corner of its toothless maw. Worst of all was its wide, sewer-plate eyes. They were perfect circles, exactly like eyes in a cartoon or kids drawing. The angle of their surface was wrong. They were flat, almost concave, closer to those of a fish or reptile. Their coloring was human, but only just about. Unblemished whites, thin grey irises, pupils the shade of bottled interstellar voids. A dead, glassy gaze that bore through me like I was so-much earth and concrete.

The bottomless pupils didn't move as the distended hands that discarded Screwloose like unwanted banana peel grabbed Big Steve.

"Arch, *help*!"

I didn't help. I couldn't. Instead of raising my shooter I listened to it clattering on the ground. My legs were numb, my mind filled with white noise. I couldn't even run to save my own neck, no matter how much what small consciousness remained wanted to. The thing pulled Big Steve towards its gaping maw and neither of us could resist. I was Archie bloody Stenworth, and in that moment I realized just how much of a joke that was when compared to the *true* power in this world.

Big Steve never managed to get another word in. The thing stuffed him head-first between its fat lips. Dull crunches were accompanied by a fresh deluge of scarlet. Steve's legs kicked and bucked for a few seconds before falling still. The thing chewed for another agonizing minute before it plucked Steve's lower half from its mouth, slavering gums sucking the last of the meat from his exposed spine. It placed the legs into the dripping sack, licking its crust-coated lips, gaze still never leaving my own.

"please don't be a bad landlord again. you interrupted my music."

I could feel its cold breath on the back of my neck as I ran. My feet found themselves again. Some things are just too much, you know? Once you get to a certain point that primal instinct kicks in and you just… you just *go*.

For me, that moment was seeing the purpose of Goon #5's injury. The thing lowered the Turk toward me, making sure I got a good view of the stringy cranial nerves in his cracked spine.

"music."

The things free hands were moving before my brain had connected the dots. By the time it had, I was already rushing through the darkness away from the insanity playing out in the flamelight. Goon #5's bestial howls started the moment a talon-tip touched an exposed nerve. That's what tipped me past the point of doing anything but running. The "music" the thing was talking about? It was the screaming we'd followed. *That's* the sight that broke the proverbial camel's back. Those avian digits plucking at the open nerves of Goon #5's spine, purposefully stimulating pain receptors, playing him like a fucking instrument.

I don't know how my legs found the tunnel, or my arms the purchase to climb. I wasn't aware again until I was sat in the Mini Cooper, sobbing uncontrollably into the steering wheel. I didn't look back as I sped off fast as I bloody could. I couldn't have even if I'd wanted to. I knew I couldn't handle seeing those glassy sewer-plate eyes watching me from the gloom behind the broken windows.

I never went back to the warehouse. I had the boys fence it off, make it appear condemned. A fair few junkies and homeless types wandered in over the years, but none of them ever wandered out. As far as the firm was concerned, I was the only survivor of a meet gone south. I only managed another fifteen-or-so years before retiring. My heart wasn't in it no more, you see? Not after finding out the horrors waiting below the streets I lorded over.

Soon enough my heart won't be in *anything* no more. Kind of funny, when you think about it. After all the things I've done and seen, in the end it'll be a bum ticker what gets me. Thanks for listening to my story. It feels good getting it off my chest. I only ask one thing of you. The kind of people that know me aren't the kind of people that stand still long enough to read something this long. If, by any chance, you hear my name mentioned in conversation, you tell 'em something. You tell 'em: "Archie Stenworth? That man weren't afraid of nuffink."

That's all I'm asking. I want you to keep up the lie, the myth, the legend. I'm trying to compromise, you see? I don't want to die with secrets, so I'm spilling them to folk I know I can trust to keep 'em. I'm Archie bloody Stenworth, and for one night I was more afraid of summink than any man before or since. Let's just keep that between us though, eh?

THE CAIRO EXPEDITION
(EXCERPTS FROM THE JOURNAL OF LORD ORWELL HARKENWILD)

June 1st, 1872, London
It's hard to believe almost a year to the day has passed since our voyage to Egypt was declared. This will no doubt be another spectacular adventure for readers of *The Gentleman's Almanac*. I'd agreed to finance and take joint leadership of the expedition at a function to celebrate that idiot Wagner's new opera house in Bayreuth. Only in Bavaria on respite after my travels through the Himalaya's, I was busy entertaining Wagner's female consorts with various tales of my exploits. After all, what is the point of a life of courage and adventure if one cannot get braggadocios about it after a few glasses of wine? The party, the opera house, and indeed Wagner himself I must admit were rather dull. After fighting with the rear-eyed Frenchman in the mountains of Nepal such things were far from stimulating enough to rouse me. The attentions of the fairer sex though? Those are never too far from my interests, just as is the case with any gentleman of honest character. That's when Obadiah introduced himself.

My stories of the Frenchman were apparently enough to foster the curiosity of not only the giggling daughters of Bavaria's nobility, however. The man I came to learn was Obadiah Bramfield had been deep in conversation with one of Wagner's protegees; a young German named Friedrich or Frederic or something along those lines, who had a moustache almost as impressive as my own. Upon overhearing my description of the nefarious red gaze and hypnotic red chimes of the Frenchman, Obadiah turned away from his dialogue on reincarnation and eternal recurrence to offer me a proposition. It turned out that Obadiah, the patron of some hospital or institution in the North American colonies, had a vested interest in whatever realm of fringe animalia the alabaster abomination I'd put down in Nepal belonged to. It was this that finally allowed him to catch my attention after a few rebuttals of his intrusion on my flirtatious boasting. His institute, which like many institutes has a name that shall forever damn elude me, was vested in the location and study of artefacts, beasts, and phenomena inexplicable by the modern sciences. He'd met the Frenchman, apparently, despite never travelling to the Himalaya's himself. It was when I scoffed at the improbability of such a thing being true that he showed me the daguerreotype. The detail of the pictograph was unmistakable; the same thin-faced Obadiah Bramfield fellow that sat before me, standing shoulder-to-sepia-shoulder with that triad of grinning maws I'd last seen tumbling off of the side of Everest. I imagine the women of Bavarian court are still indignant about the haste with which I dismissed them to probe further. By the end of the evening Obadiah and I were shaking hands on my participation, and partial funding, of his voyage to Cairo.

As usual, I didn't deign to investigate much into the *why's* of Obadiah's expedition when we first met. In the three or so decades I've scoured inside the Empire and out for adventure, I haven't yet found such information useful. Leave the justification to the Darwin's of the world, that's my motto. Scholarly pursuits are all very well for the right kind of man. I am not that kind of man though; I am the kind of man who relishes the very same dangers men of academia begrudgingly suffer through on their quests for buried knowledge. This is why I can't be too disdainful of them, despite how much of an anathema I find libraries, lecture halls, and laboratories. If there weren't men with lusts for knowledge to satiate, I'd have little reason to spend the family fortune beyond a string of just-because's and flights of fancy. It is far easier to justify a jaunt to Peru to my nagging sisters if a museum gets a nice big treasure to display with the Harkenwild name on the plaque beside it upon my return. I did ask Obadiah why we couldn't leave right away, and he mentioned something to do with the positioning of the stars around 14 months from then (August of this year). I've found the wait since then a test of perseverance, but given what I've learned since of Obadiah and his institute I know my efforts will bear fruit. After the mountains of Nepal, I'd been longing to once more traverse one of the worlds dryer, harsher climbs. The Sahara might not present the same challenge in verticality as the Himalayas, but the sandy untamed dunes are their own adventure.

So it is that, a year later, I find myself writing this on a steamer out of London, setting sail for Egypt from where we'll make our journey by rail and camel to what the archaeologist of our party, Boxstead, informs me is the location of a burial site of pre-Christian antiquity. Obadiah has come to possess the location of a tome, one that he assures me will be upend our understanding of the natural laws. The *Taealim Alrajul Al'akhir*, or *The Teachings of the Last Man* in the proper tongue. After my conquest of the Frenchman, I have been itching for more of the esoteric, the unnatural and unexplained. Obadiah has promised me adventure beyond my imagining in this regard. Since he is the only living soul I know of to also encounter the Frenchman, I believe him. Despite my pestering during our correspondence over the last twelve months he's yet to divulge much further on his other experiences with the... how shall I put it, the heretical? The unmundane? That which would upturn the natural order of the Christian world? I can tell that there's a great deal more to Obadiah than he's so far seen fit to indulge me with, especially when it comes to our shared interest in the inexplicable. Despite my urges, I shall withhold impulses to badger him on our voyage. I am assured that by the time I return to London I shall be almost as versed as he in all things unknown, but until then I must exercise just a few months more restraint.

It is not long now, though. The view through the porthole has once again got my pulse racing, in a way it hasn't since I first left England for new shores way back in 1831 when Father took me on my first, and his last, voyage. We shall head down the channel, through the Strait of Gibraltar, and then across the Mediterranean past Malta and the Isles of Sicily to dock in Alexandria, Egypt. As the sun sets over horizon waves I am, for the first time in many years, filled with genuine excitement.

June 11th, 1872, Strait of Gibraltar

Our first week at sea has been not unpleasant, but far from the most tolerable journey. At least that was the case until this evening, until the incident. Our steamer, *The Conduit,* was commissioned by Obadiah and she has held firm despite the choppy waters. The heat in these equatorial climes might be prejudicial to most Englishmen, but I am far from most Englishmen. Compared to the pressing climbs of the jungles of the Americas, or the dry heat waiting for us, a little Mediterranean humidity is no source of irksomeness for myself. Obadiah too retains his curiously calm demeanor—I've yet to see the man so much as release a bead of sweat. No, the heat is nothing for men of our ilk. The source of my annoyance on this particular voyage has been the crew.

All experienced seamen hired personally by Bramfield, I have heard little but muttered superstition come from the sailors on this vessel since the moment we left port. The further south the engines take us, the more erratic their behavior becomes. As followers of my exploits know, I don't hold the usual disdain for seamen and other lower-class professions that many men of my stock share. I started this expedition like I would any other; dining with the crew, swapping stories and scars, learning new ditties on the loose women across the ports of the world. There has been none of that on this ship. Below the deck of *The Conduit,* one will find nothing save for grim, sullen faces. No songs sung; no stories swapped. I've had to resign myself to dining with Obadiah, the geographer Boxstead, and the five other academic members of our voyage.

The conversation hasn't been entirely dull. It's also true that, although I'm loathed to admit it, dining in a manner appropriate to my station is perhaps more conducive to a successful venture. The crew would be leaving our company once we reached Alexandria. It was Obadiah, Boxstead, and the rest who'd be with me for the entirety of our expedition, so I'd be foolish to suggest my boredom didn't have some use. I'd soon be partially responsible for keeping these men alive in a desert, after all. Since many of them had never left the green pastures of Europe, knowing which of their number were likely prone to hysteria could save… well, not *my* life, but definitely one of theirs.

There is Hector Boxstead, the archaeologist I mentioned. He is a young lad, nervous but articulate, and had been in Bramfield's employ since Obadiah's own encounter with the Frenchman (in London in the 1860s, apparently). Also previously known to Obadiah are Nathaniel Harwurst and Ernst Stenworth. These two giants among men don't say much, and I knew they were with us for additional security long before Obadiah introduced them as his personal protection. Finally, from his institute there's the American Winston DeWint, an expert in esoteric languages, an Ottoman scholar in ancient idols named Arda Aydin, and finally the impatient Irish demolitions expert introduced only as Mr Darcrioch. Despite the reputation Irishmen have, I must say that of our number, it is Mr Darcrioch I worry for most. He is a small man, barely over five feet in stature, and if his frame would not shatter after even the weakest blow, I'd be genuinely flabbergasted. It seems almost comical that such a man should have mastery over gunpowder, nitroglycerin, and military grade ordnance, but there we are.

Their conversations have been focused on many dry, overly-articulated topics I invariably imbibe too much by the end of the meal to follow. Despite my hopes Obadiah might enlighten me a little on what he knew of the Frenchman, or the secrets hidden in this *Taealim Alrajul Al'akhir* we were seeking, he rarely spoke. Instead, the chugging of steam engine was cut through only by academic debates of the most tedious nature. Even if the morose behavior of the crew wasn't stretching the hours of my day to tiresomeness, the company of Obadiah's entourage every night would still have me scratching tally on the wall of my cabin as we approached Cairo. To call these men dull would be doing dullards everywhere a disservice. That's not been my only disgruntlement, though. It's also far from reason enough to make entry into this journal again, long before we've set foot in Egypt.

No. I am sitting down to write tonight not because I have been once again in the company of thin-blooded scholars, but because after the moon rose there was an incident below decks. Our meal of steamed chicken was interrupted by Jimson, the boatswain, hammering on the door to Obadiah's cabin with unrelenting panic. He was near-screeching, completely incoherent, raving about something terrible in the engine room. It took splashing a mug of gin across his face to calm him, and even then, I could tell it took him conscious effort to keep his nerves steeled. Obadiah agreed to go below decks with Jimson and bade the rest of us to stay, but I insisted on accompanying him. Remain here to listen to DeWint, Aydin, and Darcrioch rehash the same old arguments over the nature of life, death, and rebirth? As much as I've come to respect Obadiah over these last seven days as an authoritative willpower almost equal to my own, there was no chance of that happening. So it was that my co-financier begrudgingly accepted I would be joining Mr Harwurst, Mr Stenworth, and himself to investigate the source of the boatswain's unrest.

I am... not sure if this retelling will make it into my account of the expedition when it's published in *The Gentleman's Almanac*. I am no stranger to the visceral; by this point in my decorated career, I've seen more men's innards than even the great surgeon Joseph Lister. I've never been sparing with the details of accidents, mishaps, and skirmishes in my retellings for the public, either. My firsthand account of the Frenchman included a vivid recount of my guide being emptied like a leather waterskin. It would take more horsepower than any engine conceived by man can muster to turn my stomach, such is the iron from which my will is cast. What I saw in that engine room, though, I am writing here only for the purpose of exorcism. I am not a man of great religious fervor, but even I understand the stain keeping such things secret would leave on my soul. I must write this down and expel it from my thoughts lest I doom myself to a lifetime of nightmarish visions whenever my eyes close.

It was one of stokers, a boy barely out of single digits. I could only guess his age because of what little of his face remained. The rest of his skin, judging by the smell of melting fat and roasting meat, had been flayed from his body and thrown into the coals of the engine. I am glad DeWint, Ayind, and Darcrioch didn't follow us down into the dark. Even with my hardened resolve, the sight of the boy's exposed musculature was enough to have me swallowing back bile. His smile, too, unnerved me. In the jungles of Rhodesia, I'd witnessed a man's ritual disemboweling to resolve a tribal dispute. I can remember the look of pained agony on his face clearly; indeed, recounting it with avid detail was one of my first submissions to *The Gentleman's Almanac* to receive widespread acclaim. The skinless boy in that sooty darkness, propped up opposite the engine on a stool stolen from the mess, didn't look as though he'd been pained when he died. Despite having every inch of skin stripped from his body, his expression bore not one iota of distress or perturbation.

The lad was smiling.

The stoker was grinning ear-to-severed-ear on a face missing everything not immediately adjacent to his eyes, nose, and mouth. It was when the boatswain explained he'd caught the lad red handed and flaying was self-inflicted that I had to admit defeat and steady myself against the interior of the hull.

Only Mr Harwurst and Mr Stenworth didn't react at all. Obadiah looked concerned, although from his actions I don't think it was the same kind of disturbia the boatswain openly, and I secretly, felt. Obadiah spent an hour extracting every shred of information he could from the trembling Jimson. The troubled boatswain had tried to stop the boy from peeling, but nothing had worked. The lad got violent when he tried, slicing at Jimson with the same rusted knife he'd used to remove his outermost flesh inch by dripping inch. Obadiah's main concern was that the flayed lad hadn't been left to wander the rest of the ship or make contact with the rest of the crew. Jimson shook his head; he'd sealed the door when he left, not knowing what else to do, and the lad must have finished his morbid task while the boatswain went for help. The rest of the crew were aware of what happened, but wouldn't assist Jimson, refusing to go near the lad; even while he threw his removed skin into the engine furnace and sat down on his stool to laugh until he died. Cursed, they said, or so Jimson told it. I would say '*if you can believe such a thing*', but it's now dawning on me that in a world containing such nightmarish visages as the Frenchman, I in fact *can* believe such things. This is not an admission that I *do* believe, only that I find myself with newfound capacity to.

Does Obadiah believe in curses? I genuinely don't know. He is a man of science, despite the esoteric and occultish nature of his specific academic passions. Something as mundane as belief in curses and the like feels... beneath him, for lack of a better term. That being said, his reaction to one part of the boatswain's retelling left me reconsidering this assessment. Even though the engine room is lit only by the orange hues of the furnace, I could see the color draining from Obadiah's face when Jimson the boatswain revealed the word the lad muttered over and over while removing his own skin.

"*Perfection.*"

While the word means little to me beyond being the only acceptable standard of personal achievement, to Obadiah, it clearly held significance. I... I've been sworn to secrecy about what happened thereafter. *Especially* in writing. My co-financier made that part extremely clear. I'm no stranger to life at sea, and I know how these things go. Many a man overboard takes their last breath long before falling from the ship, and it's deemed in everyone's best interests if those on land never find out the truth. Obadiah assures me the boatswain's fate was in *everyone's* best interests. He remained his usual cryptic self once the deed was done, but he explained he'd expected something of this nature, tragic and unfortunate as it was. That doesn't mean it sits well with me, though. The engine furnace may reach temperatures that render all remains to ash, but what past deeds return to us in nightmares have no such cleansing fire. I hope that by committing this to paper I'll put my disquiet to rest.

Obadiah didn't explain why the boy couldn't follow Jimson into the flames. I persisted in questioning, but the only justification was that *"just because the boy is dead doesn't mean he's not still marked"*. I found his use of the word marked, rather than cursed as the boatswain had rambled, piqued my curiosity. Once more, however, my co-benefactor provided no further clarity.

I've never had much inclination towards hindsight. When I first met Obadiah, he didn't strike me as any different from the previous scholars, academics, and institutional diplomats that sought to leverage the Harkenwild fame and fortune to achieve their own scientific ends. I'd never really inquire much about them—the call to adventure in distant lands was all the justification I ever needed. It might be that my haste and haphazardness have become, as Father always predicted, my folly.

The memory of Mr Harwurst and Mr Stenworth evacuating the stoker boy's skinless smiling corpse over the ship's stern will require a drink much stiffer than mere words to bury. Thank God for gin.

June 19th, 1872, Off the Coast of Malta

I feel it would be prudent to make note of the conversation I partook in with Mr DeWint. I found the man hanging over the stern taffrail regurgitating our evening meal. I'd left Obadiah's dining quarters for some fresh air in which to enjoy my pipe, and it was the noise of DeWint's obscenely loud retching that alerted me to his presence in the inky ocean night. Were this any of the vessels I'd previously sailed on, he'd doubtless have been made mockery of by the crew for his lack of stomach. *The Conduit's* crew were nowhere to be found, however, at least not anywhere I could see them.

DeWint is a young man. I'd hazard to guess that he's not yet out of undergraduate academia, or if he is, then his student years aren't yet more than three winters behind him. We ended up striking conversation after I offered him some snuff to ease his stomach. He didn't accept the gesture, but his laughter at the notion seemed to allow him to regain some composure. After a brief back-and-forth around the general peculiarities of life at sea, I realized I'd been presented with an opportunity. Until tonight, I'd had little chance to converse with DeWint, Aydin, Darcrioch, or even Boxstead without Obadiah's presence. This hadn't been a cause for concern until the night Jimson and the stoker boy departed our company. The man was a bore, but now he was a bore that held critical information.

DeWint is far more forthcoming than Obadiah, but for all his virtuous eagerness is only marginally more informed than myself about our expedition and the man who planned it all (the plan I perhaps foolishly agreed to take part in without deigning to learn any details of). That's not to say my investigation didn't yield results, however. I may not be fully informed, but I am without doubt much less ignorant.

To summarize everything I learned over our hour-long dalliance:

- Winston DeWint cannot physically conceptualize how a man can agree to set forth on an expedition without bothering to learn details. As I said, he is a bore. An incorrigible bore.
- DeWint has been a member of Obadiah's institute for the last four years, although as far as he knows, the organization has existed for at least the last two decades.
- DeWint, Boxstead, and Aydin are experts in what the Vatican would call heresy. The broadsheets would sensationalize as the occult, but they refer to as the science of paranaturalism.
- Obadiah founded their institute, and their central offices are in "Wisconsin", a "state" in the "independent" North American colonies. My own feelings on this so-called statehood aside, DeWint notes that the asylum owned by Obadiah which partially funds their research is much older than the legally recognized territory of "Wisconsin" itself, and was one of the first buildings in the region to be erected from brick and mortar in the days of early settlement.
- DeWint seemed somewhat irate that I hadn't gleaned any of this information from our discussions over dinner. I made no attempt to hide that our evening's conversations had, until this evening, bored me to the point of distraction and absentmindedness. This only seemed to ire him further. I would be a dishonest man if I claimed I was unamused by

his irritation at the fact a person in his presence for weeks hadn't been hanging on his every word.
- I honored my own word by not discussing the boatswain. I did, however, ask if anything in the so-called paranatural sciences accounted for self-inflicted removal of one's own skin. DeWint visibly recoiled at this, not from disgust but obvious surprise, which was all the answer I needed. When I asked if the word *"perfection"* held any significance, he became genuinely riled. He suggested that *"whatever ghastly matter you're pursuing, desist if that particular word is involved, dealing with them isn't worth anything under the stars."* His forthcoming nature stopped short of extrapolation here, however.
- I decided to press with further questioning on the tome Obadiah was seeking, the *Taealim Alrajul Al'akhir*. Again, he was surprised at my lack of knowledge, given that I'd invested no small sum in its acquisition. After I'd explained that men in my position have secretaries to carry out mundane trivialities like finding out why academics need my money, he told me exactly what I'd agreed to assist in locating. The *Taealim Alrajul Al'akhir* is, according to DeWint's knowledge, one of the oldest written volumes known to exist. While its status here is debatable, there's no argument on its status as the earliest first-hand accounts of the flora, fauna, and phenomena DeWint and his paranaturalist ilk seek to understand. An undoubtably invaluable document.
- Upon dropping his voice to a whisper, DeWint disclosed some further hearsay. He had been speaking to Mr Aydin, his other colleague from the institute. Mr Darcrioch, it transpires, is a recently acquired member of their fellowship and the others are firmly within Obadiah's sphere of influence, but Winston DeWint and Arden Aydin both apparently share doubts about their longstanding employer and this particular venture. DeWint was about to ask my stance on the belief in prophecy and foretelling when we were interrupted. Mr Harwurst and Mr Stenworth manifested from the shadows, prompting DeWint into silence. Mr Stenworth spoke, bidding us to return for a secondary course. I've been on the receiving end of enough thinly veiled threats to know it wasn't a request. I might be that readers of *The*

Gentleman's Almanac will have more to read about than a mere desert adventure. I must exercise discrepancy, though.

June 28th, 1872, Kafr el-Zayyat

The crew were glad to part from our company when we docked at Alexandria. Obadiah informed me that the return leg of our trip would be mostly by land, making a stop in Constantinople. *The Conduit* was to return to London. A fine idea by my reckoning, since I hadn't set foot in Ottoman lands since the 1850s. Truth be told, I'm also beyond satisfied with a few months on solid ground. I've put the incident with the boatswain and the stoker firmly behind me, helped in no small part by the invigorating North African heat, but it would be an untruth to suggest I was eager to make further oceanic plans.

For their part, the crew hadn't made a murmur over their comrade's fate. They no doubt knew what had happened, but seamen are suspicious, and in their minds, a curse is a powerful thing. I'm sure many discussions were had below deck while Obadiah, his entourage, and I, slept in our private quarters. Conversations that ended with a resolution that we'd acted correctly, albeit for unjust reasons. To save our own hides or something along those lines, I don't doubt. Nothing was said to me, but on the few times I tried to return below deck and rouse some of the merriment I'd expected prior to departure, it was made abundantly clear I wasn't welcome.

You can imagine my relief when we met our expedition's military escort. Unlike the crew of *The Conduit,* these were men of action; men you could drink with, men with stories to share and ears to share with. To my surprise, they were all Englishmen; a regiment of defecting redcoats turned rifles for hire. I'd expected a local entourage, but Obadiah informed me Sergeant Kinnock and his squad of 7 sunbaked infantrymen had been escorting travelers across the breadth of the African Northeast for several years. They were more than qualified, apparently. Besides, he added, locals to the area haven't been the most enabling of Obadiah's institute and their goals in the past.

The presence of Sgt Kinnock and his men wasn't only welcome because they were better company than that I'd shared the expedition with so far. While my own safety was never in doubt, it's no small measure of comfort to know Mr DeWint, Mr Aydin, and Mr Darcrioch won't be a liability resting firmly on my own shoulders. That Obadiah has means to take care of himself, I haven't questioned. The man has that air about him, a steeliness in the eyes I recognize from my own reflection. Mr Harwurst and Mr Stenworth are present mainly for the look of the thing by my wager, to give the right impression. They'd still no doubt lay down their lives for their employer. I just don't believe he ultimately needs them to. I also don't believe the courtesy of their mortality extends beyond Obadiah. Kinnock is a welcome addition to our troupe.

The train journey from Alexandria to Kafr el-Zayyat took several hours. Railways are still a novelty to me, despite the decades that have passed since their invention. I was glad to have my own compartment. It allowed me to catch up on some of the sleep I'd lost in the last few days of our time on *The Conduit*. I could still hear DeWint and Aydin prattling away next door about cyclical reality or some other such dry nonsense, but not so loud as to interrupt my rest. I have not yet had a chance to converse with Mr DeWint alone since our conversation on the 28th. At no point have I been absent from either Mr Stenworth or Mr Harwurst's malevolent observation. I've tried several times over dinner to steer the topic of discussion toward the *Taealim,* or Obadiah himself to discern a little more of the man's history, but to no avail. I must admit, the longer I spend in his company, the less I am trusting of his intentions. Something seems off about the man. Not in the rank odious way something is off about the sniveling Boxstead, or in the way of clear inclination toward sadism as with Mr Harwurst and Mr Stenworth, but nonetheless there's an air to Obadiah that puts my mind ill at ease. It's not too dissimilar a feeling as I had from the Frenchman before he removed his blindfold and I bore witness to his pair of tittering maws. Still, perhaps I am being overzealous. I am, after all, on an expedition to uncover something possibly mystical and esoteric. Danger and suspense are to be expected, are they not? I'm sure that I'll

Obadiah had lodgings arranged for us when we arrived. We're boarding at an inn barely a stone's throw from the train station. I must admit, Muhammad Ali's advances to the regional infrastructure over the prior decades has born fruit. This is far from the sand-covered wilderness I'd expected. Kafr el-Zayyat is positively modern; a waypoint stretching back centuries, revitalized as a hub of trade and agriculture for the Ali dynasty's vision of an industrialized caliphate. There's been whispering in London that Egypt should have been subsumed into the Empire. I care not for statecraft, but I shall profess it would be a shame if the Khedivate fell under our occupation. This shan't make *The Almanac,* of course, as it's surely high treason, but every year I grow evermore tired of Britannia's expansion across the map. Every flag planted is an adventure lost.

Obadiah has some unrelated business to attend while in Kafr el-Zayyat, but recommended I take in the town's attractions before boarding the railway for Cairo at dawn, *"while there's still chance to partake in normalized society"*. The man has an odd way of phrasing things; I cannot lie. While the trio of academics followed this suggestion, I've already decided to opt for a night of rest. Truth be told, I am not feeling quite myself. The last few nights on *The Conduit* I found restless, troublesome, and possessing very little healthy sleep to be found. I am normally unperturbed by long waking spells, but I imagine something in the engine fumes led to the strong miasmic headacheyness which amassed over the final legs of our voyage. Respite shall provide no end of vigor. I will update once we reach Cairo, and the *real* expedition begins.

June 29th, 1872, Kafr el-Zayyat

Winston DeWint is dead. While I wrestled with the silken fabric bed sheets and tried to find sleep, he, Aydin, and Darcrioch had found their way to a hashish parlour. They'd partaken, because of course. If *Almanac* readers are hoping for a tale of a boisterous American scholar offending the locals and meeting the wrong end of a blade because of his typical colonial arrogance, they're going to be disappointed. DeWint was, by all accounts, a gentleman throughout his time indulging in Kafr el-Zayyat's exotic underside. If anything, the most problematic visitor as far as the staff and patrons of the hashish den were concerned was Aydin, who started several heated debates about the nature of Islam with a passing Imam.

No. By both Aydin and Darcrioch's recollection of events, Winston DeWint did nothing to usher in his own end. Neither can tell me *why* he died, because they can't even tell me *how* he died, even though they were both present to bear witness. According to Darcrioch, the trio had been sharing a pipe for several hours when it happened. DeWint had just exhaled; sinking back into a large cushion and continuing his conversation in fluent Arabic with one of the serving girls. What happened next, I'm unclear on, as both Aydin and Darcrioch's stories vary. I'll try to recount both versions as best I can, although several hours have passed since and already my retention begins to fail me.

According to Mr Darcrioch:
- Winston DeWint was speaking in Arabic to a beautiful woman. Despite not understanding the language himself, Mr Darcrioch could tell Mr DeWint was flirting with the hashish parlor attendee, and she seemed extremely receptive.
- Without warning, Mr DeWint stopped talking in the middle of a sentence and stared at the opposite wall. He remained there for at least a minute without moving. It wasn't until Mr Aydin shouted something at Mr DeWint that Mr Darcrioch knew something was amiss, and that Mr DeWint's behavior couldn't be attributed to the hashish.
- Again, without warning, Mr DeWint began vibrating with such velocity that he was visually rendered translucent, like a specter, with his features shifting between discernability and smoke-like obfuscation. Several of the cushions he'd been seated on ignited from the friction heat.
- The owner of the hashish parlor emptied a bucket of water over Mr DeWint in an attempt to stifle the flames. This worked to a degree, although the water that made direct contact with Mr DeWint evaporated. The hissing drew the attention of the other patrons of the parlor, many of whom began screaming or became enraged.
- After around fifty seconds, Mr DeWint came to an abrupt "rest". Mr Darcrioch didn't have another word for it, despite restful being the farthest thing from one's mind when viewing the suddenly still corpse of Winston DeWint. Mr Darcrioch didn't have a chance to inspect the body fully. The sudden violent outburst of the hashish patrons and subsequent ejection, or Mr Darcrioch and Mr Aydin from the premises, saw to that. All the former can recount is that DeWint was notably thinner, definitely dead, and his eyes were, in Mr Darcrioch's elegant words, *"blacker'n a shite in a tar pit so they were"*.

According to Mr Aydin:
- Mr DeWint was bragging about the wealth of his father's farm in Illinois, and the serving girl was feigning interest so that one of the others in the owner's harem could steal his coin purse. Mr Aydin was aware of the scheme, but decided

not to intervene as it would *"teach that upstart American a lesson"*.

- Around three minutes prior to his paralysis, Mr DeWint changed the topic of conversation rather dramatically. While he didn't revert to English or lose his braggadocios tone, his sentences became seemingly nonlinear, almost nonsensical. At first, Mr Aydin assumed the effects of the hashish had manifested linguistic limitations in Mr DeWint's Arabic. However, after listening for a while, Mr Aydin realized he appeared to be participating in conversation, although not with the confused parlor girl. Mr Aydin can't remember the specifics of what Mr DeWint said, as he himself was also influenced by the hashish, but he can recount snippets. Phrases such as *"you things aren't supposed to be here"* and *"how can you manifest so far from Wisconsin"* first drew Mr Aydin's attention, but not fully. It was when he heard Mr DeWint clearly say, *"you'll never stop him from finding the book"* that he realized DeWint wasn't simply reaching the extent of his Arabic. According to Aydin, DeWint's body language was still directed at the parlor-girl, but his eyes and words were aimed at a spot on the opposite wall, directly behind Mr Aydin. Mr Aydin couldn't see anything there, a fact he explained before I'd even asked.

- Mr Aydin felt something at his ear, a slight burning as though he'd been grazed by a bullet. He offered me a view of the lobe, and sure enough, there was indeed a small but not insignificant portion of his ear missing. There was no blood; the wound looked cauterized, freshly cauterized, but cauterized, nonetheless. It was also sizeable enough that I'd have noticed it by this point, having now spent several weeks in his company. He didn't register any visual component to the sensation, nor did he hear a gunshot, but by his own admission, it took him a few moments to register the wound's infliction. His attention was drawn to Mr DeWint. By Mr Aydin's account, Mr DeWint was now blurred as though travelling at a high speed despite remaining stationary. The velocity of his vibrations caused several of the cushions he'd been seated on to combust.

- Mr Aydin's account of the parlor owner's actions doesn't vary from Mr Darcrioch's. Given that he can speak Arabic,

Mr Aydin was able to add that the enraged patrons were screaming about curses, evil djinns, and similar local explanations *"that are customary and to be expected when a paranatural event manifests"*. When asked if he'd witnessed something like this before, Mr Aydin shrugged; a response that I found filled me with both alarm and intrigued. *"This specifically? No. I have read about possibly similar, from DeWint's reports."*

- DeWint came to an abrupt halt after nearly a minute of ceaseless motion. Mr Aydin, a man more accustomed to methods of scientific observation than Mr Darcrioch, took in several details before the locals forced them back onto the street at sword point. According to Mr Aydin his fellow paranaturalist had *"succumbed to a rapid affliction not unlike the severe malnutrition witnessed amongst the Irish peasantry during the great famine"*, a comparison Mr Darcrioch would have no doubt made himself had he not such a low tolerance to hashish. Like many academics, Winston DeWint was a rather… rotund fellow; to address the matter delicately. Mr Aydin's account of his ribs and digestive tract being visible, as though his skin were a mere veil draped across them, was disconcerting, to say the least. When I recounted Mr Darcrioch's description of DeWint's eyes, Mr Aydin nodded gravely, affirming the Irishman's appraisal. *"Such eyes on a man I have not seen, at least not by causes acknowledged with credibility in any medical institution in the civilized world, or indeed in any texts outside the Vatican archives or our own libraries,"* Mr Aydin had remarked.

Much to my frustration, our conversation was interrupted by Mr Harwurst and Mr Stenworth. Obadiah had requested my presence. I couldn't help but feel the timing was far too intrusive to be mere happenstance. He was waiting for me in his private quarters, gazing out his window into the Kafr el-Zayyat nightscape. I can hear the commotion coming from outside even now; Sgt Kinnock and his men are apparently having some difficulties placating the crowd of Kafr el-Zayyat locals amassing outside our board-house. To my surprise, Obadiah bade Mr Harwurst and Mr Stenworth leave us be, making this the first time I'd been in the man's company without his enforcers in tow since that night long, long ago in Bayreuth.

Again, I shall paraphrase the encounter as best as I am able. Several hours have passed since, and my mind is still restless.

- I must admit, our meeting began on an aggressive note, and it was myself at fault. I am not an ill-tempered man; indeed, fluster isn't a word that has so far existed in my personal lexicon. The combination of my aching head, so many unanswered questions so far into our voyage, the rabble outside, and Mr DeWint's death pushed my resolve beyond the point of composure for the first time since childhood. Obadiah didn't raise so much as an eyebrow during my rant. His thin face remained calm, placated, as indifferent as it always was on every single one of our evening meals in his quarters on board *The Conduit*.
- Once I'd calmed, which took several more minutes than I'm comfortable committing to writing even in a personal journal, Obadiah raised a hand. I found myself taking a seat on one of the cushions. I'd be dishonest if I said the movement was entirely voluntary, but I have more pressing details to preserve.
- The first words out of Obadiah's mouth disarmed me completely; they were an apology. Much to my amazement he conceded that "you're right Lord Orwell, I should have been more forthcoming about the dangers we're currently facing, and the nature of our expedition. I let my desire to not ingratiate you into this world too quickly cause a lapse in my judgement. I cannot divulge everything immediately, but I feel you're at least owed some understanding concerning Mr DeWint's untimely demise."
- Mr DeWint's death wasn't due to some malady or ailment. He was murdered, or as close to murdered as one can be considered being when meeting one's demise at the hands of the paranatural. So too was the stoker boy aboard *The Conduit*, as would the boatswain have been were it not for Mr Harwurst and Mr Stenworth's intervention. However, Mr DeWint and the deceased crewmen hadn't met their fates at the hands of the same beings. The things that ended DeWint were waiting for us when we arrived. The twin presences, as he referred to them, responsible for the stoker boy aren't limited by the constraints of physical space or geographic location. By Obadiah's reckoning, there is a strong possibility they're not even aware of each other's

existence. I don't know if I find the thought that the hostilities we faced weren't an attack from a united front, but were rather idiosyncratic assaults with unconnected but identical objectives, comforting or a cause for alarm.

- When I asked Obadiah why our compatriots had met their unfortunate end via these... entities, he informed me we had been marked since long before we'd left London. He explained that his prior secrecy and discretion had been in no small part down to this fact. It was for my safety, he assured me, that I'd had certain facts deliberately obfuscated from me. There are many abysses into which one could stare, and many will stare back. My awareness of their nature would be unto them like a beacon. So too would any overt operations by Obadiah himself. The clandestine nature of our expedition was as such to ensure nothing, be it a paranatural being or one of the many mortal cults that follow them, could catch wind of Obadiah's intent to acquire *The Taealim*.
- Obadiah then exposed what he described as his greatest conceit. He'd never needed financial backing from the Harkenwild estate, nor did he need my expertise traversing the untamed wilds and wilderness of our small, small world. What he needed was, and I quote; *"the lack of attention created by your reputation for being a man that spends exorbitant sums on quote-unquote 'scientific' expeditions with little-to-no discernible objectives. I have more enemies than there are banks; the word Bramfield can't be put to page without attracting unwanted attention. To put it simply, Lord Harkenwild, I needed your name on the paperwork."*
- It was at this point that my hands were in fists, and I was banging on the table, demanding Obadiah explain *at once* why this damn book was so important. To my amazement, he obliged. In a fashion, at least. *The Taealim,* Obadiah said, was a book written before the beginning of time itself, and that would last long after any dwindling memories of humanity had long since faded from the universe. He implored me not to try and understand how such a thing was possible. The night was already old, and we would soon be at a point where the crowd outside made haste a necessity.

- We simply didn't have the hours for me to make sense of *The Taealim's* nature.
- According to Obadiah, the shred of information he bore guilt for concealing was the lengths to which many of the entities described in *The Taealim* would go to in order to prevent him obtaining it. It was this, he said, that I should make the prize of our conversation, the uncut gem of knowledge to take with me and refine while we travelled toward Cairo.
- I, of course, wanted to know *why* something capable of alchemizing a man's eyes into spheres of obsidian would need to care that Obadiah's institute possessed a book, regardless of its contents. Surely some Darwinian catalogue of eldritch flora and fauna didn't concern beings that transcended all known laws of rational science? Obadiah actually chuckled at this. Smiles don't suit his face, and I am glad they don't outstay their welcome when he wears them.
- He assured me all would become clear when he acquired The Taealim. "When I have that book is the moment you'll understand everything there is to understand, Lord Harkenwild, this I promise you."
- For now, he said, it would suffice to know that *The Taealim* isn't just an encyclopedia of the blasphemous and inexplicable. Its nature held greater significance than its contents. Obadiah told me we'd both gain great insight when we find *The Taealim,* and part of what he'd come to learn, he revealed, was the nature of the end of all things.
- I was midway through deriding such notions of apocalyptic prophecy when we were disturbed by a third voice. Sgt Kinnock emerged from the doorway; his brow locked in a scowl. Obadiah nodded at him, then suggest I return to my room. He waved aside my protests, insisting that I'd have every answer I could want when we found *The Taealim* in the desert.

Not that it needed stating, but the rabble outside meant there'd been some changes to our prearranged schedule. Luckily, Obadiah informed me, there was a train due to leave for Cairo as soon as Mr Darcrioch, with the help of those of Sgt Kinnocks men not preoccupied with holding off the incensed mob, had finished loading his supplies. I've little with me that can't be scurried away into my satchel at a moment's notice, so I've previous few preparations to make. Rather than try and return for, at most, another restless hour's slumber, I felt it best to make note of my conversation with Obadiah, lest I forget some detail by the morrow that becomes of acute relevance in the future.

By the time we're on our way to Cairo it will be near dawn. The journey should take a few days, what with various stops. That's plenty of time. If Obadiah thinks I'm going to wait until we've blown open whatever Godforsaken desert tomb this precious book of his slumbers in, he can give himself pause. There's precious few places he can escape to for "other business" in a train car, and my willful ignorance in the face of adventure has long since perished. I have placed myself in a situation far more perilous than I'd anticipated. I will reconcile myself with the shame of that admission when I'm safely back in London. For now, I must find out exactly what the Harkenwild name has been used by this madman and his institute to facilitate. I am tired though, and Obadiah has plenty of means to excuse himself in the flurry of activity as we traverse the enraged masses to reach Kafr el-Zayyat station. This blasted headache hasn't faded, as if all the mystique and commotion wasn't enough. I will pry Obadiah's vault of secrecy open tomorrow. Tonight, once we're on the train, I must eat and rest. I shall update once I've gleamed more knowledge from Obadiah.

Despite everything, I am excited by the prospect of how much enjoyment my readership will gain from this adventure when I transcribe this for *The Almanac*.

I Don't Know The Date, They Tell Me 2003, Some Kind Of Asylum/Laboratory

I'd forgotten this journal existed. It's been so long. My belongings are alien to me, but I know they're mine. Not just because they, Bramfield's people, told me, but I feel it. Some sense that the words on the preceding pages are my own. I don't know how many years have passed since my last entry. In the literal sense, well over a century. In my mind?

They've asked me to continue, to remember. I think I can, now, maybe. There were men with us. Men with guns. I remember *them*. They're dead now. Well, I suppose everyone I've known must be long dead, but the men with muskets died before I… before Bramfield…

The desert swallowed them. There was another man with us. He was... he had bombs. Crates and crates of them. That was his purpose. They were on a steam train, the crates. *We* were on a steam train. We were fleeing some place, heading someplace else, moving earlier than we'd intended, but exactly when Bramfield planned. There'd been another man before then, too, who died. Consumed by members of the unwitnessable cabal, the K'chyzrt'thine. A warning to Bramfield, one of many. One he'd foreseen, one he'd obscured, one he'd ignored.

The man with the crates died in the blast, didn't he? Yes. Bramfield had him detonate them somehow. Maybe had one of his *other* men do it, the two I remember, the pair whose human faces hid their true nature. The explosion was such that it almost shook the stars from the heavens. *That* memory hasn't faded, despite the eons. Neither has my recollection of the hole.

We were all of us stumbling, choking, gasping for air in the fiery desert night. In was lost not only in the smoke but a haze of confusion, struggling against my blindness and the deafening ringing in my ears to make sense of what had transpired in the moments between eating a passable plate of... I can't remember, it doesn't matter, in the dinner car, and regaining consciousness prone in dunes. We were surrounded by the wreckage of the locomotive powering us through the sands not two moments prior. The man with the bombs hadn't travelled lightly; his combusted trappings left a scar on the Earth's surface some 50 feet deep. This chasm wasn't empty. The contents of the azure-iron sarcophagus in the center of the smoking pit were, without any trace of doubt, the reason Bramfield had enlisted the man with the bombs. Any pretenses of needing the nitroglycerin to gain access to a mountain-buried tomb were a rouse. Bramfield had the charges detonated at this precise point in our rail journey to liberate the thing slumbering beneath the tracks. The men with muskets weren't there to protect us from it. They were there to appease it.

The screams came before the gunshots.

I'd found the other men without arms still breathing. Bramfield and his two shadows, the Ottoman scholar, and Boxstead; he of that cursed line whose blood watches me write this. I read my previous entries before, albeit somewhat belatedly, resuming this retelling. I have since been burdened with the blasphemous understanding of the former self that I do not recognize I naively craved. Though then, at the rim of the pit, I still lived in blissful, motherly ignorance. I did not know the flashing salvo of musket fire was a testimony to the proficiency of these men; that the fact they'd found gumption to fire at all in the face of what Bramfield awakened was nothing short of miraculous. Miracles, alas, pale in comparison to the unspeakable things underpinning reality.

It took fewer seconds than there were men for their barrels to fall silent. The wet shreds and glugging crunches of human bodies being eviscerated between soft pale lips and toothless gums continued for much longer. From the other side of the pit, smoke obfuscated the cause of those dwindling cries of anguish. We didn't see what had rendered that collective of hardened desert fighters to a crimson stain on the dunes until it was already upon us. There were two screams, Boxstead and the Ottoman scholar. Bramfield was fully aware of what would emerge from those jet-black fumes, so his characteristic non-response is no cause for comment. Neither is the nonreaction of his barbaric henchbeings. I managed to still myself, at that point at least. I was close to caving though, close to succumbing to the madness of my circumstances, even at that early stage of my descent into pandemonium.

The Frenchman had left me eager to discover what rational science had denied existed. What I'd always known, deep down, lurked just out of sight no matter how deeply into the wilderness and unknown I ventured. He, that gibbering Napoleonic creature with his three mouths and hypnotic chiming, proved that every suspicion I'd had since childhood was right. When I fell to my knees in awe at the malevolent presence before us, I *knew* I would come to deeply regret my rejection of the lie I now know the rest of humanity wraps around them for comfort. Zealous adherence to the doctrine of the "rational" isn't a fallacy in understanding; it's a fortification against the undeniable lunacy of the truth. Sadly, in my lust for knowledge, I'd found wisdom too late.

"here to play, foreverman?"

The four words had my jaw clenching so hard I felt a tooth crack. A rasping whisper, loud but quiet in a way that creates instant migraines. I'd come to learn this being was known among the enlightened as The Eight Limbed Maggot Prince, The Living Idiot Curiosity Of The First Hatred, and in some corners of the universe's underbellies, He The Great Interferer. In those moments when I first heard it speak, all I knew of it was the warmth of urine in my undergarments. I'd seen elephants when visiting the India's. Ridden them. Such a vastness of bone and flesh almost defies understanding. This creature had a head the size of one, though it was human in composition; the cranium of a behemoth infant with cartwheel eyes not-too-dissimilar from that of a porcelain doll. Its octad of limbs dripped with the remains of our military escort. The long avian appendages ended in talons that I could tell were as dexterous as they were razor sharp.

"thank you for the food. i haven't eaten in decades. you know that though, it's your fault. where are my tools?"

I could smell the creature over the acrid tang of burning train car as it rounded on us. A putrid, rotting stench that left me gagging and sputtering for breath with greater intensity than any pollutant could hope to match. I could see its body for the first time then; that of a maggot easily the size of one of the remaining train cars. It protruded from the rear of the creature's scalp and the base of its skull, vast, magnificent, and grotesque. I could feel consciousness beginning to leave me again. The unknowableness of it all made me heady, weak. The Frenchman had been a malformity of the human form. He was inexplicable, but not did not defy conception. Unacclimatized eyes were never meant to behold the form mine found themselves unable to escape. The Frenchman's successor had no anchors to humanity beyond an aesthetic nod. My second experience of true reality nearly broke me. It wasn't just my inability to grasp the being towering above me, though. It wasn't even that the moment I'd expected, finding myself crushed in that glistening, blood-covered, toothless maw, never came. No. It was because when it spoke, this thing that came straight from the depths of the devil's own madness, Bramfield answered. The man whose company I'd willingly entered stood before that being so malevolent as to defy rationality, and spoke to it as an equal. If I hadn't already been on my backside, I would have collapsed. To my unending horror he started to... to *talk* to this thing, this abhorrence against reality I'd soon come to learn was but one face of an unholy trinity whose true name I dare not utter, even now. No man should be able to look such a thing in its cold, glassy, dead eyes without breaking. However, the fact that Bramfield could bring himself to calmly converse with it, nay, *command* it, made me more terrified of *him* than any conjurance from Lucifer's own nocturnal terrors. Well, there's not a Lucifer, is there? Should we be so lucky that Biblical evil was all that... no, you understand my point well enough. What follows is perhaps the last conversation I can clearly remember before I stopped being... whoever I was.

"I needed to make sure you were here when I needed you to be."

"you could have asked."

"Tried that the first time. Didn't work. This does."

"foreverman, always so cryptic. where are my—"

"You'll get them back."

"you want something."

"The book."

"you mean you don't have it?"

"It escaped. One of the Phithoxine took it thirty years ago."

"but it's arriving here?"

"Yes."

"ahaha, the foreverman always knows. when will it arrive?"

"In two minutes, thirty-seven seconds."

"and you need me to—"

"The mask had help; a Sifter was wearing it."

"and what makes the foreverman think i can do the impossible thing he asks, that I can destroy the undestroyable—"

"Because I've seen you do it, Living Idiot Curiosity. Nothing is impossible for something driven enough to know what would happen if it did."

The Living Idiot Curiosity smirked, tittering to itself. "so the foreverman needs me to break a forevermask with a lightworm stuck to it. and what if thyrtherothax says no?"

"You never say no."

"and why is—"

"Because I have your sack and a corpse-wax candle. I'm sure if I lit it, the man in charge would be very pleased to have his rogue curiosity come home, especially when he finds it out that when it broke free of him it also stole his—"

The creature's chittering laughs turned to shrieks of fury.

"for nearly half a century the foreverman had me locked in that tomb and now he has the gall to threaten! i'll remind you what happens when underscum and wastelings get ideas above—"

"The Sifter will arrive in one minute nineteen seconds. I can light this candle in a tenth of that time. Are you prepared to take the risk?"

There was no response. Instead came a flurry of lightning-fast violence, by the end of which Boxstead and the Ottoman scholar were dead. The beast hadn't taken Bramfield's threat in kind. It howled; an eardrum-shattering sound that threatened permanent deafness. I'm sure I even saw Bramfield wince in the face of it. I couldn't linger on that fact for long, though. The creature's scream of indigence was accompanied by a swipe of three taloned arms, the motion so fast my eyes couldn't register it. Two of the limbs sliced westward, the other east, crossing one-another laterally with Bramfield squarely at their intersection. I now understood why the men with muskets had been dispatched with such swiftness. The claws slid through flesh and bone like a hot scalpel through soft wax. Three of the four segments of Bramfield seemed to hang for a moment, forgetting they were now at the whims of gravity, before they sagged and peeled into a dune of steaming gore on the sand. The head didn't. Bramfield's skull had detached cleanly; the smallest portion left by Thyrtherothax' assault careening through the air, landing with a wet thud at my feet. I yelled and jabbered inanely, though not because of the warm scarlet spray that now covered my face. No. I descended into incomprehensibility because the bodyless head staring up at me from between my ankles *wasn't* Bramfield. It was the Ottoman scholar.

"Has that *ever* worked?" I heard the voice from behind me, that flat aloof drawl I'd first heard what then felt like a lifetime ago, back when I'd been a man that attended unimportant parties held for even less important men. The voice of the man I'd just seen sliced into stacked quarters by an abomination from the nightmares of my nightmares. I could hear Boxstead too, hear him yelling and roiling in his own shocked stupor while slow footsteps, and that impossible voice, moved past me on my right. "You tried that maybe thirty, forty times when we last met? You still ended up in that—"

"you have four more chances by my count, foreverman, but then you'll be put somewhere far away, plenty of time for me to—"

"Run as fast as you can and hope I don't go back to America, light the candle, and deliver the sack I wasn't stupid enough to bring with me straight to your more vengeful half, so he can finally get back his—"

I never found out what He The Great Interferer had in his sack, what could give the threats made by Bramfield such weight for a being capable of dispatching assailants so easily. Bramfield strode past me as he spoke, his eyes never leaving The Maggot Prince, his gait unwavering as he headed to once more stand before those glassy, dead orbs. Thyrtherothax continued his rueful tirade.

Though I did not yet know his full nature, I understood what the behemoth infant's face had implied when it said, *"you have four more chances by my count"*. I had my dawning dreads confirmed when the beast again cut Bramfield, the "Foreverman", off mid-sentence. Sorry, poor choice of words there. This time, the movement was vertical. Four limbs, two from each of the tumorous bulges protruding from behind the pale, pig-sized ears. Once more, Bramfield's biology could offer no resistance to the sharpness of those razor talons. Again, the two halves of his body paused for a moment, forgetting they were now separate. When they finally did come apart, the movement was agonizing and slow; a snails-pace peeling, a damp prizing apart that permeated the air with sticky, visceral noise audible even over my (by now unrestrained) wailing. Why unrestrained? Before the Living Idiot Curiosity split Bramfield for the second time, I could hear Boxstead screaming behind me. The moment birdlike claw met human flesh, I could not.

"I have twelve seconds. If you want your tools back, and my secrecy about what I found in your sack, you'll do what you always do and *break that damn mask."* Bramfield strode past me on my left, yet again striding toward the elephant-sized infant's head without so much as acknowledging his instantaneous relocation. My heart had been hammering in my chest from the moment I regained consciousness after the train exploded, but when I knew there was no denying the vertically split cadaver Bramfield casually stepped over belonged to Boxstead, it went into convulsions. I clutched at my chest, wailing, letting forth a barrage of bawled sobs the likes of which I hadn't emitted even in childhood. Three more chances; the silent lacky, the grunting one kicking me in the ribs to silence me, or… well, I knew the likelihood I could avoid the same fate as Boxstead and the Ottoman scholar was slim. I think this is when Lord Harkenwild, the man I was, truly died. Yes, I would soon find myself in a not-too-dissimilar physical state to Bramfield's other failsafes. I wouldn't be quote-unquote *"dead"* for another few minutes at least. However, mentally speaking, Orwell Harkenwild perished the moment he saw the Foreverman striding through the flamelight for the third and final time.

I remember I closed my eyes. One in three. Odds not in my favor, and when it came to it I, the great brave adventurer Lord Orwell Harkenwild, couldn't even look my death in the face. It wasn't my time, though. Not yet. Both Bramfield and The Eight Limbed Maggot Prince were suddenly far too preoccupied to continue their battle of wills. I opened my eyes, wondering why I hadn't found myself before the great terror in Bramfield's place, my entrails spewing onto the cold night sands. Then clarity cut through me. Twelve seconds had passed.

There was no grand spectacle when the Sifter arrived. For all their endless power, the living masks of Phithoxine travel the ebbs and currents of creation without pomp and ceremony. There was no flash of light, no crack of thunder or shaking of the heavens. The arrival was understated, mundane, as though the Sifter had always been there, standing between the infant-headed abomination and Bramfield's pair of bowler-hatted lackeys. One moment the air in that space was filled with naught but smoke, the sands undisturbed save for the eviscerated remains of Boxstead and the Ottoman scholar. Then, without warning and exactly two minutes and thirty-seven seconds since Bramfield foretold the arrival, the Sifter was... was there.

Soon I would learn everything of the Sifters of Hilgurinai, of their endless searching through the memories of the unfortunate souls they'd capture and lobotomize. I'd become wise to the inferiority of the intellect of man, how to the Hilgurinai, understanding even the most accomplished human philosophers is akin to those same philosophers trying to discern the motivations of amoeba. I'd understand why they stole *The Taealim* from Bramfield and his institute some three decades prior. I'd know their machinations; the end that would follow their nefarious scheming, the mass recoupling of their incorporeal species to new, more physically capable bodies, to mankind, writ large. I would come to learn all of this, but not yet. When the Sifter first materialized on that patch of soot-and-blood-soaked sand, I had no indication I was staring at anything other than a man.

Bramfield, his remaining lackeys, and Thyrtherothax reacted instantaneously, though not as instantaneously as the Sifter. Wherever it had silently apparated from, it had been under fire. I know this because the many torn holes in its decades-out-of-fashion blouse were still smoldering. However, I recognized quickly that I wasn't looking at any mere mortal man. I was still the last remaining one of *those* present. The moment I saw the Sifter's eyes, I knew, without doubt or question, I was once more witnessing something beyond my comprehension. It was his eyes, the Sifter's eyes. They flashed at Bramfield in the most literal sense; a near-blinding violet flare who malice and hatred I could feel despite being easily 10 feet from the target.

"Not possible." The glowing eyed Sifter snarled. "This Mr Danforth left you in human year eighteen twenty—"

"Sack."

Bramfield's word cut through the Sifter's overly-perfect diction. The word wasn't loud, but the authority in it seemed to stoke the furnaces of reality themselves, pushing events into the fullest of their momentum. From behind the Sifter came a deafening roar as the Eight Limbed Maggot Prince raised his talons. It was not a battle cry; no fear, fury, or bloodlust lay in it. It was a howl or irritation, indignancy from this being-beyond-being that it found itself at the whims of something as pathetic and insignificant as a human.

But Bramfield's not human, is he? Not anymore. Nor has he been in the entirety of time I, and definitely any of you, have known him. The Foreverman. If the deaths of Boxstead and the Ottoman Scholar hadn't made the meaning of that moniker abundantly clear to me, my own end would in a few short moments. Some men are immortal. I am testament to this, am I not; what with my body spending so many years ageless and naked entombed in the dunes? Immortality is a trait man is capable of possessing. Bramfield is not that. I have found myself in a position wherein my material shell will not physically expire; perpetual endurance that can still be ended, I'd wager, by significant physical trauma. Bramfield cannot die for wholly different reasons, like the universe cannot exist without him, as though time itself rewrites each moment to ensure there will *always* be an Obadiah Bramfield. He may once have been a man, but whatever fate befell him in the centuries, maybe even millennia, prior to that night in Bayreuth rendered any semblance of humanity he still possessed fleeting. Maybe he was like me once, a curious man who listened too long to his yearnings. Maybe his descent into inhumanity started with a nobler cause. I doubt I will ever know. Regardless of origination, Bramfield's ascension beyond mortality is the reason a presence as powerful as He The Great Interferer obeyed, behaving no differently than the apelike men at Bramfield's side. I've since re-read some of my prior pages to look up their names—Harwurst and Stenworth. Of course, how could I forget? Cursed lineages both, just like the unfortunate Boxstead's, tainted by their ancestors' proximity to the Foreverman before their grandfather's grandfathers had even drawn breath. At least I was the last of my line, unless my sisters found themselves unbarrened in my absence.

In any case, Harwurst, Stenforth, and Thyrtherothax moved almost in unison. Their response was fast, but the Sifter was faster. Despite the luminescence of its eyes, I'd still expected flesh and blood beneath the Sifter's waxen skin. The lack of deep crimson around any of the tattered bullet holes in its shirt should have been a clue that this wasn't the case, however. What I most assuredly *hadn't* expected, and would not have done even if I did know the "body" of the thing was little more than an artificial shell, was the sea of glistening cogs. The moment the word left Bramfield's lips, the Sifter's torso ballooned. Within less than a second it had flamelessly exploded, showering the moist vermillion sands with a horde of miniature automata. The seething mass of clicking, whirring, shrieking figurines sailed through the air in all directions, their number far greater than should have been able to squeeze into the Sifter's hollow chest cavity. They moved with incredible swiftness. Were the Sifter's adversaries mere mortals, we'd have been overwhelmed in seconds.

The Sifter hadn't arrived some thirty years in its future and found mere men waiting though, had it?

By the time the first pair of minuscule bronze feet touched the dunes, the human-sized legs below the Sifter's freshly exposed cast-iron ribs and spine were dangling in mid-air. Purple eyes disappeared beneath raptorial digits. Every vestibular limb of the infantile blasphemy was clawing at the hollow humanoid construct. Thyrtherothax lifted the Sifter, still roaring, his own glassy dead-eyed rage unshifting from Bramfield. The tide of furious mechanized shrieks didn't seem to notice their host's predicament. The glistening mass was sliding mercury-like across the sands, heading for the same once-man that The Eight Limbed Maggot Prince would love more than anything to destroy. Their trajectory wasn't clear of obstacles, however. Harwurst and Stenworth stood between them. It was here they showed just how inhuman, how masochistically in thrall to Bramfield, they really were.

Harwurst wasn't quite quick enough. He'd just about pulled the syringe of glowing red liquid from his jacket when the granular ooze found him. Were it not that I know the hell he was prepared to put himself through were his reactions more timely, I'd pity him. The rampaging miniature warriors, none taller than three inches at most, must have numbered in the millions. I remember it was at this point I finally broke and screamed myself; loud, like a babe in arms, my panic harmonized with Harwurst's own anguish, choking on smoke under waning moon and flamelight, able to do naught but watch as he met an end no man should endure.

I'd half expected the tide to pounce upon him. I'd imagined they'd weigh him down, drag him to ground level to be rendered into red mist by a wall of countless needle-thin blades. I am but a man, though, and my expectations are marred by empathy, rationality, and compassion. The Sifter's army of constructs had no such restraints. That's why they didn't wait for Harwurst to succumb to their sheer number. He started screaming the instant the first leaped from the ground and found his thigh. The distance between us wasn't great enough to obfuscate the grizzly details. The inch-high figure drove a pin-point fist into Harwurst's left leg and burrowed. The glowing syringe fell from Harwurst's grasp, and by the time it reached the ground his clothes were dripping crimson. He tore off his shirt, shrieking, and I could clearly understand why this unnaturally stoic man was suddenly so emotive. I could see them under his skin. Dozens of egg-sized lumps traversed up his body, leaving blossoming trails of purple-black bruising in their wake. Before long, Harwurst fell to his knees, his legs torn to pieces by the relentless entry-points carved into their surface. He didn't stop moving until long after they'd started emerging from his mouth, his ears, behind his eyes. When he finally collapsed into the clicking throng, his body was so empty, so utterly liquidized internally, that he didn't fall as much as crumple. A fate no man should endure, a pain no God would inflict upon his flock. I know this from first-hand experience.

However, I'd made mention of the fate Harwurst had tried to choose before meeting his unfortunate end. Seeing what happened to Stenworth after willingly driving that syringe into this chest makes it difficult to muster sympathy, no matter how agonizing the intimate invasion of the Sifter's throng.

I didn't notice Stenworth had his own syringe until he, too, started screaming. I pulled my focus from the deflating shell of Harwurst, redirecting my attention to Bramfield's other lacky. A medical implement identical to that dropped by his deceased compatriot stuck out of Stenworth's chest; the long needle rammed between two ribs, tip aorta-deep. There was no glowing red in the gilded vial, the gleaming gold plunger had been pushed down the barrel all the way to the ornate hub. The syringe may have lost its glow, but I could tell that was only because it had transferred this property to Stenworth. I think the ticking horde must have noticed too, because the glimmering bronze slime re-pooled away from Harwurst's hollow corpse, flowing with ferocity towards the glowing red man bent-double on the sands. Stenworth wasn't screaming for long, at least. He'd barely managed to reach full volume when the serum took effect.

The first ticking commando to reach Stenworth landed on his back. The automaton, a bristling inch-and-a-half creature wielding twin scimitars no longer than a sewing needle, leaped ahead of the sea of furious gears and cogs. The assailant sprang from the mass of mechanisms like a brass flea, juddering through the air and landing on Stenworth's coat. It tore through the thick material with ease. Stenworth was already bent double by this point; screaming face driven into the sand, body vibrating almost as much as the clockwork minutiae swarming him. I have no doubt the skirmisher poised at his spine would have driven those scimitars between his lumbar, parting Stenworth's vertebrae like an oyster shell, leaving him paralyzed and ready for the same hollowing as had befallen Harwurst. Before the scimitars were fully raised, however, Stenworth was already dead. The serum's maleficent intent had revealed itself. All that remained were the red flies.

His flesh was already bubbling when the finger-length assailant made contact. By the time the brass figurine was slicing through fabric, I could see the bulges; the rippling under Harwurst's skin had risen to a boiling point. It had started the moment the glowing liquid left the syringe barrel and entered his bloodstream. The dim crimson light in the man's chest was only visible a fraction of a second before the pain sent him to his knees. I could see from the exposed back of his neck that every inch of him had been sent into a state of biological pandemonium; the flesh beneath the surface bubbling and sputtering itself into new shapes, the skin above squirming and shifting like an oil canvas stretched taut over molten tallow. The rest of the clockwork horde made contact at roughly the same moment my mind began forming the question:
"*What on earth have you done to yourself, Sten—*"

Then he exploded.

The force was enough to eviscerate both his clothing and a sizeable portion of the Sifter's brass army. There was no scream. Stenworth was already screaming; the wholesale internal restructuring of one's organic mass into a swarm of fat, glowing red flies isn't a comfortable sensation, after all. His anguish didn't reach a crescendo prior to his eventual demise, however. One moment he was bent double howling, flesh convulsing in a way most unnatural, then... well, silence. He collapsed into nothingness without a sound, the vocal chords he'd used mere moments before now reconstituted into however many glowing insectoid bodies. I now knew why Bramfield, the man who had no reason to fear death, required Harwurst and Stenworth's services. They were big men, men with more than their share of body-mass. The Sifter had its own private miniature army, one more than capable of leveraging its swarm-like composition to overpower and decimate foes much larger than itself. I'd seen it with my own eyes, the way they'd torn through Harwurst, rendering him to nothing but a stain on the sands within a few short moments. Now, thanks to Stenworth's sacrifice and sizeable figure, Bramfield had a swarm of his own.

The buzzing of the scarlet Stenworth-flies rose even over my own screaming and the roars of the still-infuriated Maggot Prince. There was also a shrill whining in the air; the screeching of countless ticking infantrymen meeting their end at the mandibles and maxillae without number. The Sifter's chest cavity held an army whose total number is beyond count. The blood-red soldiers in the forces Bramfield raised from Stenworth's flesh outnumbered them a hundredfold. The air was thick with them; both with their bloated, aggressive bodies, the deafening thrum of their trillion pairs of wings, and the acrid coppery tang of their stench. One of the flies landed on my leg, and I yelped, recoiling both at the bonelike chitin of its exoskeleton and maddening humanity looking up from compound, non-mammalian eyes. Bramfield's disgusting failsafe made short work of the automated mass. I watched, jaw agape, as he strode through the glowing scarlet haze, ignoring every bloated red body skimming past his face, or the clogged and broken bronze corpses crunching underfoot. His gaze and focus were willfully singular, despite the carnage. Despite the distance and seething mass of insects and automata between us, I could see his eyes locked on one thing and one thing only—the small black leather book abandoned on the sands beneath where the Sifter dangled.

The Sifter had managed to hold off Thyrtherothax' octad of razored talons thus-far. By the time the last remaining vestiges of its brass entourage had been scattered into the smoke-filled night, however, the tide of the struggle had turned in the Maggot Prince's favor. The book, that little leather-bound black tome which I knew instantly was *The Taealim,* had fallen when the Sifter raised both arms in an attempt to halt the two arms pulling at its purple-eyed face. Its efforts were, of course, futile. Without prior signal the darkness was cut through by a thunder-flash of blinding total luminescence. There was no mystery as to where this nova of light originated. Thyrtherothax claws had found purchase, and when they pulled away from the Sifter's remarkably intact face, I realized the purple-eyed shell was never the Great Interferer's target. The Sifter, as doubtlessly fearsome as its kind are, was only ever an annoyance. It *always* was the azure-iron Phithoxine, that cantankerous living mask hiding beneath its now-broken veil of invisibility, which was the goal.

I could… *feel* it before I could see it.

It wasn't a voice… more like a presence with meaning, a coherent pressure lapping at the outermost edges of conscious understanding. It was in pain, a pain I couldn't feel physically but was emotionally totally empathetic of. The vicarious despair and anguish radiating from the plate of blue metal was overpowering, all-consuming, a greater melancholy than the collective aggregate despair of every woman to birth a breathless babe. I wasn't screaming any longer. I was weeping, tears uncontrollably cascading from my eyes to splash upon the sands, my attention now enraptured by the mask clutched and wailing in that raptorial talon.

Please… don't let him… it will be the end of us.

At the time, I believed the "us" referred to by that pressure-with-meaning was the Phithoxine and the Sifter; that chronologically unfettered pair for whom our entire expedition had, it was now apparent, been searching. I was to ascertain the actual meaning momentarily. Anyone reading this I know will be aware of our entwined fates, the Phithoxine and I, much as the prescient object was as Thyrtherothax' avian digits tightened. The Sifter was already dead when the mask's pearlescent surface began to crumple and bend in the Maggot Prince's vice grip. Once the Phithoxine was removed the remaining arms made short worth of that gutless shell. The luminescent purple eyes, still glowing, shattered like glass as two talon-tips lanced each pupil, driving through the sockets beneath in a haze of sparks and chaffing fuselage. If the Sifter screamed when the Living Idiot Curiosity liquidized the being living behind that violet gaze, I didn't hear it. The mask's penetration of my awareness made registering anything outside the totalitarian sense of loss it projected impossible. I was dimly able to note Bramfield's silhouette stooping low on the other side of the curtain of tears, scooping *The Taealim* from the dunes while its previous owner was tossed over Thyrtherothax' behemoth maggot shoulder like unwanted chicken bones. I noticed, like I said. Care though? No. My *concerns* were only with the mask folding slowly in on itself under the pressure of that unholy fist.

"And now, Lord Harkenwild, I make good on my promise." I remember Bramfield's words to me only because I have had more time than time itself to revisit that moment, to experience it through the lens of infinite variation. At the time I didn't know he'd turned from Thyrtherothax, that he'd walked over to where I wept on the ground, tucking *The Taealim* in his back pocket without so much as giving its cover a cursory glance. "I promised you'd know everything when I acquired *The Taealim*. It's your destiny, Lord Harkenwild, to know. It always is, every time. Next time we meet, you'll have a holistic understanding of everything that is, everything that isn't, and most importantly, how both will come to an end... on this occasion, at least."

I remember Bramfield's words through the... ha, *gift* of cosmic awakening. I would have needed no such enlightenment to remember the feeling of his hand on my shoulder, the unease I felt at the sudden wry smile on his usually expressionless thin face. I'd also need no assistance to recollect the sight of one of the Sifter's clockwork hordes, a refugee that survived the assault of red flies still choking out the moonlight by hiding in a fold of my coat-tail, emerging from its hiding place. My mortal memory would be more than capable of repainting, with crystal clarity, time grinding to a stand-still as it launched itself from my forearm and landed on Bramfield's thigh. I especially would require effort to forget, rather than recount, the way his grin widened when it drove its minuscule-but-deadly brass fists into his flesh.

And then it happened, the reason Bramfield had arranged our expedition, the true purpose of his interest in me; in my being present on that night, in that exact spot of desert, and meeting my end at the precise moment, the Phithoxine mask finally succumbed to the will of The Eight Limbed Maggot Prince and shattered. Arranging such a circumstance seems nigh-on impossible, does it not? Once more, I draw you to the utter inhumanity of the man you call Director. He knew how events would proceed down to the second. He knew because he'd already experienced more repetitions of every single one of those seconds than there are stars in the sky. After all, it might have been the first time *I'd* died, but I'm far from the first Lord Orwell Harkenwild that the Foreverman had led to that stretch of dune on a warm night in an 1872, am I?

The transition was instantaneous. I'd not even registered the inch-high figure burrowing into Bramfield's leg when I was standing, Bramfield on his backside at my feet on the sand in the space where I was... where I *should* have been, completely unscathed.

I buckled almost immediately. The agony shooting up my leftside was everything, even when accounting for the final few shrieks of incorporeal despair that pulsed from the Phithoxine mask. My left leg was numb, and I was standing for less than a tenth of a second. There was a burning near my groin that turned briefly to an ice-cold chill as the burrowing, drilling metal carved through the tender flesh of my crotch and bladder. I howled as I felt my dangling manhood decouple from my form, the warmth of liberated blood and urine washing across my breaches like a tidal surge. Then the bulge burrowed inward, mulching my innards as it ascended toward the heart, hammering out hellfire against my ribcage. I saw Bramfield pull another expression; mild annoyance, mainly at the deluge of vomit he couldn't roll sideways fast enough to fully avoid when the swarm of white-hot tearing pushed up through my intestines and stomach. When did I finally lose consciousness? I don't know. It could be when I felt my lungs deflate in my chest, forcing the breaths I clung onto with panicked tenacity forever from me, along with my ability to scream. I could have lapsed into the darkness at the sensation of my heart beating itself into a pulp against the dervish of razor-thin bronze scaling my ribcage like a ladder beneath my skin. Maybe it was feeling the warmth of smoke pooling in my near-hollow chest, allowed entry via a new orifice when the automaton finally reemerged from my throat. Who can truly say. What I'm certain of is that, at the exact, precise moment, my final conscious thought was about to fizzle out of existence. Thyrtherothax destroyed the mask.

There was a second flash, although this one I was already too blind to notice. The last physical sounds I heard as the final nerves in my ears ceased firing were Bramfield's words as he pulled himself once more to his feet. "Find out how it ends, Lord Harkenwild, and when you return, we'll bring it about together, as we must do, as we *always* do."

Then Lord Orwell Harkenwild died. *I* didn't stop, though.

I felt consciousness leaving me. I recall being grateful to finally be at an end, for the infinite burning in my gut and churning of my sanity to be over at long last. Then something... *hit* me, for lack of a better word. Something despairing, and mournful, and freshly untethered to the azure-iron mask it had always inhabited, the mask that the universe was unable to process it *not* inhabiting. My last relatable, human sensations were vague confusion. All perception of my physical body had left me, of which I had no shortage of gratitude, but the cessation of *being* I'd expected never came. I remember thinking... no, *becoming* a question in that intangible void.

Why?

Then I was plummeting. Not just down, but forward, backward, laterally to each side, outward, inward. I fell up. Not flying or elevating. Falling upward. A sensation nobody can comprehend until they've experienced it. I fell in every direction at once, impossibly, in a way only explainable if I was experiencing a multitude of events simultaneously. It was a feeling made all the more harrowing by the fact I *no longer had a body to feel with.* This inertia resonated with every fiber of my being, yet I had no being within which there were fibers to resonate. I had no mouth. I had no lungs. I couldn't scream, but I could *become* scream. And so I did, for longer than there are cycles of time in infinity.

I saw and heard things in that timeless space. This void wasn't a vacuum. This place was full, though with what my mind simply won't let me recall. I have no inclination to try and unblock the memories, either. If my subconscious measured my fortitude as fit to retain recollection of my own death, I shudder to think what my senses were subjected to during the eons I was the scream. If my mind wiped itself of the memories once I returned to a physical body, it did so for a reason. Time became an irrelevance, concepts of place were rendered moot, the idea of a self was abjectly laughable. I was nothing, but the nothing I became knew it wasn't alone.

The mask, that carved piece of living metal that exists both within and outside of reality, was with me. Or, rather, it's... how to put it... it's spirit, its essence, was with me. Homeless and blasphemous to the laws of reality, natural or paranatural, a perpetually captive thing which should be unfreeable had latched onto my departing soul, steering me as far away from the universe that would soon seek to erase it as it could.

Together we... we ran. Yes, that's the easiest way to explain it to you. We ran for so long even the ageless Phithoxine presence meshed with my aware non-self grew weary. It's not possible for anyone to comprehend such spans of time. Even Bramfield, I think. He's existed for as long as there's been an existence to exist in, but even he elects to push someone else... push *me*... through this necessary step in his perpetual design. Were it not for my impossible merging of being with the destroyed mask, I would have been pulled apart entirely, deprived even of an afterlife.

Well, I suppose I *have* been denied an afterlife, haven't I?

To clarify then; if it weren't for entwining with my Phithoxine half, if not for my very essence becoming more than it had been when wearing the shell of Lord Orwell Harkenwild, I would have become the scream permanently. I would have *been* the scream for longer than forever, an existence that dwarfs an eternity as countless fractured disembodied madnesses to be devoured by the teeming void. I wasn't alone, though. We were together. Just as Bramfield intended.

He needed me intact; you see. This was Bramfield's end goal all along – for me to witness, to watch, and centuries later, when your little institute exhumed my body from the sands, to report.

I'd seen the conversations Bramfield and I had in previous timelines. I've witnessed the almost endless repetitions of those conversations he and I share when I come around in this labyrinth of horrors, this palace to the obscene Bramfield has constructed beneath the North Sea. That's why I haven't been able to stop laughing while I watch your nervous faces scurrying around on the other side of the glass, why his raging fury when all you can do is shrug amuses me so, so much.

He's going to have to tell you what he's looking for sooner or later, isn't he? What he expected me to reveal to him after he pumped my corpse full of his blasted serum and pulled us back from the endless teeming nothingness outside creation. It's all to do with prophecy, you see. Bramfield and I have danced this dance more times than there are times. He has all you thinking he's saving the world. You all think that what you're doing is protecting humanity, keeping the world safe from the near-limitless number of horrors and nightmares that would see it end.

You're protecting nothing, you foolish bastards. This world faces no greater threat than the Foreverman. Or, at least, it didn't.

Obadiah Bramfield has kept this universe endlessly reincarnating, spinning the wheel over and over. The world will always end, and Bramfield will always be the one to end it. He waits until that night in 1872 every single time, has Thyrtherothax "destroy" the Phithoxine mask, and flings our newly shared consciousness through the roiling nexus. He never needed *The Taealim*—it was the sequence of events that played out when he tried to reacquire it the first time, on the universe's virginal run, that he knew he needed. I'd emerge back into my reformed body with the one thing he needed to know – how the universe is supposed to end.

It's different every time, you see. Sometimes the alien god Hhdufj frees themselves and remakes reality in its own image. Sometimes the man in charge regains what his wayward Maggot-Bodied Curiosity stole. Sometimes a pair of unspeakable things finally get humanity to understand the true meaning of perception.

It doesn't really matter. You've experienced all of the above already, although you don't remember. You'll experience it all again too. The wheel will always turn, but only Bramfield and I are standing far enough back from it to see. And this, you feckless idiots in your white coats, is why he's panicking, why he's pooling so many of your limited resources into his adopted daughter and her book. Oh yes, I saw all of that. That was the vision this time, you see.

There's never been a Geraldine Eastley before. There's never been a Hahre. Bramfield's never been *afraid*.

That's why he's having me write this all out, and why you people are under strict orders to deliver it straight to him without reading. The Buddhists were half right about reincarnation. *We* don't reincarnate, though, not in the born-into-a-new body sense. The *universe* reincarnates. We live the same lives over and over in proceeding incarnations of the universe, with marginal differences each time, each of our 'lives' taking place in the latest grand version of cosmic events.

In every version of history, something happens to the man that Bramfield is born as, the "Obadiah Bramfield" in the traditional sense. When it does, Bramfield the Foreverman picks up in his body, ready to usher in the end times. Because of whatever happened to him during the very first incarnation of the universe, Bramfield remembers every single universal cycle he's experienced. That's just the tip of the iceberg with the Foreverman, of course, but you only need to know that single key fact to understand why he's making me write this all down.

I see something when he throws my soul from reality; you see. The one thing my mind allows me to recall with clarity. How *everything* ends. It all has to come to a conclusion a certain way, you see. Different every time. Bramfield knows them all – he's had infinite lifetimes to study *The Taealim*, after all. He just needs me, his prophet, to look forward at the gaping abyss ahead and show him. He needs me to look outside of all things and report back with which of the millions of creation-ending abominations has been granted the privilege by the Great Listener, the Keeper of Stories.

Normally he pulls my body from the sand, the reason for the date known only to him, and injects my corpse with his serum. My soul, *our* soul, is pulled back and, in my madness, I grab him and let forth one of the multitudes of expected prophecies, the ones he's heard each a million times over.

That's why he's panicking, you see?

This time I didn't return with familiar prophecy. We came back from the abyss with the one thing the Foreverman fears. The one thing that *shouldn't be.* A single word, and what the word was quaked the man whose soul outlives the universe to his very core.

Why did it scare him so? Because of what it was.

It was new.

Hahre.

So now he's trying everything he never has just to make sense of it. I must admit, after all the prodding with electrodes, journaling makes a nice change. I don't know what your dear Director is planning to do about the first unknown he's ever faced. But if you think for a second that following him will... ha... *save* humanity, I speak from incomprehensible experience when I say that you could not be more wrong.

HE LAST MRS. DANFORTH

I met it… him… the husband, two years ago. I don't want to get side-tracked by the story of how I became (as the English call it) a mail-order bride. *That* story is harrowing and depressing enough in itself. *The War* left a lot of orphans on both sides of the new border. Many have similar stories to mine. I don't want to waste however long I've got by sharing experiences that differ little from any other girl whose childhood died in *The War*.

So many of us ended up press-ganged by hungry communities into going in the Russian men's vans. So many ended up here, or America, or Saudi Arabia, to share beds with disgusting men so families back home could keep coal in the furnace one more winter. A tale retold a thousand times over by every woman that's lived it.

Their stories have nothing mine does not. Where my story differs is the ending. None of those other daughters of *The War* ended up with someone like the husband. This I guarantee.

It called itself Mr. Danforth. The first thing it said to me when I arrived at Heathrow was, *"you are called Mrs. Danforth."* It wasn't a question. It was a command. Despite what you're thinking, this didn't raise suspicion. I'd had very few conversations with men that *didn't* start with them barking orders. My first thoughts of the husband were that he would be a man like all those except Father. All I was thinking as he walked me to his SUV was, *"and so I go from the hands of one pig into the hands of another."*

How wrong I was.

I didn't properly inspect the husband until I was in the back seat. I hadn't looked at him much in the airport. I'd kept my head down, staring at the floor, because that's what the Russian men told me to do. It took a few hours to reach the house. Plenty of time for me to stare at the husband in the rear-view mirror, to get a proper look at the man whose bed I'd been sold into. *That* was when alarm bells started ringing.

As the SUV trundled down increasingly less maintained roads, my mind was running through possible explanations for my new husband's face. It was rigid, stiff. None of the muscles of his wide brow or angular jaw twitched, clenched, or moved. At all. For three whole hours. His skin was off, too. Not literally, but something about it troubled me for reasons I couldn't place. I think it was the tone. The hues of his face were too uniform, too smooth. Almost the exact same shade of grey almost-peach all over. There was no ruddiness to his cheeks, no darkness under his eyes. For a man I'd been told was in his 40s he had none of the scars, laughter-lines, or crow's feet I'd expected. His face had almost no crevices and creases at all.

His eyes created a distrust I had no trouble explaining. They remained as still as his face throughout our silent journey. Even when we'd turn corners, his gaze remained locked straight ahead. I tried coughing once or twice to see if I could attract his attention. Nothing. Despite the unease this caused, I couldn't ignore that there was something to those eyes that was undeniably beautiful. Mesmerizing, even. Part of me wonders if that's why he/it had no trouble enticing the unfortunate souls in the basement.

The husband's eyes have a shimmer to them. A majestic light. That's the only way I can describe it. In my native Serbian the word I'd use is *sveti,* but even that doesn't feel quite right. Everything in those sockets, from the unblemished whites to the smooth perfectly circular pupils, sparkles like the rarest of ocean pearls. In any other context that shine would be awe-inspiring, beautiful, wondrous. In the face of the husband, the man that doesn't blink, the enticing gleam has new undertones. In that face, the twinkling feels less like gazing at stars in distant galaxies, and more like realizing the light you've followed through murky waters is attached to a deep-sea monstrosity.

For three hours, we sat in silence. I actually jumped a little when the wheels ground to a halt. The husband didn't say anything, not until he'd left the car and opened the passenger-side door.

"This is Mr and Mrs Danforth's building. Follow."

Now the Russian men were safely a plane journey behind me, I allowed myself to pay more attention to the husband's words. I recognized immediately what I'd been too shell-shocked to notice before. He was speaking fluent Serbian. I mean *fluent*, too. His pronunciation was so perfect he could easily have landed a job as a newsreader back home. This was a shock. I'd been implicitly told that he *wouldn't* speak Serbian, that almost no English people did. The Russian men loved to remind us of that. We all knew why. It made sure we knew we were alone, that we were isolated, that if we tried to flee our new homes, nobody could understand enough to help.

Isolated. *Zabačen*, in the language I knew. I couldn't think of a more fitting word for my new accommodation.

The bungalow stood alone. For miles in every direction were nothing but fields of wilted and rotting vegetables. The muted grumble of motorway gridlock could be picked up when the wind blew the right way, but only on the absolute edges of my hearing. In a few spots on the horizon, I could see the amber haze of light pollution reflected on the underbellies of rolling clouds pregnant with rain. These telltale signs of civilization were distant, so distant that I knew if I ran, it would be days before I reached one.

Inside, I found no respite for my clenched jaw or shallow breathing. There were… There *are* four rooms. The largest are the kitchen/dining area and bedroom. Even they are poky, though. The bedroom barely fits the cast iron bed I'm hiding under. The bathroom has full working amenities, which is something at least. The other room was the first item of discussion on the husband's agenda. The basement. Entry is strictly forbidden. He made the punishment for transgression clear, too.

"Not first Mrs. Danforth. Can find more Mrs. Danforth's."

His warning sent a chill down my spine. After instructing me to cook us both a meal of baked beans (which he didn't eat), he commanded me to retire to bed. I didn't sleep at all that night. I lay in the dark, tears streaming down my face, listening to the creaking footsteps from the kitchen. Every time they'd clump closer to the door, my heart skipped a beat, breath catching in my throat. That moment I was expecting, when I'd feel his weight sagging the mattress, hear the groan of the springs that signaled the initiation of the wifely duties he'd paid for, never came.

This was a small relief, at least. In fact, by a week or two, I managed to sleep in relative peace for a few hours each night.

Within a month, I only found I *couldn't* on the nights that... well, we'll get to that.

Here's the thing, until last night I played by the rules. It's been two years and I'm still Mrs. Danforth. There hasn't been a single day in that time the husband *hasn't* terrified me. However, he's never laid a hand on me, in *any* context. Two years is a long time. There have been nights when... God, I hate myself for this... I would have let him just for something resembling human contact. The only bodies I've touched in two whole years were cold, clammy, and covered in loose soil. Other than that, I haven't had so much as a handshake. Not speaking to a real person for two years drives your mind to dark places, but touch starvation is a different madness entirely. If I ever make it out from under this bed, if I can make it through the rotting vegetables and find civilization beneath those amber clouds, I'm hugging the first person I see and never letting go.

The first night was the blueprint for each that followed. My fear never subsided, but it did change. With every month it became evermore tinted with hopelessness, a despairing melancholy.

Tears have been a large part of my day. It was about 6 months into my marriage that the weight of it all broke me so much I couldn't stop them falling. It only took a week to realize I *didn't* need to conceal them from the husband. His smooth, motionless face never reacted to sobbing or anything else. I've tried screaming at him, insulting him, pleading, questioning, talking about inane nonsense even. Nothing. I must have retold my life story three dozen times to those gazeless shimmering eyes. Yelled every curse, cracked every joke. Nothing. Aside from commands in stunted Serbian like *"you will wake up now"* and *"reading prevents mental degradation, you will read",* he's never said a word to me.

Every day has the same routine. He has me cook meals that he never eats, do menial cleaning tasks, and when he goes in the SUV to one of the patches of amber clouds, he instructs me to read. It's also my job to answer the door. This, I think, is the reason why he... why *it,* purchased my hand in marriage from the Russian men. Despite our isolation, there were *many* knockings. I was told on the first night that Mrs. Danforth's main role was ensuring that Mr. Danforth wasn't disturbed. That meant telling the various council workers, local political candidates, cold-calling salesmen, and preaching religious types that he was away on business.

Always he'd stand behind the door, just out of sight of the visitors, looking down at me with that rippling glow as I rattled off the textbook excuse. It went the same way every time.

Well, *almost* every time. Sometimes, such as with the third visitor, the husband would intervene.

I'm sure that by this point you have wondered *"are you telling me that for two years you've never tried to escape or stand up to him, even though he's never laid a hand on you?!"* This question I understand, and it is one I can answer. As I said, the husband never laid a hand on *me*. The same can't be said for visitors to the house. I don't know what criteria it had for deciding which visitors became victims. All I know is that the third visitor, a poor boy barely out of his teenage years raising money for some cause or other, ticked the right boxes.

"Mr. Danforth isn't on a business trip." The husband's words rang out from the shadow behind the open door. He was speaking in English now, accent as clipped and precise in the British tongue as it had been in Serbian. He stepped out into the light, standing just behind me at the threshold of the shack. I'd barely been married to him for a week, but already I knew him enough for this sudden change in behavior to sound alarm bells.

"Mrs. Danforth was confused," the husband said, "please excuse her, she is not well."

I gulped. So did the young man on the porch. He was trembling in his father's suit, a bead of sweat trickling down his forehead to pool at the crease of his brow.

"R-r-right, yes, well, Mr. Danforth, The lad stammered, fumbling with his clipboard and pen, "I'm here... um... I'm-I'm-I'm here to talk about..."

"You will come inside Mr. Danforth's house." It wasn't a question. I stood in the doorway, trying my best to ignore the prickling chill of the husband's breath on the back of my neck. For a few drawn-out moments, I watched the boy's face twist into visible discomfort. In the end, his vulnerable mind couldn't win. I stood aside to let him slouch into the kitchen, wincing as the husband slammed the door behind him.

"Mrs. Danforth will go to sleep." Again, the husband's words weren't an inquiry. It was obvious they were addressed at me, if for no other reason than because he'd effortlessly switched back to Serbian.

"But it's two-thirty." The second set of Serbian words I heard came from my own lips. I blinked at the husband, perplexed at my own outburst but nonetheless suddenly inspired. The mixture of confusion and defiance had me rooted to the spot. I said nothing further, but still didn't move.

Behind the husband, the trembling boy took a seat at the kitchen table. There were tears streaming down his face. I could tell that somewhere beyond those watering eyes was a voice, a voice screaming at the boy to get out of that chair and run. The boy's body wasn't listening. It had stopped listening the moment Mr. Danforth addressed it. All that body could do now was obey in a way that I found myself, for the first time, *not* doing.

The reason it took two years to work up the courage to be under this bed is because of how the husband reacted to my first (and only) flirtation with disobedience. I was expecting him to raise his fists, to fly across the room in a fit of fury to beat me back into submissiveness. The moment never came. As I said, he's never laid a hand on me. He doesn't have to.

I felt the sharp stab at the base of my skull the instant his eyes narrowed. Before I had time to fully register its existence, the pain had spread across my entire head, drowning every nerve in acidic burning agony. My nails were digging into my scalp around the moment I noticed I was screaming. Through the white and black spots peppering my vision, I could see the husband standing over me. The change in perspective was the only reason I knew I'd collapsed. For the first time since meeting him, his expression had changed. He wasn't staring blankly ahead anymore. He was glaring.

His eyes were thin slits, allowing only slithers of their intense otherworldly iridescence through. The beams weren't pointing directly ahead, but down at the floor, down at me. Lips that had only so far moved to form words were crunched into a scowl. The muscles in his jaw bulged so much that I'm amazed his near-perfect teeth didn't crack under the pressure. That was the moment I first understood the depth of my true fear of this man... this *thing*. It was when I was writhing in unexplainable agony, seeing him towering over me in his ironed polo shirt and jeans, seeing him *notice* me for the first time. It's *that* fear which has kept me docile and trembling for two long years, and it was there on those freshly-scrubbed tiles that I cowered before it for the first time.

When the husband spoke again, it was through clenched teeth. "Mrs. Danforth will go to sleep."

"Y… y-yes…" Once more, I heard words leave my lips. The instant they did, my head was released from the invisible barrage of fire. The husband relaxed back into his usual blank-slate state. I couldn't bring myself to look over my shoulder as I crawled to the bedroom door. I caught a quick glance while I pulled myself up to my trembling feet using the handle, though. Brief, accidental, but enough to paint a clear picture for the darkest places my wandering mind can go in the quiet hours.

The husband had turned his back to me. He was facing the kitchen table, standing above the acne-scarred young man. The boy hadn't said a word throughout my ordeal. One look at his face told me why. He was as terrified as I was. Enough tears had fallen from his cheeks that a small puddle formed on the tabletop. He was doing his best to stare straight ahead, but every so often he'd be unable to stop his gaze flicking to meet the husband. Whenever their eyes met, he'd let out a soft whimper. One of his legs broke out into violent judders as I closed the door behind me. I curled up under the thread-bare duvet, willing myself to forget the nauseating thought that the spasms were from a trapped mind resisting induced paralysis.

Lying awake with tears in my eyes was the norm. That night, the reason I had to bite down on my hand to muffle my cries was new, though. The sounds that snaked and writhed through the cracks around that door were… what's the best way to convey it… haunting? Yes. Haunting I can't think of a better word, actually. They lived on as earworms for many months after. Spectres that teased explanations for the thuds and scrapes in the nights that followed from the worst depths of my imagination.

The screams started as soon as the bedclothes were over my head. High pitched, ragged. Screams I knew all-too-well from hiding in my parent's closet during *The War*, feeling relieved that the men with their AK-47's had chosen the family next door. It was no relief hearing screams like that now. Even worse when they changed to the *other* kind of screaming I recognized. The kind I'd also heard in my parent's closet, the kind my father did when the men with AK-47's *hadn't* chosen a family next door, or down the street. The kind he'd made when they'd beaten him senseless, tied him to a chair, and taken out their box of DIY tools…

Hearing a barely-grown man's howls of torment is harrowing enough. Were I a lucky woman, that would have been *all* I heard. Such as it is, luck has never been in my favor. The wet slurps of flesh tearing, muted snaps as bones cracked, the tightening of eardrums when the drill whirred into life; none of the sounds I associated with screams like that were present. Instead, there were noises that nothing in my memory could reconcile. It started with clicking, a prolonged barrage of ever-faster skittering like ball-bearings bouncing off a car windshield. The boy was babbling something when they ended, but his words were muffled by the thick wood of the door. His terror wasn't.

Once the clicks fell silent, the second unexplained noise started. This was humming. A deep, electronic, unwavering thrum that even through the door I could tell came from machinery. Within twenty seconds, it ceased, abruptly and without indication. The exact moment the lad's wailing grew from panic-induced to pained.

The unexplained noises, the ones coming from whatever it was the husband was doing, had also taken a turn. There was a... I don't know what to call it, like a *whistling*? A shrill continuous note, breathy but definitely not organic. It was far too monotonous and unbending for that. There was a metallic tint to it too, something I can't quite put into words but nevertheless conjured visions of rusted piped and creaking gears. This continued for a full fifteen minutes, long after the screaming from the young man fell silent. My teeth were clamped on my hand with such pressure that I tasted blood by the time it ended. I waited at least an hour until the *thump-thump-thump* of something heavy being dragged down to the basement had ceased. I fell asleep shaking as I always did, although harder than I had since *The War*.

The husband said nothing of the previous night when he woke me to cook a breakfast he once again didn't eat. My instruction for that day was simple: *"Mrs. Danforth will clean"*. I could see why as soon as I left the bedroom. The young man's chair sat at the epicentre of an explosion of dark red stains. Stains that sprayed out from a specific point. When I realised that point was roughly where the boy's head would have been, I couldn't stop myself from breaking down into uncontrolled sobs. These continued throughout cooking the requested porridge, and through the silent meal. The memory of what happened when he... when *it* stared at me, when it started boiling my brain with nothing but a glare, was the only reason I could finish the meal as instructed. Every mouthful took willpower to prevent returning once swallowed. This has been perhaps one of the hardest conditions of my situation to endure. There are only two places at the kitchen table, and the one the husband chooses for his "guests" *isn't* the one he sits at to not-eat. I'm not instructed to clean until after breakfast. The husband does this deliberately, I think. The message is clear: *look at the blood you sit in. There were other Mrs. Danforth's.*

These nights happen at least once every two weeks, although it can sometimes be more (highest frequency was four in as many days). After a while, I couldn't help but start asking questions. I did try fielding them directly to him, which received the same response as every other interaction I've tried to initiate. Since that got me nowhere, I was left to muse, hypothesize, and (when I could stomach it), listen. After two years of this, I still had no clue what he was doing or why he was doing it.

The *why* I can still only guess. I found out the *what* last night, but we'll cover that. I've got to tell you about the phone in the basement first.

It was yesterday, and one of those mornings, that I sat in a 6 foot scab. The husband had not long ventured out to one of the distant amber hazes to purchase food he would never eat. I was scrubbing the red stains left by an unfortunate fundraiser for endangered pandas when, dangling almost out of earshot, I heard it. It was coming from the basement, oozing up through the cracks beneath the sponge and soapsuds. I thought it was a bell at first, or a wind chime. Then the buzzing started. It had been so long since I heard one that I almost didn't recognise.

It was a phone ringing.

My heart skipped several beats. I had to manually restart my breaths, refusing to believe what my ears were telling me. A quick glance at the window was all the reassurance I needed. The husband had only just left; he was always gone for at least two hours. I had time. Hands shaking, I put down the sponge. Checking the moldy fields one last time, the memory of that mind-stab glare still fresh despite two years passing, I gulped. Every step took more willpower than I think you'd ever believe, but I stopped following my instructions. Instead, I walked toward the basement door. It amazes me still that it wasn't locked this entire time. I guess he doesn't care about any Mrs. Danforth discovering his secrets, although why would he, if he can just replace us? The smell hit me first. It rolled out the doorway the second I cracked it ajar. Pungent, acrid, heavy, and with a sweetness that brings no comfort. Once more in my mind I was a little girl in *The War*, finally daring to leave my home after three days staring at my father's glassy unmoving eyes through the gap in the closet door.

In the basement, I was fortunate enough that the angle of the sun through the kitchen window hit the doorway just enough to provide some light. Enough to see that there'd been dozens of air fresheners of every conceivable shape, scent, and size nailed to the ceiling. This at least explained why the cloying stench of human decay hadn't reached the kitchen. There was a small vent in one corner, but I knew this alone wouldn't have been enough to mask the smell of all those corpses.

There were *dozens* of them. A mass of bodies heaped in the far corner that spread almost to the stairs. I recognized all of them, despite the varying stages of decay. Every single one, from the near-skeletal postman through to the bloated, purifying lost hiker that picked the wrong place to ask for directions. This I expect is no surprise, though. It wasn't to me. Recognizing those bodies wasn't why I collapsed into a wailing mess at the foot of the basement stairs. It was the machine down here with them. In the opposite corner, underneath the feeble ventilation shaft, was an oven. Not a small one like the pathetic thing in the kitchen. This was an industrial unit, the kind of furnace found in morgues and crematoriums.

It was the implication more than anything. The oven had clearly been there a while, judging by the rust and soot. He hadn't been bluffing about the other Mrs. Danforth's. The presence of that furnace confirmed two things; the husband had been at this since long before I arrived, and that he's had to make no effort to conceal his activities. Either nobody's tried to stop him, or nobody can. I'm praying it's the former.

The phone restarting its jingle snapped me out of my despair. My stomach dropped when I pinpointed the source. *No,* I thought, *no no no please, anything but this.* It only took one blink for the basement to vanish. I was back in *The War*, reaching for the keys in my father's pocket so I could leave our flat and find food, screaming as his cold stiff form fell on top of me from the bed, wailing for help that wasn't there as I struggled to free myself from underneath the dead weight of a man four times my size.

No, snap out of it.

I swallowed, deciding to obey the inner defiance, finding encouragement in yet another buzzing tinkle from within the pile. I had to beat back the intrusive memories every second my arm was in that heap of decaying flesh. I was only feeling my way through clammy limbs and blood-crusted fabric for about thirty seconds, but my perception managed to stretch them to decades. The feeling of slick waxy skin on my arm, the noxious tang of rotting human meat mere inches from my nostrils, the moist groans and creaks as I disturbed built up gasses and fluids inside bloated organs… all of it merged into a sensory overload I'm still amazed I managed to push through. When my hand wrapped around something hard, plastic, and vibrating, I couldn't pull it out fast enough.

I didn't stop to look at my prize until I was certain I was back in the bedroom and not having some kind of fever dream. The phone, *this* phone, had 50% charge remaining. I turned it off immediately, not wanting to waste one second of precious battery life. But where to hide it? The solution seemed so stupid I caught myself laughing for the first time in… well, long enough that I'm getting tearful trying to work it out. A while. The one place in the house the husband has *never* been (aside from the bathroom, which offered no hiding spaces).

I heard the crunch of tires on dirt at the same time I finished rearranging the pillow to make triply sure there was no indication of the treasure stuffed inside. I'm quite impressed with my quick thinking for this next part. Obviously, I'd not done the cleaning as instructed. I needed an excuse, something that wouldn't arouse suspicion. So, what did I do? I lay on the ground in the unwashed blood and claimed I'd passed out. The husband queried, and I fed it a whole yarn about collapsing on the floor and having no idea how much time has passed. It worked. He instructed me to "*cook and consume chicken soup*", and then continue with the cleaning as instructed.

The day became one of the longest of my two-year hell. For the first time, I had to force crying, moroseness, defeat. I couldn't remember when I'd last had reason to smile, and now I was willing my lips not to curl upward. All I could think about was this phone, this message. I can barely speak any English. Phoning the police is pointless; I can't explain where I am, let alone what's happening. Writing it though? I've had two years with no mental stimulation besides reading classic literature with the assistance of an English-Serbian dictionary. I was mentally planning this message all yesterday afternoon. I didn't anticipate writing it so soon, but a lot's changed since I found this phone.

Last night was one of *those* nights, you see. This one was a woman, older than me by several decades, meeting constituents on behalf of some local politician. The scene played out the same as it always did.

"Mrs. Danforth will go to sleep."

I didn't protest. The woman was doing the standard paralysis panic dance when I shut the door behind me. As usual, I did my best to avoid her face, to spare myself the mental image of the terrified pleading look they *always* had in their eyes. Once more I was laying under the bedclothes. I could feel the coolness of the phone in my palm when the whimpers and screams started. The perfect cover to start writing, right? I wish I'd thought so.

Instead, for some reason, the reminder of my successful venture into the basement emboldened me. I found myself not hurriedly sending out an SOS to anyone on the internet that could help, but instead creeping back toward the door. I needed to know; you see. I'd never be able to put this behind me if I didn't know.

Idiot.

Once more, the pressure of teeth on my palm drew blood. Through the crack in the door, I saw... I saw *everything*. Immediately I regretted my decision, but so powerful was the morbid curiosity cultivated over two long years that I couldn't look away. By last night, I already had incredibly strong suspicions about the husband, that *he* was probably better referred to as *it*. The nightmare playing out in front of me confirmed every single one of them.

Both the husband and the woman were sitting at the kitchen table, exactly as he and I did for every meal he didn't eat. She was still ensnared by whatever kept his victim's docile and obedient. She'd managed to wrestle back just enough control to start screaming, for one of her hands to occasionally spasm and flap on the laminate tabletop, but that's it. For his part, the husband was moving the most he ever had in our two-year marriage. I now knew what the clicking sounds were. Already the urge to scream was so much I felt light-headed, and he... it... *they* were only just getting warmed up.

There were hundreds of them. Miniature clockwork men of varying proportions and sizes, the largest of which stood barely over two inches tall. They were pouring out of the husband's slack, open jaw. Some rappelled down on ropes made of string and twine, others opted to freefall. The clicking I'd heard on every one of *those* nights? It was the sound of them hitting the table, of uncountable pairs of tiny brass feet scurrying around on the laminate. They moved fast, so fast that some were barely a blur. The larger ones pointed and directed the runts of the horde, ushering them to their assigned tasks with cracks of spark-tipped prods no longer than a toothpick. Each knew their role. It took them almost no time at all to set up the shoebox-sized machine they dragged out of the husband's open chest cavity.

The husband's response to all this? The same as his response to everything else. There was no reaction to the sea of copper and bronze cascading from his wide maw. He didn't flinch when some of them clambered up his shirt to unbutton it, when they pulled at seams on his hairless chest to peel back that rubbery skin. As his innards were revealed inch by inch, he didn't even blink. Why? Because "he" didn't exist. It, the husband, was just a shell, a vessel for this mass of clanking mechanical activity to travel amongst us undetected.

His iron ribcage held no organs. There was no beating heart, no rising and falling lungs, no gurgling stomach. Behind it lay nothing save for a large pearlescent blue steel box. As I watched, eyes welling with tears, some of the clockwork men started pulling levers and crank handles set into the husband's spine. There was a faint *whoosh* of unseen steam valves as the miniature locking mechanisms holding the blue-steel box in place released. It landed with a heavy thud where the writhing heap of cogs and gears was thickest. To my amazement, none of the rusted figures were crushed. Instead, there was a flurry of skittering metallic limbs. Then, much like a dead tarantula carried by ravenous ants, the box glided toward the trembling woman.

That's when I learned the source of the second sound. The unwavering motor-like humming. It came from the array of pistons, gears, and other pneumatic components hidden behind the husband's face. Whilst some of the clockwork throng got to adjusting the knobs and dials on the blue-steel box, the husband's head was opening. A great split ran vertically along its center, rising from his chin like he was being unzipped from within. The whirring started when the segments started rising up and outward on the arrangement of intricate pneumatic extenders. Those eyes that barely moved? They were lenses. Thick one-way lenses so that the thing sitting within, the source of that mesmerising paralysis-inducing glow, could view the outside world.

I've never seen something be so ugly and beautiful at once.

The body was grotesque, an aberration that went against everything sane and decent. It was barely twelve inches long, and most of its mass lay in its bulbous body. The quivering yellowish belly pulsated in a small metal chair that emerged from the husband's open throat. Around it were dozens of wheels, switches, levers, and valves. The aberration manipulated these with its seven wiry arms. These thin appendages wormed their way from the creature's neck, moving and flicking like reptilian tongues around the maddeningly complex interface. Above the ring of purplish tendrils were two gnarled horns protruding from behind its tiny collarbone. These were thicker than the tentacle arms and half as short. They weren't mobile either; the darker flesh of their surface seemed scarred, burned. Open sores on its surface wept a whitish liquid I could smell as soon as the face segments drifted apart. A rancid smell, a smell far too close to the cloying miasma in the basement.

Between those sore-crusted stumps, though? What hovered between them was... *sveti*. Holy. There's no other word.

It was the light. An orb of it, floating between the bony horns. I can't tell you what color it was because it was all of them. Not in the way that white is all colors of light, either. Your brain registers white light as white. My brain was registering the orb as white, black, red, yellow, green, purple... every color I can name simultaneously (and even some that I can't). Exposed to the world, it was bright, almost blindingly so. If I hadn't spent my nights under blankets facing the wall, I'd have noticed it flashing through the cracks between floor and door. The orb was no larger than a chicken's egg. Somehow, the moment I saw it, I knew its truths; that it was sentient, aware, and that it and the phlegm-coated blight beneath were one. The instantaneous awareness of the power of the thing was overwhelming. My tears flowed more freely than they ever had, even during *The War*. I was only in its presence a few minutes, but during that time all cognitive freedom left me. My sense of time, place, self, all gone. There was nothing except the light.

The woman's screech snapped me out of my awe. A wave of nausea welled up to my throat. It was obvious why she was screaming, and it took everything in my power not to scream too.

The brass army had finished setting up the blue-steel box. The woman was screaming because two sharp needles, each about a foot and a half long, had launched themselves from the machine on the table. They'd found the corners of her eyes. She wasn't crying tears now, but rivers of dark red. The chrome needles drilled through her tear ducts, deep into her sockets, tearing through bone and optical nerves. I knew *exactly* what they were trying to find. I'd read enough classics with medical protagonists to recognize lobotomies.

What I'd never read about were the apparitions. The whistling sound was... well, I don't know *what* it was. All I know is that it started the moment those needles began to glow red-hot. A small crystal had risen from a port at the box's center. It, too, shone with crimson heat. Above the fist-sized rock was a constantly-shifting horde of spectral figures. Only one of them I recognized; the woman in the chair, the one whose eyes were rolling back in her skull. It didn't take me long to put the pieces together. I was seeing her life. A montage of ghostly scenes from her past, pulled from her brain to be displayed and dissected by the aberration in the husband's head. It was leaning forward in its chair, the seven worm arms quivering excitedly. I could tell it was searching for something, that there was some vision the glowing orb was hoping to witness. I had no idea what and still don't. I don't want to find out either.

Whatever it was, the glowing orb didn't find it in this particular set of memories. I could sense the frustration ebbing from it when the husband's face began to retract. I almost tore a ligament in my hand when the needles retracted. They left the woman's head with a snap. Such force was there that her head wrenched back with an audible crack as vertebrae in her neck split. A wide cone of blood and cranial fluid sprayed from the wounds, covering the table while the last beats of life twitched out of her body.

So yeah, that was last night. The night I found out. He... it... *they* didn't notice me watching, the orb-headed aberration or his clockwork minions. This morning was the same as all the others. That is, until they left to get the food they had no reason to consume. Right now, they're grabbing the keys to the SUV to drive after me. They think I've run off into the woods, fields, and bushes in front of the house. That's because I spent half an hour running in said direction. But, you see, I then spent another half hour running *backward.* By the time they've figured it out, I'll have run off into the fields *behind* the house. The ones with the brightest amber in the clouds, where the roar of motorway life comes loudest.

I deliberately left the door open and did everything I could to make it look like I'd already run. Thank God it worked. While I was writing this, they were in a rage, tearing about the kitchen and smashing everything they could find. Thanks for providing enough distraction to keep my breathing steady and quiet. Whatever they are, they don't understand people enough to check under a bed.

They're driving off now, so I've got to give it two minutes, then run as fast as I damn can toward those clouds. I'm turning this phone off. 20% battery. I may need it. I'll send an update when… who am I kidding, *if* I make it. In the meantime, if the place I'm describing seems familiar, my warning is this. Stay the hell away. Whatever they are, they don't have to be shy. They *want* you to come looking. I've never had a choice in where life takes me. You do. Don't waste it.

WHAT AWAITS

Let's cross off the obvious questions you have. I didn't invent, find, or use a time machine. Nobody came back to summon me to fulfill a glorious destiny. Everything happened totally by accident, and to be honest, part of the reason I'm writing this all down is to put the pieces together myself. To make sense of it a bit, you know?

It started when Bill (my husband) and I purchased this dusty old maritime museum. Quaint place, one of those little time capsules of a small town's local history. We'd moved to the coast for a better life. Our marriage is legal in our home state, sure, but the court of public opinion still isn't sold. We figured it'd be easier to set up roots where we could hold hands without the staring. The place was a steal, too. Came with all the exhibits, a ready-to-run business. Family-owned until we signed the deeds. Previous owner was the last of the line, apparently. Either that or none of the old codger's distant great nephews or nieces wanted it. Maybe they knew?

We hadn't planned to keep running it as a museum, of course. This prime slice of commercial real estate we'd envisioned as becoming the most 'gram-worthy coffee place on the boardwalk. We wanted that influencer-powered Spring Breaker money. I'm not going to be dramatic and say things like "we should have known" or "it was too good to be true", because we had no way to, and it wasn't. Yes, the place was a steal. It wasn't daylight robbery though. We didn't get the place for free from Bill's long-lost creepy uncle or anything cliché like that. It was cheap, but not curse, haunting, or previous-tenant-murdered cheap. There was no reason to think buying that quaint little local museum was an invitation for paranormal shenanigans like… well, like whatever it was that just happened in the basement.

Nobody told us the place had one. It wasn't on the layout plans, or in the *extensive* (read: beggy) write-up of the property we got from the realtor. We were sitting through the remaining maritime bric-a-brac when I found the trapdoor. It was almost invisible, a square of faint grooves hidden just behind the massive model of a fishing ship. I thought the thing was ugly personally, but Bill *insisted* we keep it (the model boat, that is). All the actually important historical stuff had been donated to *proper* museums already, leaving us with only the various waxworks and dioramas to work with for decoration. The ship was Bill's favorite. Well, to be more accurate, the long tentacled Kraken thing rising from the waves to devour it was. Horrible looking things if you asked me. Bill didn't ask, but I told him anyway. I found his taste for old horror movies and the macabre endearing (especially around Halloween), but still, I protested about keeping the ship.

"Look at it William, it's horrid; nobody wants *that* in the background of their story. We're going for pirate shanties and bubble tea, not Davy Jones and freezing seawater."

He'd just laughed at that.

"Look at it *Benjamin*, it's Kitsch, they'll love it. It's got Pirates of the Caribbean vibes coming out the wazoo."

"Those tentacles have *human teeth* glued to them, Bill!"

"Yeah, but… they're milk teeth. They're probably not from dead people. Probably."

The excuse didn't really wash, but this place was Bill's baby and so, ultimately, I knew I'd oblige. Full disclosure here, I was much more interested in the sunsets and mojitos side of the move than the running-a-business bit. Bill, though, Bill was like a kid with a new video game about the commercial venture aspects. I'd decided weeks ago to show interest but stay out the way. That's why I ended up helping him lift the heavy glass case containing the painted wood, clay, resin, twine, and human teeth.

It was *big*. The ship itself was easily 2 feet long, and the glass case that contained it came up to Bill's shoulders (meaning it was well overhead height for me). Damn thing weighed a tonne. If it hadn't been so… so off-putting, I'd probably have agreed with him about incorporating it into the decor. The level of craftsmanship was phenomenal. Despite my distaste, I had to give credit to the fact that I knew I was looking at somebody's life's work. There was something about it, though, something that rubbed me up the wrong way. It wasn't just the sight of a sea monster with human teeth, either. It was a little too realistic for my tastes; I think. Plus, for some reason, the model maker had decided to include a historically inaccurate figure amongst the sailors. I remember pointing this out to Bill, wondering aloud why there was a kid in skinny jeans and hoodie standing on the deck with 19th-century seamen. Our guess was that the out-of-time figure was a little joke on the part of the artist, or maybe someone they knew included as some kind of pseudo-gesture. Even though they were only a few inches tall, the level of detail on their face was harrowingly accurate. I found out just how accurate a little while after we learned what the tooth-kraken diorama concealed. The trapdoor was so well hidden that I thought I'd accidentally dislodged a floorboard when I tripped over one of its edges.

"Oh shit! Bill, mind your feet!"

I stumbled and felt the weight of the diorama case leave my grasp. It only had a few inches to drop, but the heavy *thud* was so loud a few precariously balanced trinkets fell from their perches.

"Ah! Jesus Christ, Benny! Watch what you're doing!"

Luckily, the heavy display missed Bill's toes, but not by much. If he'd have been half an inch closer, we'd have spent the night in A&E. We only bickered for a few short minutes before I bent down to inspect the trap door. A short conversation about not realizing we had a basement later and Bill was prizing it open with the crowbar from our van. We could hear the moaning the moment it swung open.

"Bill! I think there's someone—"

"*Shh*—I hear it too."

There were cries coming from down there. A man's sobs, deep and ragged and pained. A tingle of adrenaline burst through me. My mind was racing through every story I'd ever read about squatters living in wall cavities, or violent junkies taking up shelter in the cellars of abandoned buildings. I fretted over the morning news, of the headlines that would say things like "newly local couple butchered in grizzly double homicide". My husband's response to the noise turned my stomach almost as much as the wails themselves.

Bill nodded to me and, despite my protests, descended the ladder into the dark. I peered down the trapdoor. He was standing in a small room, shining around the flashlight on his cell phone.

"There's a storage room down here Benny. I think it's unlocked—"

He stepped out of view of the trapdoor, and a moment later I heard the creaking of heavy wood on rusted hinges. The soft whimpering grew significantly louder.

"William Groaker, you get back up here right now. We are calling the police."

His shouts echoed back from somewhere beyond my field of view.

"No need to call the cops Benny. It's probably just some lost homeless guy. He's crying for God's sake. Let me deal with it; I don't want to be responsible for yet another unarmed man being shot because of white fragility…"

I rolled my eyes, drowning out Bill's virtuous rant about the dangers of law enforcement. I loved that he cared about all that stuff, but finding out there's a stranger living on the property you've just purchased is *not* the time. After a minute or so Bill's echoes quietened to silence. I was alone with the trapdoor, peculiar maritime oddities, and distant sounds of suburban traffic.

It took me about three minutes to go from "as usual, I think something's wrong" to "OK, I may not be being my usual paranoid self, something *might* actually be wrong here." After four, I was shout-whispering down the hole.

"Bill? *Bill??* What's going on down there?!"

No response.

I sat for ten more long seconds, straining my ears to hear any sign of my husband. None came. The only sounds wafting up from the open trapdoor were the soft sobbing. I gulped, every hair on my body straightening to attention. My intrusive imagination started a slideshow of terror, of the man I loved maimed and mutilated in the thousands of ways characters in his horror movies snuffed it. Another agonizingly lengthy ten seconds later, I was doing something incredibly stupid. I should have called the cops, right? I didn't though. I respected Bill's sanctimonious instruction too much. So, what did I do? I climbed down the ladder. Idiot.

My screams when I saw the skull were so loud that more bric-a-brac clattered on the floorboards upstairs.

I'd turned my phone's flashlight on before I'd descended, holding it in my mouth as I navigated the steel rungs in the dark. My hands were shaking when I got to the bottom. Typical klutzy Benny, what did I do? Dropped the damn thing. After bending down to fumble around on the dirty ground for a few moments, I found it, picked it up, and turned around. There, a few inches from my face, was a lipless, bony grin. Like I said, I *screamed*. I nearly fell back onto my ass. It took me several deep shaking breaths to realize the empty sockets leering down at me *didn't* belong to a specter, ghoul, or some other apparition. No. Opposite the ladder, through the open door marked "STORAGE: MANAGEMENT ONLY", was a skeleton hanging in a glass case. An anatomical display for physicians from way-back-when. You know the sort, the one that cartoons taught us all doctors' offices had. I was so embarrassed that I almost forgot why I'd come down here in the first place. The still-uninterrupted wailing from the shadows beyond the grinning skull made sure it was *only* almost, though.

I gulped, clinging to my fears for Bill's safety as motivation to penetrate the shadows of the storage room.

The secret space was much larger than the building above. It stretched back much further than my feeble phone flashlight could reach, a semi-cavernous space with a lofty distant ceiling bordered by high cinder block walls. I kept shout-whispering for Bill as I crept through the narrow alleys and passageways between the piles of stored exhibits. Never did I hear a response, or anything save for the progressively louder wails from the maniac who I couldn't help but picture hacking Bill to pieces. Well, at first I couldn't help panicking over such mental images. As I got further into the storage room, I started to take notice of the exhibits, though. By the time I actually found Bill, I was so lost in trying to make sense of them that I nearly tripped over him.

As I said, I'm still trying to piece all this together myself. This happened… about three hours ago, I think. Maybe four (from your perspective, at least). I can't recall everything that's down there, but I'll try to remember what I can. I need to, even if the details end up hazy. I think it'll help give what happened to Bill and me some perspective. Neither of us had ever really believed in the supernatural, paranormal, or any of that (as I thought until a few hours back) rubbish. We weren't staunch skeptics, but by the same token, our general outlook was that 99.999% of it all was explainable.

I doubt there are *any* explanations for some of the things hidden beneath our affordable slice of a happy future.

The first few exhibits I saw were odd and borderline unsettling, but nothing I would be writing about out of context. I'll give you an example. Directly behind the mocking skeleton was a wooden pallet; the kind forklifts drivers use their aforementioned forklifts to move about. On this particular pallet were a dozen or so rectangular stone blocks. Each was no taller than my shin, and none would have been remarkable at all, were it not for the intricate hieroglyphs. They were like none I recognized (although admittedly I'm no archaeologist). I'm pretty sure I never heard of any ancient civilization that carved depictions of themselves as lizard people, though. The reptilian figures were carved into every stone, more often than not shown throwing spears at groups of taller figures. Figures that were very clearly meant to be human. There was also the figure with an ear for a face. Appearing on several of the stones, this third symbol-character unsettled me not so much because its entire head was an ear. No. It unsettled me because the hieroglyphs were clearly thousands of years old. Reptilian figures and ear-faces could be explained away with tribal imagination. The fact that the ear-head was wearing a grey suit complete with black tie couldn't.

Many of the artifacts close to the doorway were of a similar nature. Dozens of rusted devices that looked modern in design, piles of time-corroded relics so complex their purpose defied understanding. It wasn't until I'd been walking for a minute or two, still following the moans and calling for bill, that the exhibits inspired greater emotion than mere unease. At some point, an 8 foot fish tank containing a red book suspended in clear resin blocked my path, forcing me to duck left between a cloth-covered cabinet and a stack of dusty crates. I turned the corner and screamed once more.

The rim of my juddering phone light had caught the edges of something. Something long, pink, nail-tipped, and fleshy. Fingers. It was when my beam traveled up the arm they were attached to that I yelled. The feeble glow from my phone should have found a chest attached to that limb. It didn't.

I had to take a step or two back and blink a few times before I could fully make sense of what I was seeing. I was looking at a suit. I didn't figure it was a suit at first though, and it was understanding the suit aspect that pushed me squarely into nopeville.

The skin of the fingertips I'd caught was a dull peach-colored rubbery stuff. Not latex, it looked more like skin than latex, but not enough like skin to fool the senses. The figure had all its limbs. Arms, legs, even the neck were all intact. It was the head and chest that meant I had to stop for a double take. The chest and torso were open. A vertical slit ran down from the base of the throat to the Ken Doll-smooth crotch, the rubbery flesh pulled apart like curtains. Inside was an angular skeletal structure made of dark iron-like metal. It was vaguely human, but only in the places where the structural utility of the human skeleton made sense. There were no superfluous nubs of bone, no excessively complex joints. Also, not gonna lie, I don't think any human being has an assortment of miniature valves, knobs, and levers on their spinal cord. I'm also pretty darn certain no person on earth has a small chair in their skull.

The head of the figure was split vertically, much like the torso. However, this split ran through iron bone as well as plastic skin. The opposing hemispheres were suspended either side of the neck on several brass pistons, each no longer or thicker than a knitting needle. Surrounding the opening to the iron cylinder spine was a plethora of more dials, widgets, and buttons. It was the chair at their center, a small iron cup-shaped seat, that drew the most of my attention. There was something in it. A sagging, pus-colored thing that looked like a halfway point between a slug and a starfish. I screamed because this thing was... it was breathing. Slow, ragged breaths, breaths so clear I could hear the pain and labor required to make them.

That was the point I made an executive decision for Bill and me. I swore to myself that when I found him we were getting out of this place, and then we were selling it. No amount of coastal happiness would be a worthwhile tradeoff for whatever we'd stumbled into. Speaking of stumbling, I did that as fast as I could, *away* from the wheezing creature in the non-functional man suit. I don't think thankfully is quite the right word, but the whimpering in the distance hadn't stopped. I was weirdly relieved, though only because it meant finding my direction again was no issue. Somehow, I knew that wherever I found the sobbing man was where I'd also find Bill. I was right about that, sadly. I was also right about there being nothing sunsets and margaritas could bring worth what we'd unwittingly inherited when we shook hands and accepted keys.

For the first time ever I hate being right.

I was fumbling my way through cramped darkness and dusty shadows for at least ten minutes. For context, you could walk the length of the museum in about twelve seconds with a spring in your step. The oddities I was passing were truly in the realms of the disturbing by this point. Any of them would have rattled my absent-minded wandering thoughts for weeks. I didn't just see one, though. I saw...

Jesus. I'm not going to be OK, am I?

There were paintings so horrific that several made me mumble "no... please no..." under my breath. One was so bad that it only took a brief glimpse for me to stop running and cough up my lunch. Seriously. My flashlight was on it for barely a tenth of a second and I was puking. It was a person; of what gender it was impossible to tell. Why? Because the figure in the portrait had no face. Atop the neck in the immaculate oil painting was a glistening mass of gore and bone. So talented was the painter that the phone light seemed to glisten and dance on the exposed muscles and dripping sinew. Like I said, I only caught a glimpse. One split-second glance was enough for me to be on my knees, throat burning as bile and half-digested sushi forced their way from my stomach. Let's think about that, shall we? A painting of a jawless, eyeless, skinless face is a grizzly thought, yeah? It's not instant-vomit grizzly, though. I don't think Bill and I would have lasted long if I were *that* squeamish. There was something wrong about that painting. Something unnatural that both my mind and body rejected with zero hesitation. Even writing about it now is making me a little queasy, just being honest.

I forced myself to keep the light on the ground after that. Every so often though, my arm would jolt, or I'd forget myself and sweep the beam over some fresh monstrosity. I was in tears before long, though I don't know which specific exhibit got them going. It could have been the aquarium tank full of dead men. No... that's not right. It wasn't dead *men*. It was a dead *man*. A dozen or so copies of the same man's corpse, floating in clear blue liquid. A long, thin, wrinkled old face repeated over and over again with varying shades of pain, anger, and fear. Still, I might have been crying by the time I saw that. My panic might have risen to hysterics-level when I made the mistake of finding the eye in the little black box. The one that moved and followed me, the one that fell to the ground with a wet *splat* and scattering of organic mess when my klutzy elbow knocked it from its shelf. Ignoring the parade of aberrations got harder and harder the longer I hurtled onward. I kept running toward the sobs, toward where I *knew* Bill would be. My feet weren't pounding in the dark much longer. The taste of vomit was still fresh when I felt the tug at my ankle.

"What the hell! Bill?!"

I'd been going so fast by that point that skidding to a halt had me damn near crashing into another stack of dust-coated crates. Bill was lying on the floor, sprawled at the opening to a clearing amongst the piles of unspeakable objects. I didn't need my phone flashlight anymore. So lost was I in my panic that I didn't register the flicker of the trashcan fire until after I felt Bill's hand clawing at my pants leg. Shortly after I became aware of the faint orange glow, the stench hit me. Whoever these trespassers were, they'd been here a while. Several weeks at least judging from the pungency of the human waste odor and smoky grilled rat aroma.

Oh, and you read that right. It was trespass*ers*. Plural.

Both were men no further along in life than their late twenties. As soon as I saw them, I had my explanation for the sobbing. One of them, the one furthest from Bill and I, had a face that gleamed with the wet slick of tears. He was bawling like a toddler, curled up in the fetal position on a retro-looking orange living room chair, hugging his knees so his bare feet didn't touch the cold granite floor. His back-and-forth rocking was so vigorous that the wooden chair legs scraped and scratched on the ground. The other figure, the one standing on our side of the flaming trash can and dead rat spit, drew the most of my attention, however. His wild eyes met my bewildered ones, and for a moment, we both stared at each other. He was no doubt wondering why yet another intruder had stumbled into their makeshift camp. I was wondering what he'd done to Bill that meant my husband's eyes were rolling back in his skull, and his jaw wouldn't stop grinding. I can't remember which of us acted first. I know we both lunged though.

Listen, let's not paint this situation as heroic or inspiring. I leapt at the guy like a cornered animal. I wasn't He-Man; I was a slave in the Roman gladiator pit charging at a hungry lion because the 0.0001% of survival was still their best chance at seeing another morning. The way *he* came at *me* was very different. There was no fear, no panic or terror. The way he moved was determined, practiced, predatory. The quote-unquote "fight" was over before it started. One moment I was in the air, and the next the darkness was getting darker in time with waves of hot pain from the base of my skull.

The dull ache hadn't abated when I came to.

"Ethan… Ethan. please don't… just leave them. Ethan…"

The sobbed pleading roused me pretty sharpish. The events leading up to being knocked out cold came flooding back. The trapdoor, the sobbing, the things in the basement, the trashcan fire, Bill. Oh God, my first coherent thoughts said, Bill. I've got to find Bill. Trying to stand let me know that my assailant had tied me to a chair. My vision was still blurry, so I couldn't make sense of my surroundings at first, but every second brought more focus. I soon realized that I'd been moved deeper into the bowels of the museum storage, away from their makeshift camp. To my relief, I could see Bill, although that relief quickly gave way to concern. He wasn't moving.

"Bill?! *BILL!* I swear to God if you've hurt—"

"Shut up." My half-screamed threat was cut short by a palm slamming into my left cheek. The *smack* of skin-on-skin panged around the cramped shadows, and to my shame, I found myself obeying the command.

"That's better."

The man that slapped me was the same predatory figure I'd been overpowered by back at the trashcan fire clearing. There were a few more trashcan fires in this new, larger space, and the increase in light allowed for a better look at him. Tired was the first word that sprang to mind. The face hovering inches from my own held eyes so bloodshot that the pupils looked as though they were set into two scrunched-up balls of post-nosebleed tissue paper. The bags under them were the deep brown-purple of an old bruise, and I could smell the dryness of his mouth on his rancid breath. I didn't have to know a thing about this man to know that he hadn't slept in days.

"Ethan… Ethan. please leave them alone…" This second round of tear-choked begging had me looking over Ethan's (I'm assuming) shoulder. His companion, the one I'd last seen rocking up on the orange '70s living room chair, was sitting on the floor a few feet away from Bill. Thanks to the multiple trash can fires here, I could see this man's features clearer too. You know that cliché expression about feeling the color drain from your face? Doesn't feel so cliché once you experience it yourself. I recognized the tear-stained face, you see. In the brighter orange haze. I realized where I'd seen it before. I couldn't mistake that face, despite the fact that the last time I'd seen it was when it was attached to a wooden body about two inches tall.

I knew that sobbing man. He was the out-of-time figurine from the human-toothed sea monster display.

That wasn't the only thing I could work out about him. His words carried the telltale bending of the hearing impaired, which would have been obvious anyway with the visible hearing aids. This man looked tired too, but not anywhere near the same level as Ethan. There were several bruises around his lips, eyes, and across his arms. Whatever kind of relationship these two shared wasn't a happy one. The power dynamic here was obvious. Even though I didn't know the sobbing man from Adam, I could tell instantly that I was this Ethan character's third, not second, captive. I'll be honest, though, I wasn't too concerned with how he found himself down here with this madman. I was still trying to comprehend the fact was a miniature version of him on the antique model ship upstairs.

"You…" I heard myself mumbling, unable to look away from him.

"You're… you were on the ship."

"He was, but he can't hear you." Ethan was standing above me, smirking.

"The mask took his hearing. Do you know sign language?" I shook my head, no. Ethan shrugged.

"Me neither. I've been writing stuff down for him on a notepad. We seem to be getting on OK. You don't really care though, do you?"

I found my head shaking again before I could stop it. Thankfully, the maniac didn't take offense. Instead. he laughed, which in hindsight might actually have been worse. It was a shrill laugh, a barely audible titter that my eardrums could find no way to make palatable.

"Heeeheeehe… no, I wouldn't care if I was tied to a chair. Why would you? You're tied to a chair. I bet the only thing you care about right now is how to *not* be tied to a chair, right?"

I struggled against my bindings once more. They were tight, tight enough that it only took three or four strains against them for my ankles and wrists to protest. I glared at the madman towering over me and tried my best to mask the machine-gun hammering of my pulse.

"What—what are you doing here?" I stammered.

"What have you done to Bill? What's going—"

Another skin-on-skin crack, this time across my right cheek.

"No questions from you, only from me. I'm guessing Bill is that guy on the floor, yeah?" I nodded, ashamed at the prickling coming from the corners of my eyes. Ethan's smirk widened.

"Cool. Thought so. Bill's fine. Well… fine is a bit of a stretch. He's not dead, since that's what I'd be worried about in your position. You worried he's dead?"

I found myself nodding again. The prickling was a warmth now, two long trails of hot moisture framing my cheekbones.

"Yeah, I thought so. Well, like I said, he's not. But, like I *also* said, *you're not the one who gets to find stuff out."* He pinched one of my cheeks and gave it a few tugs, just like an overbearing uncle with a bewildered infant.

"*I'm* the question guy here, Friend-Of-Bill. First one: what are you doing here?"

I blinked a few times, taken aback by the audacity of the question. "What am *I* doing here?!"

"You and Bill, yes. What are you both doing down here?"

"We own the place!"

"Do you?" Ethan's smirk faltered a little. He was genuinely surprised by the news. "What happened to the old man? Did he die?"

"Yes! Although I don't see—"

Ethan ignored me, clicking his tongue a few times before rambling on. "That's a shame, a real shame. That makes things a bit tricky. For you and Bill, I mean. Not for Riley and me. We're close. So close. Six months down here with the mask and we're so damn close."

"Did Mr Pembroke know you were down here?" I was a little surprised to hear the words flutter from my lips. So was Ethan.

"Were my slaps not hard enough? *NO QUESTIONS FROM YOU!"* His roar was so loud that, for a harrowing life-flashing-before-eyes instant, I thought he was about to snap my neck. He grabbed me by the shoulders. The grip was so tight that long, unwashed fingernails broke skin through my shirt, causing small scarlet clouds to bloom on the fabric.

"No. Questions. From. You. This *isn't* about you, Friend-Of-Bill. This isn't *your* story. It's ours, me and Riley, Riley and me. Well, not *ours*. I'm an extra too. Mainly it's his."

I was so relieved to feel the stinging claw pressure on my left shoulder release. Ethan pointed at the sobbing deaf man behind him, the Riley whose story I'd been accused of trespassing on. Once more I was listening to an incredulity I felt far too terrified to possess leaving my lips.

"What... what the hell are you talking about! Are you *high?* Is that what this is?! Did Mr Pembroke let you use this place to—"

Another slap.

"Shut up, Friend-Of-Bill. This is the *last* warning, OK? Laaaaaaast. But yeah, the old man let us stay down here. Drugs though? Heeeheeehe. Drugs. I wish. No. No no no, Friend-Of-Bill. I think for this to make sense you need to see. You need to *know.*"

Ethan walked behind me, and I heard the sound of a bag being unzipped. Riley, who'd been watching the scene unfold, started wailing louder than ever before.

"Ethan, please no don't, please don't Ethan, just leave it in the bag. Look what it did to the first one, Ethan, ETHAN!"

Ethan carried on rambling, as though oblivious to his friends' protests.

"We broke in here, you see, a while back now. Well, we broke in up *there*, not down here. We found down here by accident. Funny things, aren't they, accidents?"

His semi-nonsense was whispered into my left ear by the end of the last sentence. He was standing directly behind me, one hand again placed on my right shoulder. I couldn't help but wince at the sharp stinging from the papercut gouging his nails left. Especially when he started rubbing my shoulder blade with a clammy palm.

"You see, Friend-Of-Bill, he was the first to put it on." Ethan crooned; his hushed tone barely audible over Riley's hysteric protests.

"The rest of us watched him. We watched him flicker and shift, watched him go and then return, coming back with burst ears and screams about hearing God speak. He ran after that though, didn't you, Riley? Took me ages to track him down and bring him back here. The other two didn't want to, but I was determined. I *had* to know. I put it on too, you know, Friend-Of-Bill. We all did in the end. We were going to take it to the police but... well, there's something about it, you know? It's part of something *bigger* than laws and morality and nations and men. You can't resist it. All three of us caved. The other two, they didn't make it. They ended up like poor Bill, but *I* was stronger. It shows you things. No, not just shows... *takes* you to them. It took me to so many places, showed me what I have to do. That we'd find the end to all this if we wait down here. I have to help him, you see. I have to help him by finding somebody else that God will speak to."

I think Riley knew what Ethan was rambling about, because even though he couldn't hear the words, his wails fit the insanity leaving his captor's lips.

"*ETHAN PLEASE, YOU DON'T HAVE TO DO THIS, IT WASN'T GOD, I WANT TO GO HOME, PLEASE LET US GO ETHAN—*"

The hysteria had no effect. Ethan carried on as though his other captor didn't exist.

"The old man knew. He'd put it on, too. Course he had. He knew we were coming, you see, that's one of the things it showed him. That's why he helped me keep Riley down here. But you don't know what it is, do you, Friend-Of-Bill? I must admit, I owe him an apology, that Bill of yours. I just kind of ambushed him without showing him what it was, without explaining. Just jumped out the shadows and put it on his face. Kind of rude, no?"

Ethan let go of my shoulder for the final time. My chest tightened as he walked back around to my field of view. He was holding something, turning it over and over delicately in his grimy hands. It was a mask. A nearly flat, almost featureless mask cast entirely from a single piece of metal. I've never seen any material like it. With the exception of the velvet lining of the interior, the mask was made of pearlescent mottled steel. If I had to give it a color I'd have said blue, but only just. Reflections of the orange trash can fires cycled through hues as they danced. The blue of the steel felt more like an illusion than a color, like it was a trick my mind was pulling to shield me from some spectrum-defying shade. I didn't have long to inspect it. Whether or not that's a good thing, I'm still unsure.

I was partway through trying to process the thin circular patterns scratched into the blue steel when Ethan struck.

"*TELL US WHAT IT SHOWS YOU, FRIEND-OF-BILL! LET IT TAKE YOU TO GOD!*"

I had enough time to register the velvet lining sucking at my face. It pulled me inward, latching onto my head, and before I could scream, my every sense was cut to blackness and silence.

I was rising. I couldn't see a thing, but I could feel the pressure of motion all across my back. Some unseen force had me by the navel, yanking me upward with such velocity the air was knocked from my lungs. I wasn't in the museum basement anymore. The sounds of Riley's whimpers, Ethan's tittering, the crackle of the trash can fires, all of them had gone. The only sound in my ears was the deafening rush of hurtling through nothingness at God knows how many miles per hour. I wanted to scream. I wanted to scream and yell so loud that my ribs snapped. The situation I'd left was PTSD creating levels of horrific. Being held captive by a crazy guy is... well, it's not *normal,* but there's nothing about that situation that science can't explain (hidden museum exhibits aside). Having a mask thrust on your face and getting plucked from reality, though? That's a whole different level of messed-up sanity-breaking disturbia.

Jesus... I can see how crazy this all sounds. I'm going to need therapy for a long, long time, aren't I? Ha, who am I kidding; no couch and conversation will help me deal with this. This is straitjacket and padded room territory. Hell, if it wasn't for the fact I have *proof,* I'd be checking into an asylum right now. I just want you to know that. I understand how you're going to react to all this and... just trust me; *I know.* If this hadn't happened to *me, I* would be *you* right now. All doubtful and full of disbelief. Fuck, I *wish* I could be you right now. Life was better when I didn't believe in stuff like this. No, believe isn't the right word. It's not believing in something if you *know* that it's real.

I can't tell you how long I was ascending in that void. From an outside perspective, I was only gone half a minute or so, and I know that because clocks are a thing and I checked mine shortly after I'd managed to stop vomiting. That wasn't until later though, until after I'd run from that museum so fast I tore muscles in both legs. From *inside* where the mask had taken me, from that endless empty place, the rise through nothingness felt like it went on for years. Maybe even decades. It's difficult to tell. What I do know is that there was no warning when I finally stopped.

THUMP

I was still trying to find air to scream with when something crashed into my back. The pain was immediate, like I'd been thrown into a brick wall by a steroid-addicted pro wrestler. The sound of my own coughing was the first sensory stimulation I registered. Next, I noted that I wasn't cold anymore. The subterranean storage room had been chilly, and the void I'd flown through was freezing to the point my lack of frostbite was still a little disconcerting. This place, though, this place was warm. The air had the steady artificial heat of an advanced temperature control system. For context, the museum Bill and I purchased was kept warm during the short mild winters by a few outlet-powered electric radiators. Despite being blind, I knew I wasn't in the storage room anymore.

Yeah, that's right. I couldn't see. My eyes had been deprived of light for so long that it took a few minutes for vision to return. It wasn't until I'd tried blinking a few times that I realized they weren't closed. That was far from my only problem, though. Shortly after the wind-knocking slam, there was an unpleasant lurching sensation in my stomach. Almost like I was in a barrel being rolled over a cliff edge in slow motion. It didn't take me long to figure out what the unusual nausea was. It was gravity returning. Wherever I was, I was lying on my back.

A few more blinks later, I had enough vision to piece together that I was indoors again. It wasn't the museum basement anymore, though. I have no idea where I was, but it wasn't somewhere I'd been before. This new place was brightly lit by rows of long bulbs screwed into cages hanging above. The ceiling and walls were completely painted a dull, depressing grey, save for waist-high tiling that also covered the floor. The tiles must have been white once. Once being the optimum word there. By the time I'd been dropped on them, they were a browning yellow, the unique tone of years of janitorial neglect. There was no time to dwell on filthy tiles, however. I wasn't alone.

When I pulled myself up, it only took one frantic whip-around of my head to see this place was a long corridor. Despite the filth, I could smell a variety of industrial-strength cleaning chemicals. While the eyes said abandoned abattoir, the nose said wartime field hospital. The white coats worn by the four or five perplexed men and women surrounding me fuelled this suspicion.

"*WOAH!* What the hell?!" One of them said, an Indian man with a name badge that outed him as Dr Anand.

"What the actual God damn hell! See, this is what happens when you redirect 90% of the Security Research budget into chasing a madwoman with a book and a grudge! Where did you come from, how you did spontaneously manifest in here?! *Who are you?!*"

I held my hands up, pulse once again racing when I saw the slick black handles of the pistols each of them carried in hip-holsters.

"I-I-I'm Benjamin… B-Benjamin Groaker… p-p-p-please I—"

I never got to finish my sentence. Not because of the pistols, or because of the group of doctors who looked just as confused and alarmed by my presence here as I was. It was because of the howl.

It came from down the corridor, from around the corner barely 15 feet behind a man whose badge informed me was named Dr Harper-Girard.

"Oh bloody hell," he said, speaking with a thick British accent as he spun 180 degrees and drew his pistol, "bloody hell it's happening, they're here."

I didn't have to guess who "they" were. The howls grew louder with every split second that passed, reaching their crescendo before Dr Anand had time to bark his response.

"Robert, find Leona and get to the vessel."

"But—"

"*Now,* Robert. I don't care what year it is, if they get to the hangar, you make the jump."

The color drained from Dr Harper-Girard's face. He sprinted past me, shooting another confused look my way as he went. I didn't care. I'll be honest, I wasn't paying him much attention. Dr Anand and the other science types weren't paying *me* much attention anymore, either. We were all focused on the tide of shrieking, roaring monstrosities barrelling around the corner and rolling as a foul tide towards us.

I could smell them before I saw them. A reeking stench that cut above even the tangy miasma of industrial chemicals. I'd never smelled anything like it, like a mixture of bread, mold, and gasoline. The things moved fast though. I'd barely even started being repulsed by noxious fumes in my nostrils when I stopped to start screaming at the sight of their source. I couldn't count how many there were. It could have been anywhere between dozens and hundreds. A seething mass of slick, glistening bodies, a pressurized onslaught of slug-fleshed beings twice the size of any man. I only knew the tsunami of mucus-coated grey abominations wasn't a single creature because of all the mouths. They'd rise from the phlegmy surface as the things writhed and slithered over each other, vanishing again as the next howling being pushed the maw back beneath the slimy waves.

Their teeth struck me the most. More angular than any I'd seen, even on statues. Perfect squares. The kind of teeth cartoon characters have. Charming in animation, sure, but to see them in real life? Haunting. Harrowing. Terrifying. Pick your adjective, any work. So straight were the angles of those teeth that the sight of so many ignited the flare of a migraine at my temples. I'm trying not to picture them as I write this, but... Jesus. Double Jesus. Behemoth slug monstrosities are bad enough in their own right. A set of gnashers that defy natural design so much they create headaches feels like overkill.

Goddammit, Bill. Why'd you have to fall for the charm of anchors and dried starfish? We could have picked up that nice lodge in Wisconsin. But no, you had to cave to my need for ocean air.

I'm so sorry.

I felt another hand tugging on my shoulder. This grip was strong as Ethan's, although thankfully it didn't come with skin-piercing dirty fingernails.

"I don't know who you are, but you've got to move!"

I turned, following the arm to gaze into a pair of wide, green eyes. They were on a young face, and the name badge on *this* lab coat revealed that face to belong to one Assistant Researcher Fisher.

"Come on!" She repeated, yanking my shoulder again. "Move!"

I couldn't move. I couldn't do anything except blubber shrill nonsense, knees weak and breaths rapid as they were shallow. Fisher pulled again, and I fell into her, knocking us both to the ground.

BLAM-BLAM-BLAM

"Fisher, leave him!" I looked up to see Dr Anand. He'd drawn his pistol and was firing round after round into the oncoming grin-covered biomass.

"But why'd he show up *now*? It has to mean some—"

BLAM-BLAM

Dr Anand screamed down at her over the gunfire, his furious gaze never leaving the tsunami of shrieking gunk. "FISHER LEAVE HIM GODDAMMIT, THAT'S A BLOODY ORDER!"

BLAM-BLAM-BLAM

"ARGH!"

The salvo of pistol fire was ineffective. Fisher was still struggling to get out from under me when the slathering tide reached the first of the lab coats. I didn't catch the name on their badge, the one that got pulled into the gaping square-toothed orifice. I heard them scream, though. We all did, even over the deafening choral howling of the countless Cheshire-cat man slugs. The unfortunate first victim had stood barely four feet from where Fisher and I lay. One of the pulsating things had whipped itself, mouth first, from the mass. The angular teeth dug through the lab coat and flesh beneath like it was half-set jelly. Before any one of us cottoned on to what had just happened, the jaws around his torso snapped back into the throng, taking the bloodied lab coat-wearing mess with them. The man barely had time to scream. Within less than a second, the seething tide had consumed him, the rolling twisting mouths fighting each other to claim the largest chunks of meat.

This was when *I* started screaming again. It was a different scream than any I'd made so far. There's not a word for the emotion in that scream. It was a primordial panic, long hidden in our DNA, a cocktail of hormones unused since long before we came down from the trees. Assistant Researcher Fisher was yelling, although I think this was because she still couldn't push me off of her.

"Get up! Get up, you idiot, or we're going to—"

Then she started screaming too. I was aware of the smell before anything else. This close, it was so powerful my diaphragm instantly began to convulse. I turned round to see what Fisher had been screaming at, although despite my undiluted panic, I knew what I'd see above me.

At full height, it was easily 10 feet tall.

One of the beings had reached us. But, instead of pulling us into the throng, it had decided it wanted us to itself. It had stood upright, launching itself ahead of the encroaching horde and erecting to full size with one disgusting movement. Up close, the teeth were even worse. Each was the size of my face, and the unblemished white of their surface was so bright I'm genuinely amazed they weren't illuminated. I knew where the smell came from now, too. It was their breath. The nauseating stench magnified a thousandfold as the beast opened its garbage chute wide maw. It bent over until its teeth were inches from our screaming faces. Then it howled. The sound cut through every nerve ending in me. My bones rattled, sinew and tendons tensed to the point of nearly snapping. The hot mold-scented breath billowed over us, spewing from the roaring abomination with such force the air was once more knocked from my lungs.

I couldn't help but close my eyes. Fisher stopped struggling. I could feel her grip on me tighten, her fear now overpowering her as much as mine was me. There was no getting away. Those maddening teeth were too close.

I screwed my face as tight as I could and wailed.

Do you know what having monstrous jaws cut through your flesh like freshly baked cake feels like? Me neither. I'd been expecting to find out, but I never did. Neither did Assistant Researcher Fisher.

One moment all I could hear was the abyssal howls of the grey tide and the blam-blam-blam of pistol fire. The next there was nothing save for whimpers, yells, and babbling of my own continued panic. Instead of hot pain as alabaster enamel carves my intestines, all I felt was the rush of unexplained wind on my back. I was once again ascending the void. I wasn't alone this time, though. Fisher was still beneath me. Unlike me, she wasn't screaming. I think she was *too* scared and confused to scream. Like Ethan, her nails began to dig into my back, but unlike with him, it wasn't intentional. She was glaring up at me, holding tight as she could, mouth flapping open and closed as her brain failed to make sense of what was happening.

THUMP

Again, there was no warning when our seconds/years-long journey up through the void ended. It happened exactly the same; the unpleasant crashing, the nauseating flip-flop of gravity in my guts, the rapid blinking to return vision to blinded eyes.

Wherever I was this time was outdoors. I knew that because I could feel the stinging whip of cold night air even before I'd blinked the moon and stars into focus.

"How'd they find us… How'd they find us… How'd they find us…"

I became aware of a woman's voice next to me, repeating a shell-shocked mantra over and over. It only took a few seconds for my memory to catch up.

"You're here!"

She turned to me and blinked a couple of times before responding.

"*I'm* here?! What do you mean *I'm* here! Don't you think you should explain why *you're* here first! And where *here* is?!"

It was my turn to need a few seconds to cognitively process this nonsensical exchange.

"Do you even know about the mask?" I eventually hazarded.

"Mask, what? What are you talking about? No." Fisher stammered, the color still not returned to her cheeks. "Masks this guy tells me, honestly, I—look, fuck your mask, what were you doing in the London Facility? How did you—"

"London Facility?! Did you say *London!*"

"Yes, London! Where did you think—"

"California!"

Once more, the lab-coated woman looked. "California?"

"Yes, California! One minute Bill and I were moving old museum stuff, and the next—"

"You've teleported me from London to California?!"

"What?! No—"

Before I could react, Fisher was up on her feet. Her sleek black pistol was drawn and bearing down on me. I gulped, but it wasn't like I was calm beforehand. By this point, having a gun pointed at me was a drop in the ocean when it came to reasons to panic.

"P-please," I stammered, "please just wait a minute, I think there's been some kind of—"

"No, no *you* wait a minute. I want answers *now*. Were you even there for me? No, of course you weren't. Dr Anand? No... no... You were... you were there for *him,* weren't you? For Robert? Yes! To make sure the Director couldn't reset the—" She let out a sudden gasp, clapping a hand to her mouth and nearly dropping her pistol.

"You're with *her,* aren't you?! *She* told them where to find us. That bitch, when they finally find her, I'm going to—"

"You're going to do what, Samantha?"

Fisher and I both froze. Fisher somehow lost even more color in her cheeks; her bottom lip started to tremble. This new voice also belonged to a woman, and at first, I was confused as to why Fisher responded to it with such... well, with such fear. It was the same way she'd responded to the tide of mucus-coated abominations. I couldn't see any reason for her panic. The voice was soothing, if anything, calm and level, a rich female voice that drummed up mental images of freshly baked pies, drawings on fridges, and stories before bed. A mother's voice, if that makes any sense (I'm not sure it does, because I'm reading this back and I don't think it conveys what I'm trying to convey *at all,* but it'll have to do). Fisher though? The way Fisher reacted, you'd think she'd heard the voice of Hitler. She even dropped her pistol. I didn't wait around when I saw it thud on the soil. The dirt had barely settled when I was back on my feet, heart racing, brain working overtime to make sense of both my new surroundings *and* the woman Fisher was backing slowly away from.

All I could see for miles were fields of rotting vegetables. I knew they were rotting because the air had that faint sweetness to it, the same kind you get by the trash behind Vegan restaurants. The woman had approached us from behind where Fisher stood, meaning the latter woman went from aiming a gun at me to trying to cower behind me and use me as a shield to protect her from… well, I was about to find out what from.

The former woman, the one Fisher was as afraid of as slug things from my nightmares, was striking to look at. Again, I'm going to have to make some attempts with language here. Beautiful isn't the word. She definitely *wasn't* what you'd call sexy, hot, foxy, any of those "want to put penis in" terms that straight men use. That's not to say they *wouldn't* want to, far from it. The lust appeal wasn't what made her features captivating, though. She was… well, perfect. That's the closest word I have. What I can't tell you is exactly what quality it was she'd perfected; some kind of combination of grace, beauty, innocence, wisdom, danger, and hope that no human language has words for.

Juxtaposed to the Auburn hair and unknowable perfect qualities of her head was the body beneath it. In terms of shape, it wasn't anything to write home about, nothing that would get heads turning. Well, apart from the arm, that is. Her left one was missing. In its place was a robotic appendage, the most advanced prosthetic limb I'd ever seen. It was sleek, almost liquid in how it moved. I felt my stomach drop when I saw the metal surface of this arm, the mottled almost-blue pearlescent plates forged from a strange metal I was far too familiar with. What wasn't so sleek were the scars and burns where cutting-edge mechanisms met her living flesh. Even though she was lit only by the pallid moonlight, I could see the pain in that gnarled scarring, the agony that must have been endured to produce marks so red and raw-looking.

"G-G-G-Geraldine." It was Fisher's turn to stammer.

"What—What are you—"

"*G-G-G-Geraldine,* pah!" The woman mocked Fisher's fear, putting on a whiney mock-child voice.

"*Puh-lease.* Pull yourself together, Samantha. Oh, and it's still Dr Eastley to you. I didn't get my PhD for nothing."

My gaze played tennis between the two; the trembling girl in a lab coat cowering behind me, and the cyborg paragon of womanhood in her tracksuit bottoms and tank top still approaching her.

"Now, Sammy, I think the *real* question is, what are *you* doing here, and who is *he?*"

I could feel the confusion in Fisher's response.

"What—what do you mean, who is he? He's one of yours, you sent him!"

Eastley shook her head.

"No, he doesn't work for me. I haven't needed anyone to work for me in about oh… what is it… five years now?"

"What in God's name are you talking about?! We found the mole who'd been leaking the database to you last week!"

"Last week?" Dr Eastley raised an eyebrow. "But Boxstead died… wait, what year do you think it is?"

"Don't play games with me, *Geraldine.* I know that you're the one who told the Formtakers that Bramfield's being kept at the London—"

Fisher never got to finish her sentence. The moment she mentioned the word Bramfield, Dr Eastley burst out into fits of unrestrained laughter.

"Bramfield? London Facility?! Ha! Well, that explains it then. So what happened, did you sneak into the Harper-Girard Chamber? Finally got curious about *how* your esteemed Director would… oh… *ohhh*…"

Dr Eastley's gaze shifted from Fisher to myself.

"Ahh… well, isn't this too priceless. So tell me, which version of the mask did you put on? I know it's not the one that *they* have, the one he keeps fused to that poor clone of himself for special occasions… Was it the one in Russia then, the one under the Eiffel tower, or perhaps California…"

"California, it was in California." I swallowed; my mouth dry. With every word she spoke, Dr Eastley's voice felt less and less comforting.

"Ah yes, the one in the Pembroke collection. Thought so. How was young Ethan when you—"

"Pembroke collection?!" Fisher piped up from behind me, suddenly finding some courage. "What are you talking about?! I was on the team that recovered the Pembroke collection. There wasn't a—"

Eastley laughed again. "Ha! On the team. Good one, Samantha. Bringing the field researchers their coffee hardly counts. Were you even *allowed* to enter the premises?"

Silence from behind my shoulder.

"Thought not. Well, this bewildered fellow here is a little out of time, aren't you my friend? I mean, you *both* are, but this poor sod is further from where he should be. I'm guessing he thinks it's... what, 2021?"

I nodded.

"Oh, bless you. See Fisher, he's not one of mine. He's just some unlucky fool that found the Pembroke collection before you guys cordoned it off and demolished the place."

"What are you talking about, Eastley?!" Fisher was yelling now. "How can he—the Pembroke building was destroyed three years ago, it's—"

I never saw the arm move. Neither did Fisher, which is why I think she didn't get out of the way. One moment, Dr Eastley stood, one eyebrow cocked, hands on her hips. Next, she was on the tips of her feet, face locked in a snarl, her human hand balled into a fist. Her artificial one wasn't really a hand anymore. The blue-steel limb had whipped forward, extending and wrapping itself thrice around Fisher so fast that she was dangling in the air before I'd even realized Eastley's arm wasn't an arm anymore.

"Don't you get it, Samantha? There's *no* London Facility. There's not even an IPSET anymore. It was destroyed, demolished on the same night you hitch-hiked a ride with *this* guy." Eastley nodded in my direction, but her wild eyes never left the screaming Fisher suspended about 10 feet above us.

"You get it now? I won. By the time that night ended, I'd invited the All-Parent. Jesus, seems so long ago now... I've had to be so patient; you know? They're here now, though. Tonight is the night the universe ends, forever, no restarts, and anyone that could have hoped to stop it died *years* ago. I wiped them *all* off the map, even Bramfield. I'd always assumed the Formtakers got *you*. They were nothing to do with me, FYI. Them figuring out where Bramfield was and deciding to act on it that same night was just a happy fluke. Quite convenient, actually. Having them all in the same place made wiping them out en masse *so* much easier. Have you ever killed a God? Trust me, it's a rush."

Dr Eastley was smirking now. There was zero comfort in her words by this point. Truth be told, I was starting to feel like an idiot for ever having questioned Fisher's fear of her. In case you're wondering, I still have *no fucking clue* what any of the stuff they were back-and-forthing over meant. At the time, all that went through my head was the mantra "pleasewakeuppleasewakeuppleasewakeup" on loop. I wish I'd been more with it. Something tells me if I had been, I could have got some answers out of that Dr Eastley. Despite the fact she grew more terrifying with every passing second, she was the only person who seemed to have the faintest clue what was happening to me. Fisher knew a little more than me, although, apparently, not much. Besides, even if I did have the wherewithal to question Fisher, she wouldn't have been able to tell me much without a head.

Fisher's screams will be with me until the day I die. This whole messed up experience will be, no doubt, but her death wails will take up a special rent-free space in my head, I'm sure. As the coils of pearlescent almost-blue tightened around her, she howled at a pitch hitherto unreached by any human-born sound I've ever heard. The volume was near-deafening, almost as loud as the shrieking sea of phlegm-coated abominations had been. Almost loud enough to mask the dull snaps of her bones cracking under the pressure of the steel. Sadly, *only* almost, though. Fisher was still conscious for an alarming number of those thick organic crunches. Her jaw was still flapping when the pressure popped her eyes from their sockets, legs still kicked even as her steaming, dripping innards were squeezed from both ends like a stamped-on tube of toothpaste. The screams only stopped when Fisher's skull, unable to fight the tendril coiling around it any longer, imploded.

"I'm sorry you had to see that. Truly, I am." Eastleys smirk made the sincerity of her words difficult to believe.

"I didn't want any loose ends though, you know? Speaking of, it's probably in my interests to get rid of you, too."

"P-please don't! Please! I don't know what's happening, I really don't, I just want this to end—wait no, not like *that,* I just want to go home, I just want to—"

I stopped begging for my life when I realized the boa-constrictor appendage wasn't snaking around to squeeze the last breaths from my body. Dr Eastley was still smirking, but the traces of venomous snarl had vanished. I was far from calmed by this, but it did at least let me know that the fate she had in store for me was different from that of Fisher.

"Kill you? Oh my dear, no. No no no. What would be the point? That's why I'm doing this, you see, so you and Fisher and all the rest of them never have to die again. This is the *last time.* That's why it brought you here, I think, to show you. It's mischievous like that. It doesn't want me to succeed, you see. None of them do. They enjoy preying on you... preying on *us,* far too much. They don't want the ride to stop."

I gulped, but said nothing. What was I supposed to say? I had no idea what in fucks name she was talking about. All I could think was how much I didn't want to end up like Fisher, how much I wanted to wake up next to Bill in our normal bed in our normal life, for this to have been some twisted, uncharacteristically vivid, imaginative nightmare. No such luck.

Eastley continued her spiel, head angled, gazing at me as a chef does the lobster they're yet to decide how to cook.

"Well, I hope it knows that its plan won't work. Hhdufj couldn't stop me, the *Taealim* couldn't stop me, the man in charge couldn't stop me. Hell, even Bramfield couldn't stop me. What chance do *you* have?"

Something happened when she said the word *you.* It was brief, so fast that I almost didn't notice. A weight, a momentary heaviness accompanied by the fleeting sensation of warm velvet.

"Disrupt the timeline as much as you want, you devious little object. I've known all about you and your little games from the beginning. You won't survive this time. This is the end. *Permanent.* It's done. You lost, you and all the rest of the parasites and predators that fed on us over and over for eternity. Game over. The charade ends tonight. In fact, if you'll both do me a favor and look up..."

Now, this next part you'll have to bear with me on. *A lot* happened that I'm not sure I have the language to explain. Again, I felt the weight on my face, the softness of velvet. It wasn't brief this time, though. It lingered, pulling my head until I was staring at the night sky above. I'm getting tired of telling you that I screamed, but... well, what do you want me to do? I did; I screamed so hard that hot stabs of pain shot through my jaw and throat from tearing vocal cords.

The stars above had gone. At an insurmountable speed, they vanished one by one. Within a second or two I was staring not at a starry sky but at vast, empty darkness that stretched quite literally until the ends of the universe. Then the humming started. It wasn't a sound you understand; it was a feeling. A physical vibration rattling every cell in my body individually, like they were sought out, and each inflicted with their own personal earthquake. I was shaking, but I wasn't being shaken. The ground wasn't rumbling, there was no shifting and grinding of tectonic plates beneath my feet. This shaking came from within, as though my body was being urged by some inexplicable force to tear itself apart at an atomic level. It didn't take long for the pain to become unbearable. I couldn't hear if I was screaming anymore. I couldn't hear anything except for a deep, low, deafening white noise that seemed to be coming from everywhere at once.

That's when the eyes started opening.

There were millions of them. They revealed themselves almost in unison, emerging in the pitch darkness where the stars once shone. Distressingly human looking-eyes of all sizes, an uncountable number of gazes staring down at Earth, the last morsel left of a universe-sized feast. Suddenly I was reminded of Ethan, of his rambling about Riley, and what Riley had wailed as he begged his friend to understand.

"It's not God."

If Riley had described anything remotely like what I witnessed, then it's understandable why Ethan jumped to divine conclusions. The weight on my face grew heavier with each passing moment, the sensation of the hitherto absent mask becoming ever more real in the presence of... of whatever it was bearing down on our infinitely tiny planet. Somehow, I knew that those eyes belonged to one being. This was the... the *All Parent* that Eastley had been raving about. It had to be. Why else would the invisible weight on my face be trembling?

I think the mask pulled us out of there just in time. The seething thrum from my cells had evolved into an all-body burning. I was actually grateful to feel the cold rush of the void, the soothing chill of nothingness rushing past me for minutes/decades on end. The more distance I put between myself and that glaring, hateful horizon, the better. In the few seconds before my vision cut to shifting blackness, the ground beneath me had started... splitting, I guess is the word? There weren't chasms forming in the soil; that's not what I'm trying to say. It's like every grain of dirt on earth lost its connection to gravity simultaneously. Rocks turned to sand in a heartbeat, distant mountains collapsed into liquid as though they'd been faking solid status this whole time and just had their surface tension broken. The low rumbling sound had reached a crescendo that gave Riley's deafness a sudden, harrowing context. I think if the mask wasn't so afraid, I'd have suffered the same fate. Thankfully, I seem to have gotten away with a real bad case of tinnitus.

The last thing I remember of my time in the rotting vegetables was, despite the pain, trying to comprehend the being above me. The sheer scale of it… it gives me brain freeze trying to think about it now (for lack of a better term). A being larger than a universe, a living thing so vast that enveloped the entirety of visible space in a matter of seconds. It was all I could think about as I rose through the void for the penultimate time. Whatever this… this *All Parent* was, it couldn't possibly exist. Even though I'd seen it with my own eyes, felt it gazing down at *me* personally with its infinite trillion-eyed gaze, my mind refused to accept it. Remember when I said I was writing this partly to make sense of it for myself? Yeah. 90% of that effort is trying to wrap my head around the fact something like… like *that*, could be real. I couldn't imagine it, you see. Never could I have conceived of something that colossal, that hopelessly vast. Even writing about it now is making me a little queasy.

As I said, this was my second-to-last trip through the void. The mask had one last place to take me, one last stop in its last-ditch attempt to (if Eastley was to be believed) prevent whatever I'd just witnessed from becoming true. I think that's what she meant, at least. Even though her words felt like the most important I'd ever heard, I could barely keep up with what she was saying. I was hoping that by the time I wrote it all down, I'd understand it a bit better. No joy. I've never been a big ideas guy. Doing an overnight crash course in going mad hasn't changed that, it seems.

I didn't know I only had one more stop at the time. I was just glad that wherever I'd end up next couldn't be as sanity-undoing as the possible universal apocalypse I'd just left. Wherever I was about to go, I told myself, nothing could be as bad as that.

It will probably surprise none of you to know that this assumption was laughably wrong.

THUMP.

This time, the pressing void didn't fade, no matter how much I blinked. It lingered long after the impact pains subsided, when the flip-flop of yet again readjusting to gravity had been and gone. It wasn't until I looked on either side of me that I could breathe a sigh of relief. The blindness wasn't permanent, thank God. I know this because I could see clearly wherever else I looked. It was only above me that my vision couldn't penetrate, and by the time I'd got to my feet for a better understanding of my surroundings, I'd found this *wasn't* because of problems with my sight. Darkness hung above this new place, a thick cloud of gaseous inky nothingness that no light could disturb. The same blackness I'd been falling through for hours and/or centuries. It was roiling above me in all directions as far as I could see, covering every horizon in a blanket of non-light deeper than even the starlessness that preceded those God damn eyes.

The darkness was uniform and unbroken. Somehow, I knew it wasn't still though, although *please* don't ask me to elaborate on this. It was moving, writhing, alive, and I was aware of this despite having literally zero reasons to be. My face was wet with tears by the time my feet were moving. I was too broken to argue with them by then. I'd seen far too much already, had my mind torn and restitched only to go through it all over again a moment later. Nothing, though, not even possibly witnessing the end of the universe, could have toughened my psyche enough for this.

I wasn't on Earth anymore.

Notice how I *didn't* tell you what I could hear, what I could smell, the temperature of the air? That's because there was nothing to report. The void the mask kept yanking me up through was freezing, as I've mentioned several times already. The moment I landed, that chill left (which was, as always, a relief). It wasn't replaced by warmth, though. It wasn't replaced by *anything*. I wasn't numb per se, I could *definitely* feel still. The aching from my back after a third fling through endless nothing was testament enough to that. It's more like the nerve endings responsible for reporting air temperature had been silenced. The tears on my face were still warm and wet, the vague awareness of weight and velvet on my face hadn't gone. Only the air was a mystery (if there was even any at all). I can't stress this enough: *please* don't ask me to try and expand on that. I genuinely don't think my mind could take it. Hell, I'm starting to doubt it can take what little I've already put together.

Maybe I should stop writing this? No. No, if I don't do this now, then I never will. I need to get this out while I'm still coherent, especially if this all means what I think it does. I owe Bill that much.

The faint velvet tugging pulled me through this unknowable place for what must have been weeks. I know it must have been weeks because I shaved yesterday morning, and now I have a beard down to my collarbone. I've given up trying to work out how time worked in the void, so I'm sure as hell not going to bother trying to figure why I aged in that library but didn't die of starvation.

Oh yeah. That's where I was, you see. The landscape the mask marched me through was an endless plane of towering, rickety wooden bookshelves. A Goddamn library waiting at the bottom of an infinite void. Or maybe it was the top; it's difficult to tell. My idea of up/down has been pulled to pieces almost as much as my sense of time. There was no sun that I could see, no vast bulbs or burning pyres to explain the total and unbroken illumination of this flat realm of books and silence. Every inch of it was visible as though directly under a spotlight. I had no trouble at all reading the titles on the spines of some of the volumes while the mask pulled me onward. I'm not going to tell you all the ones I remember, because some of them... well, fuck, I don't want to believe they could even exist. A whole section of *For Dummies* books detailing how to do every unspeakable thing you could conceive of. Rows of what appeared to be photo albums, each labeled with the name of some atrocity from human history (the majority of which occurred long before the invention of cameras). There were miles and miles of autobiographies by figures I know for a fact never wrote one. People like Heinrich Himmler, Jeffrey Epstein, Emperor Nero, Charles Manson, and Idi Amin, to name a few. There were many names amongst the infamous that I didn't recognize, and never want to, if the titles of their life stories are any indication. Whoever *H. Yardley* is or was, anyone associated with a book called *"Eating my son: How I learned to stop worrying and love my truth"* isn't somebody I want to learn about. And *that's* just the example I can bring myself to share.

There was no uniformity to the shelves themselves beyond them all being wooden. The tallest of them was around 10 to 12 feet, the shortest only just reaching my ankle. Rows was a bit of a generous way to describe their arrangement, too. There were passages and corridors through the maze of wood and pages, sure, but none felt deliberate. This wasn't planned like a regular library. None of the spaces between shelves we ventured down were straight, spacious, or even seemed intentional. Once or twice, I could have sworn new pathways opened up in front of us, like some of the bookcases moved aside to grant us entry when they thought I wasn't looking.

Not once did I feel tempted to pick up and read any of those books. It wasn't anything to do with their titles, either. Read, are you kidding? I couldn't even think straight. I was a shell by that point, an empty blubbering vessel being led through an impossible place by an invisible malicious object I could only half-feel. Of course, I tried taking it off; I'm not a dumbass. That was the *first* thing I tried when I realized the weight of it wasn't going away this time. Why do you think I was so dejected, so morose and hopeless, as it led me through the endless shelves for all those weeks? There was nothing I could do except wait to die. Alone, in a library that was either at the end of known creation or somehow outside it entirely.

"You again! I thought I told you to bugger off!"

I can't remember what exactly I was despairing about at the moment I heard the voice. It could have been my fading memories of Bill; it could have been the growing realization that I hadn't starved to death yet and might be walking this maze of books forever. Who knows. What I *do* know is that when I heard it, I damn near had a heart attack. It had been weeks since I'd last spoken to anyone, and that person had been Dr Eastley. Suffice to say I wasn't exactly expecting conversation. I especially wasn't expecting conversation to start from behind me, from the passage I'd just trudged down; the one I knew for a fact was empty.

I whirled around, lungs getting ready to scream again for the first time in God knows how long. They didn't, though. I was too surprised to scream. Not shocked, not terrified (no more so than I already was at least), just… surprised.

Standing between two bookshelves containing large dictionaries of languages I didn't recognize was an old woman. Not a witchy, hag-like old woman. Not the kind of woman you got on fairy tales, the ones that were all bones and edges and malice. If I had to choose a word to describe the tiny wrinkled dear in front of me, I would have said *homely*. Her face was as round as her ample waistline, her eyes were sunken but still glinted with memories of mischief long gone. Well, they would have done if the toothless mouth under her creased bulbous nose wasn't locked in a scowl.

"Oi! I said I thought I told you to bugger off! Go on, get lost!"

She dropped the stack of books she'd been carrying and raised her arms, brushing at the air with her wrists as she walked towards me, shooing me away to… well, who the hell knows where. It was when the invisible velveteen weight on my face grew heavier that I realized she wasn't talking to me.

The invisible mask juddered, rattling my teeth. That look Eastley had, the one where she was almost looking *through* me, was in the eyes of this new, much older, woman. The wrinkled dear cocked an ear, like she was listening to words outside the scope of my woefully inadequate human hearing. There was a long, oppressively-silent pause. Throughout it, the pressure on my face bucked and shook. The old woman would tut occasionally, sometimes saying things like "a likely story" and "pull the other one". Eventually, she held up her palms and shook her head.

"Look, look, I don't want to hear it." She said.

"You know how it is the same as I do. It ends and begins again. I'm not having you pissing about round here for however many billions of years while you wait for them to come down from the trees again. The master was *very* clear last time when you—"

More bucking and kicking on my face, this time so violently that I actually let out a little yelp. The old woman rolled her eyes at this, but the invisible commotion didn't stop until her expression started to change from annoyance to concern.

"That can't be right." She eventually said. "They made it, but they're not supposed to end it. What did you say that woman's name was, Eastley?"

Another round of painful thumping on my head.

"Ok ok, calm down! Don't blame me for asking questions. I've never heard of a Geraldine Eastley, not that one at least."

The largest thump yet, so hard that a trickle of blood gushed from my nose. I raised my shirt to stem the blood. The dissonance when my hands didn't touch the steel and velvet my face felt caused instant nausea, but I managed to contain myself. It's not like I had anything in me to spew.

"Look, of *course* it matters that I haven't heard of her." The woman continued, ignoring both me and the scarlet leaking from my nostrils.

"I've heard of *everyone*. If I haven't heard of 'em then they don't exist, and if they don't exist, then we've got a big bloody problem."

She turned, beckoning over her shoulder for me... for us, to follow. I could hear her muttering to herself as she stomped through the void-ceilinged labyrinthine wilderness of spines, covers, and shelves.

"The master is not going to like this, yet another bleeding mess they're going to have to sort out, you know they're going to be *pissed,* why can't any of you lot play your bloody parts, an infinitely recurring universe full of endlessly reincarnating life and you *still* find ways to bugger it up, that *thing* wouldn't even care if you idiots inside weren't making such a bloody ruckus every cycle, bloody Hahre throwing a bloody temper tantrum and now I'm going to be the one that gets it in the buggering neck..."

On and on she ranted. I wish I understood any of what she was saying. Sanity be damned, sometimes you hear things that you don't really comprehend, but you know are important. Rapid-fire T's and C's at the end of ads are a good example, right? Well, this old woman's borderline nonsensical mutterings felt like the T's and C's of life itself. Like I was listening to somebody laying out the fundamental rules underpinning all of known existence, but in a way that my monkey brain couldn't grasp enough to make use of. One of my biggest challenges recovering from this will be letting go of my memories of her British-curse-filled ranting. If I don't, I'll tear myself apart trying to make sense of it. I know the answer to... well, to *everything* is in there, but I also know I'll destroy myself trying to find it long before I even come close.

I was relieved that we weren't walking for long. I'd trekked through that library more than enough; I was *beyond* sick of it. I didn't know we were approaching the final destination of my journey, of course. I was just eager for something to happen, anything to break the insanity of marching through those endless bookcases alone. The old woman was still mid-rant when she showed us around a corner into... that place.

Of everything I witnessed since finding the trapdoor, the room waiting for us beyond the final bookshelf was the most language-defying of all. My screams were both instantaneous and made all the more violent by the fact I couldn't hear them. The old woman had taken us to a small space that wasn't small at all. Physically, it was small, but in the *other* dimensions, the ones that a simple human being like me *wasn't* supposed to be able to perceive, it was *huge*. It was also full. What of I can't tell you. Not because I'm not allowed to, or because I don't want to, but because I literally can't. I don't know what the things rolling and sliding over and through each other beyond where the physical space ended were. I don't know what words I'd use to describe them, either. They had qualities to them, sure, but none of these qualities were familiar. There was nothing I could define as color, or shape, or substance. I was aware of their angles, their lines, their curves, but I couldn't *see* them. I knew they were talking, discussing, communicating, but I couldn't *hear* them. I was registering them with senses I didn't know I had... no, senses that I know I *don't* have and never have done *outside* that reasonless place. There was no floor beneath us, but I walked on solid ground. Only one of the room's occupants was inside the physical boundaries, the walls that occupied the dimensions you and I understand. It was to this figure, somehow miles away yet reached in a few steps, that the old woman spoke after she cleared her throat.

"*Ahem*—Sorry to disturb you, master. A version of the Phithoxine Mask is back again, the most current one. I told it to bugger off master, of course, but it... well, it's here about a hundred years earlier than expected and... umm... There's a *problem,* master. Things didn't end like they should this time."

The invisible weight was trembling again. I could feel the mask's fear, a noxious wave of unchecked panic that washed over me from the head down. My knees weakened; a few seconds of tingling at my fingers and toes preceded a total numbness of the extremities. I was sobbing again, but it wasn't a stream of steady tears anymore. It was uncontrollably, unrestrainedly, unashamedly in ways that only newborn babies are capable. Could I hear it though? No. The only sounds were the machinegun *batump-batump-batump-batump* of my heartbeat in my ears. A splitting migraine bloomed behind my eyes in a matter of seconds, the weeks of sleepless, endless walking catching up and mixing with the nauseating pseudo-sensory overstimulation. All ties to life before the mask left me... hell, to life before the library even. I passed out and awoke and passed out again, over and over in quick succession, never being unconscious long enough for my head to droop more than an inch or two. My brain forgot how to correct my vision, flipping everything 180 degrees. The *batumping* in my ears fused into a crescendo of white noise. With no voice, I opened my mouth and begged the tiny infinite around me for death.

And all of this before the thing had even turned around.

From right next to me and miles away, I could hear the old woman mumbling her feeble excuses. "I am *truly* sorry for disturbing you, master, especially with something as trivial as creation, but like I said, this version of the Phithoxine Mask... well, I'm sure I don't need to remind your eminent self that this cycle is... *was*... due to end when G'ir'thyrx became powerful enough to penetrate the barrier, about a century from this mask's present from what I gather, as it always is when the cycle decides to end that way..."

The thing in front of us bore down on her. I almost don't want to describe it to you. If I do, you might make the mistake of feeling prepared, and then if you were ever unfortunate enough to meet it, you'd break under the weight of your cosmically hopeless naivety. I could see it, but the fraction of it I could *see* was far from the whole. The rest of it I can't translate into words because, much like its... its *lair*, I guess, I wasn't perceiving it with any senses that human beings were built to experience. Despite being no taller than around 7 feet in our three familiar dimensions, in those I wish I didn't know about, it was vaster even than the eyes that swallowed the universe. *Much* vaster.

The thing's *appearance*, which as I said mattered little, was itself far from normal. Like much of what I witnessed after opening the trapdoor, it was therapy-inducing in its own right. The figure was humanoid; androgynous, gangly, and dressed in a crinkled grey suit with polished black dress shows, complete with a skinny equally-black tie and pressed wide-collar shirt the same shade of white as a dying star. The centerpiece was the face, though. Or rather, the ear. That's all there was at the end of its long neck, you see. A massive human ear about three feet long. An ear that was *looking* at us.

"But, well, the thing is master... it's Hahre. They've found a way to sneak a bit of themselves in. They're bloody ending it, master, as in *ending*-ending it. Like I said, I would *never* normally disturb you about anything as insignificant as creation but... well, without the recurrence cycle, things could get *messy,* master..."

That's the last I remember of the conversation that followed. The mask, the old woman, and the ear discussed subjects beyond my comprehension, but it didn't matter. Even if I could have understood, I still wouldn't have been able to listen. Both my body and mind had reached the limits of their endurance. The head-splitting... whatever-it-was that started when we entered the cramped-but-open space finally pushed me beyond cognitive reasoning. My only memories are a flash of... well, not even images. Not sounds or sights or anything like that. When I cast my mind back, all I get is a rolling tide of sensation, of concepts and ideas and emotions I can't define, but that's it. I remember the ear. *That* sticks through. I remember the rage, too. More than *anything*, I remember the rage. If you're like me, and you're a bit of a... well, a shit-stirrer, you'll know what it feels like when somebody is so angry with you they're imagining ways to kill you. Like when they're actively visualizing it in their head, and that little vein starts popping on their neck or temple. You know the kind of fury I'm talking about, the kind you can basically feel. *That* was the rage that oozed from the ear-thing. Except instead of coming from one person, imagine it coming from an entire football stadium of them, every single one glaring down at you alone on the center of the field. A pure, concentrated hatred. Hate I didn't know it was possible for *anything* to feel, let alone *be*...

No. I think the less we dwell on that, the better. As I said, I was experiencing things with senses I don't fully understand. I think.. I think I *was* that hate at one point. Not like I was the subject of it, or that I experienced feeling it... I was *being* it... living *as* it while it brewed within the ear-thing...

Yeah, you know what; I was right, let's *not*. If even a shred of that hate still exists in me, somehow, I don't want to risk reawakening it.

I don't know if losing consciousness is the right word for it, but I was unaware long enough for it to be a shock when I found myself laying on solid ground. Adjusting to life with only five senses took me a few moments. It took a few more to pull myself together enough to realize that, for the first time in weeks, I was experiencing the familiar. The cool underground dampness, the smokey scent of rats spit-roasting over a trash-can fire, the jabbering of a raving sleep-deprived lunatic...

"He's back! He's back! Did you speak to them; did you speak to God?!"

I was lying on the cold concrete floor of the museum basement. Ethan was standing over me, his sunken eyes wide and eager.

"What... what is... what are..." I stammered. From my perspective, it had been, at the *absolute* least, years since I'd been in that basement. My head was spinning. Memories that felt several lifetimes old came flooding back. I was Benjamin Groaker, I'd been assaulted in my basement; Ethan had put a strange mask on me; I'd come down here looking for my husband Bill...

"*BILL!*"

I launched myself to my feet, shoving Ethan out of the way. Bill was laying where I'd left him all those years... all those *minutes* ago. He wasn't moving or talking, but he was, thank Christ, still breathing. I vaguely remember Ethan screaming questions at me as I tried to pick Bill up, to carry him to safety, to put this damn nightmare behind us. I remember Ethan shoving his weight into me, Bill's weight sliding off my shoulders as the younger man wrestled me to the ground. I remember him punching me, and I remember punching back. There are some vague flashbacks to him pleading. There's also, of course, the faint recollections of my fist pounding into his face over and over until my knuckles connected with wet concrete. I have glimpses of knowing that Riley was still there, that he was there when we left still, that he didn't try and stop us, that he only wanted to sit and hold the mask tightly to his chest. That's about it, though. I had so much adrenaline flowing through me that my mind didn't really start jotting memories down until I'd managed to drag Bill into the car and drive halfway down the street. I managed to rouse him just enough to walk, but getting him to climb the ladder was a challenge. We made it, though. Somehow.

It was when I'd finally managed to stop screaming into the steering wheel and drive away that I got my "proof", my horrifying confirmation that what happened wasn't some kind of hallucination. I wish it had been. More than anything, I wish it'd been the product of schizophrenia or a terminal brain tumor. No such luck. Vans had pulled up to the museum while I was screaming and Bill mumbled eye-roll nonsense in the seat next to me, you see. Vans that were clown-car-filled with both SWAT-looking gunmen and bumbling figures in lab coats. Even though rear-view mirrors are small, and my vision was still recovering from so long without proper light, I recognized the first scientist to get out of those vans. Even though her young face was eager and excited instead of terrified or angry, even though she was several years younger than when I'd last seen her, how could I mistake her?

It was Fisher.

Nothing else of note happened between driving as fast as I could away from Fisher and when I started writing this. I've put Bill on the couch for now. Wrapped him up warm. I don't think he was, umm, *away,* for as long as I was. He doesn't have a beard, you see, although there's definitely much more fuzz on his face than what would have grown in a few hours. He's talking now, which is something. Nothing sensical, though. Mostly he just keeps saying "it's got a baby's face, it's got a baby's face, it's got a baby's face" over and over again. Lord knows what the mask showed him, what he saw in the few minutes before I caught up to him in the basement. Whatever it was, it's broken him.

Am I intact? No, truth be told. I can already feel the breakdown coming. My leg hasn't stopped shaking for half an hour, and seeing through the white spots in my vision to write this is a challenge. All I want to do is curl up next to Bill and weep for a thousand years.

We don't have a thousand years, though, do we? Seeing Fisher means I can't hide from it. If she hadn't showed up, maybe I could have pretended everything I saw was some kind of mental fabrication, the birth song of a long-dormant imagination. But no, she had to be *real,* didn't she? That means the rest of it must be too.

Fuck.

The mask took me through time. I think I've been to the future, and there's not much of it left to travel. I think... no, not think. I *know* that I've seen the end of the universe. I've seen a lot of other things too, but the destruction of everything is the only part of whatever the fuck just happened I can actually wrap my head around. If I'm not completely insane by tomorrow morning, then maybe, *maybe,* I can start piecing together the rest of what I saw, what I heard, what I learned. That's a problem for tomorrow's Benjamin Groaker though, (if the consciousness behind these eyes can be still called that by then, at least). For now, I'm going to wrap Bill's arms around me and sob into his chest until I fall asleep. It's been years since he held me... or it feels that way, at least. I've earned this. I'm owed it.

Go and hold your loved ones. Pull them to you so tight your ribs start to hurt. Hug them until you can't breathe and then hug them harder still. Never let them go, ever. You've got a few years left with them at most. Use them wisely.

Printed in Great Britain
by Amazon